HOTEL DARE™

Terry Blas • Claudia Aguirre

kaboom!™

Logo Designer
Grace Park

Designer
Kara Leopard

Associate Editor
Sophie Philips-Roberts

Editor
Whitney Leopard

Special thanks to Rocio Peñuñuri Romero, Camila Oroza,
and Fen Garza for their help making the colors beautiful,
and to Jimmy Pressler for his work on the map design.

Ross Richie CEO & Founder
Joy Huffman CFO
Matt Gagnon Editor-in-Chief
Filip Sablik President, Publishing & Marketing
Stephen Christy President, Development
Lance Kreiter Vice President, Licensing & Merchandising
Phil Barbaro Vice President, Finance & Human Resources
Arune Singh Vice President, Marketing
Bryce Carlson Vice President, Editorial & Creative Strategy
Scott Newman Manager, Production Design
Kate Henning Manager, Operations
Spencer Simpson Manager, Sales
Sierra Hahn Executive Editor
Jeanine Schaefer Executive Editor
Dafna Pleban Senior Editor
Shannon Watters Senior Editor
Eric Harburn Senior Editor
Chris Rosa Editor
Matthew Levine Editor
Sophie Philips-Roberts Associate Editor
Gavin Gronenthal Assistant Editor

Michael Moccio Assistant Editor
Gwen Waller Assistant Editor
Amanda LaFranco Executive Assistant
Jillian Crab Design Coordinator
Michelle Ankley Design Coordinator
Kara Leopard Production Designer
Marie Krupina Production Designer
Grace Park Production Designer
Chelsea Roberts Production Design Assistant
Samantha Knapp Production Design Assistant
Elizabeth Loughridge Accounting Coordinator
José Meza Live Events Lead
Stephanie Hocutt Digital Marketing Lead
Esther Kim Marketing Coordinator
Cat O'Grady Digital Marketing Coordinator
Holly Aitchison Digital Sales Coordinator
Morgan Perry Retail Sales Coordinator
Megan Christopher Operations Coordinator
Rodrigo Hernandez Mailroom Assistant
Breanna Sarpy Executive Assistant

HOTEL DARE, JUNE 2019. Published by KaBOOM!, a division of Boom Entertainment, Inc. Hotel Dare is ™ & © 2019 Terry
Blas. All rights reserved. KaBOOM!™ and the KaBOOM! logo are trademarks of Boom Entertainment, Inc., registered in
various countries and categories. All characters, events, and institutions depicted herein are fictional. Any similarity between
any of the names, characters, persons, events, and/or institutions in this publication to actual names, characters, and
persons, whether living or dead, events, and/or institutions is unintended and purely coincidental. KaBOOM! does not read
or accept unsolicited submissions of ideas, stories, or artwork.

For information regarding the CPSIA on this printed material, call: (203) 595-3636 and provide reference #RICH – 839747.

BOOM! Studios, 5670 Wilshire Boulevard, Suite 400, Los Angeles, CA 90036-5679. Printed in USA. First Printing.

ISBN: 978-1-68415-205-6, eISBN: 978-1-64144-020-2

Written by

Terry Blas

Illustrated by

Claudia Aguirre

Letters by
Mike Fiorentino

For my family.
The one I was given
and the one that I found.
—T.B.

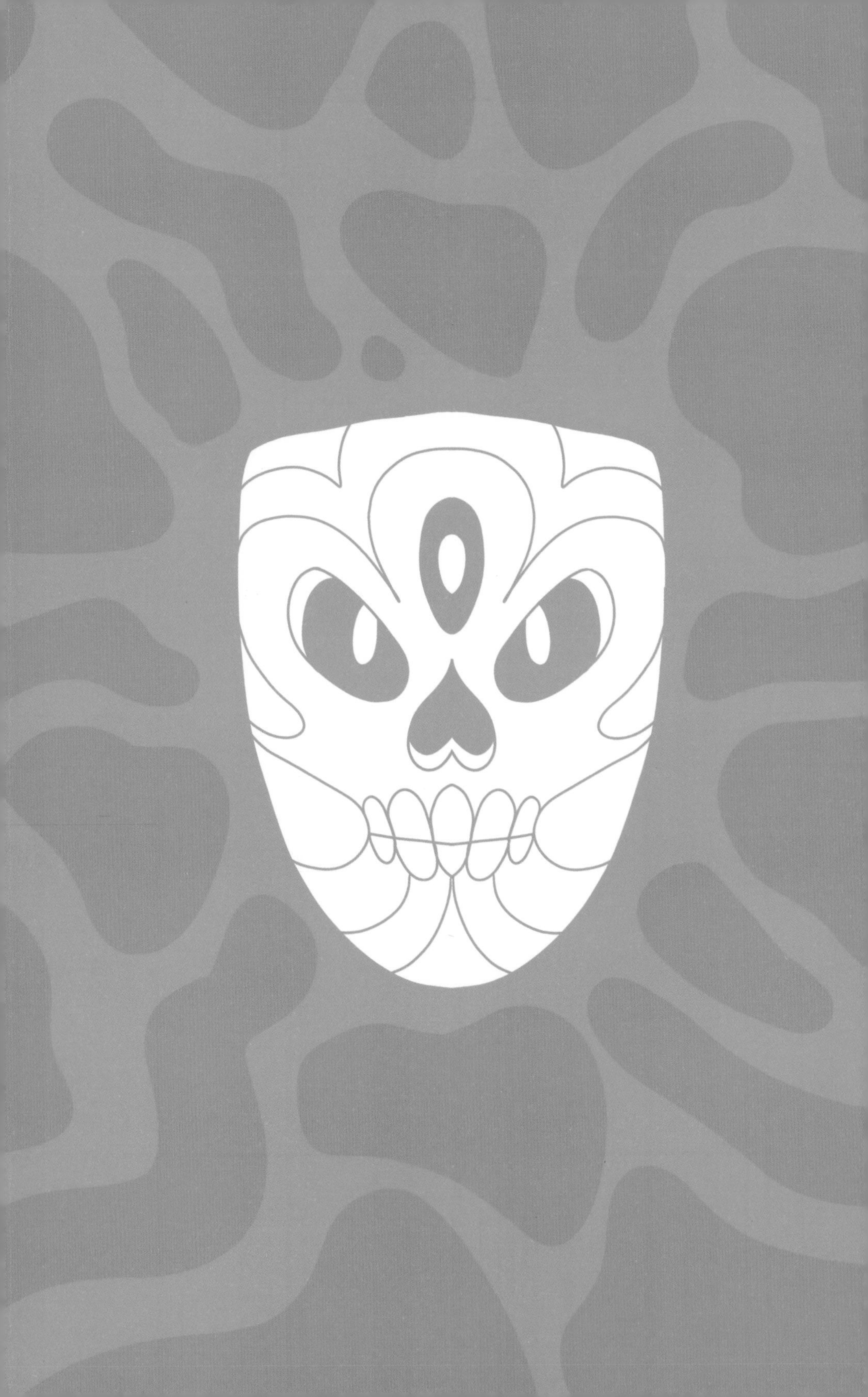

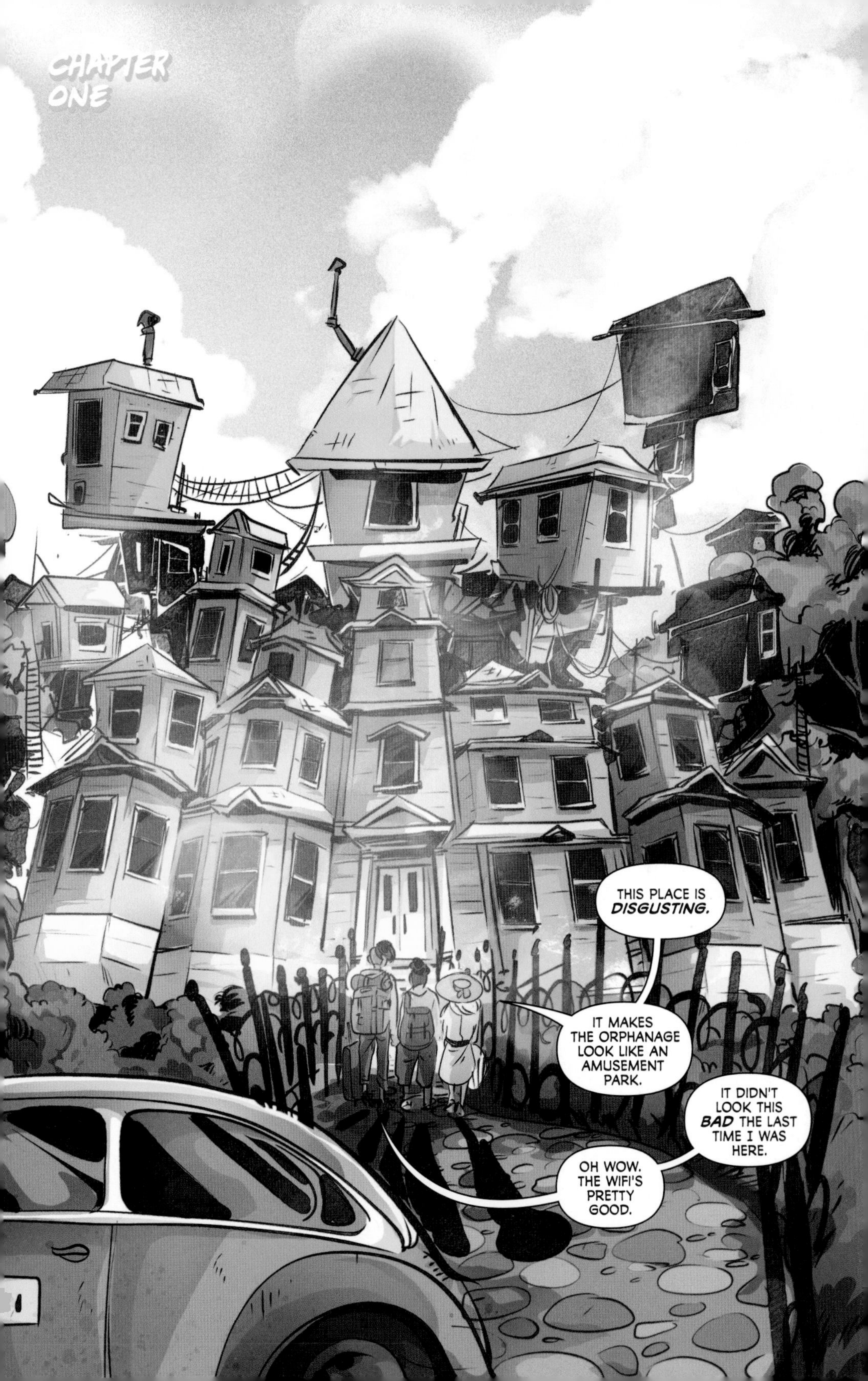
CHAPTER ONE
THIS PLACE IS DISGUSTING.
IT MAKES THE ORPHANAGE LOOK LIKE AN AMUSEMENT PARK.
IT DIDN'T LOOK THIS BAD THE LAST TIME I WAS HERE.
OH WOW. THE WIFI'S PRETTY GOOD.

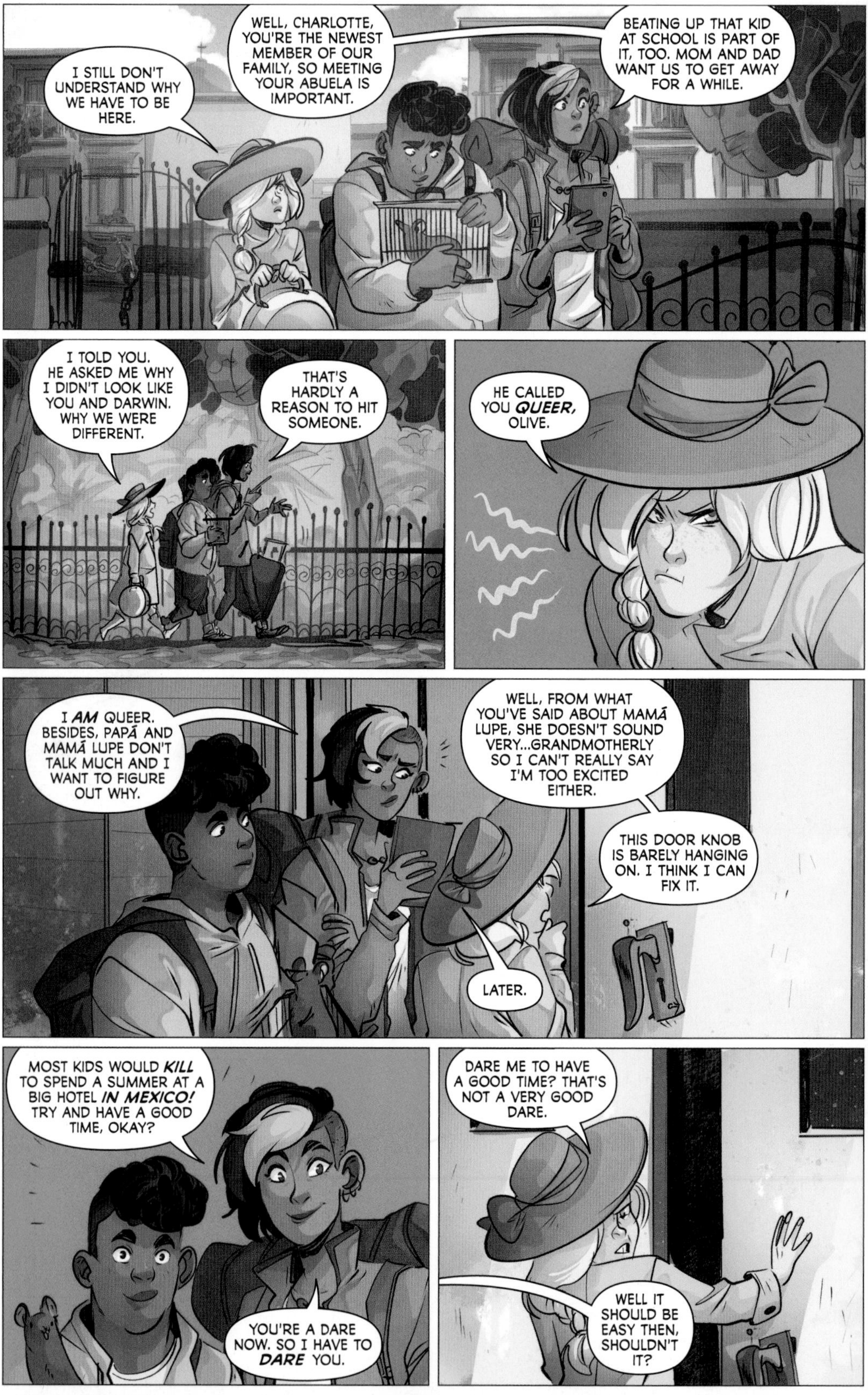
I STILL DON'T UNDERSTAND WHY WE HAVE TO BE HERE.
WELL, CHARLOTTE, YOU'RE THE NEWEST MEMBER OF OUR FAMILY, SO MEETING YOUR ABUELA IS IMPORTANT.
BEATING UP THAT KID AT SCHOOL IS PART OF IT, TOO. MOM AND DAD WANT US TO GET AWAY FOR A WHILE.
I TOLD YOU. HE ASKED ME WHY I DIDN'T LOOK LIKE YOU AND DARWIN. WHY WE WERE DIFFERENT.
THAT'S HARDLY A REASON TO HIT SOMEONE.
HE CALLED YOU QUEER, OLIVE.
I AM QUEER. BESIDES, PAPÁ AND MAMÁ LUPE DON'T TALK MUCH AND I WANT TO FIGURE OUT WHY.
WELL, FROM WHAT YOU'VE SAID ABOUT MAMÁ LUPE, SHE DOESN'T SOUND VERY...GRANDMOTHERLY SO I CAN'T REALLY SAY I'M TOO EXCITED EITHER.
THIS DOOR KNOB IS BARELY HANGING ON. I THINK I CAN FIX IT.
LATER.
MOST KIDS WOULD KILL TO SPEND A SUMMER AT A BIG HOTEL IN MEXICO! TRY AND HAVE A GOOD TIME, OKAY?
YOU'RE A DARE NOW. SO I HAVE TO DARE YOU.
DARE ME TO HAVE A GOOD TIME? THAT'S NOT A VERY GOOD DARE.
WELL IT SHOULD BE EASY THEN, SHOULDN'T IT?

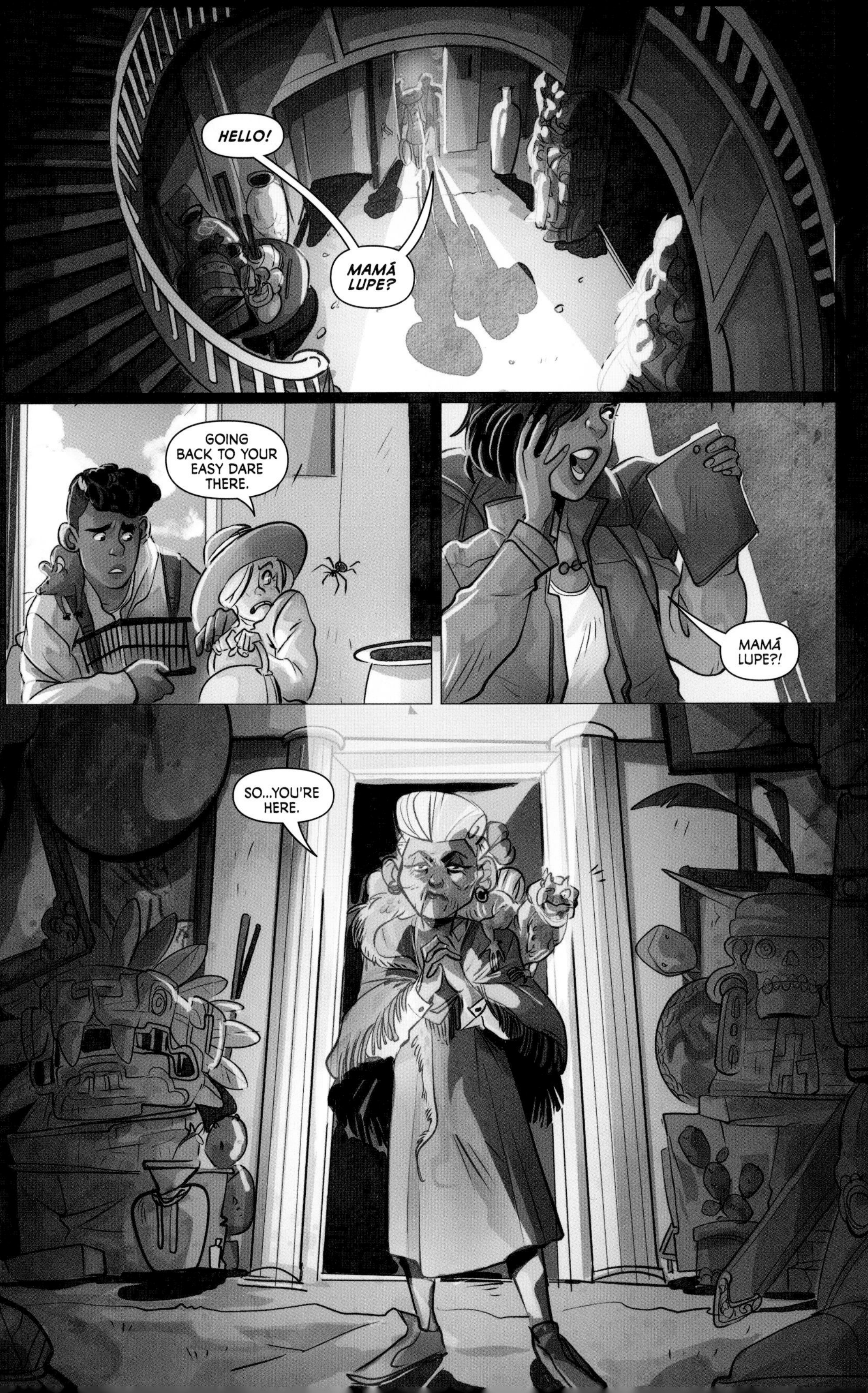
HELLO!
MAMÁ LUPE?
GOING BACK TO YOUR EASY DARE THERE.
MAMÁ LUPE?!
SO...YOU'RE HERE.

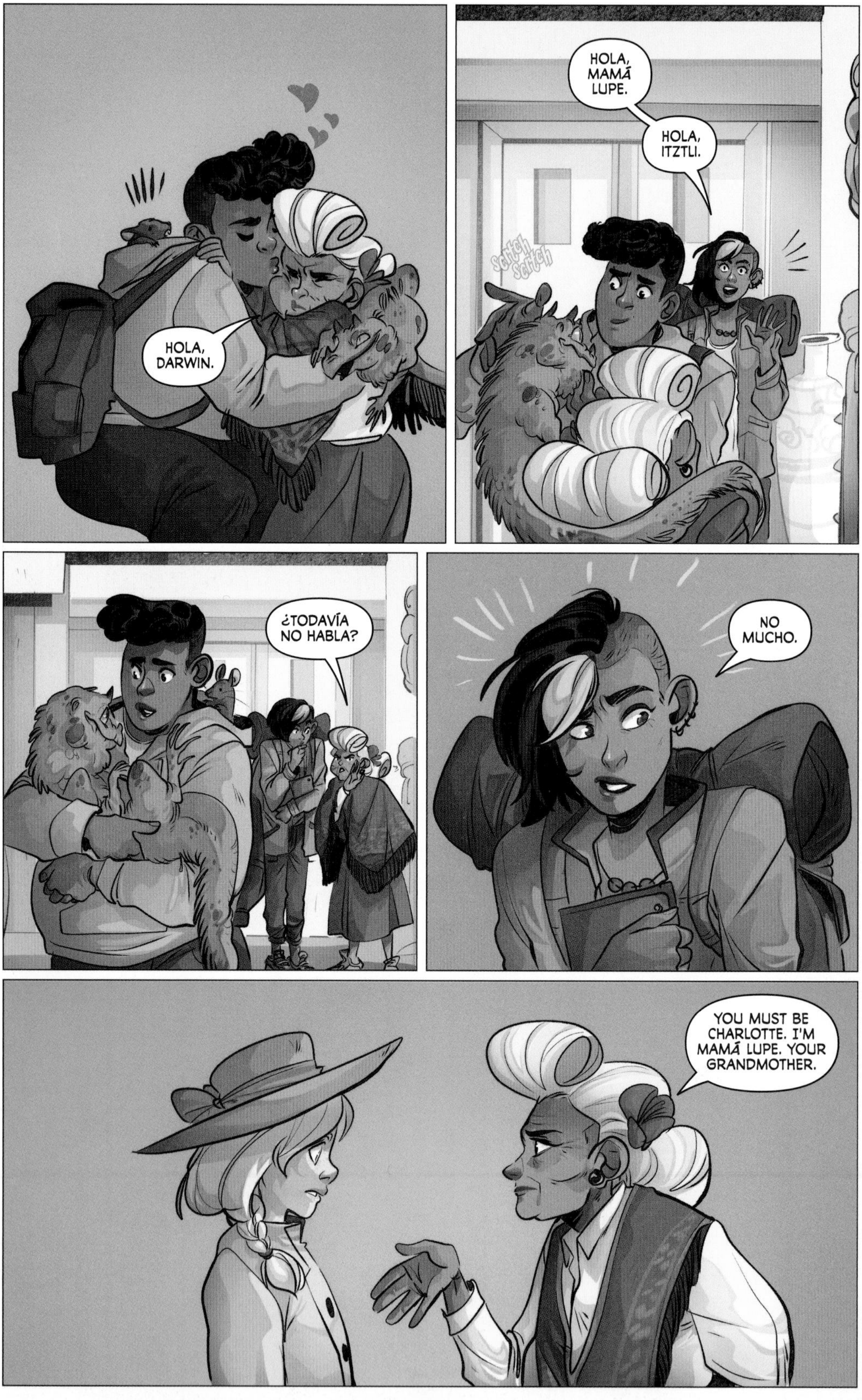
HOLA, DARWIN.
HOLA, MAMÁ LUPE.
HOLA, ITZTLI.
SCRTCH SCRTCH
¿TODAVÍA NO HABLA?
NO MUCHO.
YOU MUST BE CHARLOTTE. I'M MAMÁ LUPE. YOUR GRANDMOTHER.

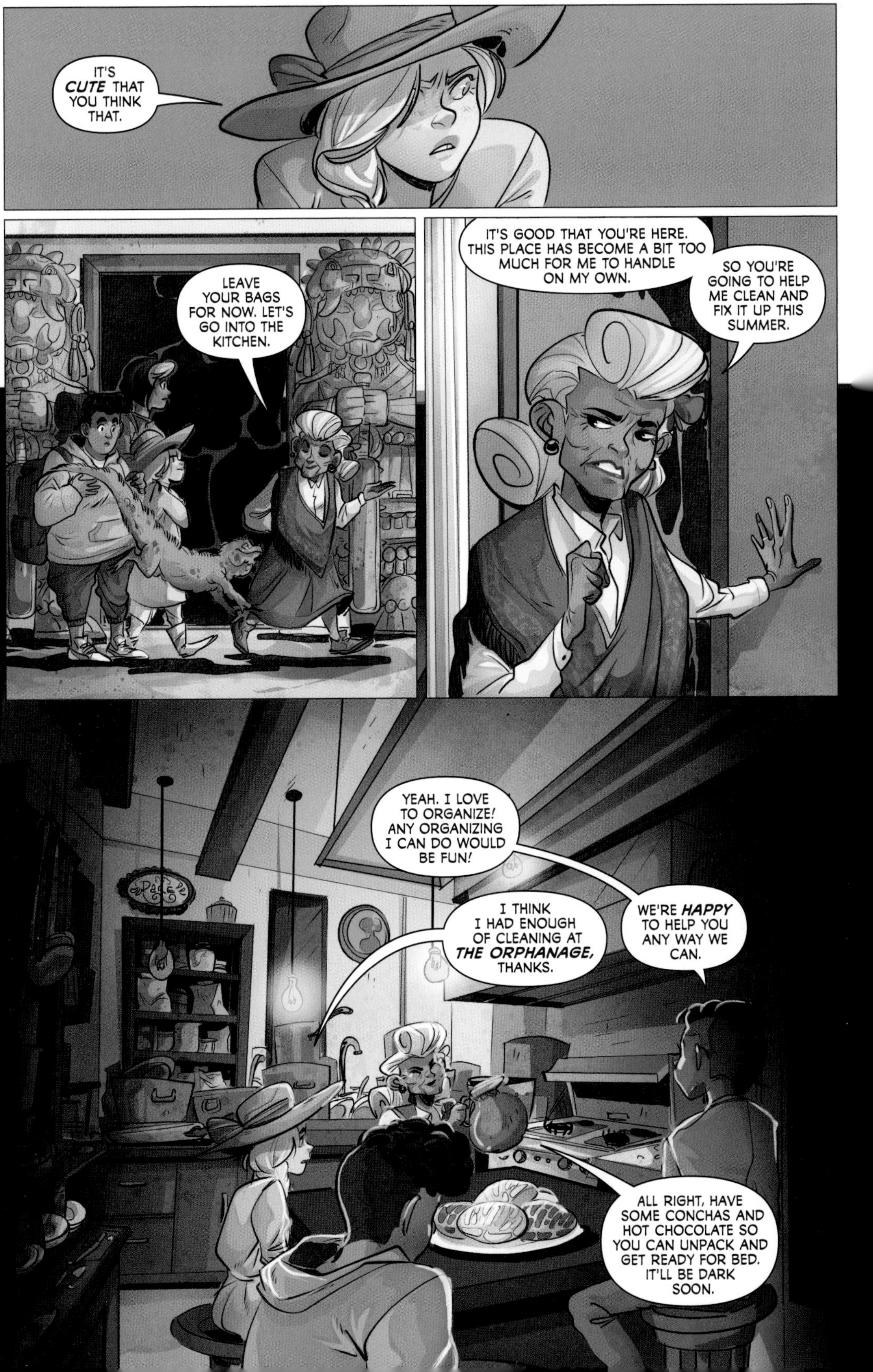
IT'S *CUTE* THAT YOU THINK THAT.
LEAVE YOUR BAGS FOR NOW. LET'S GO INTO THE KITCHEN.
IT'S GOOD THAT YOU'RE HERE. THIS PLACE HAS BECOME A BIT TOO MUCH FOR ME TO HANDLE ON MY OWN.
SO YOU'RE GOING TO HELP ME CLEAN AND FIX IT UP THIS SUMMER.
YEAH. I LOVE TO ORGANIZE! ANY ORGANIZING I CAN DO WOULD BE FUN!
I THINK I HAD ENOUGH OF CLEANING AT *THE ORPHANAGE,* THANKS.
WE'RE *HAPPY* TO HELP YOU ANY WAY WE CAN.
ALL RIGHT, HAVE SOME CONCHAS AND HOT CHOCOLATE SO YOU CAN UNPACK AND GET READY FOR BED. IT'LL BE DARK SOON.

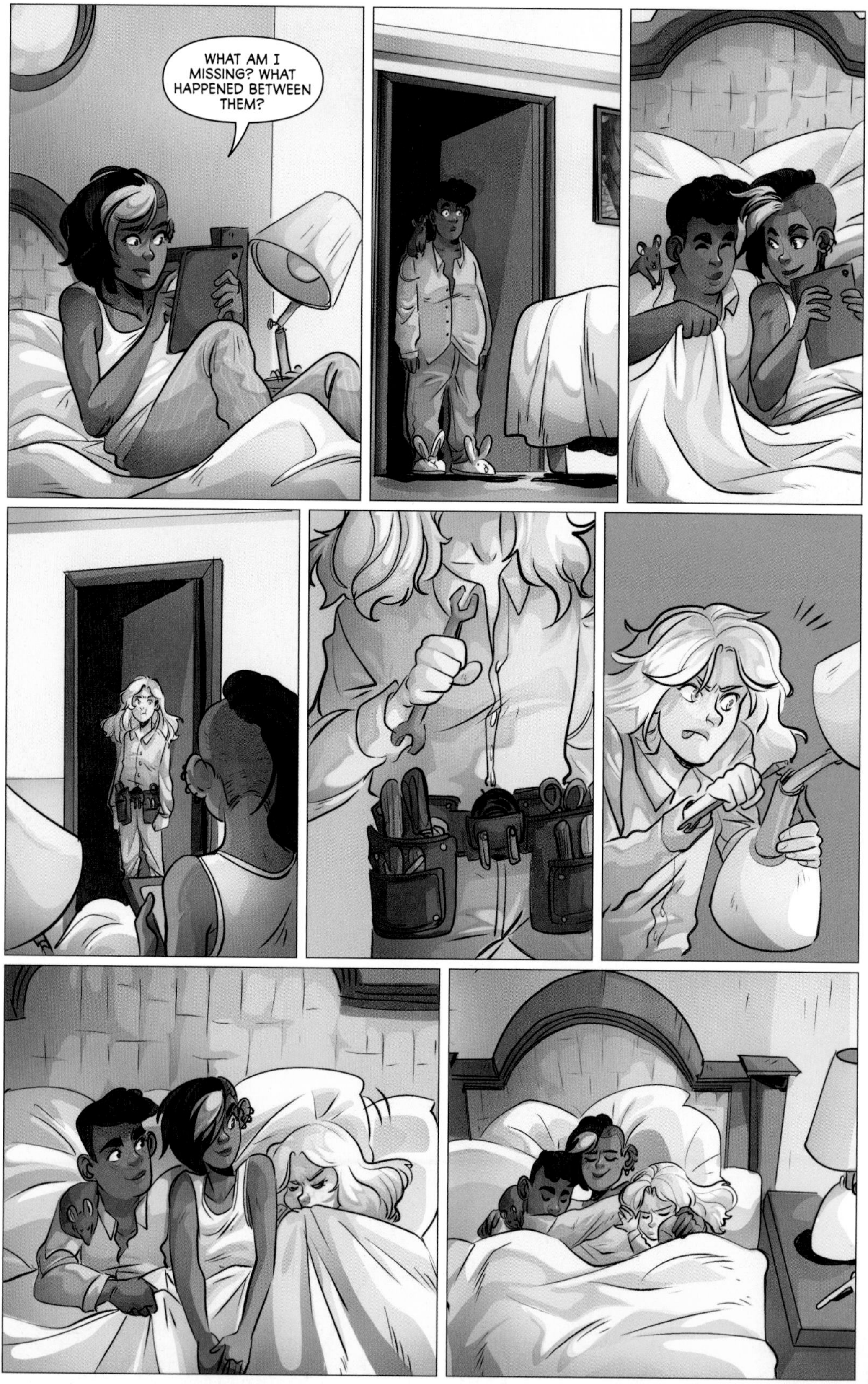
WHAT AM I MISSING? WHAT HAPPENED BETWEEN THEM?

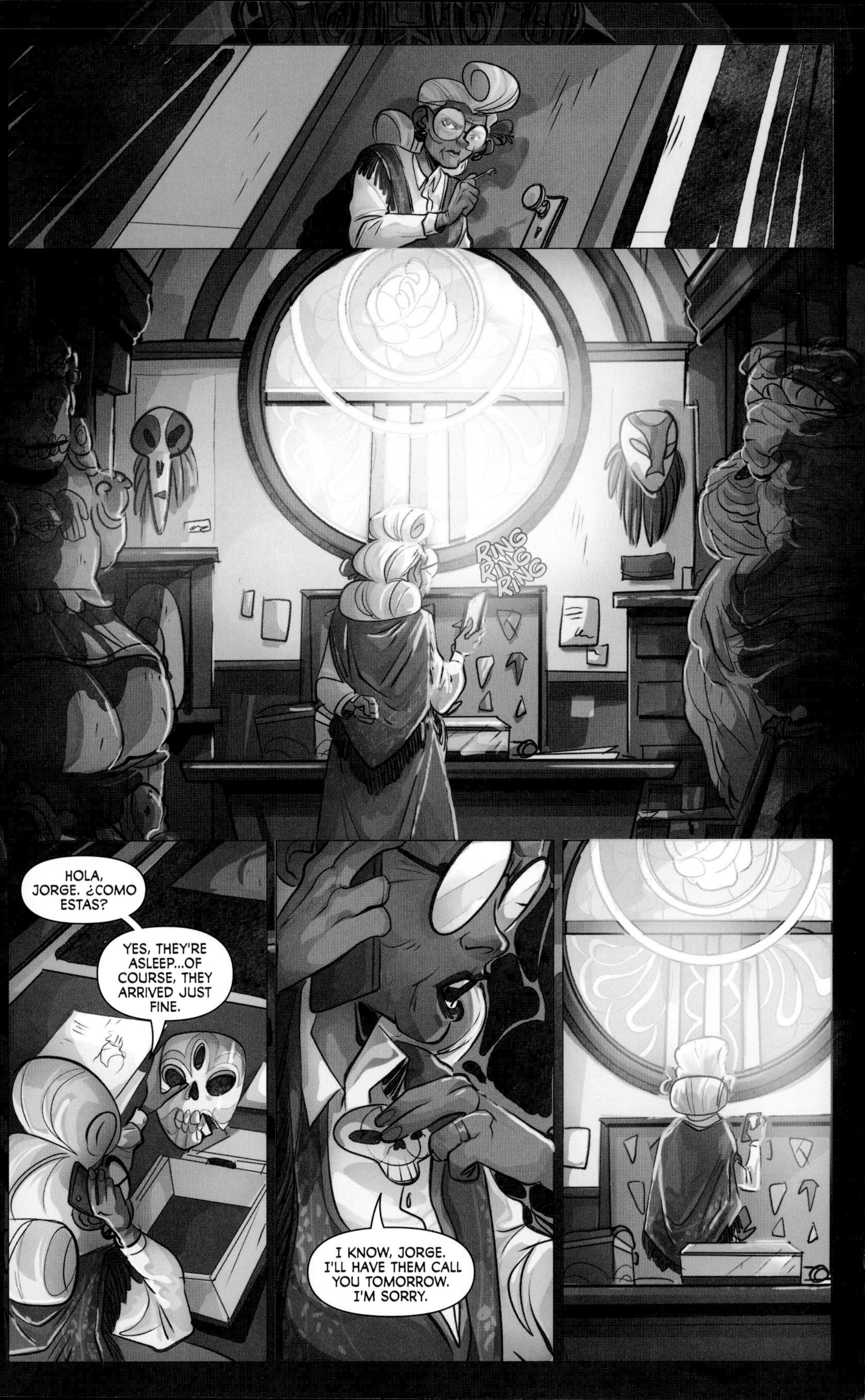
RING RING RING
HOLA, JORGE. ¿COMO ESTAS?
YES, THEY'RE ASLEEP...OF COURSE, THEY ARRIVED JUST FINE.
I KNOW, JORGE. I'LL HAVE THEM CALL YOU TOMORROW. I'M SORRY.

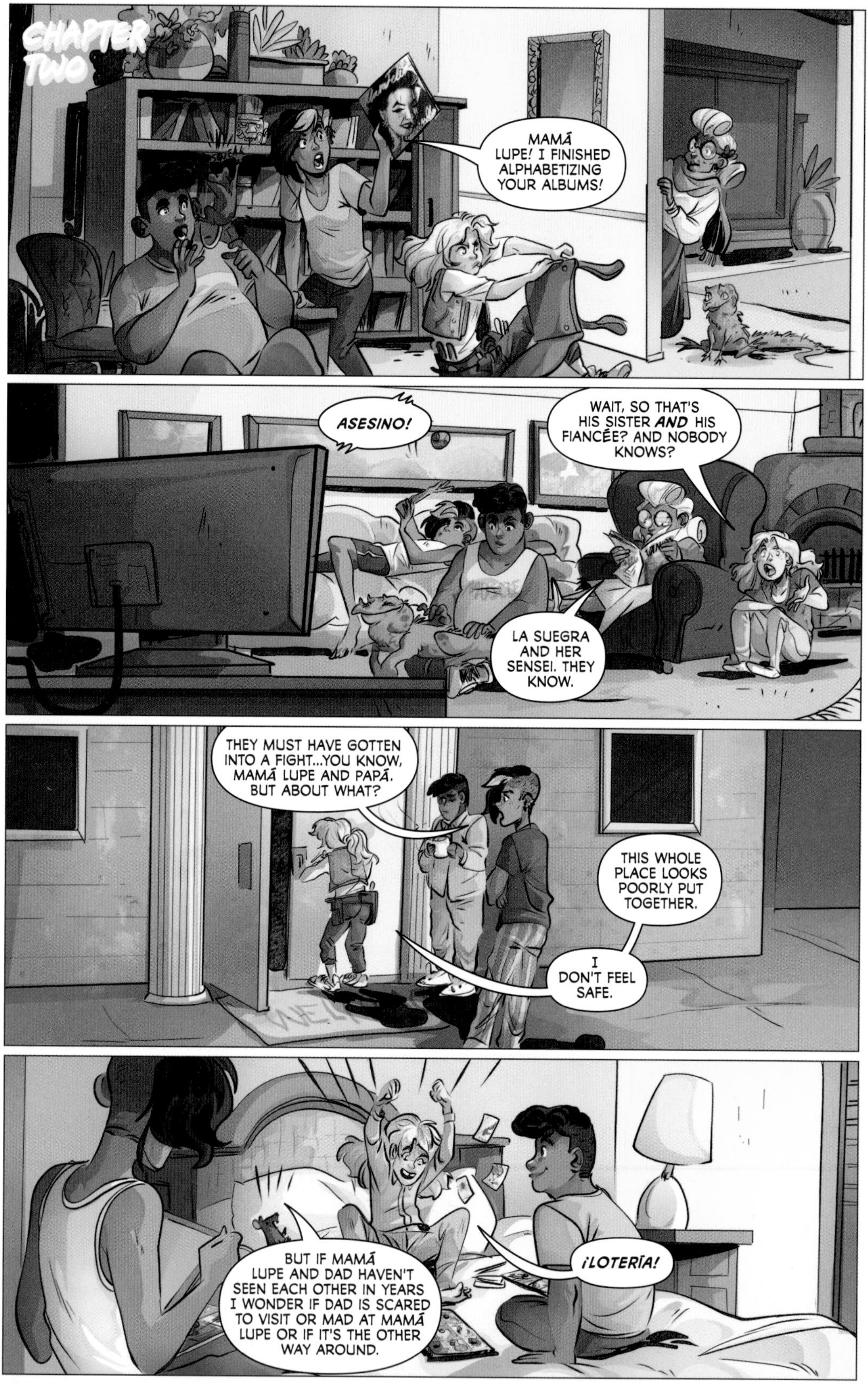
CHAPTER TWO
MAMÁ LUPE! I FINISHED ALPHABETIZING YOUR ALBUMS!
ASESINO!
WAIT, SO THAT'S HIS SISTER *AND* HIS FIANCÉE? AND NOBODY KNOWS?
LA SUEGRA AND HER SENSEI. THEY KNOW.
THEY MUST HAVE GOTTEN INTO A FIGHT...YOU KNOW, MAMÁ LUPE AND PAPÁ. BUT ABOUT WHAT?
THIS WHOLE PLACE LOOKS POORLY PUT TOGETHER.
I DON'T FEEL SAFE.
BUT IF MAMÁ LUPE AND DAD HAVEN'T SEEN EACH OTHER IN YEARS I WONDER IF DAD IS SCARED TO VISIT OR MAD AT MAMÁ LUPE OR IF IT'S THE OTHER WAY AROUND.
¡LOTERÍA!

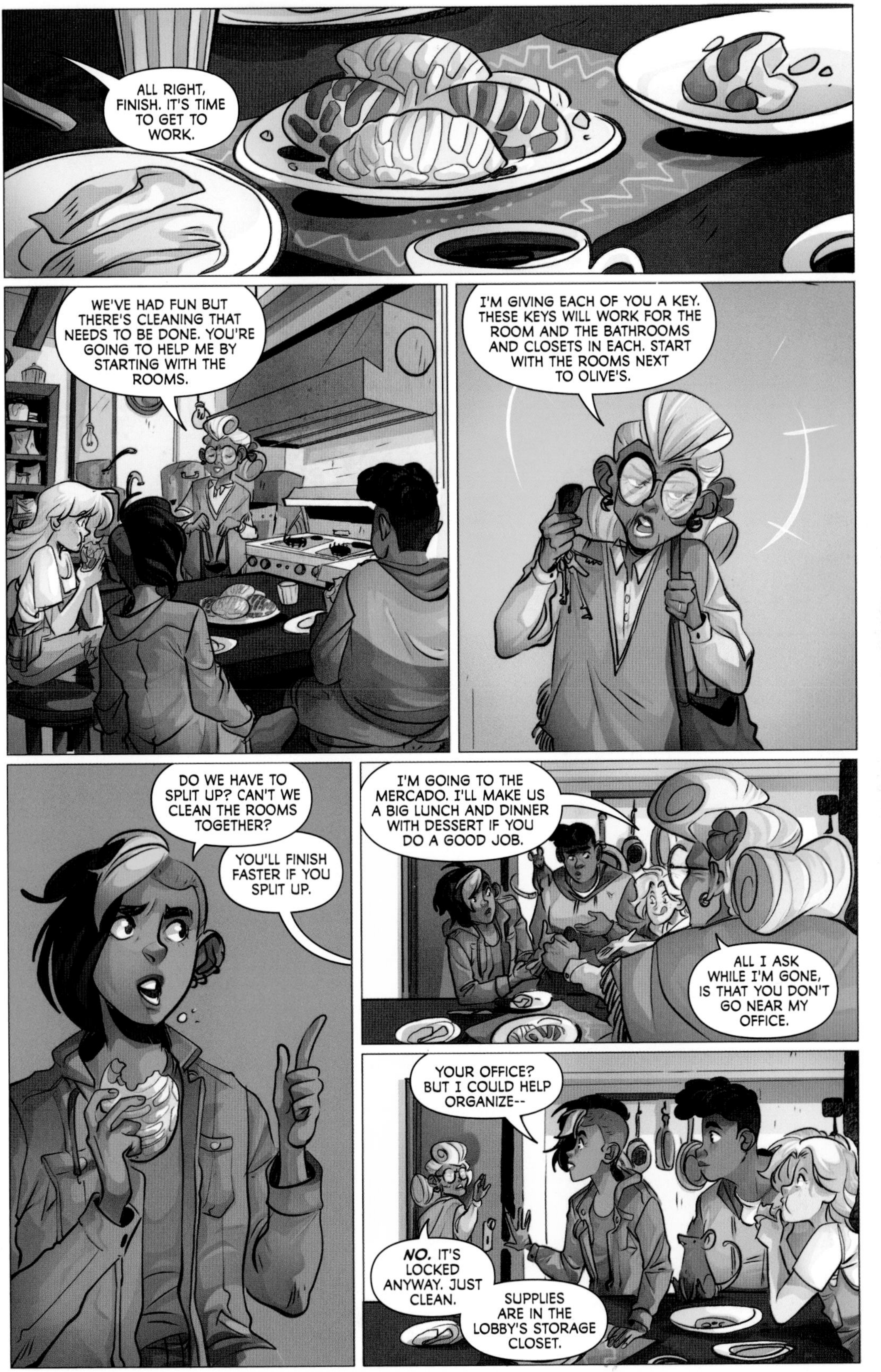
ALL RIGHT, FINISH. IT'S TIME TO GET TO WORK.
WE'VE HAD FUN BUT THERE'S CLEANING THAT NEEDS TO BE DONE. YOU'RE GOING TO HELP ME BY STARTING WITH THE ROOMS.
I'M GIVING EACH OF YOU A KEY. THESE KEYS WILL WORK FOR THE ROOM AND THE BATHROOMS AND CLOSETS IN EACH. START WITH THE ROOMS NEXT TO OLIVE'S.
DO WE HAVE TO SPLIT UP? CAN'T WE CLEAN THE ROOMS TOGETHER?
YOU'LL FINISH FASTER IF YOU SPLIT UP.
I'M GOING TO THE MERCADO. I'LL MAKE US A BIG LUNCH AND DINNER WITH DESSERT IF YOU DO A GOOD JOB.
ALL I ASK WHILE I'M GONE, IS THAT YOU DON'T GO NEAR MY OFFICE.
YOUR OFFICE? BUT I COULD HELP ORGANIZE--
NO. IT'S LOCKED ANYWAY. JUST CLEAN.
SUPPLIES ARE IN THE LOBBY'S STORAGE CLOSET.

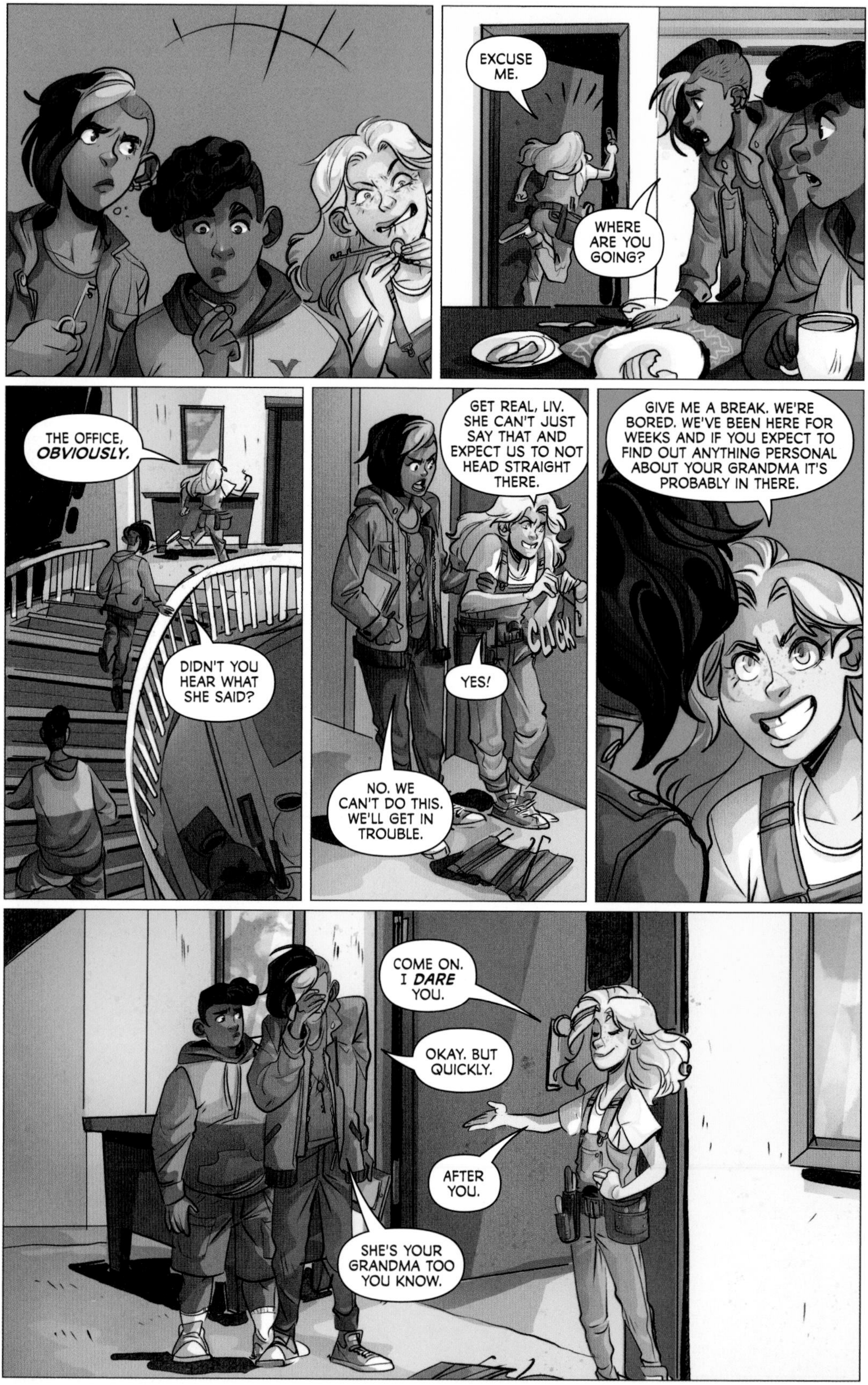
EXCUSE ME.
WHERE ARE YOU GOING?
THE OFFICE, *OBVIOUSLY.*
DIDN'T YOU HEAR WHAT SHE SAID?
GET REAL, LIV. SHE CAN'T JUST SAY THAT AND EXPECT US TO NOT HEAD STRAIGHT THERE.
CLICK
YES!
NO. WE CAN'T DO THIS. WE'LL GET IN TROUBLE.
GIVE ME A BREAK. WE'RE BORED. WE'VE BEEN HERE FOR WEEKS AND IF YOU EXPECT TO FIND OUT ANYTHING PERSONAL ABOUT YOUR GRANDMA IT'S PROBABLY IN THERE.
COME ON. I *DARE* YOU.
OKAY. BUT QUICKLY.
AFTER YOU.
SHE'S YOUR GRANDMA TOO YOU KNOW.

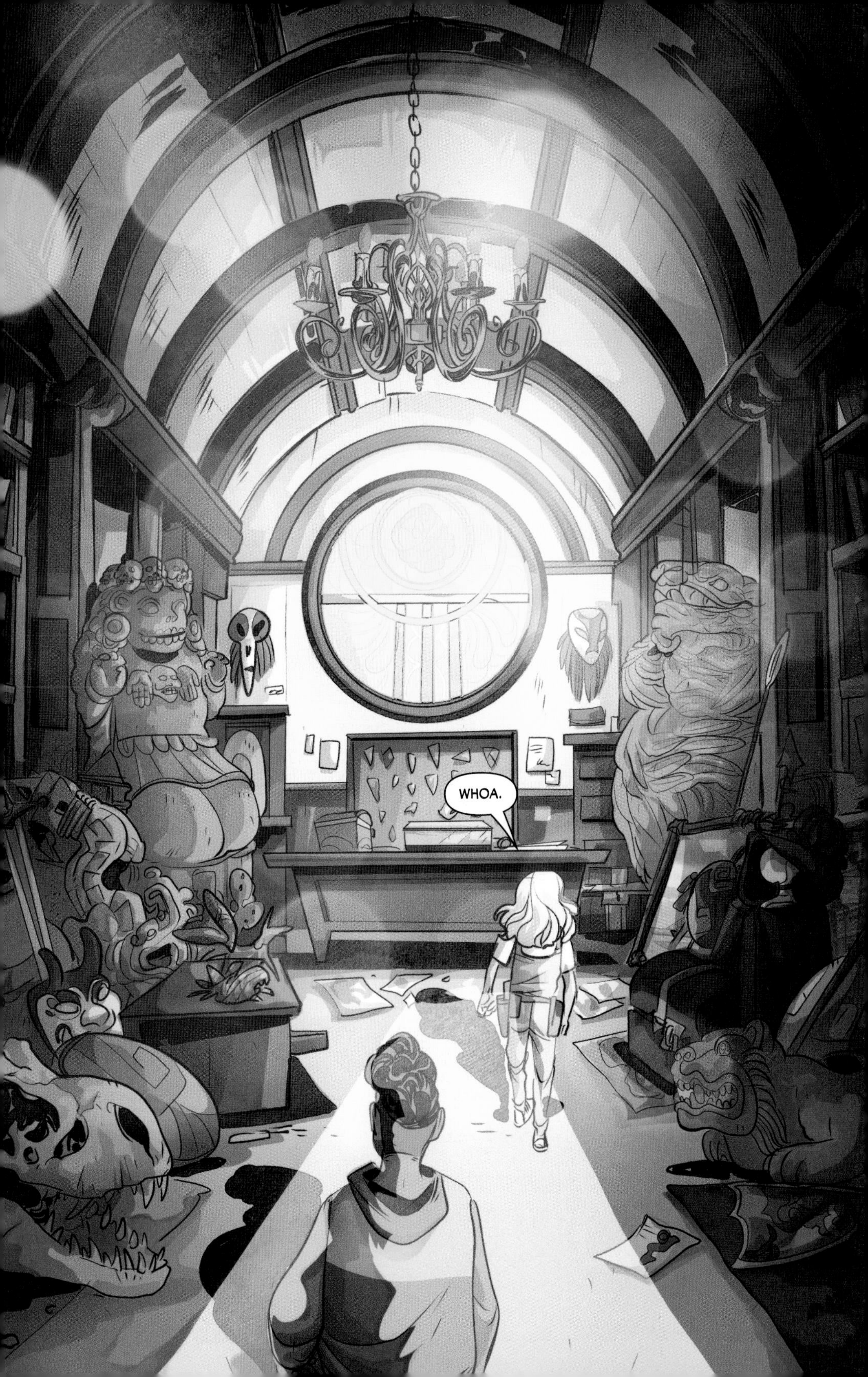
WHOA.

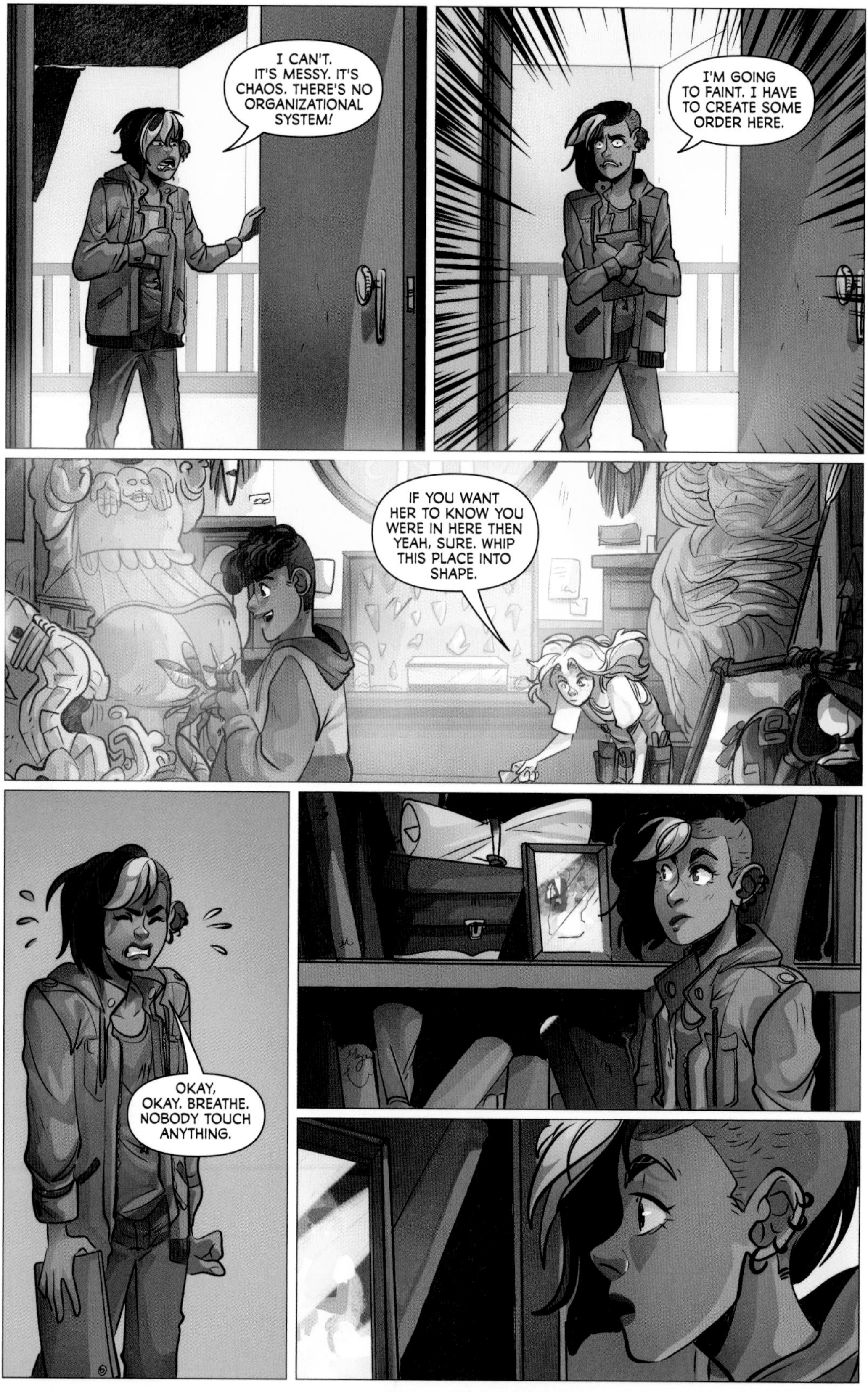
I CAN'T. IT'S MESSY. IT'S CHAOS. THERE'S NO ORGANIZATIONAL SYSTEM!
I'M GOING TO FAINT. I HAVE TO CREATE SOME ORDER HERE.
IF YOU WANT HER TO KNOW YOU WERE IN HERE THEN YEAH, SURE. WHIP THIS PLACE INTO SHAPE.
OKAY, OKAY. BREATHE. NOBODY TOUCH ANYTHING.

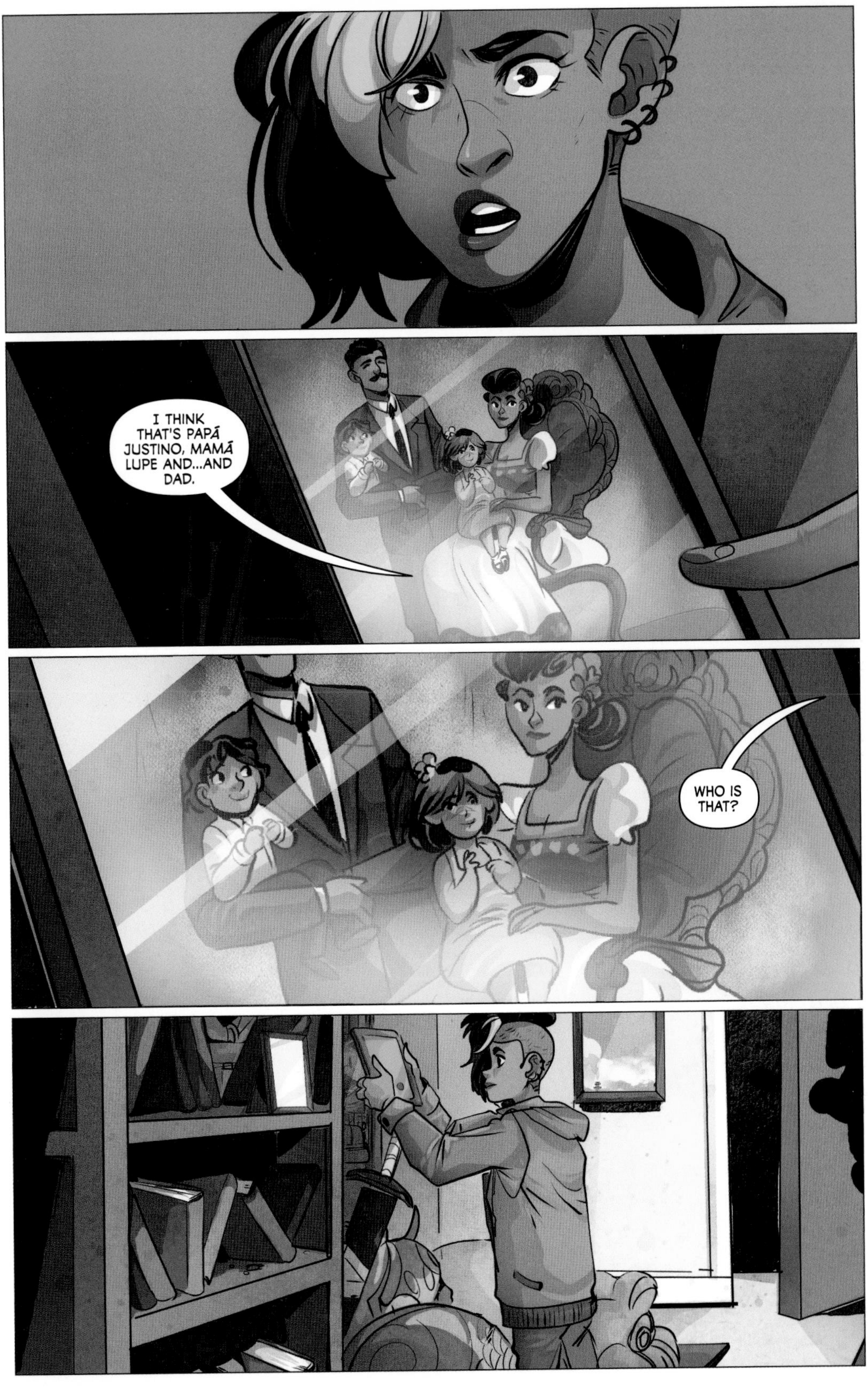
I THINK THAT'S PAPÁ JUSTINO, MAMÁ LUPE AND...AND DAD.
WHO IS THAT?

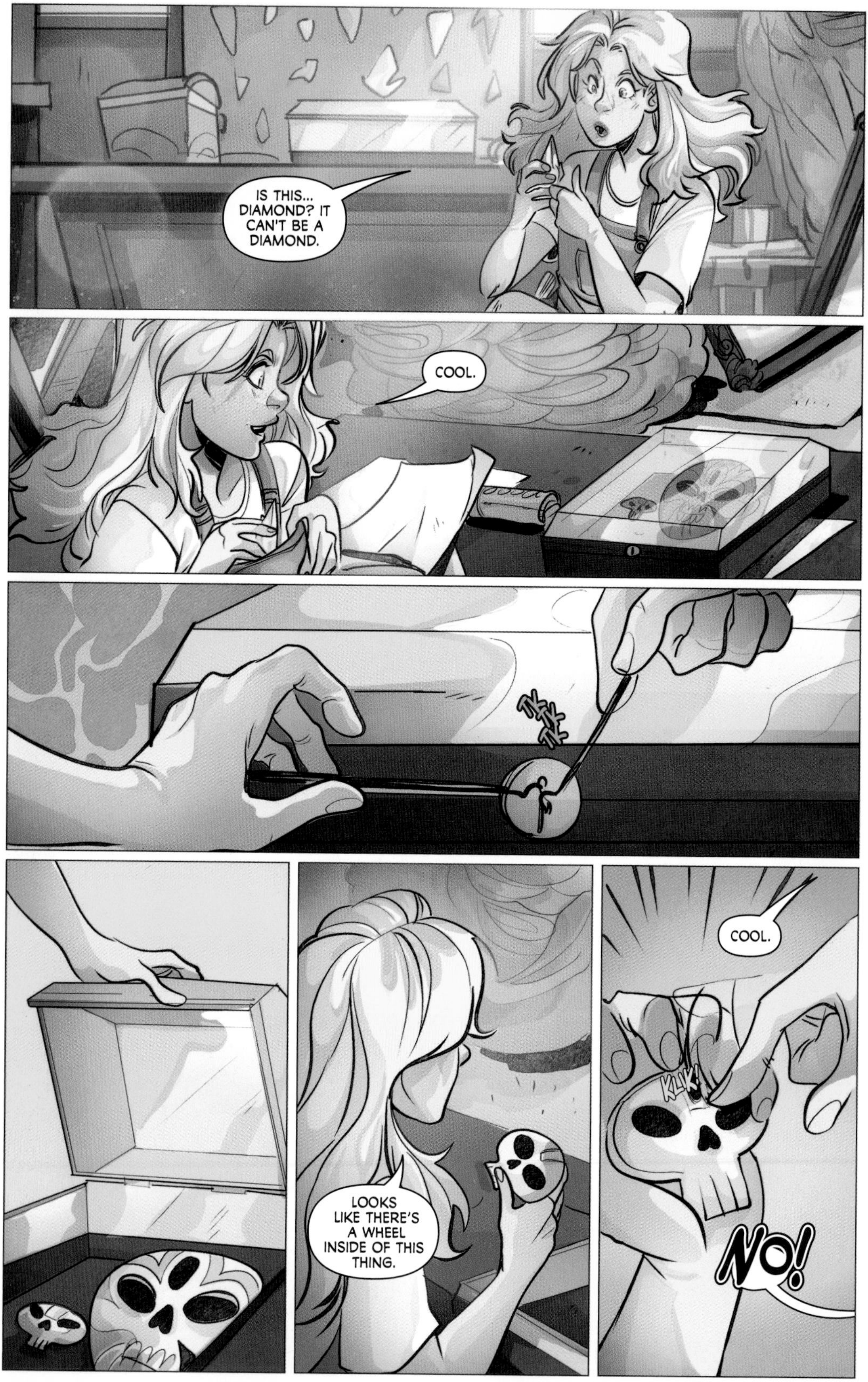
IS THIS... DIAMOND? IT CAN'T BE A DIAMOND.
COOL.
TK TK TK
LOOKS LIKE THERE'S A WHEEL INSIDE OF THIS THING.
COOL.
KLIK!
NO!

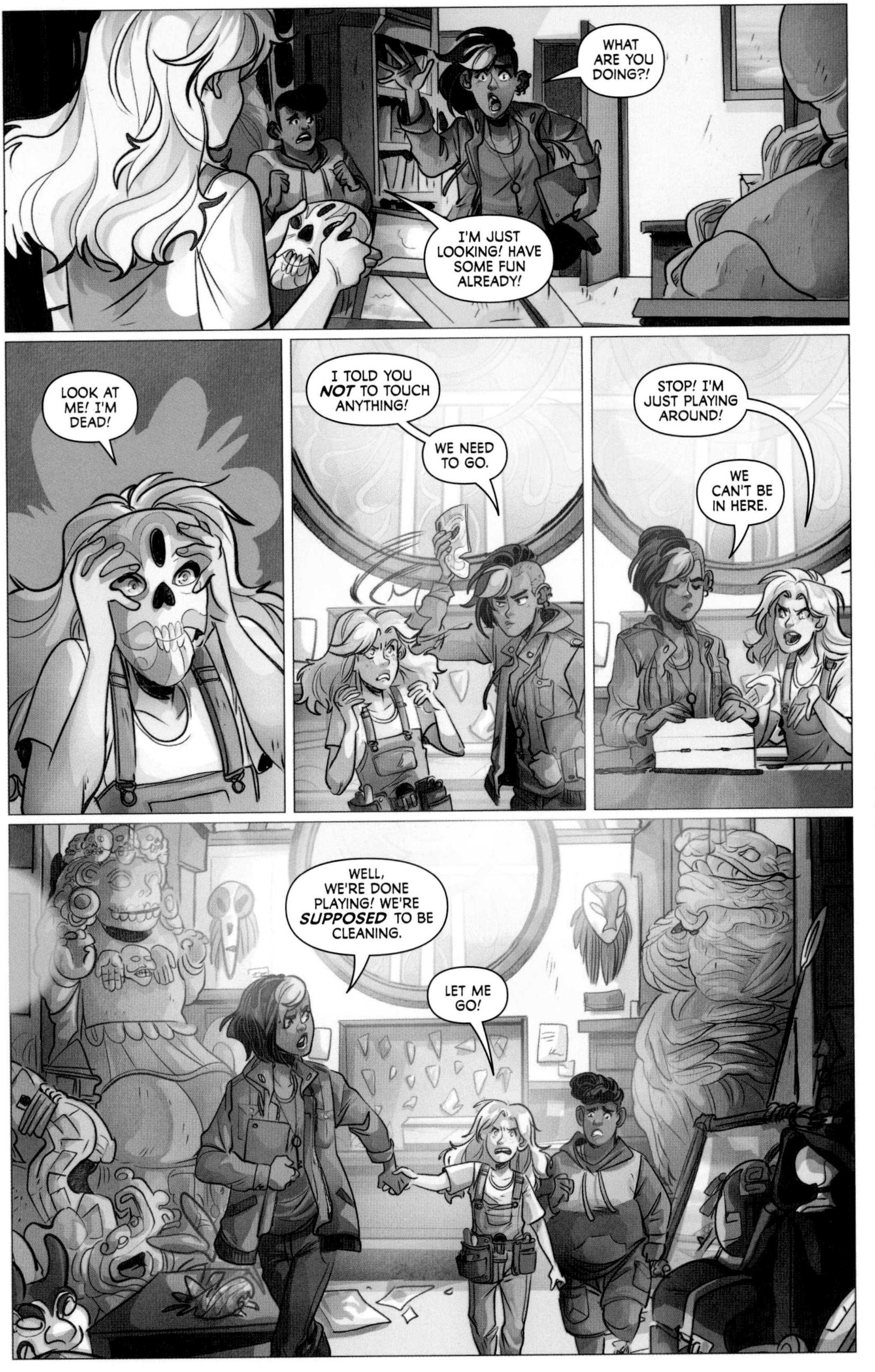
WHAT ARE YOU DOING?!
I'M JUST LOOKING! HAVE SOME FUN ALREADY!
LOOK AT ME! I'M DEAD!
I TOLD YOU *NOT* TO TOUCH ANYTHING!
WE NEED TO GO.
STOP! I'M JUST PLAYING AROUND!
WE CAN'T BE IN HERE.
WELL, WE'RE DONE PLAYING! WE'RE *SUPPOSED* TO BE CLEANING.
LET ME GO!

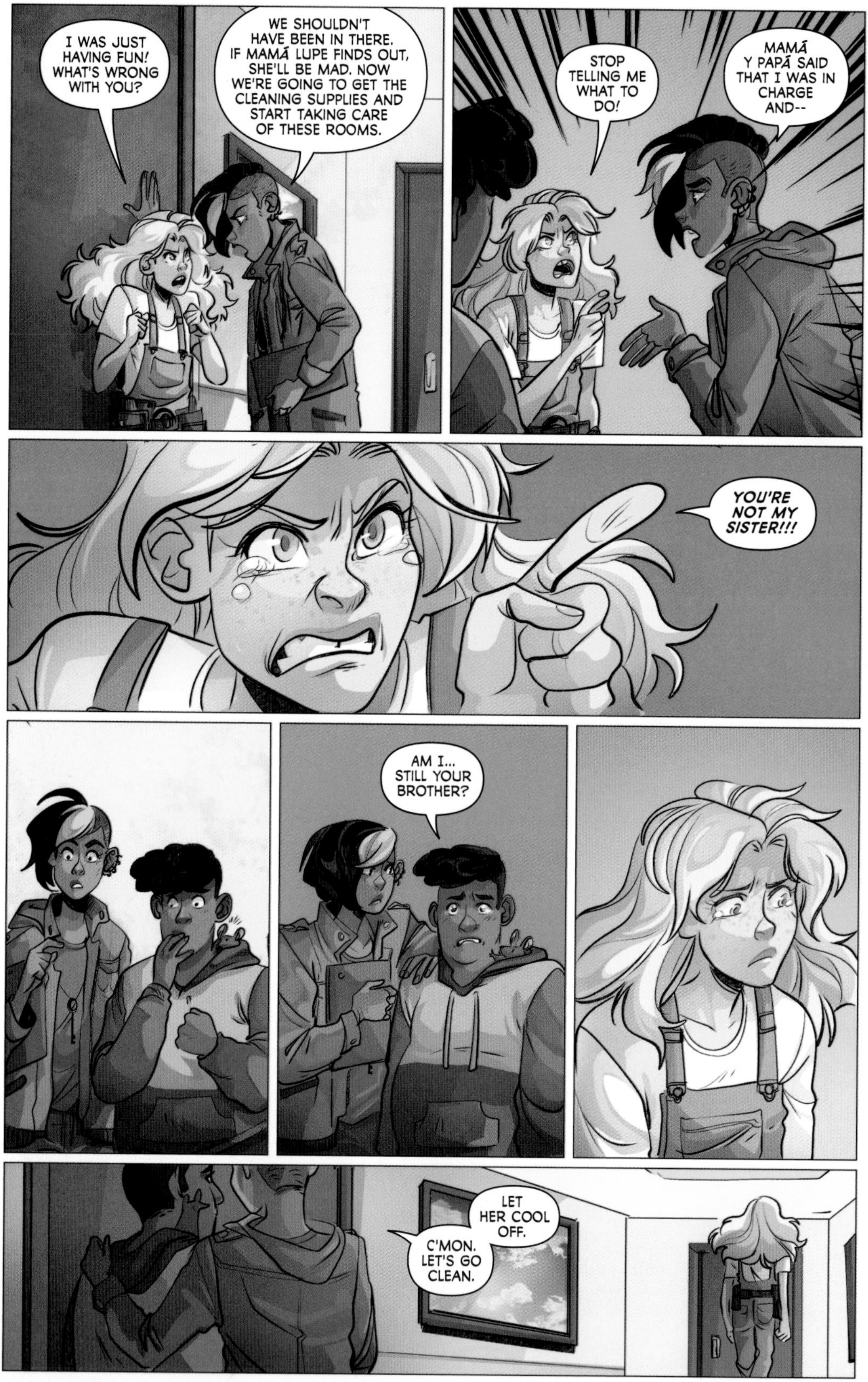
I WAS JUST HAVING FUN! WHAT'S WRONG WITH YOU?
WE SHOULDN'T HAVE BEEN IN THERE. IF MAMÁ LUPE FINDS OUT, SHE'LL BE MAD. NOW WE'RE GOING TO GET THE CLEANING SUPPLIES AND START TAKING CARE OF THESE ROOMS.
STOP TELLING ME WHAT TO DO!
MAMÁ Y PAPÁ SAID THAT I WAS IN CHARGE AND--
YOU'RE NOT MY SISTER!!!
AM I... STILL YOUR BROTHER?
LET HER COOL OFF.
C'MON. LET'S GO CLEAN.

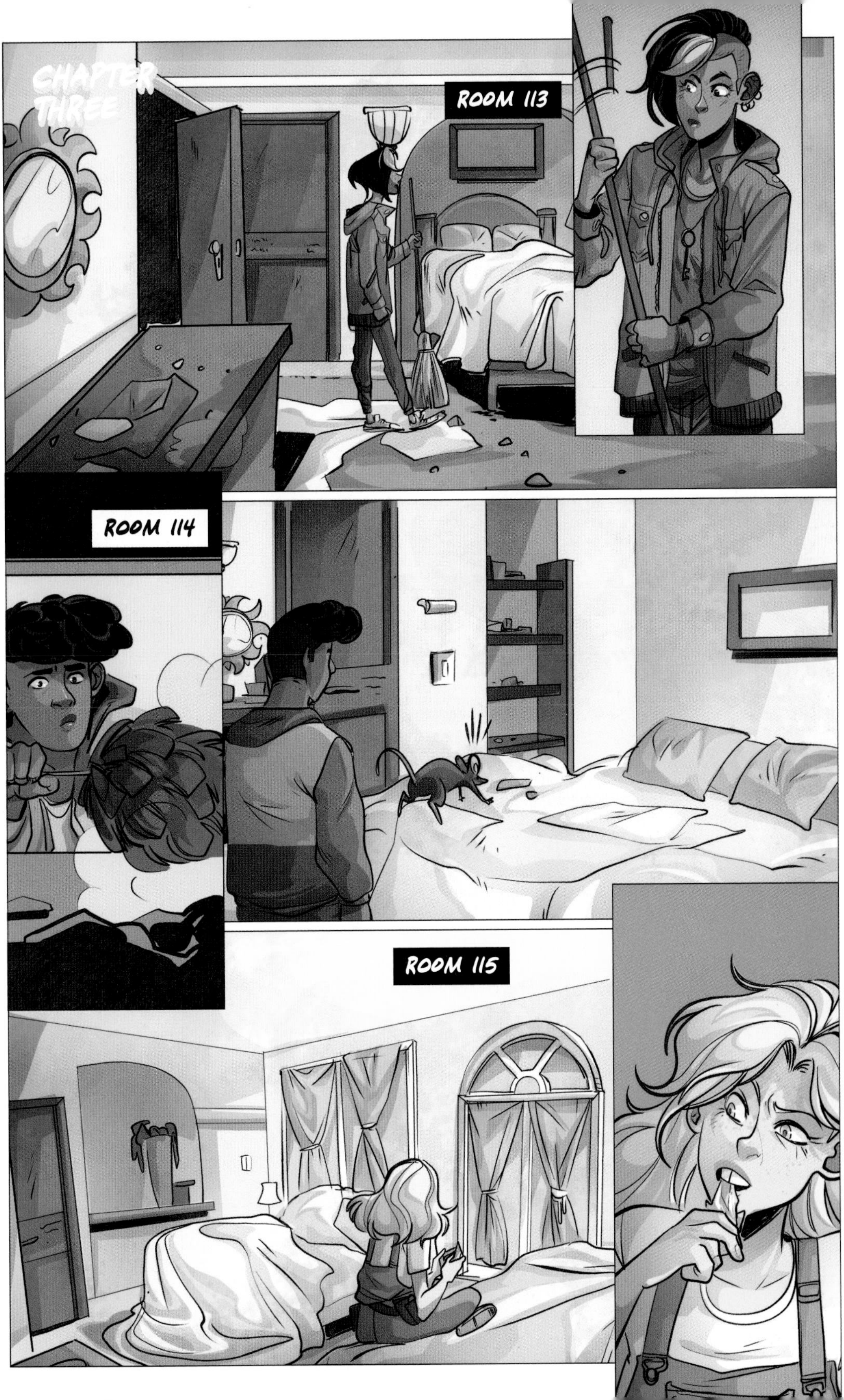
CHAPTER THREE
ROOM 113
ROOM 114
ROOM 115

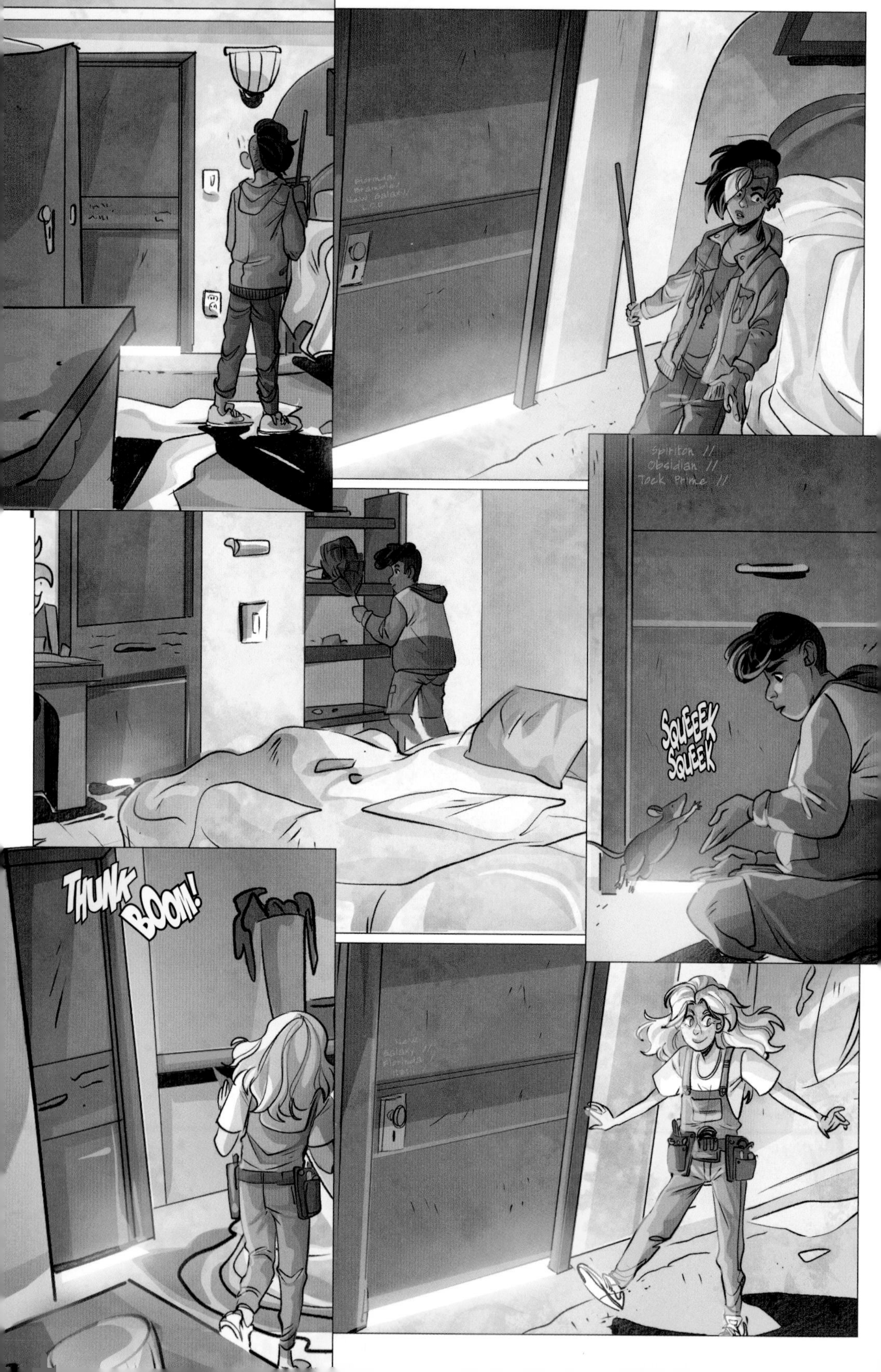
Spiriton //
Obsidian //
Tock Prime //
SQUEEEK
SQUEEK
THUNK
BOOM!

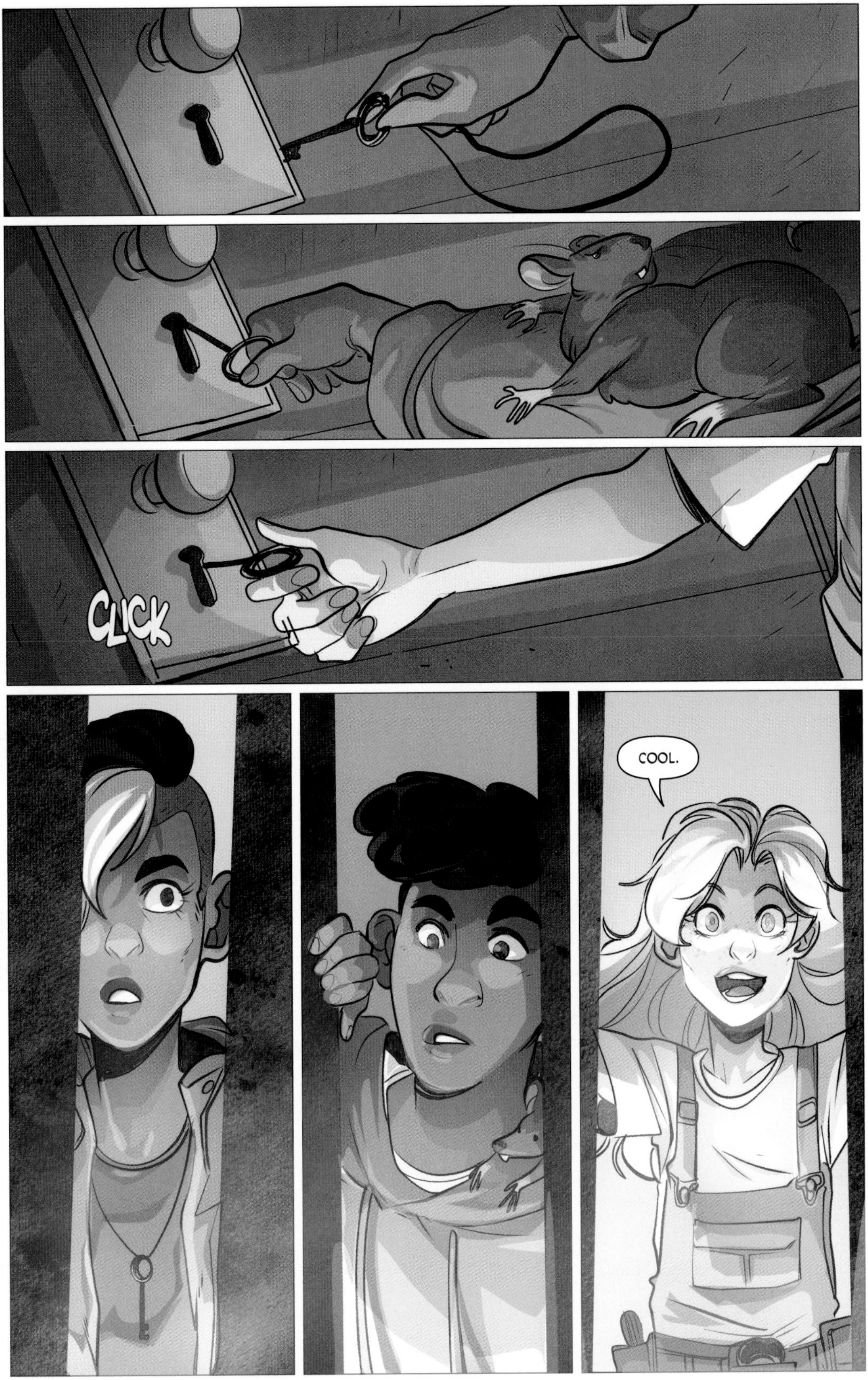
CLICK
COOL.

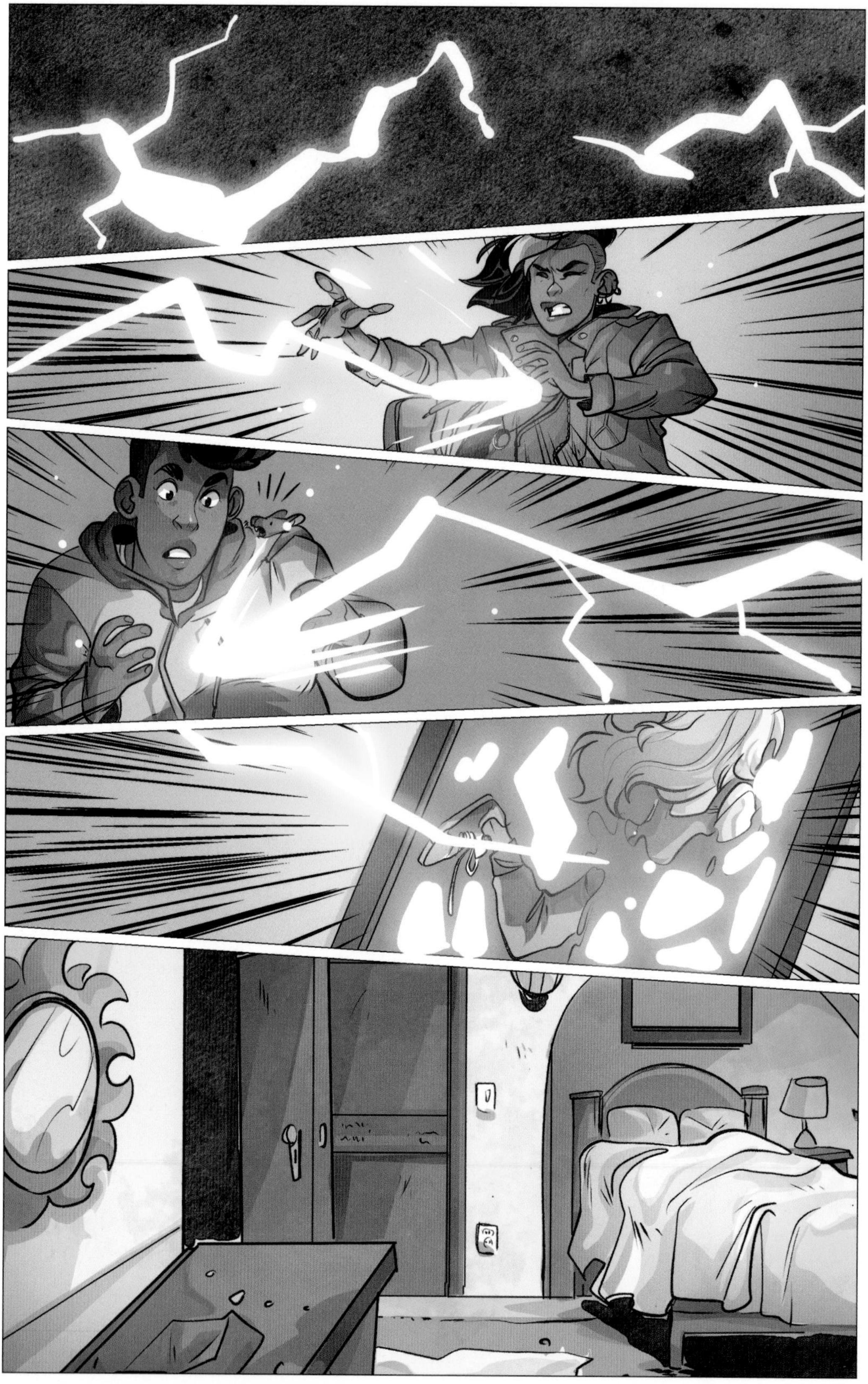

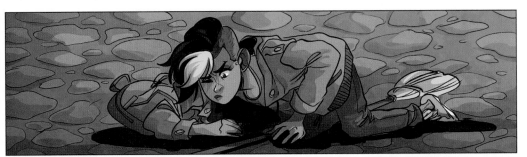

WHERE THE--

SNIFFLE.

*SNIFFLE.
SNIFFLE.*

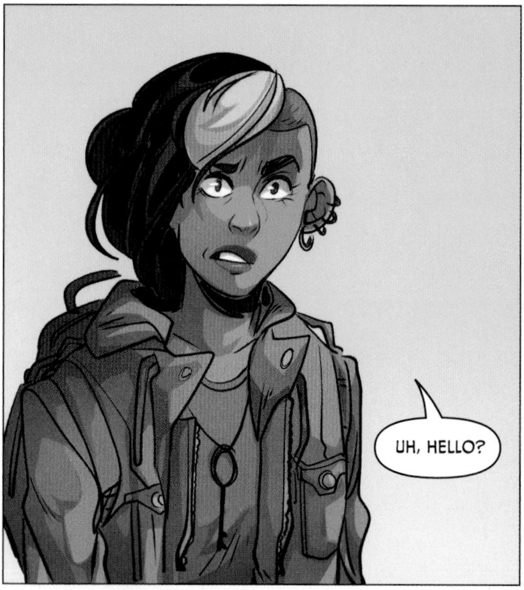
UH, HELLO?

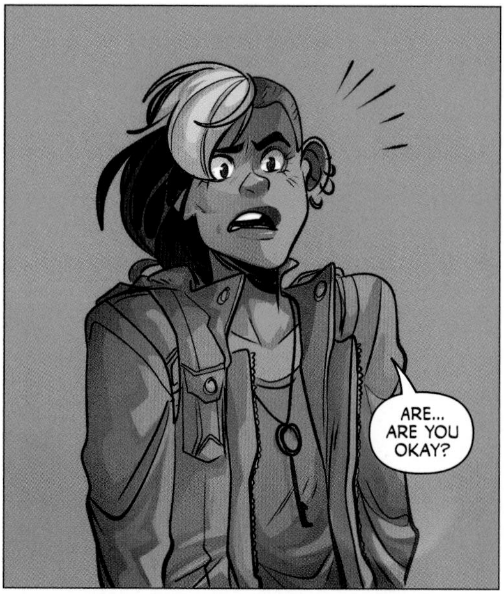
ARE... ARE YOU OKAY?

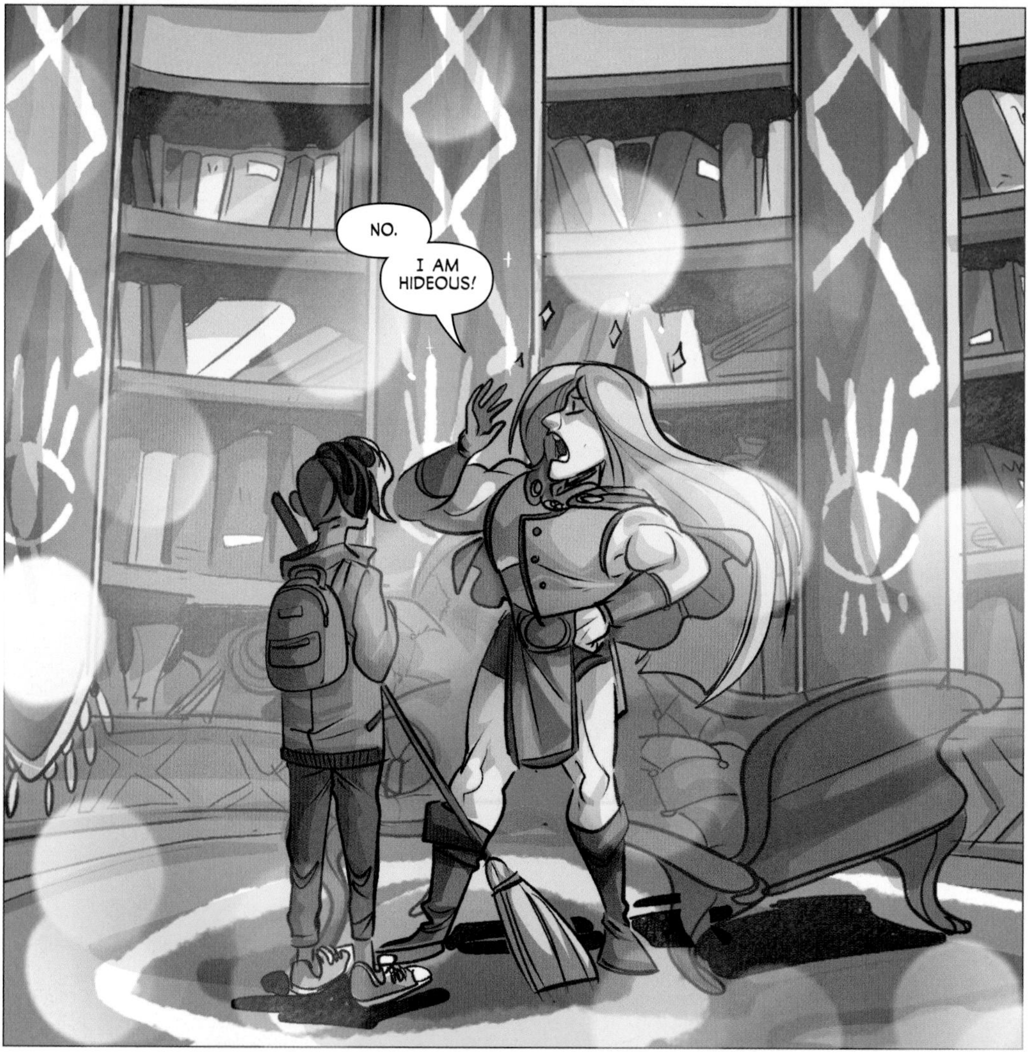
NO.
I AM HIDEOUS!

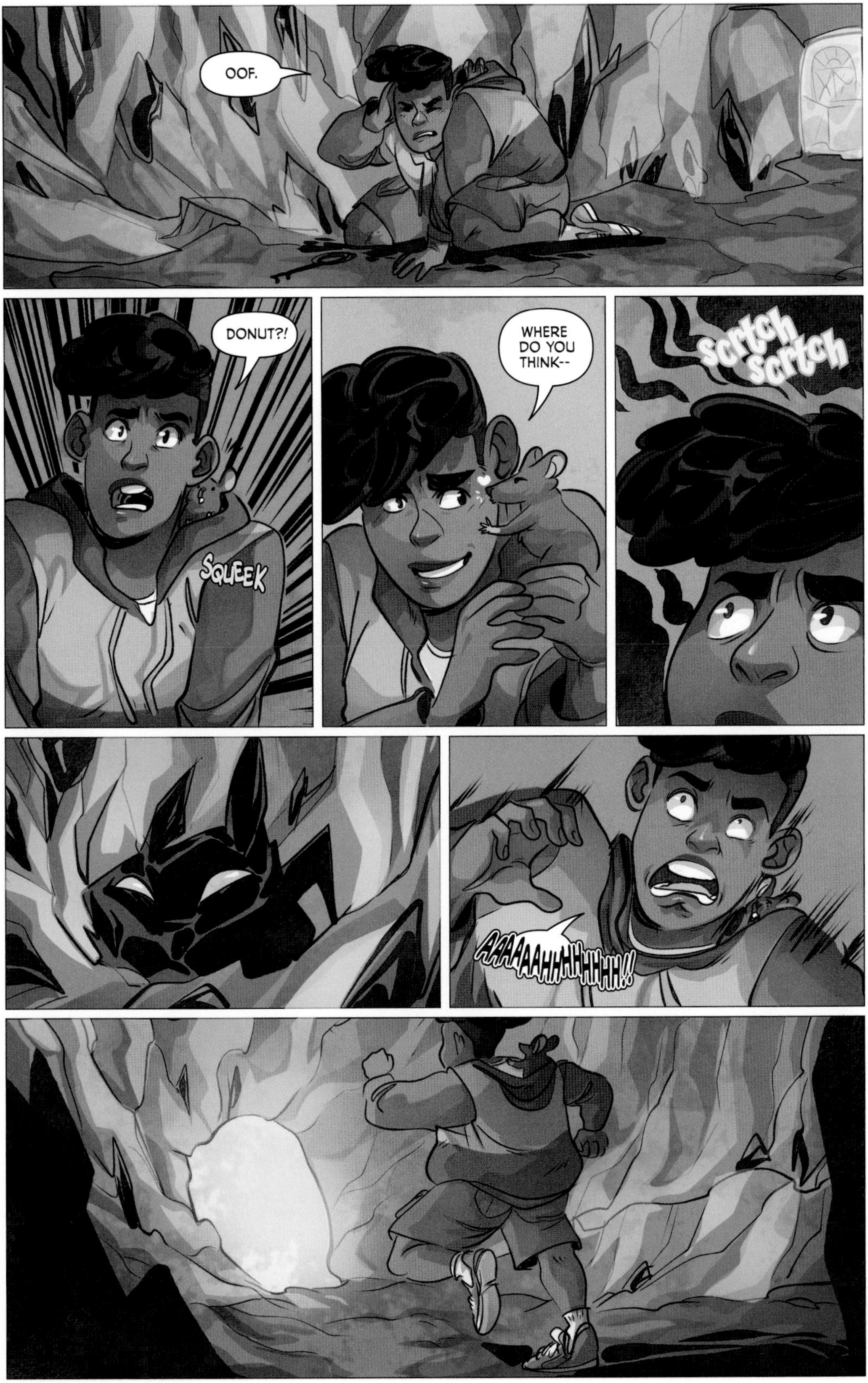
OOF.
DONUT?!
SQUEEK
WHERE DO YOU THINK--
SCRTCH SCRTCH
AAAAAAHHHHHHHH!!

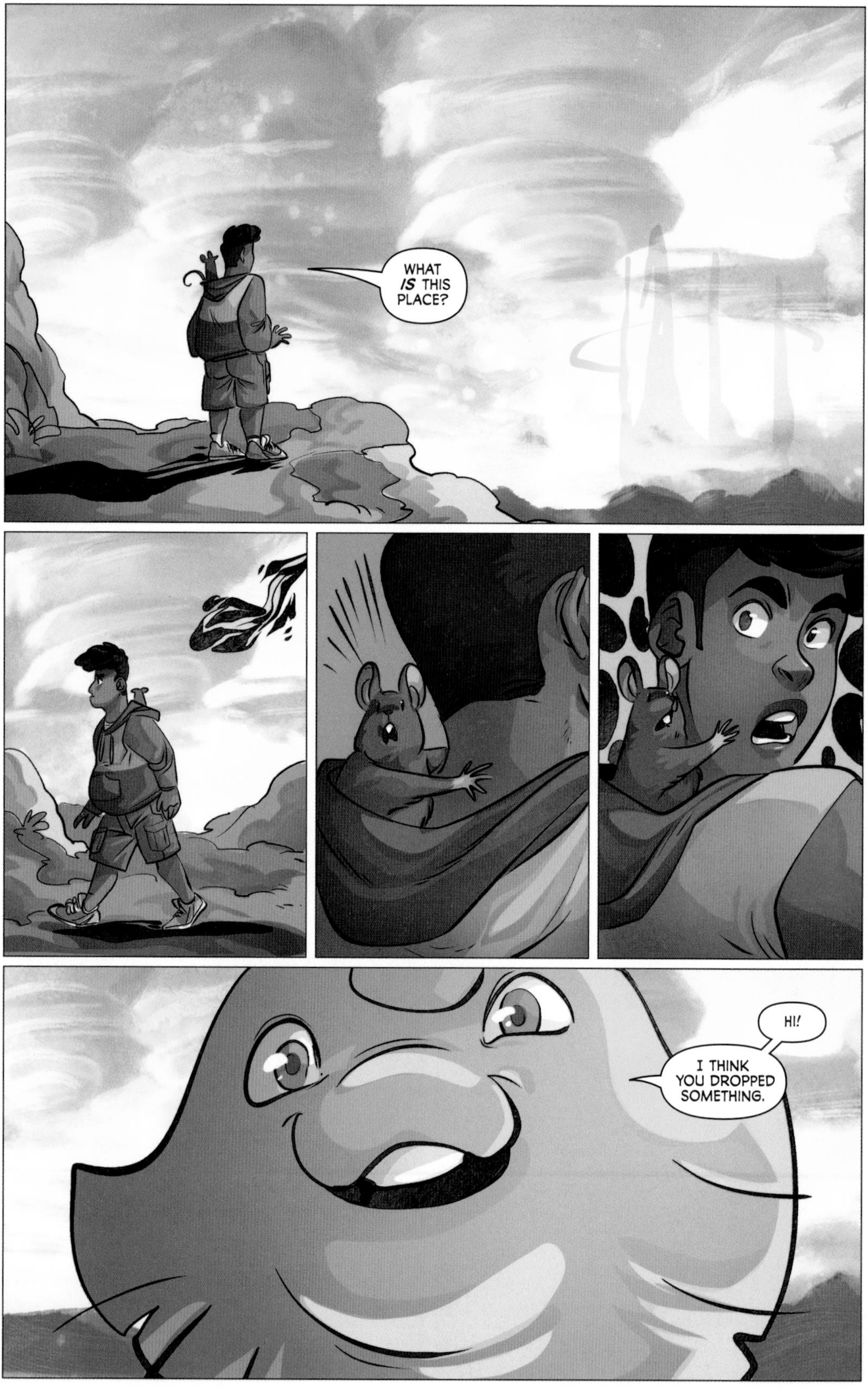
WHAT *IS* THIS PLACE?
HI!
I THINK YOU DROPPED SOMETHING.

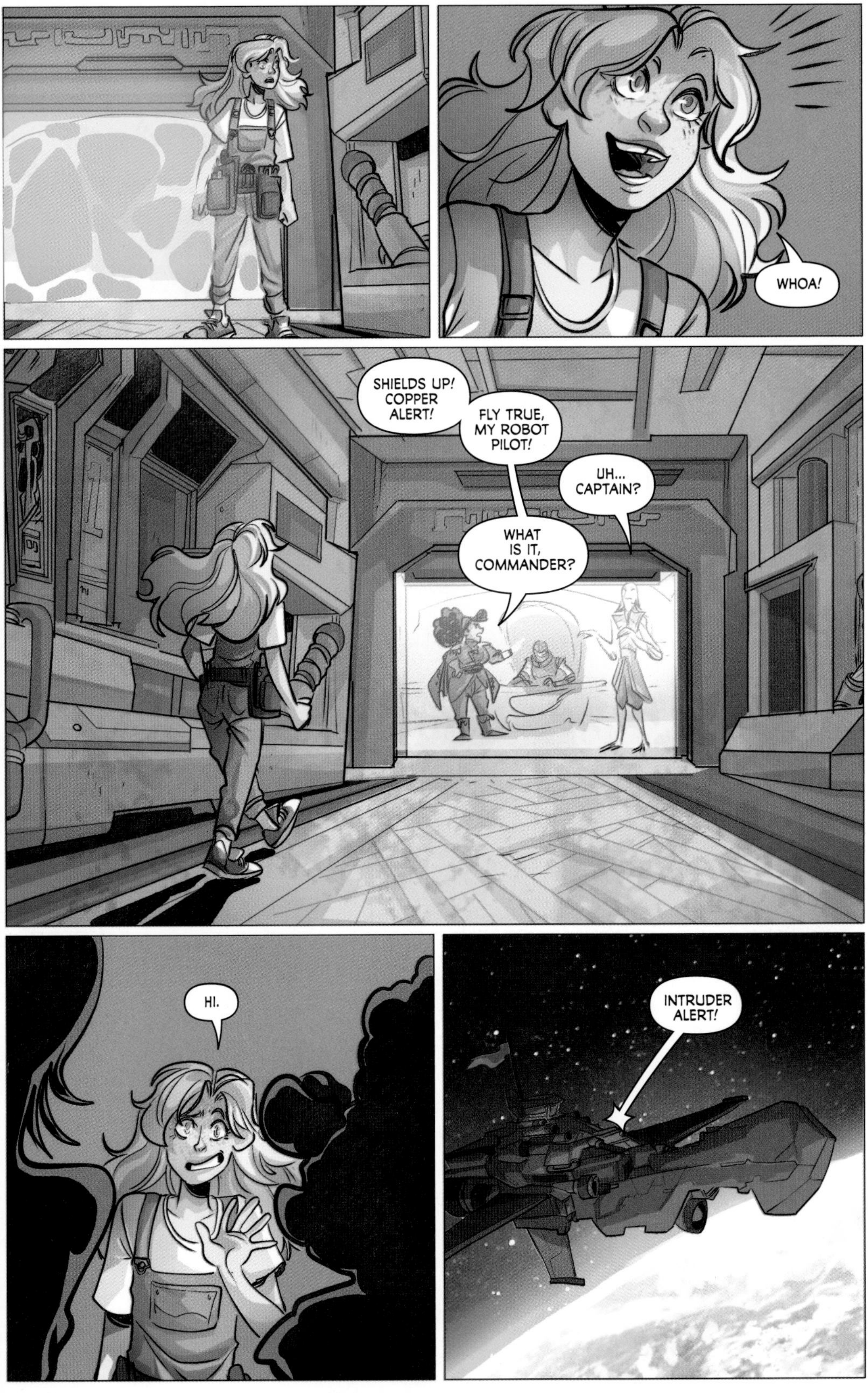
WHOA!
SHIELDS UP! COPPER ALERT!
FLY TRUE, MY ROBOT PILOT!
UH... CAPTAIN?
WHAT IS IT, COMMANDER?
HI.
INTRUDER ALERT!

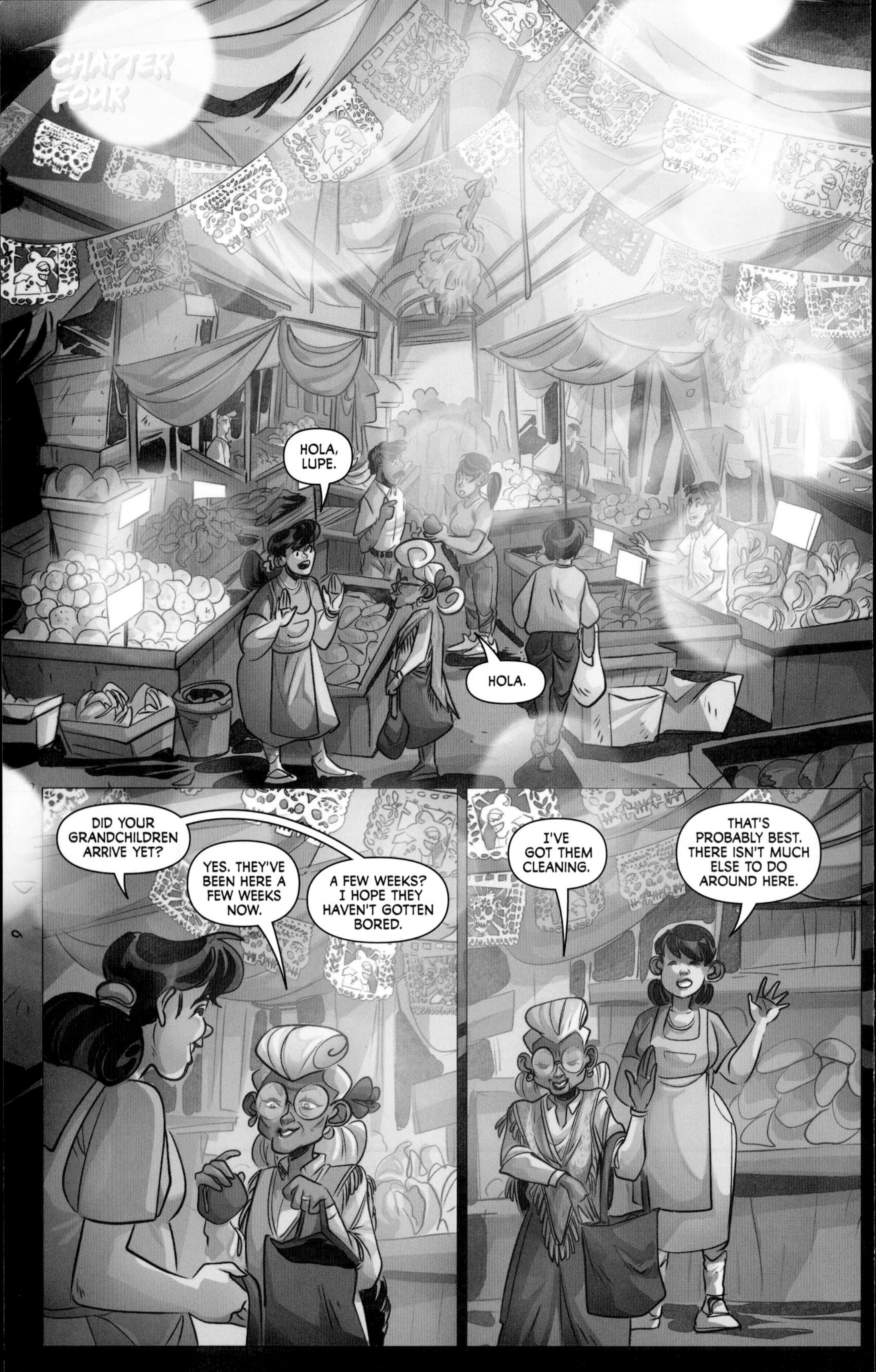
CHAPTER FOUR
HOLA, LUPE.
HOLA.
DID YOUR GRANDCHILDREN ARRIVE YET?
YES. THEY'VE BEEN HERE A FEW WEEKS NOW.
A FEW WEEKS? I HOPE THEY HAVEN'T GOTTEN BORED.
I'VE GOT THEM CLEANING.
THAT'S PROBABLY BEST. THERE ISN'T MUCH ELSE TO DO AROUND HERE.

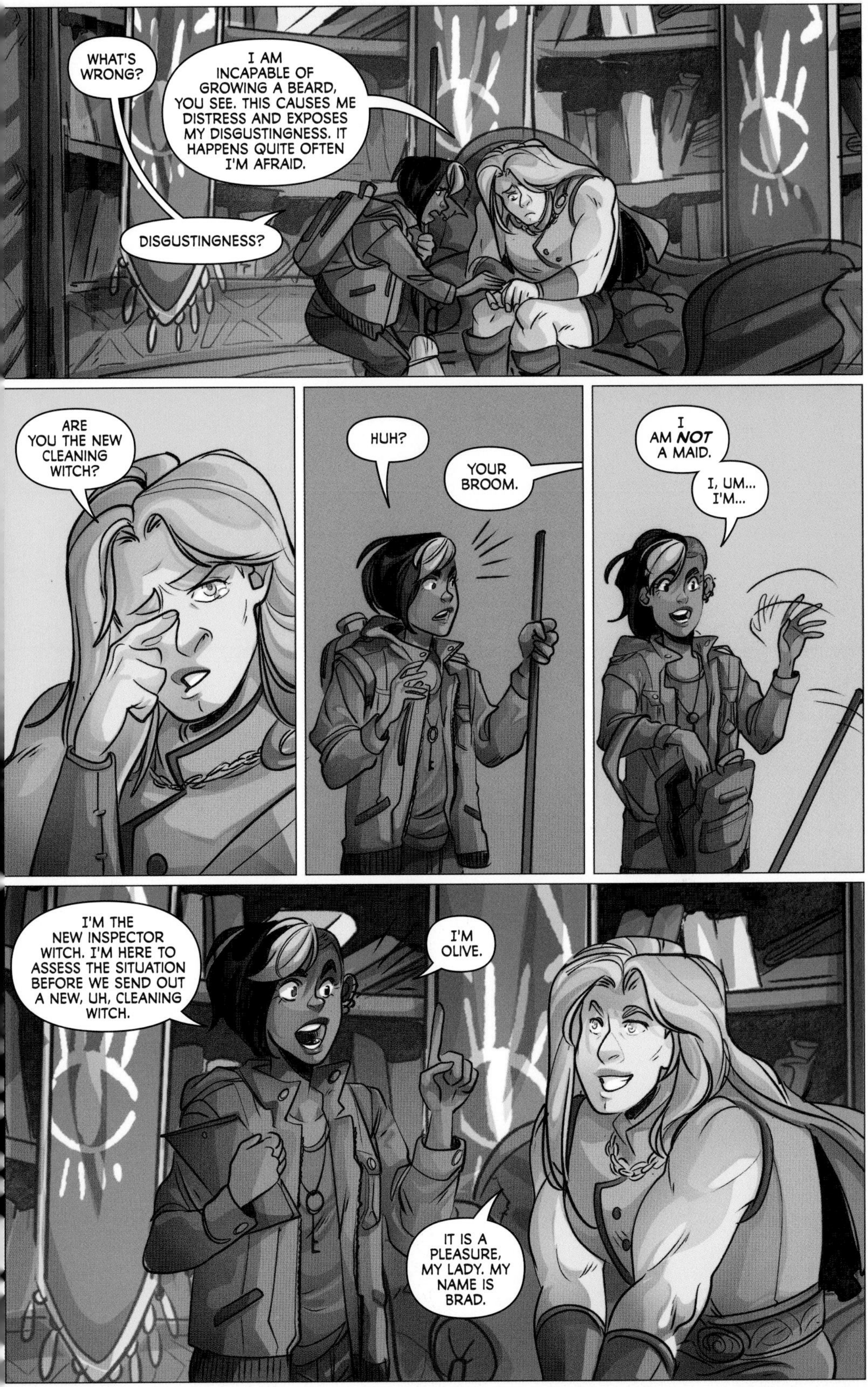

WHAT'S WRONG?
I AM INCAPABLE OF GROWING A BEARD, YOU SEE. THIS CAUSES ME DISTRESS AND EXPOSES MY DISGUSTINGNESS. IT HAPPENS QUITE OFTEN I'M AFRAID.
DISGUSTINGNESS?
ARE YOU THE NEW CLEANING WITCH?
HUH?
YOUR BROOM.
I AM *NOT* A MAID.
I, UM... I'M...
I'M THE NEW INSPECTOR WITCH. I'M HERE TO ASSESS THE SITUATION BEFORE WE SEND OUT A NEW, UH, CLEANING WITCH.
I'M OLIVE.
IT IS A PLEASURE, MY LADY. MY NAME IS BRAD.

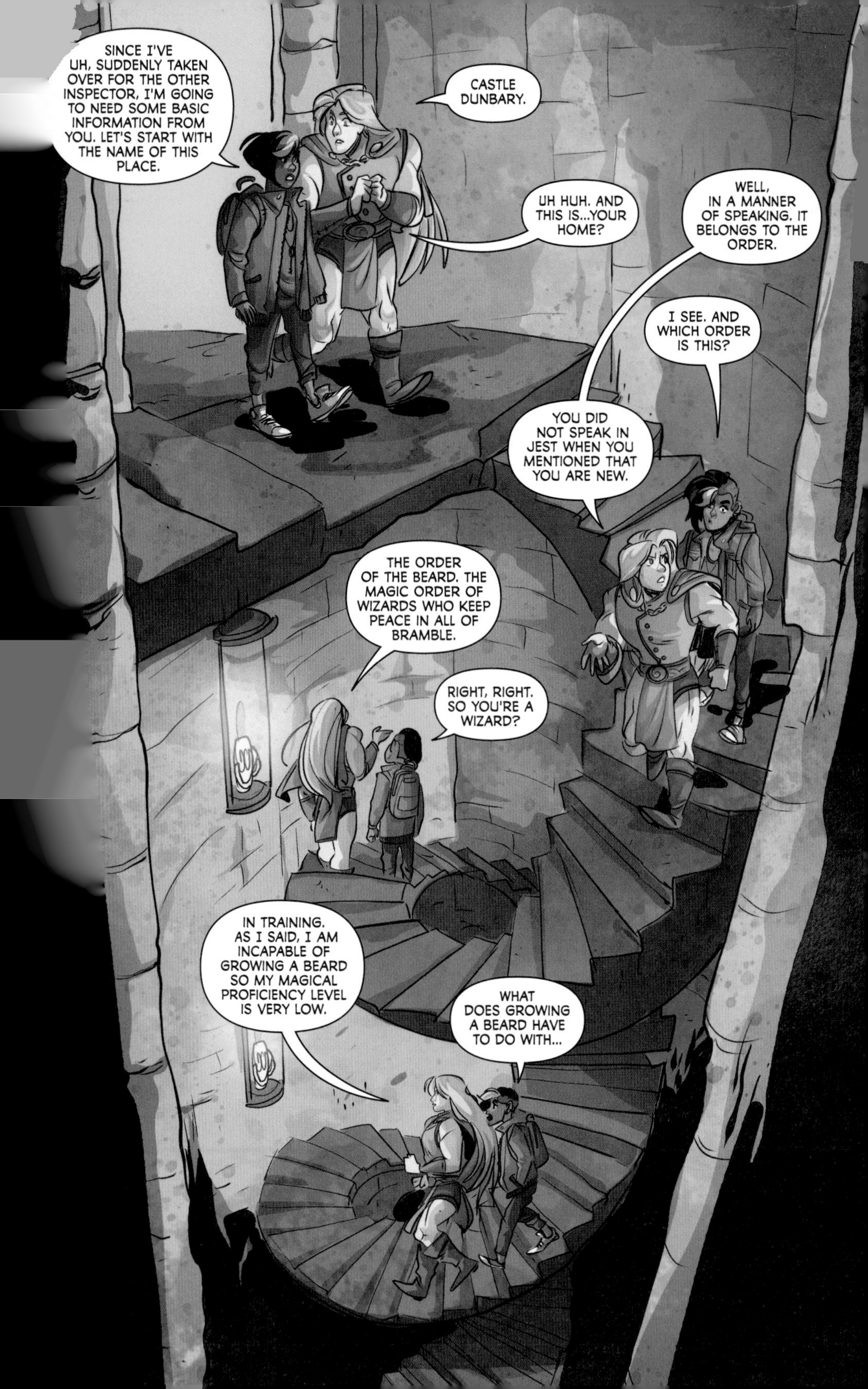
SINCE I'VE UH, SUDDENLY TAKEN OVER FOR THE OTHER INSPECTOR, I'M GOING TO NEED SOME BASIC INFORMATION FROM YOU. LET'S START WITH THE NAME OF THIS PLACE.
CASTLE DUNBARY.
UH HUH. AND THIS IS...YOUR HOME?
WELL, IN A MANNER OF SPEAKING. IT BELONGS TO THE ORDER.
I SEE. AND WHICH ORDER IS THIS?
YOU DID NOT SPEAK IN JEST WHEN YOU MENTIONED THAT YOU ARE NEW.
THE ORDER OF THE BEARD. THE MAGIC ORDER OF WIZARDS WHO KEEP PEACE IN ALL OF BRAMBLE.
RIGHT, RIGHT. SO YOU'RE A WIZARD?
IN TRAINING. AS I SAID, I AM INCAPABLE OF GROWING A BEARD SO MY MAGICAL PROFICIENCY LEVEL IS VERY LOW.
WHAT DOES GROWING A BEARD HAVE TO DO WITH...

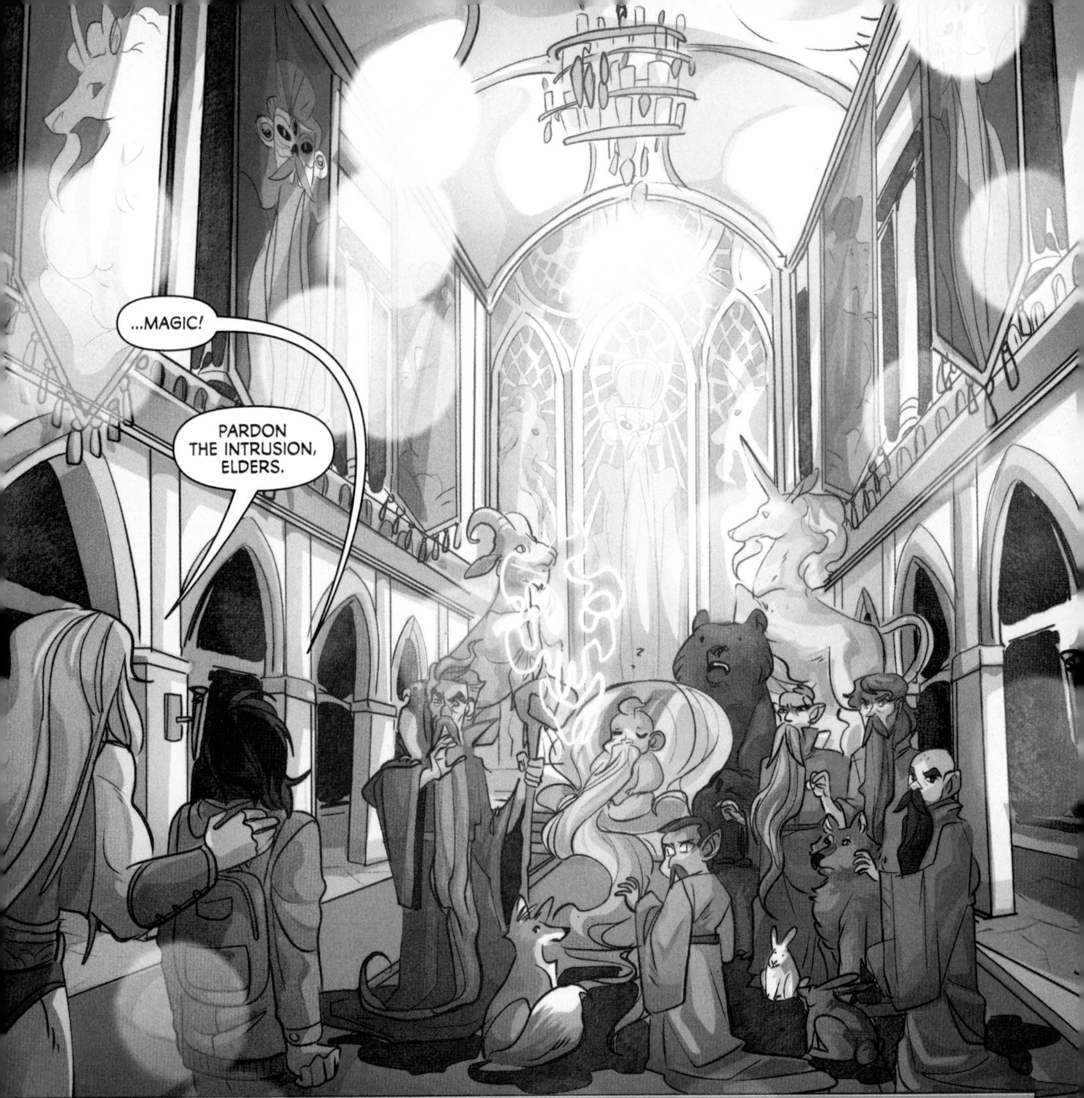
...MAGIC!
PARDON THE INTRUSION, ELDERS.

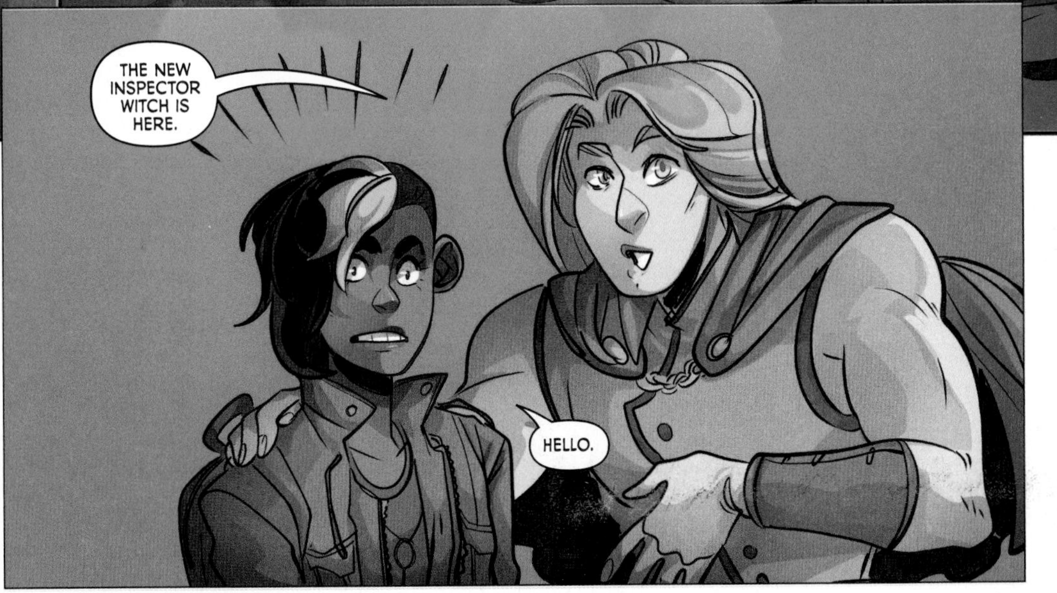
THE NEW INSPECTOR WITCH IS HERE.
HELLO.

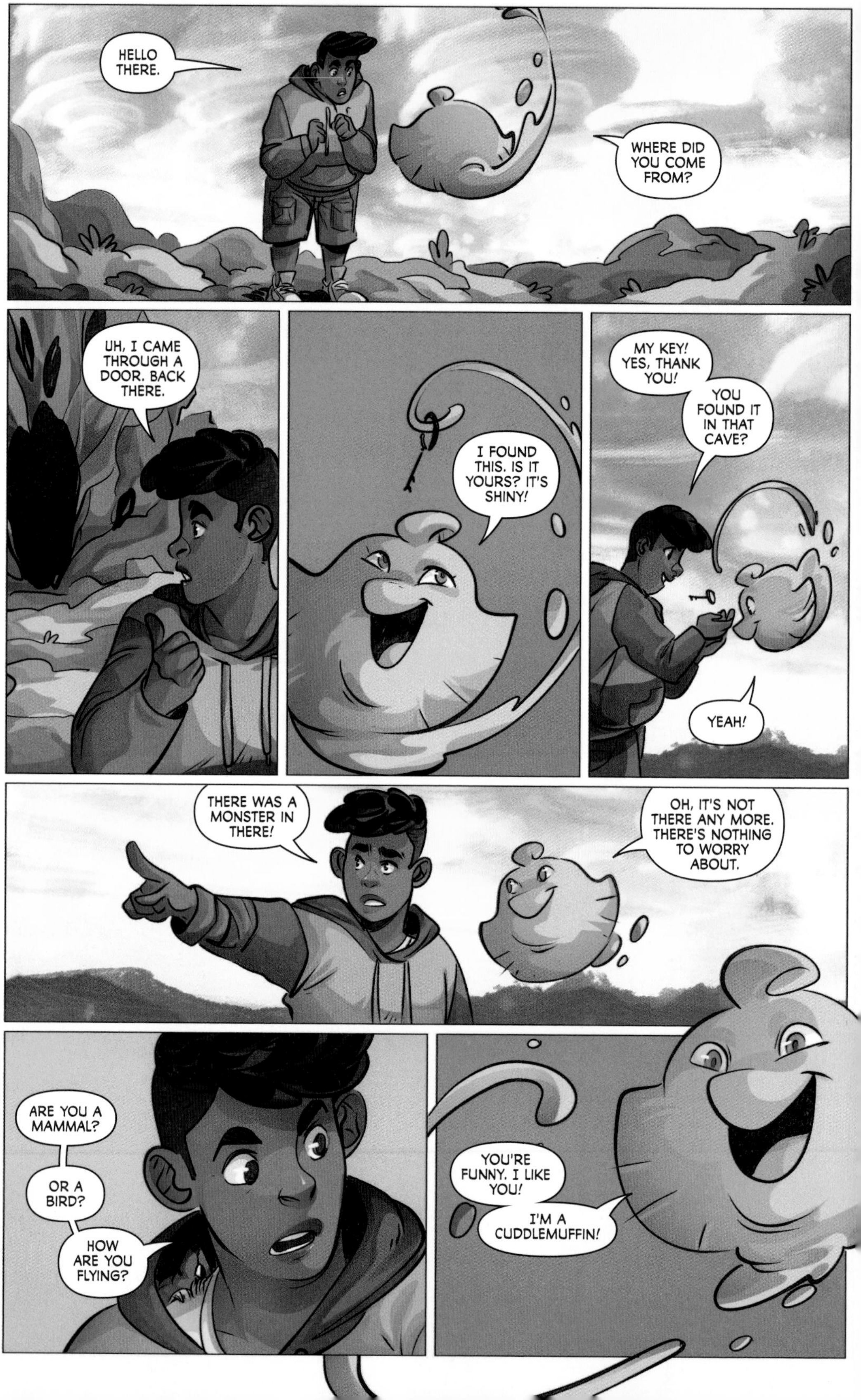
HELLO THERE.
WHERE DID YOU COME FROM?
UH, I CAME THROUGH A DOOR. BACK THERE.
I FOUND THIS. IS IT YOURS? IT'S SHINY!
MY KEY! YES, THANK YOU!
YOU FOUND IT IN THAT CAVE?
YEAH!
THERE WAS A MONSTER IN THERE!
OH, IT'S NOT THERE ANY MORE. THERE'S NOTHING TO WORRY ABOUT.
ARE YOU A MAMMAL?
OR A BIRD?
HOW ARE YOU FLYING?
YOU'RE FUNNY. I LIKE YOU!
I'M A CUDDLEMUFFIN!

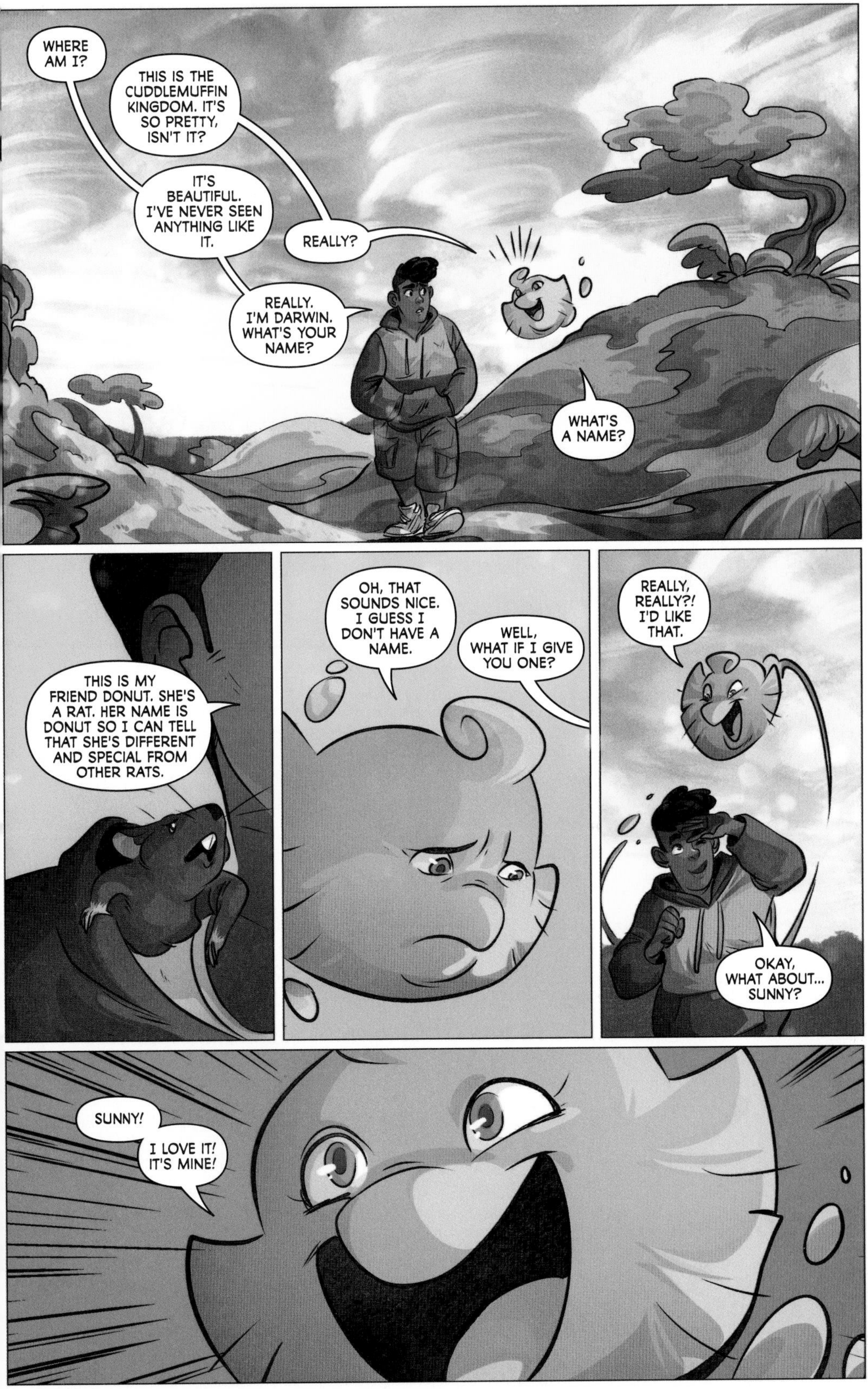
WHERE AM I?
THIS IS THE CUDDLEMUFFIN KINGDOM. IT'S SO PRETTY, ISN'T IT?
IT'S BEAUTIFUL. I'VE NEVER SEEN ANYTHING LIKE IT.
REALLY?
REALLY. I'M DARWIN. WHAT'S YOUR NAME?
WHAT'S A NAME?
THIS IS MY FRIEND DONUT. SHE'S A RAT. HER NAME IS DONUT SO I CAN TELL THAT SHE'S DIFFERENT AND SPECIAL FROM OTHER RATS.
OH, THAT SOUNDS NICE. I GUESS I DON'T HAVE A NAME.
WELL, WHAT IF I GIVE YOU ONE?
REALLY, REALLY?! I'D LIKE THAT.
OKAY, WHAT ABOUT... SUNNY?
SUNNY!
I LOVE IT! IT'S MINE!

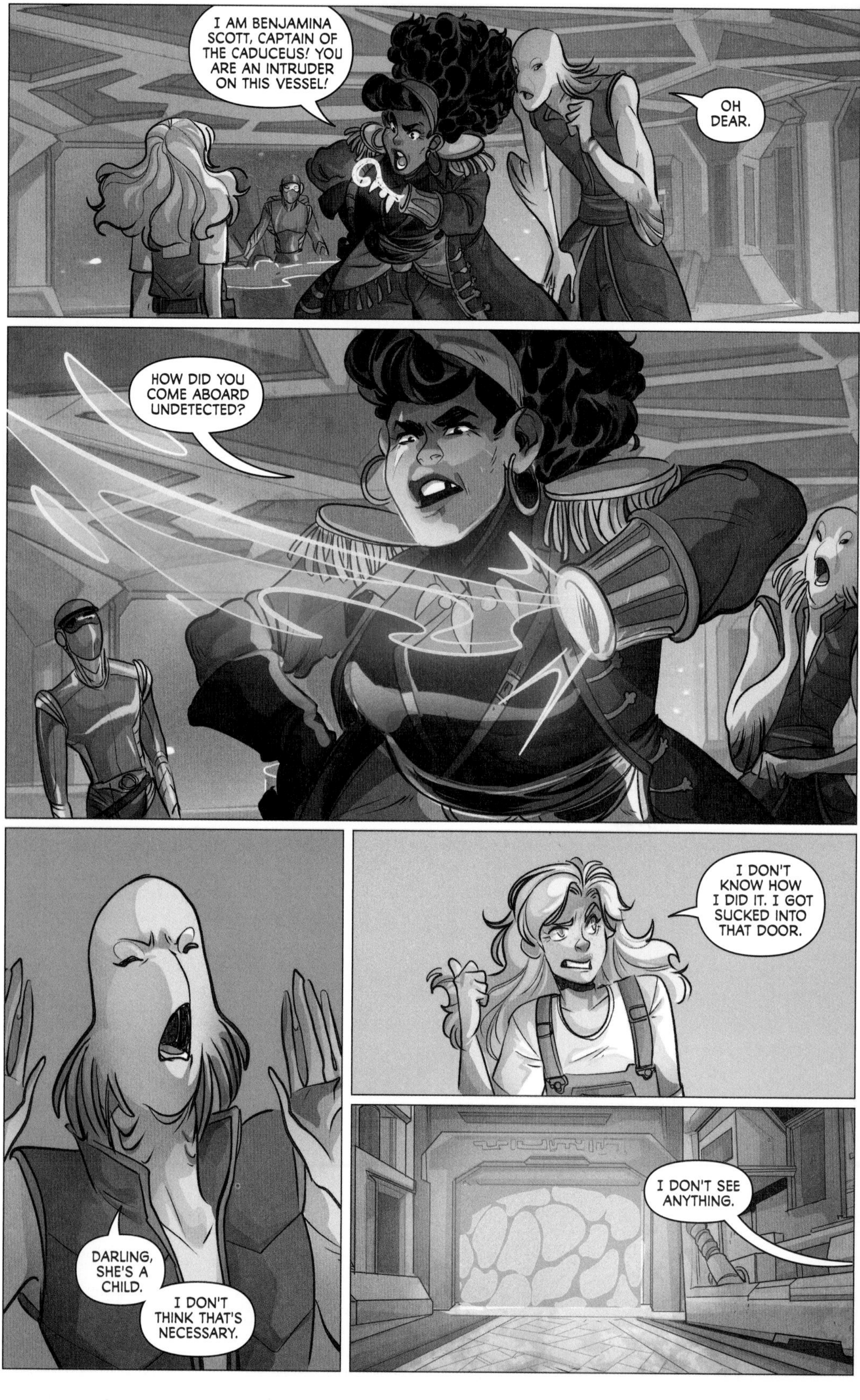
I AM BENJAMINA SCOTT, CAPTAIN OF THE CADUCEUS! YOU ARE AN INTRUDER ON THIS VESSEL!
OH DEAR.
HOW DID YOU COME ABOARD UNDETECTED?
I DON'T KNOW HOW I DID IT. I GOT SUCKED INTO THAT DOOR.
DARLING, SHE'S A CHILD.
I DON'T THINK THAT'S NECESSARY.
I DON'T SEE ANYTHING.

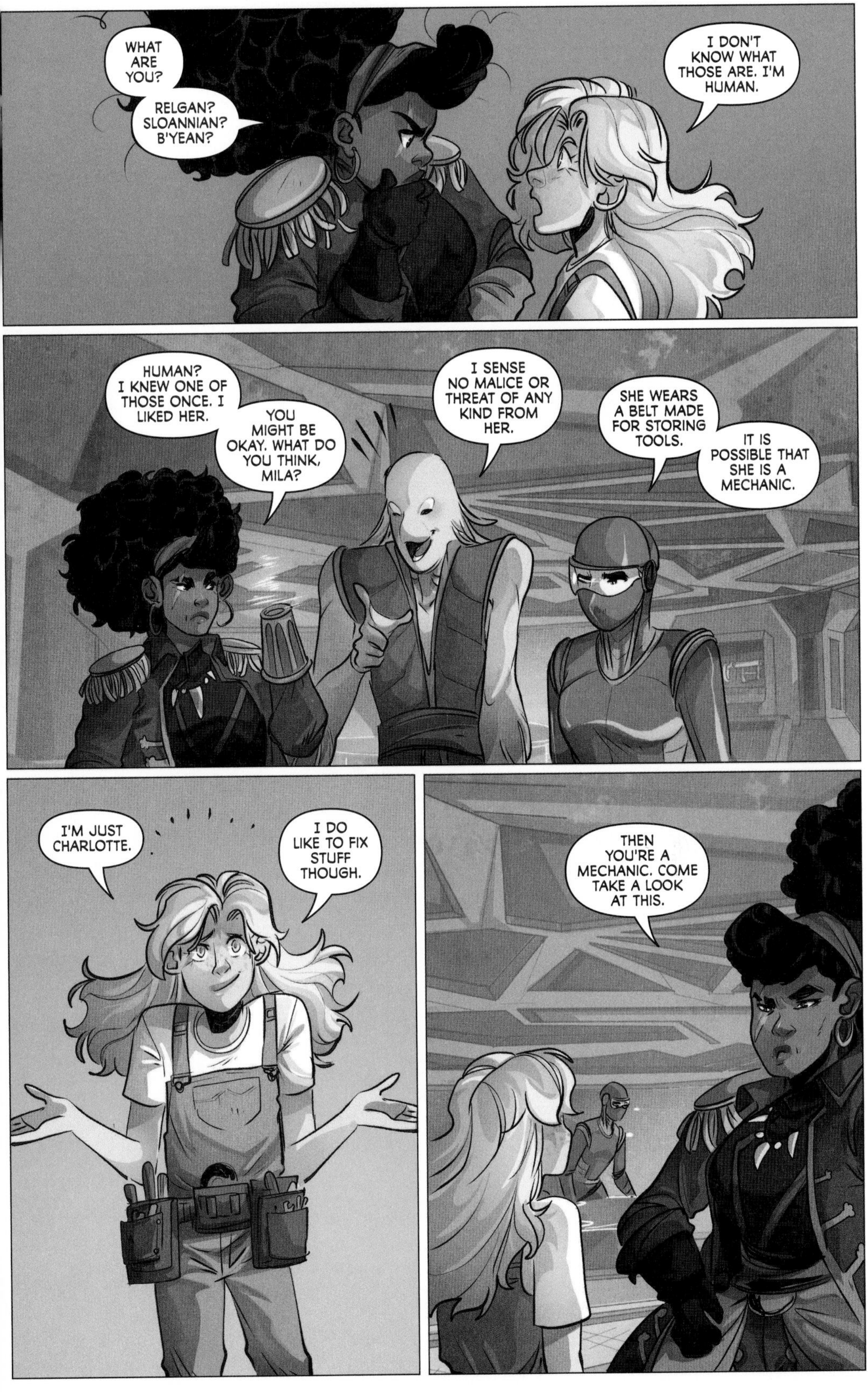
WHAT ARE YOU?
RELGAN? SLOANNIAN? B'YEAN?
I DON'T KNOW WHAT THOSE ARE. I'M HUMAN.
HUMAN? I KNEW ONE OF THOSE ONCE. I LIKED HER.
YOU MIGHT BE OKAY. WHAT DO YOU THINK, MILA?
I SENSE NO MALICE OR THREAT OF ANY KIND FROM HER.
SHE WEARS A BELT MADE FOR STORING TOOLS.
IT IS POSSIBLE THAT SHE IS A MECHANIC.
I'M JUST CHARLOTTE.
I DO LIKE TO FIX STUFF THOUGH.
THEN YOU'RE A MECHANIC. COME TAKE A LOOK AT THIS.

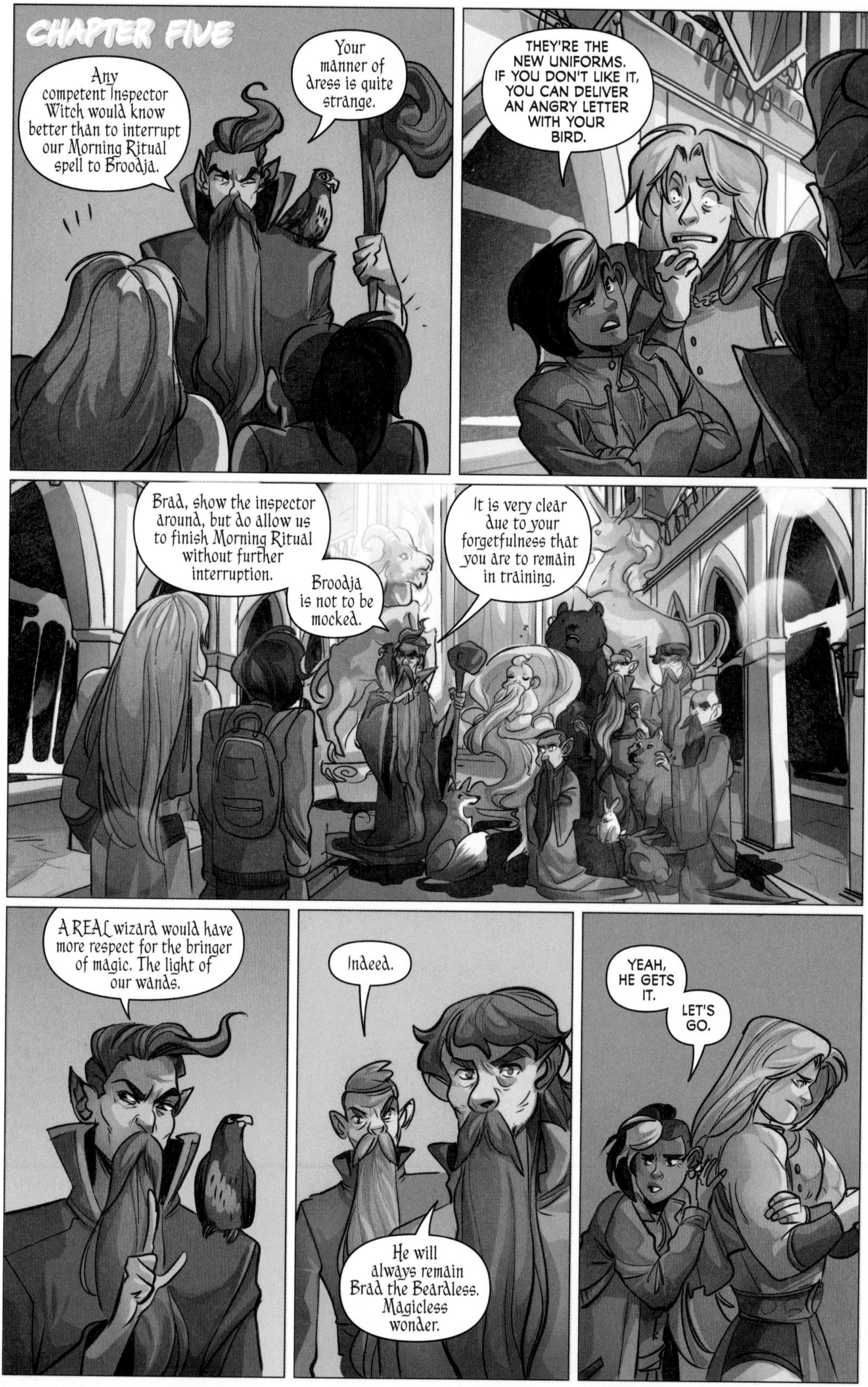
CHAPTER FIVE
Any competent Inspector Witch would know better than to interrupt our Morning Ritual spell to Broodja.
Your manner of dress is quite strange.
THEY'RE THE NEW UNIFORMS. IF YOU DON'T LIKE IT, YOU CAN DELIVER AN ANGRY LETTER WITH YOUR BIRD.
Brad, show the inspector around, but do allow us to finish Morning Ritual without further interruption.
Broodja is not to be mocked.
It is very clear due to your forgetfulness that you are to remain in training.
A REAL wizard would have more respect for the bringer of magic. The light of our wands.
Indeed.
He will always remain Brad the Beardless. Magicless wonder.
YEAH, HE GETS IT.
LET'S GO.

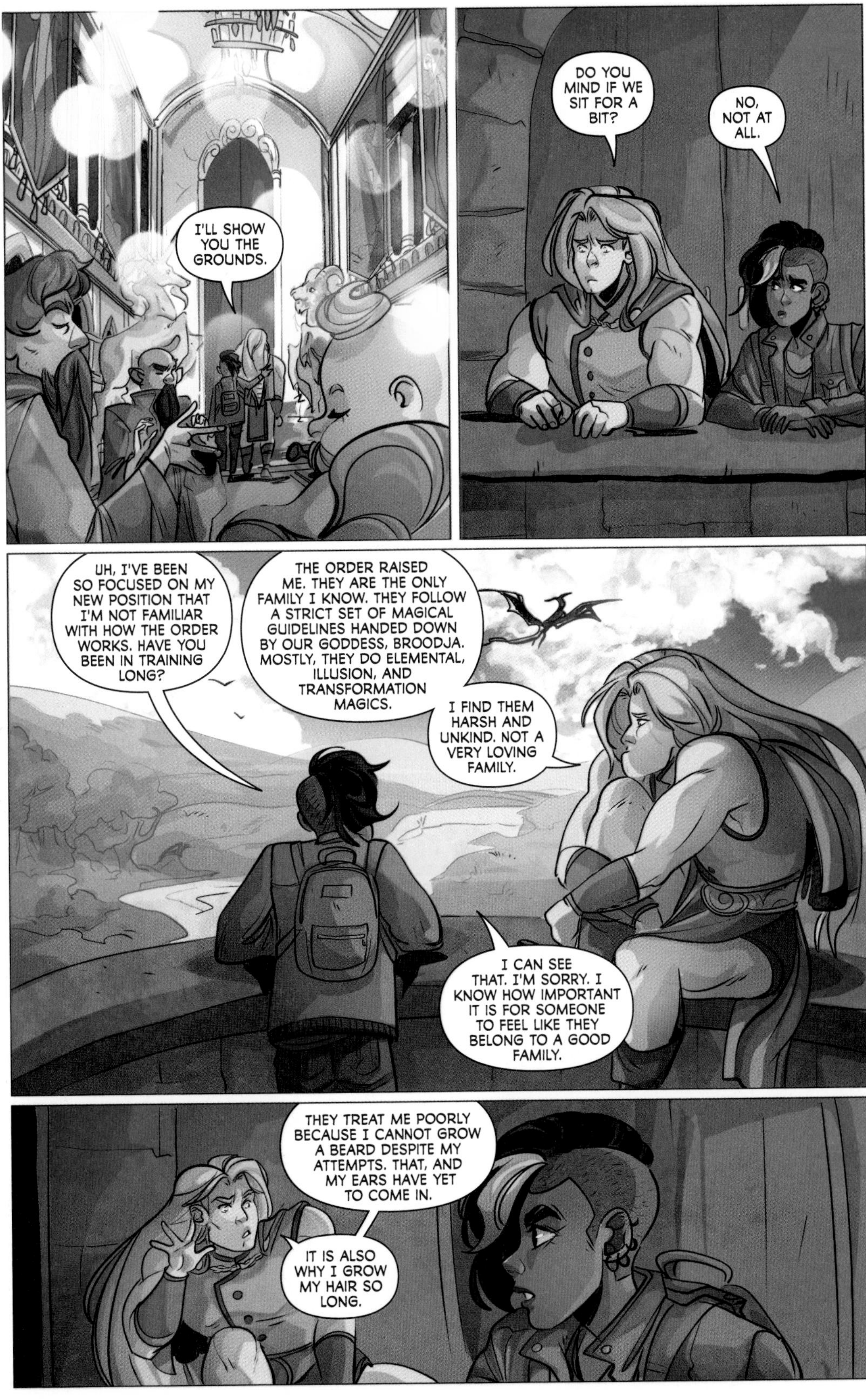
I'LL SHOW YOU THE GROUNDS.
DO YOU MIND IF WE SIT FOR A BIT?
NO, NOT AT ALL.
UH, I'VE BEEN SO FOCUSED ON MY NEW POSITION THAT I'M NOT FAMILIAR WITH HOW THE ORDER WORKS. HAVE YOU BEEN IN TRAINING LONG?
THE ORDER RAISED ME. THEY ARE THE ONLY FAMILY I KNOW. THEY FOLLOW A STRICT SET OF MAGICAL GUIDELINES HANDED DOWN BY OUR GODDESS, BROODJA. MOSTLY, THEY DO ELEMENTAL, ILLUSION, AND TRANSFORMATION MAGICS.
I FIND THEM HARSH AND UNKIND. NOT A VERY LOVING FAMILY.
I CAN SEE THAT. I'M SORRY. I KNOW HOW IMPORTANT IT IS FOR SOMEONE TO FEEL LIKE THEY BELONG TO A GOOD FAMILY.
THEY TREAT ME POORLY BECAUSE I CANNOT GROW A BEARD DESPITE MY ATTEMPTS. THAT, AND MY EARS HAVE YET TO COME IN.
IT IS ALSO WHY I GROW MY HAIR SO LONG.

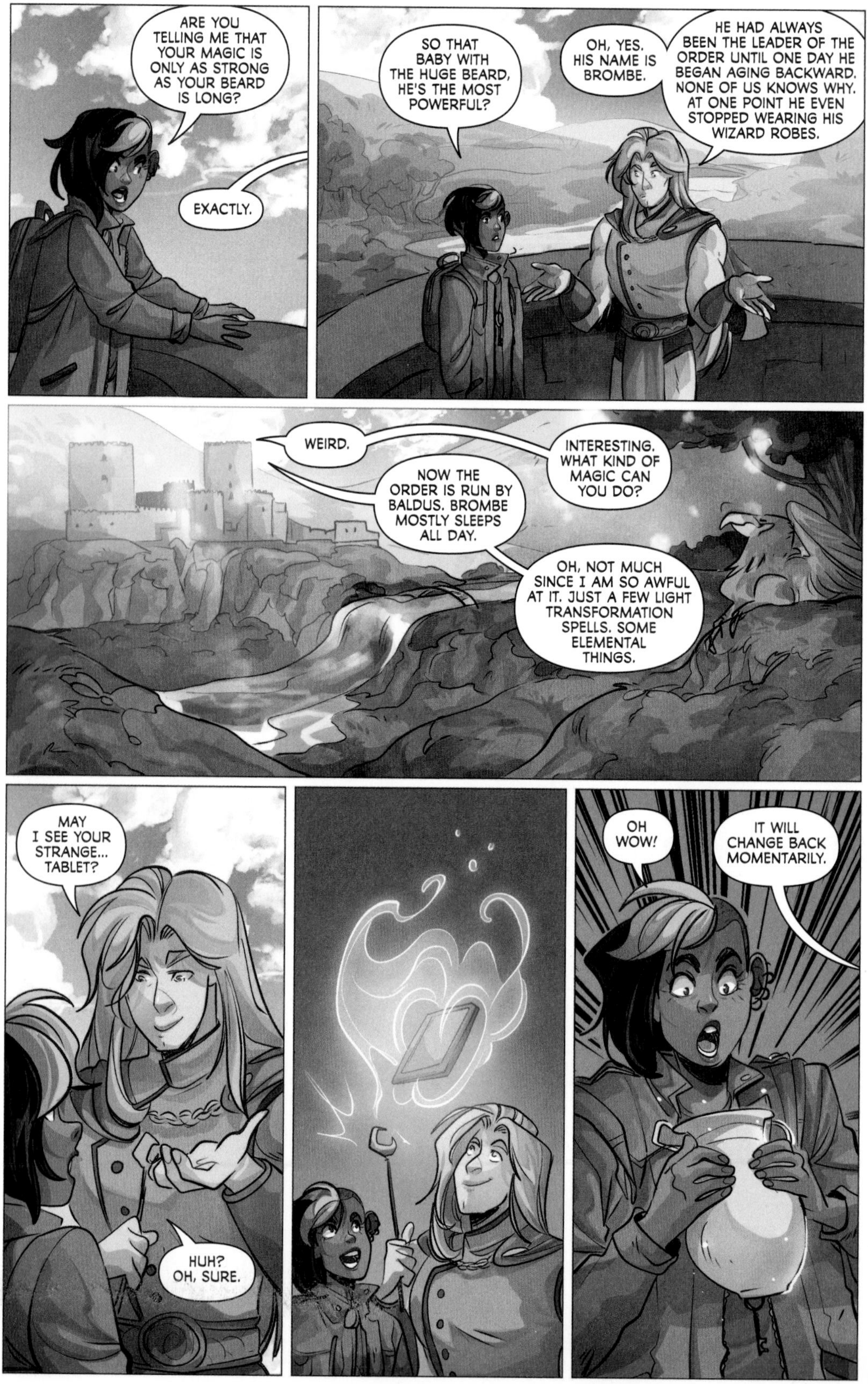
ARE YOU TELLING ME THAT YOUR MAGIC IS ONLY AS STRONG AS YOUR BEARD IS LONG?
EXACTLY.
SO THAT BABY WITH THE HUGE BEARD, HE'S THE MOST POWERFUL?
OH, YES. HIS NAME IS BROMBE.
HE HAD ALWAYS BEEN THE LEADER OF THE ORDER UNTIL ONE DAY HE BEGAN AGING BACKWARD. NONE OF US KNOWS WHY. AT ONE POINT HE EVEN STOPPED WEARING HIS WIZARD ROBES.
WEIRD.
NOW THE ORDER IS RUN BY BALDUS. BROMBE MOSTLY SLEEPS ALL DAY.
INTERESTING. WHAT KIND OF MAGIC CAN YOU DO?
OH, NOT MUCH SINCE I AM SO AWFUL AT IT. JUST A FEW LIGHT TRANSFORMATION SPELLS. SOME ELEMENTAL THINGS.
MAY I SEE YOUR STRANGE... TABLET?
HUH? OH, SURE.
OH WOW!
IT WILL CHANGE BACK MOMENTARILY.

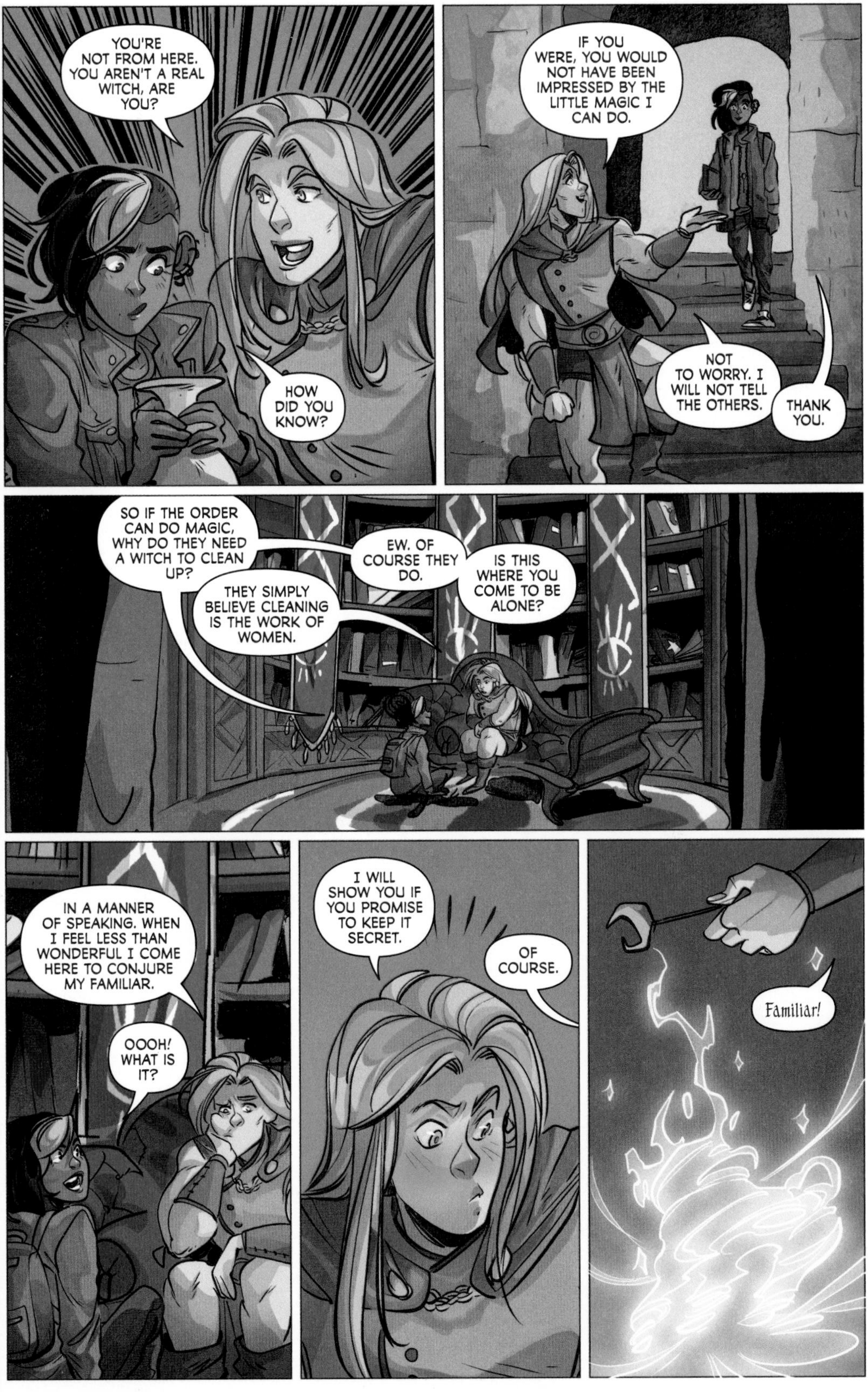
YOU'RE NOT FROM HERE. YOU AREN'T A REAL WITCH, ARE YOU?
HOW DID YOU KNOW?
IF YOU WERE, YOU WOULD NOT HAVE BEEN IMPRESSED BY THE LITTLE MAGIC I CAN DO.
NOT TO WORRY. I WILL NOT TELL THE OTHERS.
THANK YOU.
SO IF THE ORDER CAN DO MAGIC, WHY DO THEY NEED A WITCH TO CLEAN UP?
THEY SIMPLY BELIEVE CLEANING IS THE WORK OF WOMEN.
EW. OF COURSE THEY DO.
IS THIS WHERE YOU COME TO BE ALONE?
IN A MANNER OF SPEAKING. WHEN I FEEL LESS THAN WONDERFUL I COME HERE TO CONJURE MY FAMILIAR.
OOOH! WHAT IS IT?
I WILL SHOW YOU IF YOU PROMISE TO KEEP IT SECRET.
OF COURSE.
Familiar!

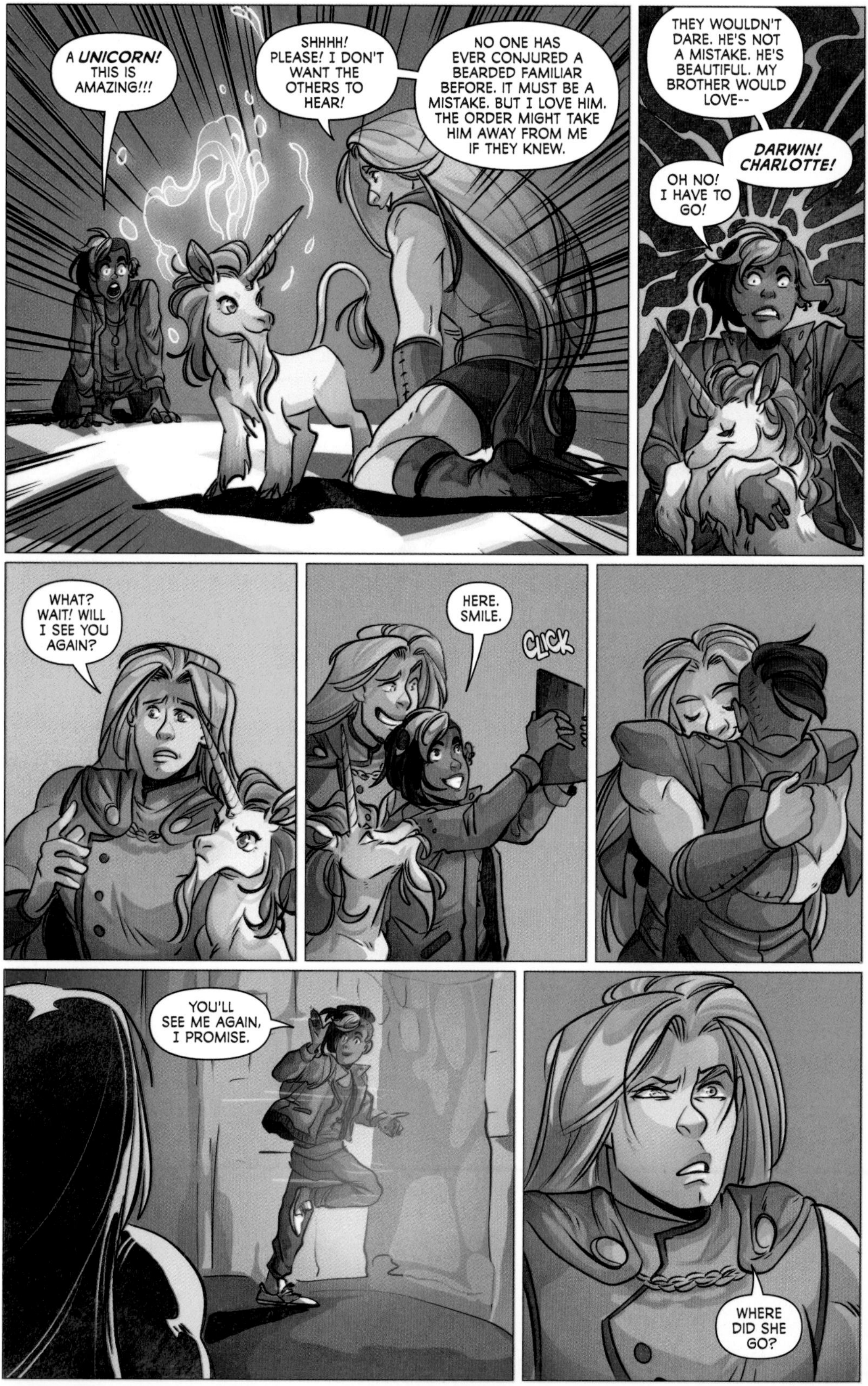
A **UNICORN!** THIS IS AMAZING!!!
SHHHH! PLEASE! I DON'T WANT THE OTHERS TO HEAR!
NO ONE HAS EVER CONJURED A BEARDED FAMILIAR BEFORE. IT MUST BE A MISTAKE. BUT I LOVE HIM. THE ORDER MIGHT TAKE HIM AWAY FROM ME IF THEY KNEW.
THEY WOULDN'T DARE. HE'S NOT A MISTAKE. HE'S BEAUTIFUL. MY BROTHER WOULD LOVE--
DARWIN! CHARLOTTE!
OH NO! I HAVE TO GO!
WHAT? WAIT! WILL I SEE YOU AGAIN?
HERE. SMILE.
CLICK
YOU'LL SEE ME AGAIN, I PROMISE.
WHERE DID SHE GO?

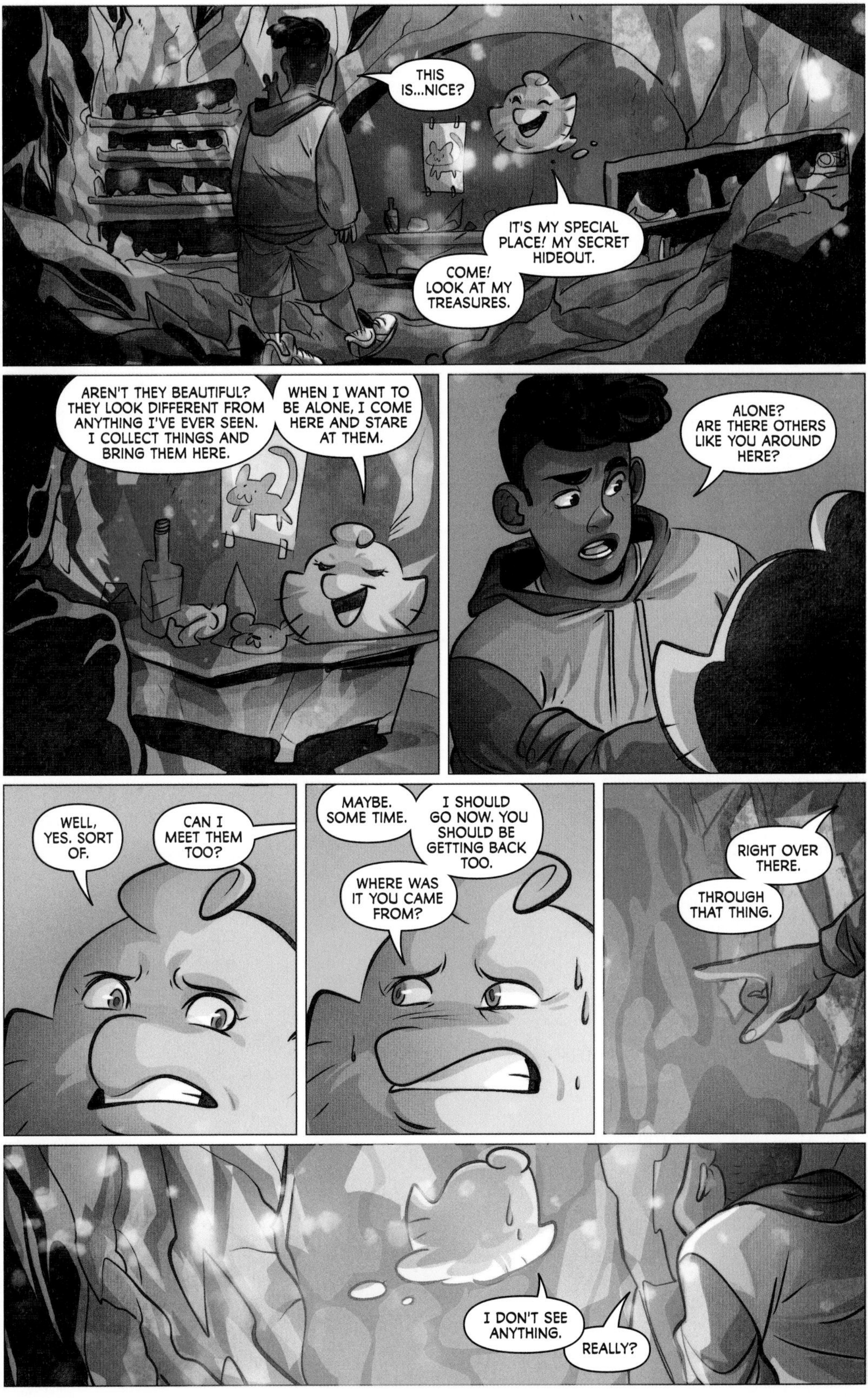

THIS IS...NICE?
IT'S MY SPECIAL PLACE! MY SECRET HIDEOUT.
COME! LOOK AT MY TREASURES.
AREN'T THEY BEAUTIFUL? THEY LOOK DIFFERENT FROM ANYTHING I'VE EVER SEEN. I COLLECT THINGS AND BRING THEM HERE.
WHEN I WANT TO BE ALONE, I COME HERE AND STARE AT THEM.
ALONE? ARE THERE OTHERS LIKE YOU AROUND HERE?
WELL, YES. SORT OF.
CAN I MEET THEM TOO?
MAYBE. SOME TIME.
I SHOULD GO NOW. YOU SHOULD BE GETTING BACK TOO.
WHERE WAS IT YOU CAME FROM?
RIGHT OVER THERE.
THROUGH THAT THING.
I DON'T SEE ANYTHING.
REALLY?

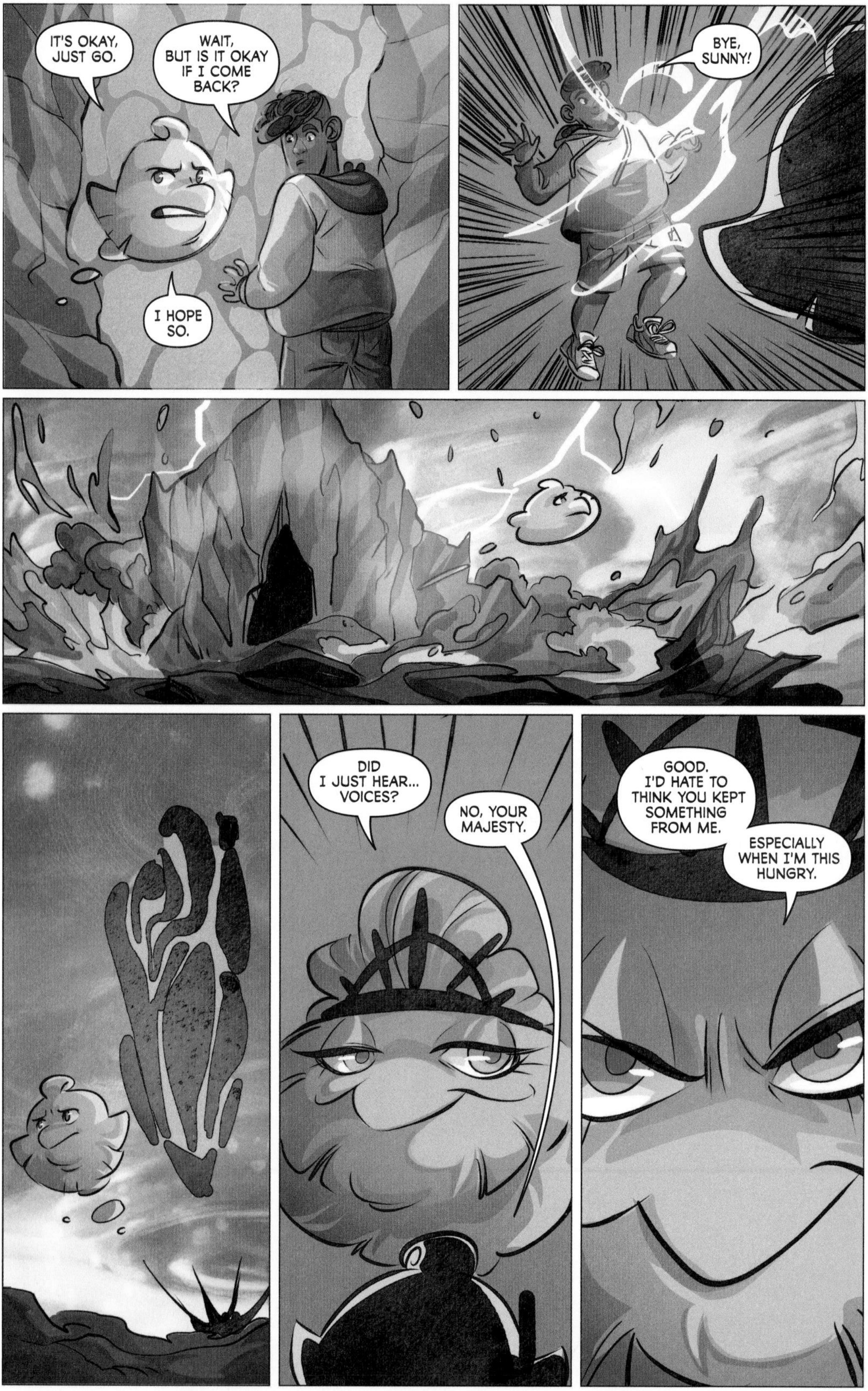
IT'S OKAY, JUST GO.
WAIT, BUT IS IT OKAY IF I COME BACK?
I HOPE SO.
BYE, SUNNY!
DID I JUST HEAR... VOICES?
NO, YOUR MAJESTY.
GOOD. I'D HATE TO THINK YOU KEPT SOMETHING FROM ME.
ESPECIALLY WHEN I'M THIS HUNGRY.

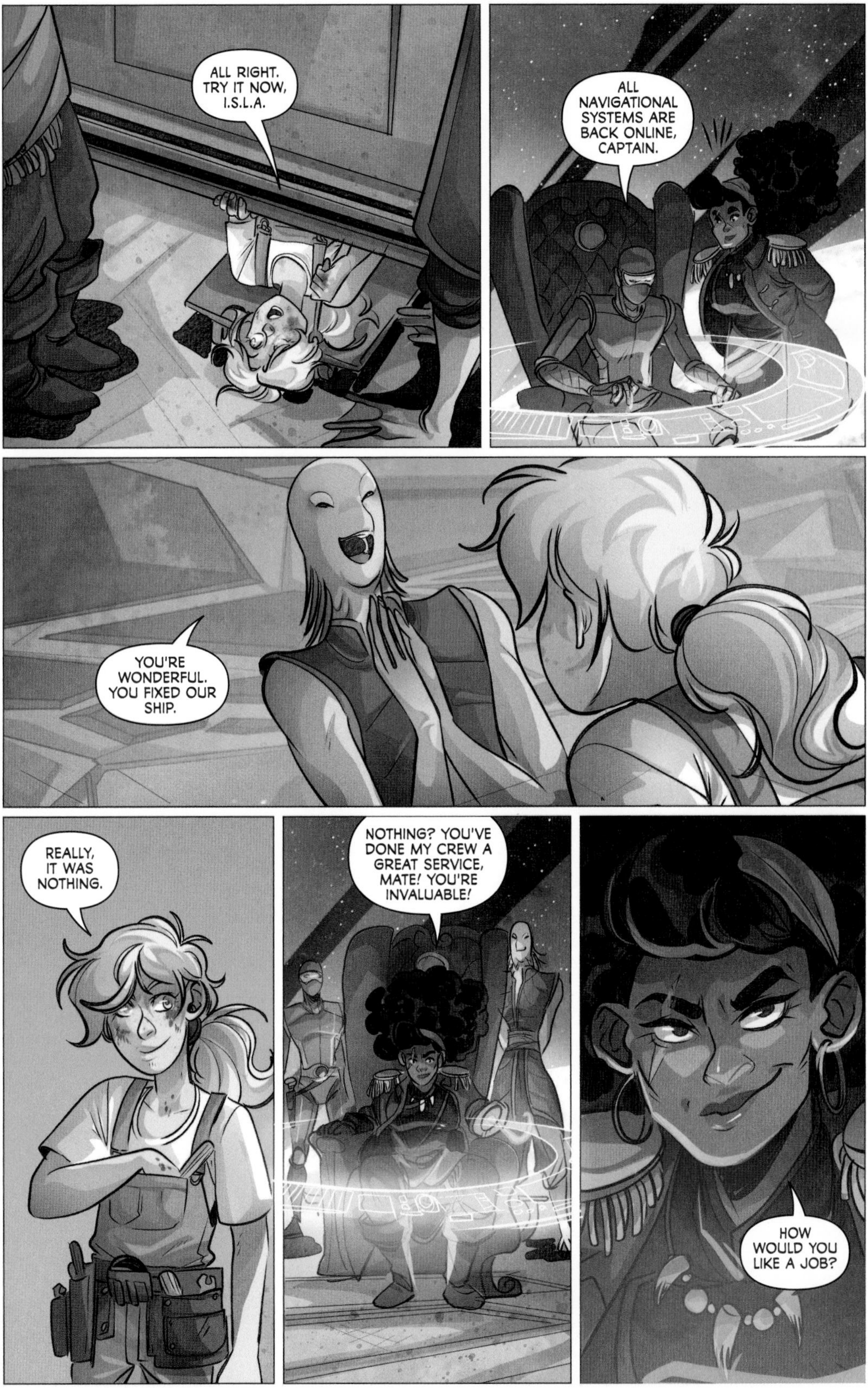
ALL RIGHT. TRY IT NOW, I.S.L.A.
ALL NAVIGATIONAL SYSTEMS ARE BACK ONLINE, CAPTAIN.
YOU'RE WONDERFUL. YOU FIXED OUR SHIP.
REALLY, IT WAS NOTHING.
NOTHING? YOU'VE DONE MY CREW A GREAT SERVICE, MATE! YOU'RE INVALUABLE!
HOW WOULD YOU LIKE A JOB?

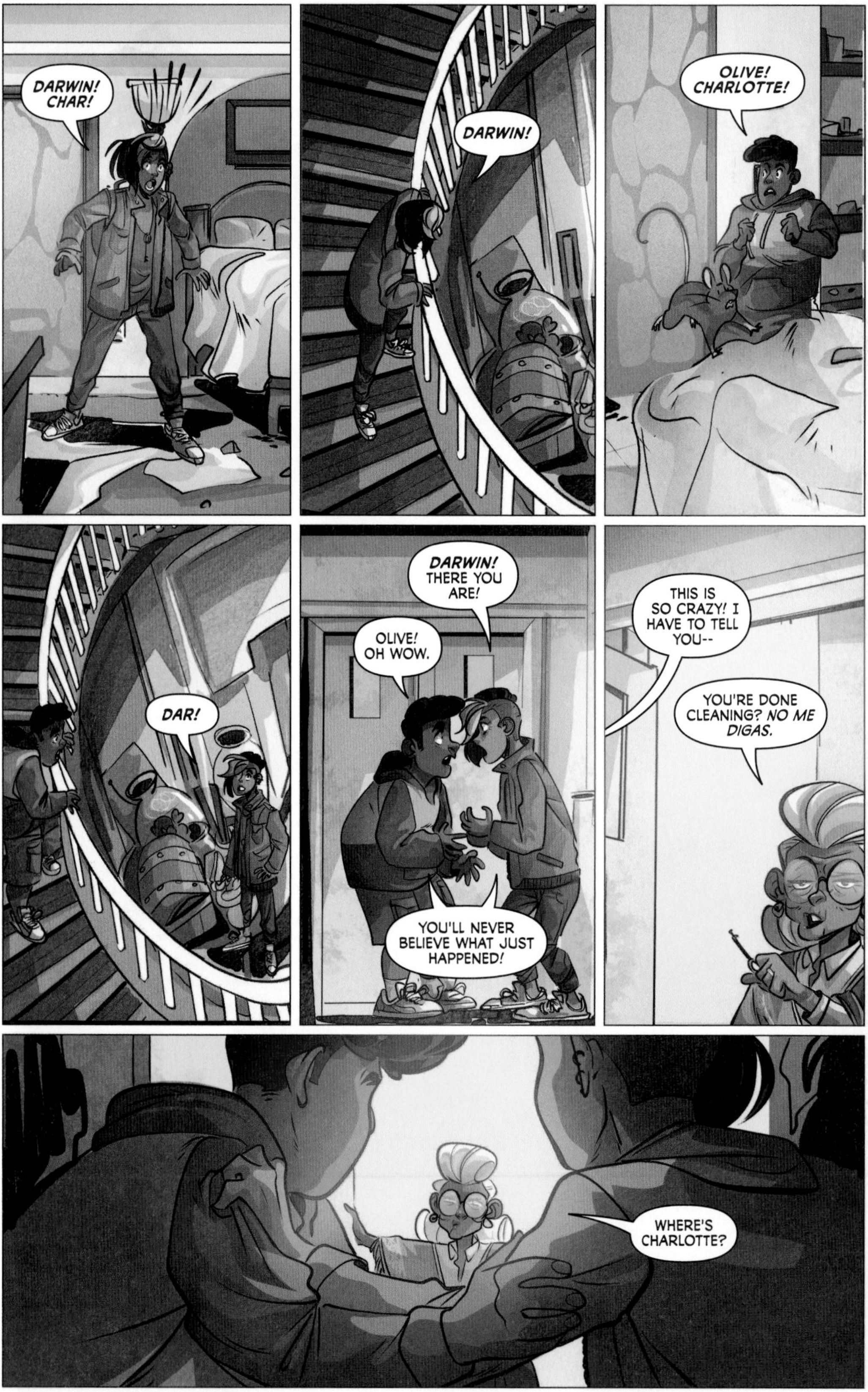

DARWIN! CHAR!
DARWIN!
OLIVE! CHARLOTTE!
DAR!
DARWIN! THERE YOU ARE!
OLIVE! OH WOW.
YOU'LL NEVER BELIEVE WHAT JUST HAPPENED!
THIS IS SO CRAZY! I HAVE TO TELL YOU--
YOU'RE DONE CLEANING? NO ME DIGAS.
WHERE'S CHARLOTTE?

CHAPTER SIX

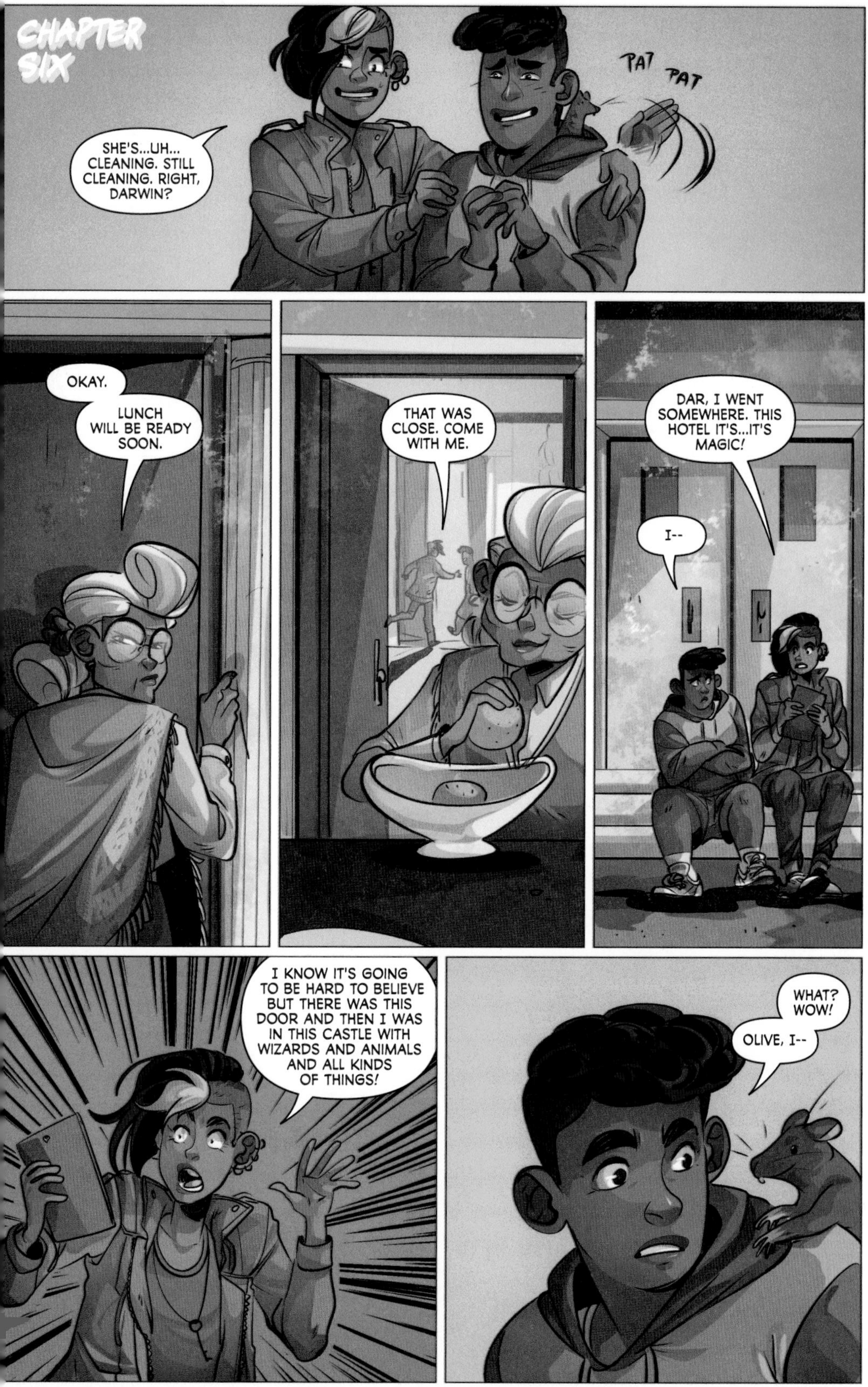
PAT PAT
SHE'S...UH... CLEANING. STILL CLEANING. RIGHT, DARWIN?
OKAY.
LUNCH WILL BE READY SOON.
THAT WAS CLOSE. COME WITH ME.
DAR, I WENT SOMEWHERE. THIS HOTEL IT'S...IT'S MAGIC!
I--
I KNOW IT'S GOING TO BE HARD TO BELIEVE BUT THERE WAS THIS DOOR AND THEN I WAS IN THIS CASTLE WITH WIZARDS AND ANIMALS AND ALL KINDS OF THINGS!
WHAT? WOW!
OLIVE, I--

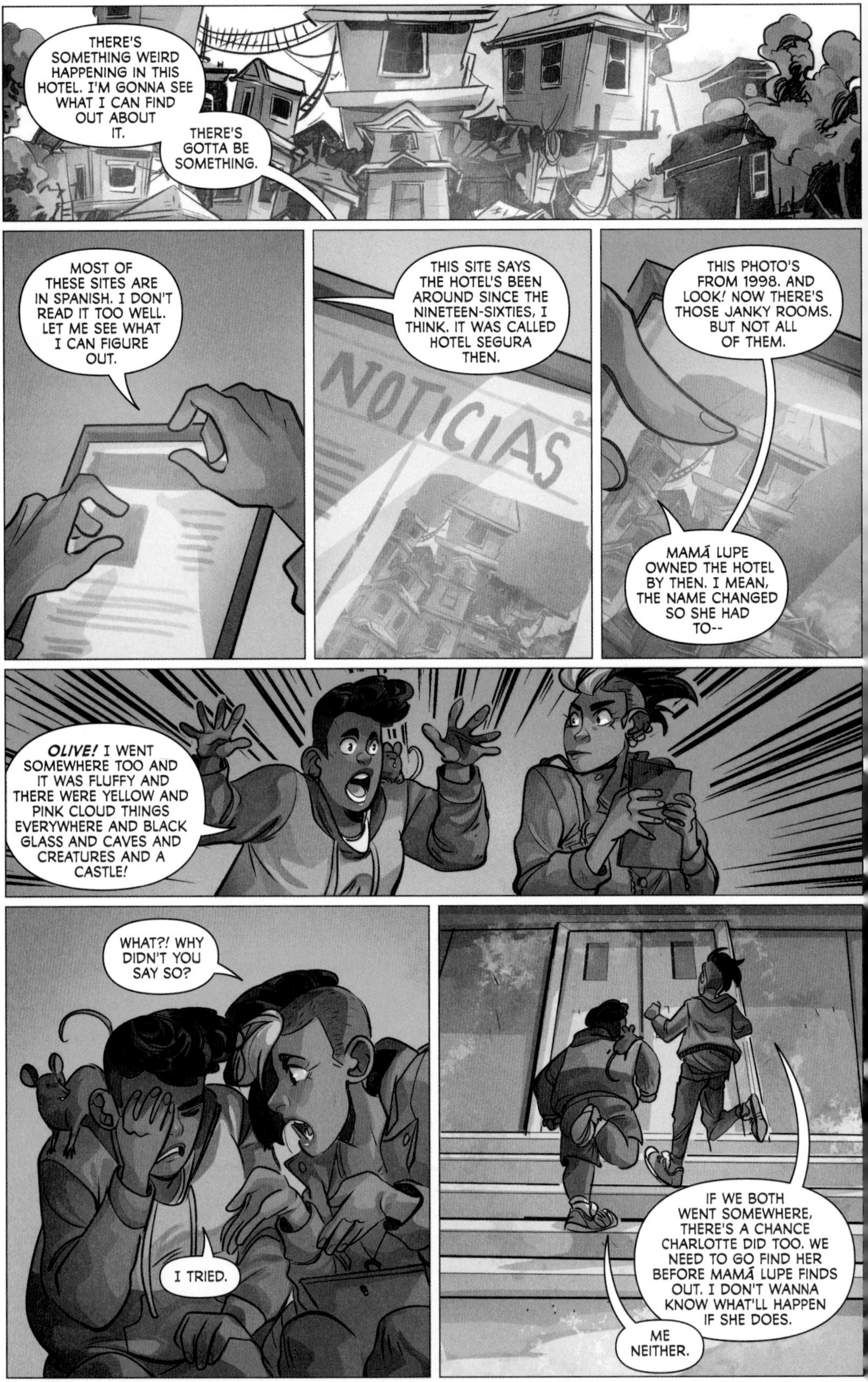
THERE'S SOMETHING WEIRD HAPPENING IN THIS HOTEL. I'M GONNA SEE WHAT I CAN FIND OUT ABOUT IT.
THERE'S GOTTA BE SOMETHING.
MOST OF THESE SITES ARE IN SPANISH. I DON'T READ IT TOO WELL. LET ME SEE WHAT I CAN FIGURE OUT.
THIS SITE SAYS THE HOTEL'S BEEN AROUND SINCE THE NINETEEN-SIXTIES, I THINK. IT WAS CALLED HOTEL SEGURA THEN.
NOTICIAS
THIS PHOTO'S FROM 1998. AND LOOK! NOW THERE'S THOSE JANKY ROOMS. BUT NOT ALL OF THEM.
MAMÁ LUPE OWNED THE HOTEL BY THEN. I MEAN, THE NAME CHANGED SO SHE HAD TO--
OLIVE! I WENT SOMEWHERE TOO AND IT WAS FLUFFY AND THERE WERE YELLOW AND PINK CLOUD THINGS EVERYWHERE AND BLACK GLASS AND CAVES AND CREATURES AND A CASTLE!
WHAT?! WHY DIDN'T YOU SAY SO?
I TRIED.
IF WE BOTH WENT SOMEWHERE, THERE'S A CHANCE CHARLOTTE DID TOO. WE NEED TO GO FIND HER BEFORE MAMÁ LUPE FINDS OUT. I DON'T WANNA KNOW WHAT'LL HAPPEN IF SHE DOES.
ME NEITHER.

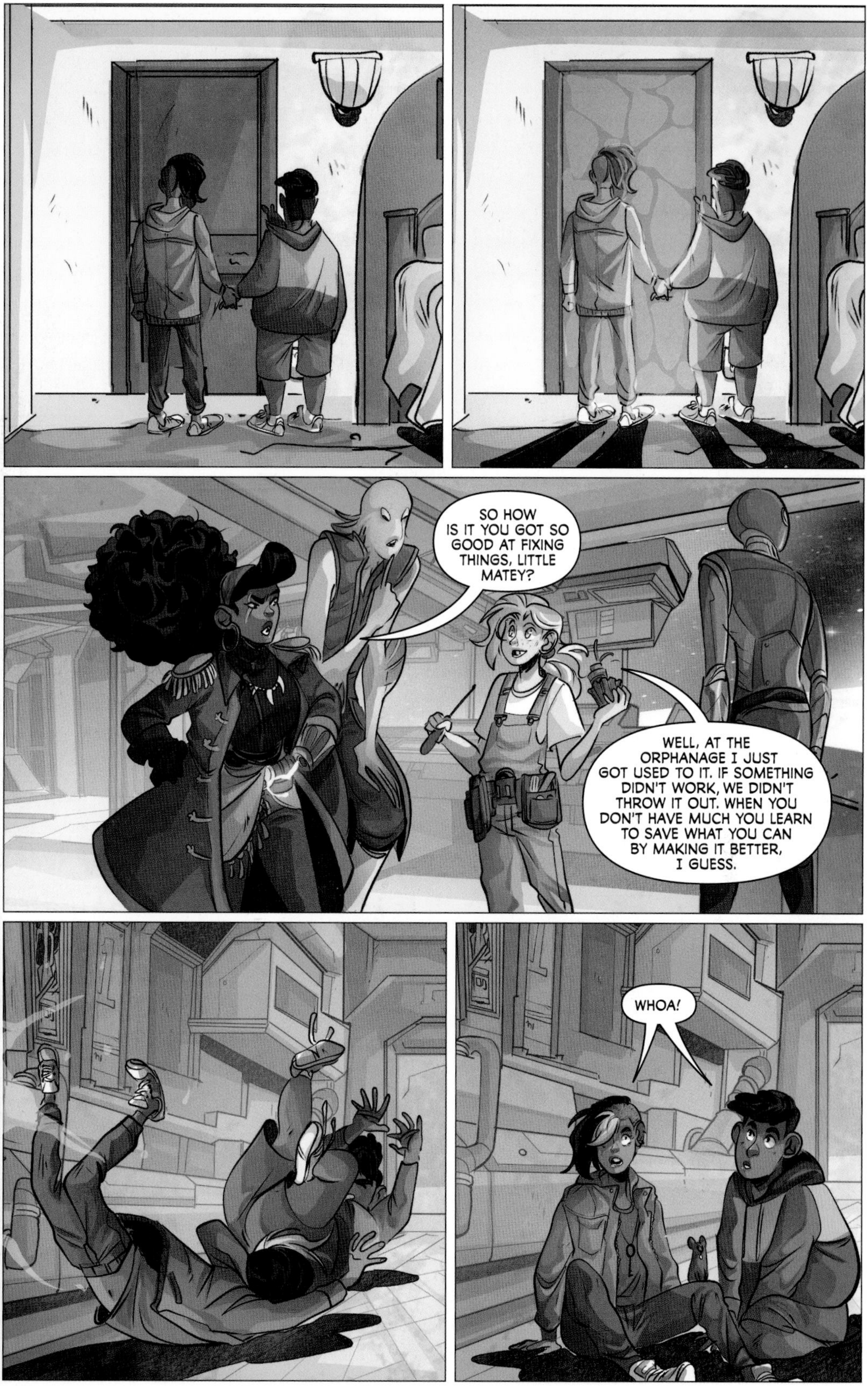
SO HOW IS IT YOU GOT SO GOOD AT FIXING THINGS, LITTLE MATEY?
WELL, AT THE ORPHANAGE I JUST GOT USED TO IT. IF SOMETHING DIDN'T WORK, WE DIDN'T THROW IT OUT. WHEN YOU DON'T HAVE MUCH YOU LEARN TO SAVE WHAT YOU CAN BY MAKING IT BETTER, I GUESS.
WHOA!

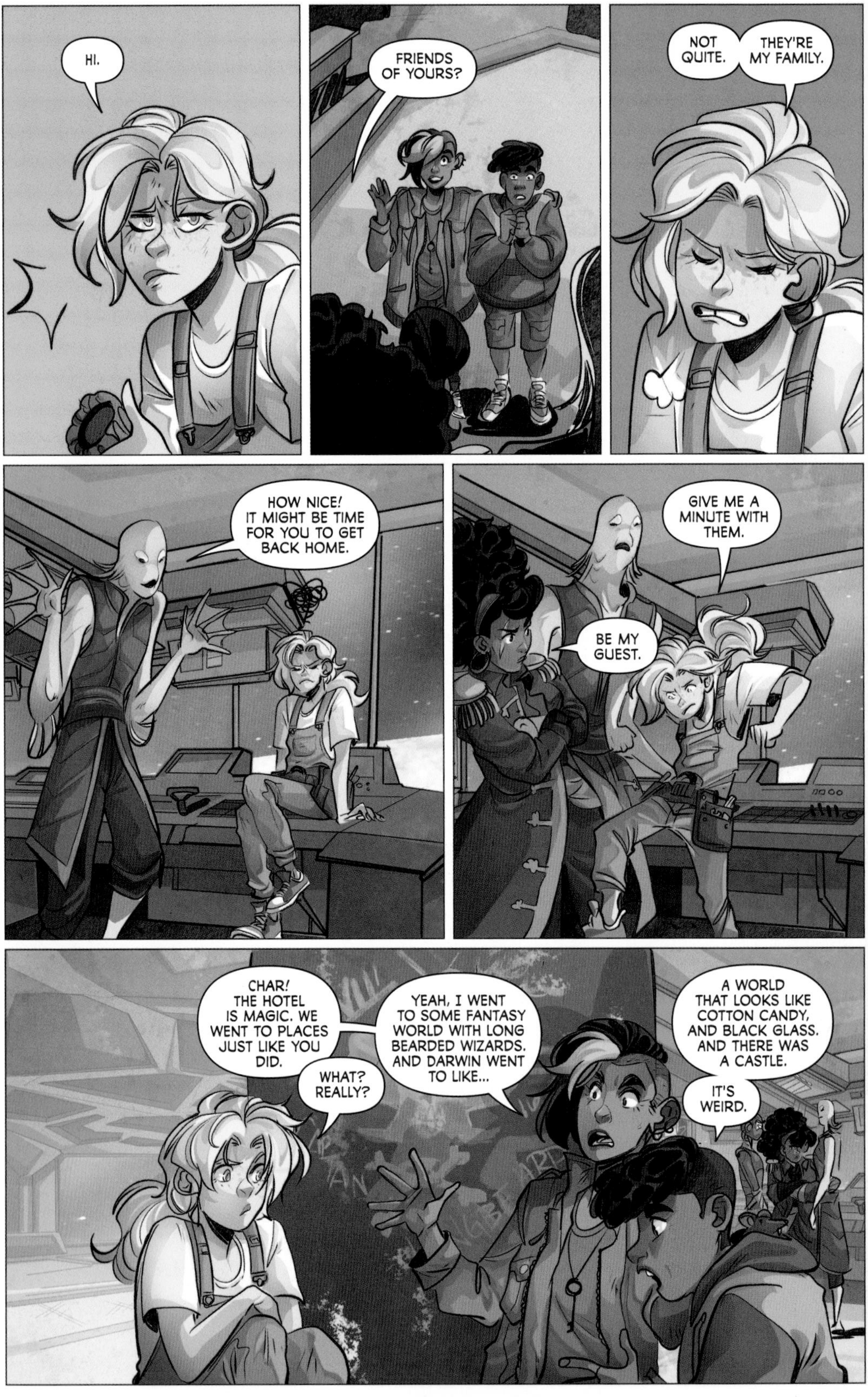
HI.
FRIENDS OF YOURS?
NOT QUITE.
THEY'RE MY FAMILY.
HOW NICE! IT MIGHT BE TIME FOR YOU TO GET BACK HOME.
GIVE ME A MINUTE WITH THEM.
BE MY GUEST.
CHAR! THE HOTEL IS MAGIC. WE WENT TO PLACES JUST LIKE YOU DID.
WHAT? REALLY?
YEAH, I WENT TO SOME FANTASY WORLD WITH LONG BEARDED WIZARDS. AND DARWIN WENT TO LIKE...
A WORLD THAT LOOKS LIKE COTTON CANDY, AND BLACK GLASS. AND THERE WAS A CASTLE.
IT'S WEIRD.

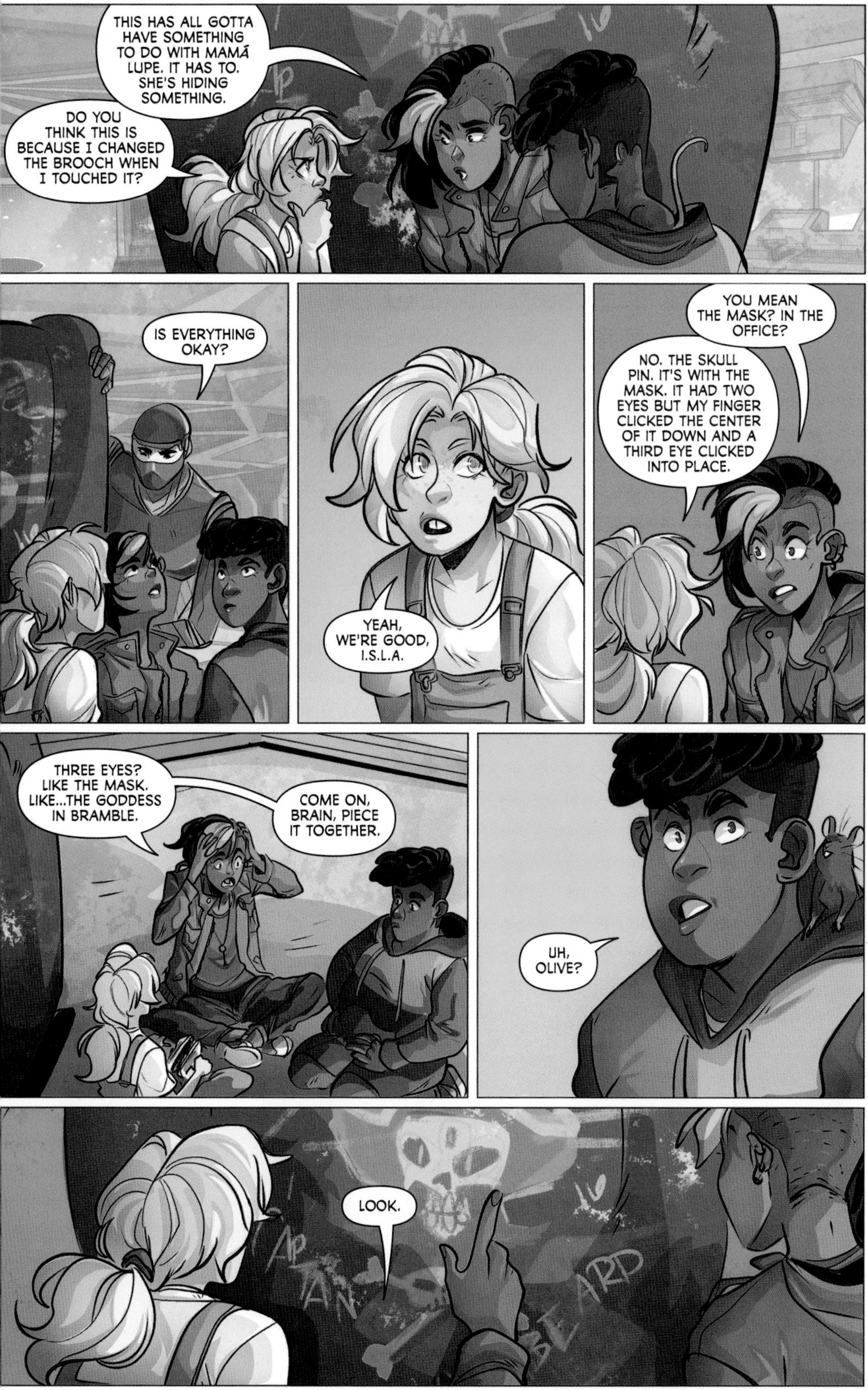

THIS HAS ALL GOTTA HAVE SOMETHING TO DO WITH MAMÁ LUPE. IT HAS TO. SHE'S HIDING SOMETHING.
DO YOU THINK THIS IS BECAUSE I CHANGED THE BROOCH WHEN I TOUCHED IT?
IS EVERYTHING OKAY?
YEAH, WE'RE GOOD, I.S.L.A.
YOU MEAN THE MASK? IN THE OFFICE?
NO. THE SKULL PIN. IT'S WITH THE MASK. IT HAD TWO EYES BUT MY FINGER CLICKED THE CENTER OF IT DOWN AND A THIRD EYE CLICKED INTO PLACE.
THREE EYES? LIKE THE MASK. LIKE...THE GODDESS IN BRAMBLE.
COME ON, BRAIN, PIECE IT TOGETHER.
UH, OLIVE?
LOOK.

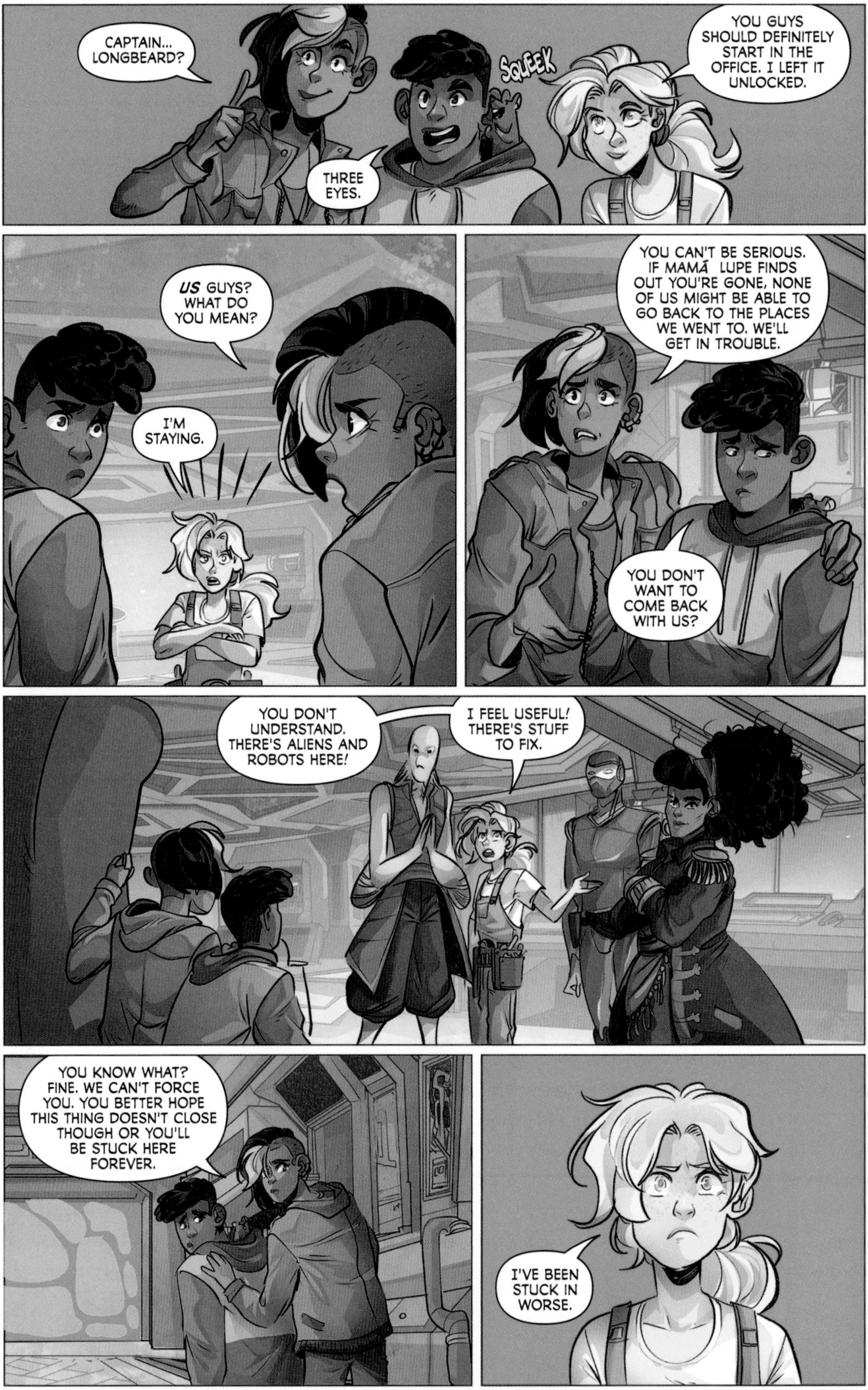

CAPTAIN... LONGBEARD?
THREE EYES.
SQUEEK
YOU GUYS SHOULD DEFINITELY START IN THE OFFICE. I LEFT IT UNLOCKED.
US GUYS? WHAT DO YOU MEAN?
I'M STAYING.
YOU CAN'T BE SERIOUS. IF *MAMÁ* LUPE FINDS OUT YOU'RE GONE, NONE OF US MIGHT BE ABLE TO GO BACK TO THE PLACES WE WENT TO. WE'LL GET IN TROUBLE.
YOU DON'T WANT TO COME BACK WITH US?
YOU DON'T UNDERSTAND. THERE'S ALIENS AND ROBOTS HERE!
I FEEL USEFUL! THERE'S STUFF TO FIX.
YOU KNOW WHAT? FINE. WE CAN'T FORCE YOU. YOU BETTER HOPE THIS THING DOESN'T CLOSE THOUGH OR YOU'LL BE STUCK HERE FOREVER.
I'VE BEEN STUCK IN WORSE.

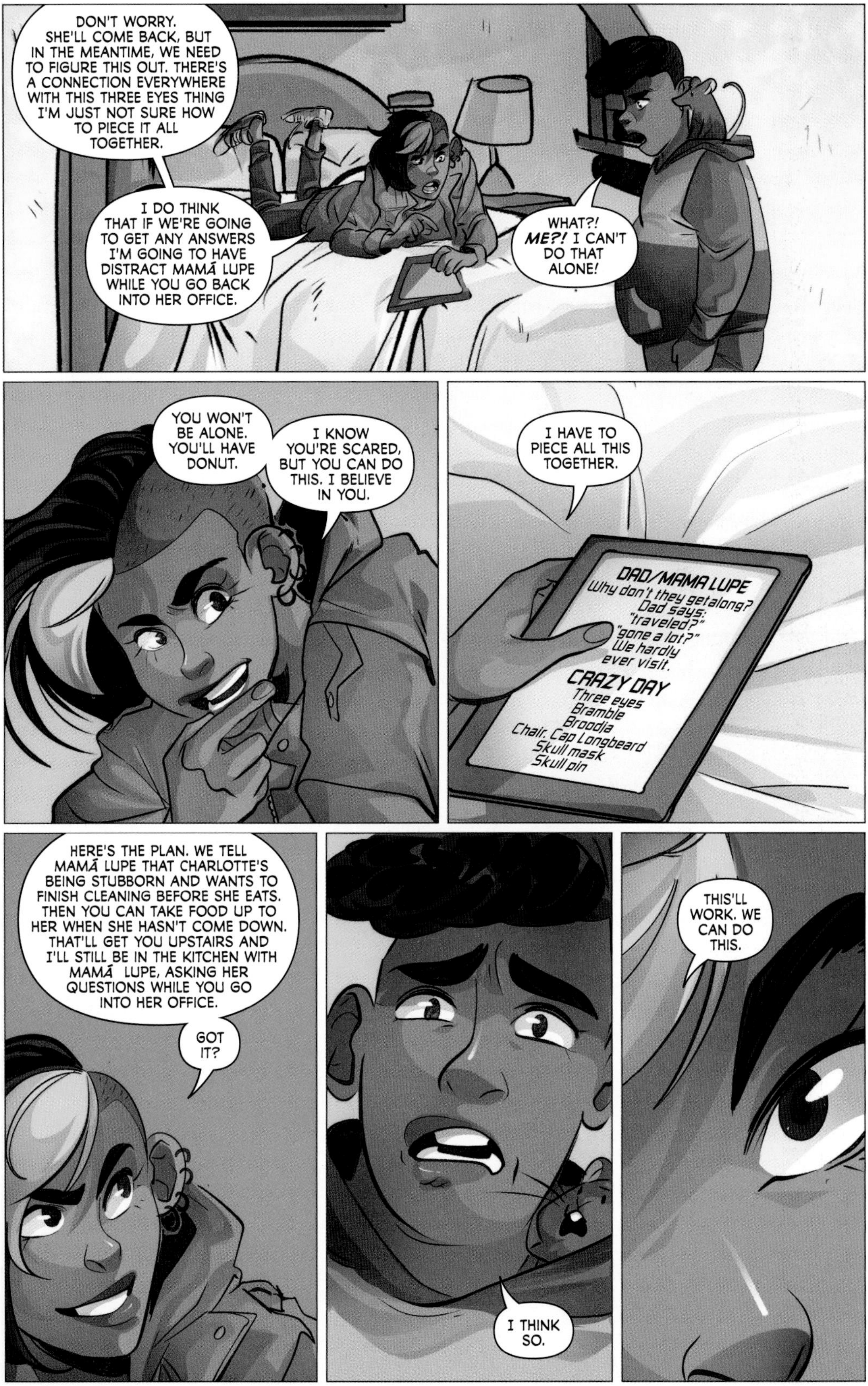
DON'T WORRY. SHE'LL COME BACK, BUT IN THE MEANTIME, WE NEED TO FIGURE THIS OUT. THERE'S A CONNECTION EVERYWHERE WITH THIS THREE EYES THING I'M JUST NOT SURE HOW TO PIECE IT ALL TOGETHER.
I DO THINK THAT IF WE'RE GOING TO GET ANY ANSWERS I'M GOING TO HAVE DISTRACT MAMÁ LUPE WHILE YOU GO BACK INTO HER OFFICE.
WHAT?! ME?! I CAN'T DO THAT ALONE!
YOU WON'T BE ALONE. YOU'LL HAVE DONUT.
I KNOW YOU'RE SCARED, BUT YOU CAN DO THIS. I BELIEVE IN YOU.
I HAVE TO PIECE ALL THIS TOGETHER.
DAD/MAMA LUPE
Why don't they get along?
Dad says:
"traveled?"
"gone a lot?"
We hardly ever visit.
CRAZY DAY
Three eyes
Bramble
Broodja
Chair. Cap Longbeard
Skull mask
Skull pin
HERE'S THE PLAN. WE TELL MAMÁ LUPE THAT CHARLOTTE'S BEING STUBBORN AND WANTS TO FINISH CLEANING BEFORE SHE EATS. THEN YOU CAN TAKE FOOD UP TO HER WHEN SHE HASN'T COME DOWN. THAT'LL GET YOU UPSTAIRS AND I'LL STILL BE IN THE KITCHEN WITH MAMÁ LUPE, ASKING HER QUESTIONS WHILE YOU GO INTO HER OFFICE.
GOT IT?
I THINK SO.
THIS'LL WORK. WE CAN DO THIS.

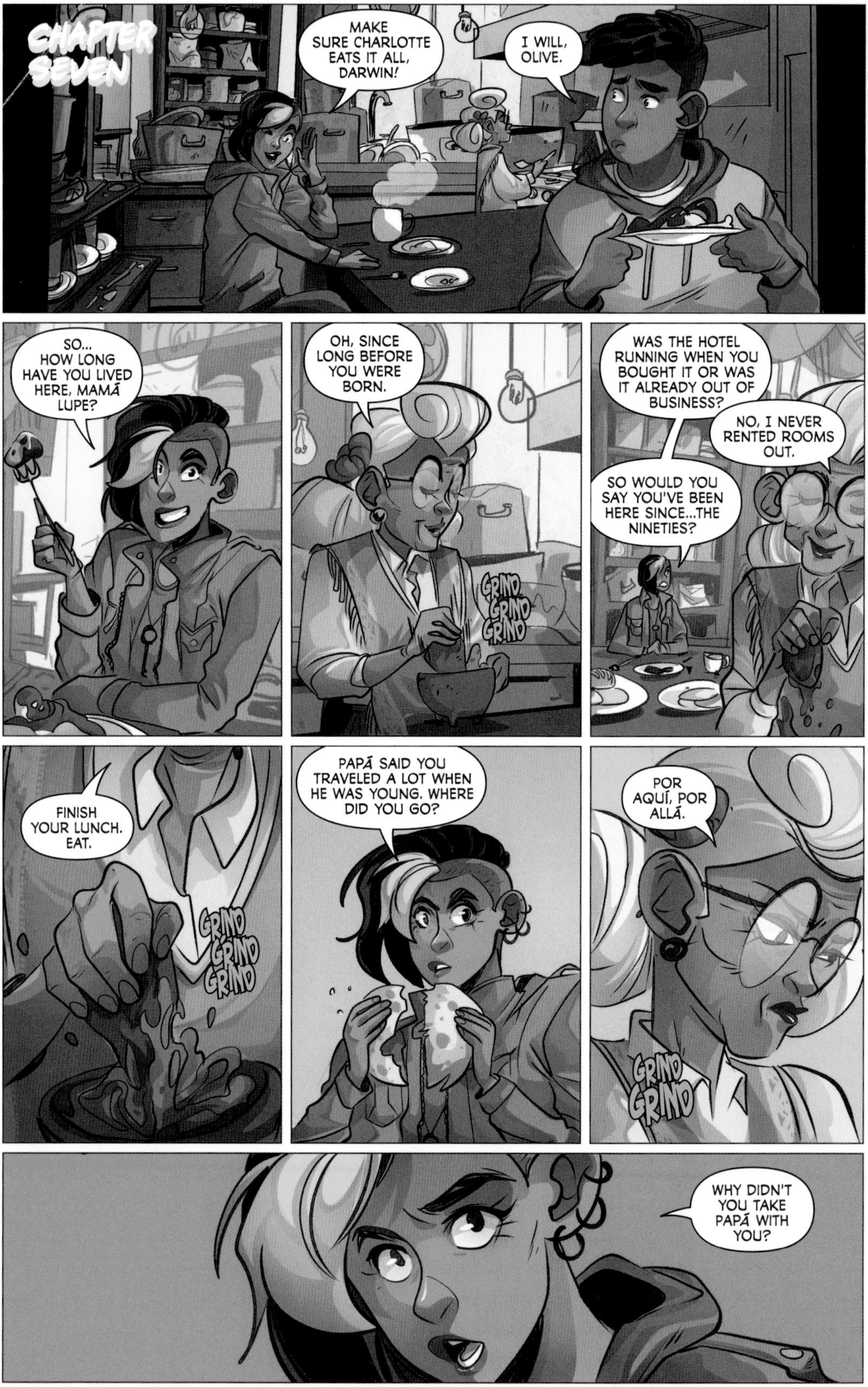
CHAPTER SEVEN
MAKE SURE CHARLOTTE EATS IT ALL, DARWIN!
I WILL, OLIVE.
SO... HOW LONG HAVE YOU LIVED HERE, MAMÁ LUPE?
OH, SINCE LONG BEFORE YOU WERE BORN.
GRIND GRIND GRIND
WAS THE HOTEL RUNNING WHEN YOU BOUGHT IT OR WAS IT ALREADY OUT OF BUSINESS?
NO, I NEVER RENTED ROOMS OUT.
SO WOULD YOU SAY YOU'VE BEEN HERE SINCE...THE NINETIES?
FINISH YOUR LUNCH. EAT.
GRIND GRIND GRIND
PAPÁ SAID YOU TRAVELED A LOT WHEN HE WAS YOUNG. WHERE DID YOU GO?
POR AQUÍ, POR ALLÁ.
GRIND GRIND
WHY DIDN'T YOU TAKE PAPÁ WITH YOU?

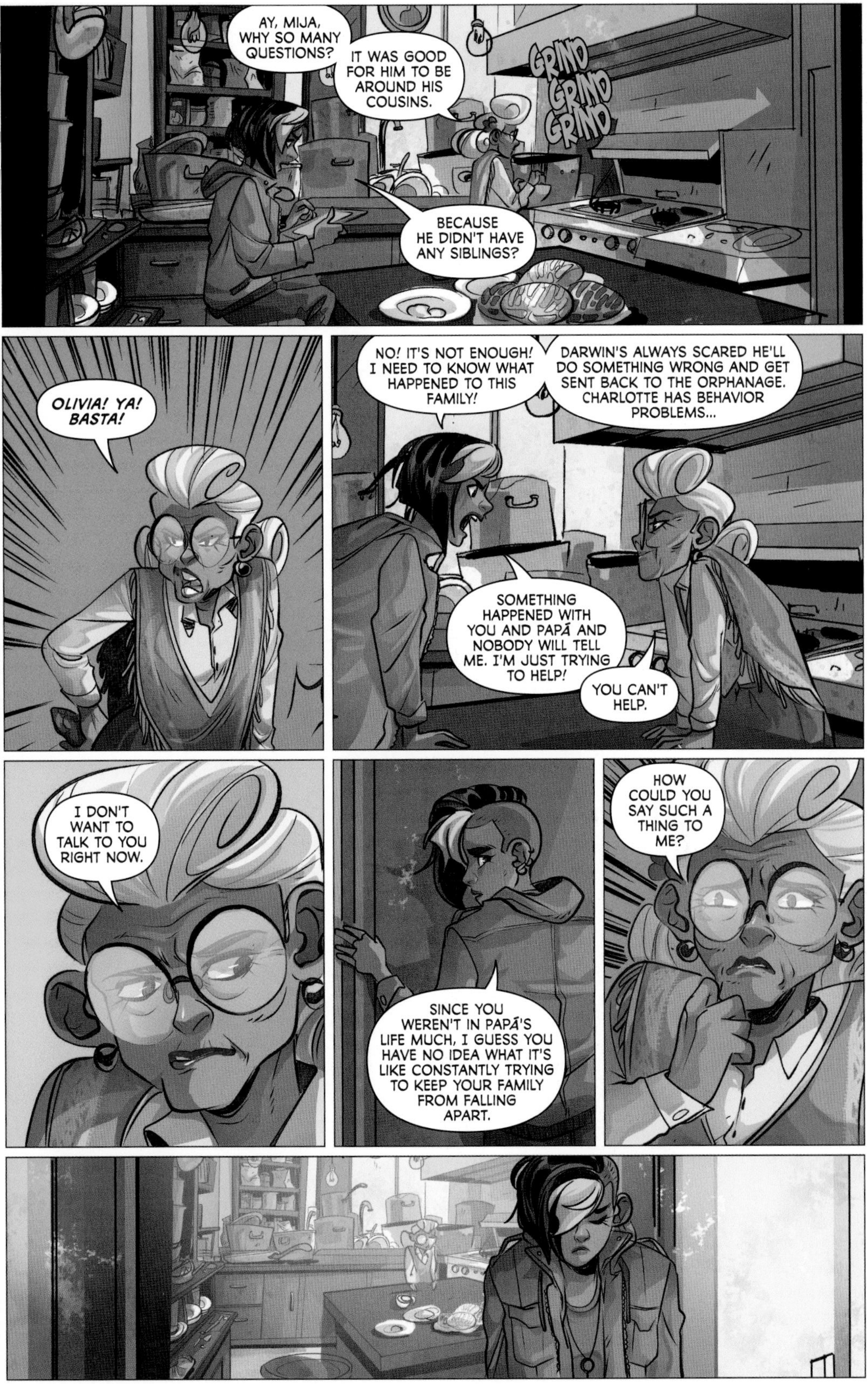
AY, MIJA, WHY SO MANY QUESTIONS?
IT WAS GOOD FOR HIM TO BE AROUND HIS COUSINS.
GRIND GRIND GRIND
BECAUSE HE DIDN'T HAVE ANY SIBLINGS?
OLIVIA! YA! BASTA!
NO! IT'S NOT ENOUGH! I NEED TO KNOW WHAT HAPPENED TO THIS FAMILY!
DARWIN'S ALWAYS SCARED HE'LL DO SOMETHING WRONG AND GET SENT BACK TO THE ORPHANAGE. CHARLOTTE HAS BEHAVIOR PROBLEMS...
SOMETHING HAPPENED WITH YOU AND PAPÁ AND NOBODY WILL TELL ME. I'M JUST TRYING TO HELP!
YOU CAN'T HELP.
I DON'T WANT TO TALK TO YOU RIGHT NOW.
SINCE YOU WEREN'T IN PAPÁ'S LIFE MUCH, I GUESS YOU HAVE NO IDEA WHAT IT'S LIKE CONSTANTLY TRYING TO KEEP YOUR FAMILY FROM FALLING APART.
HOW COULD YOU SAY SUCH A THING TO ME?

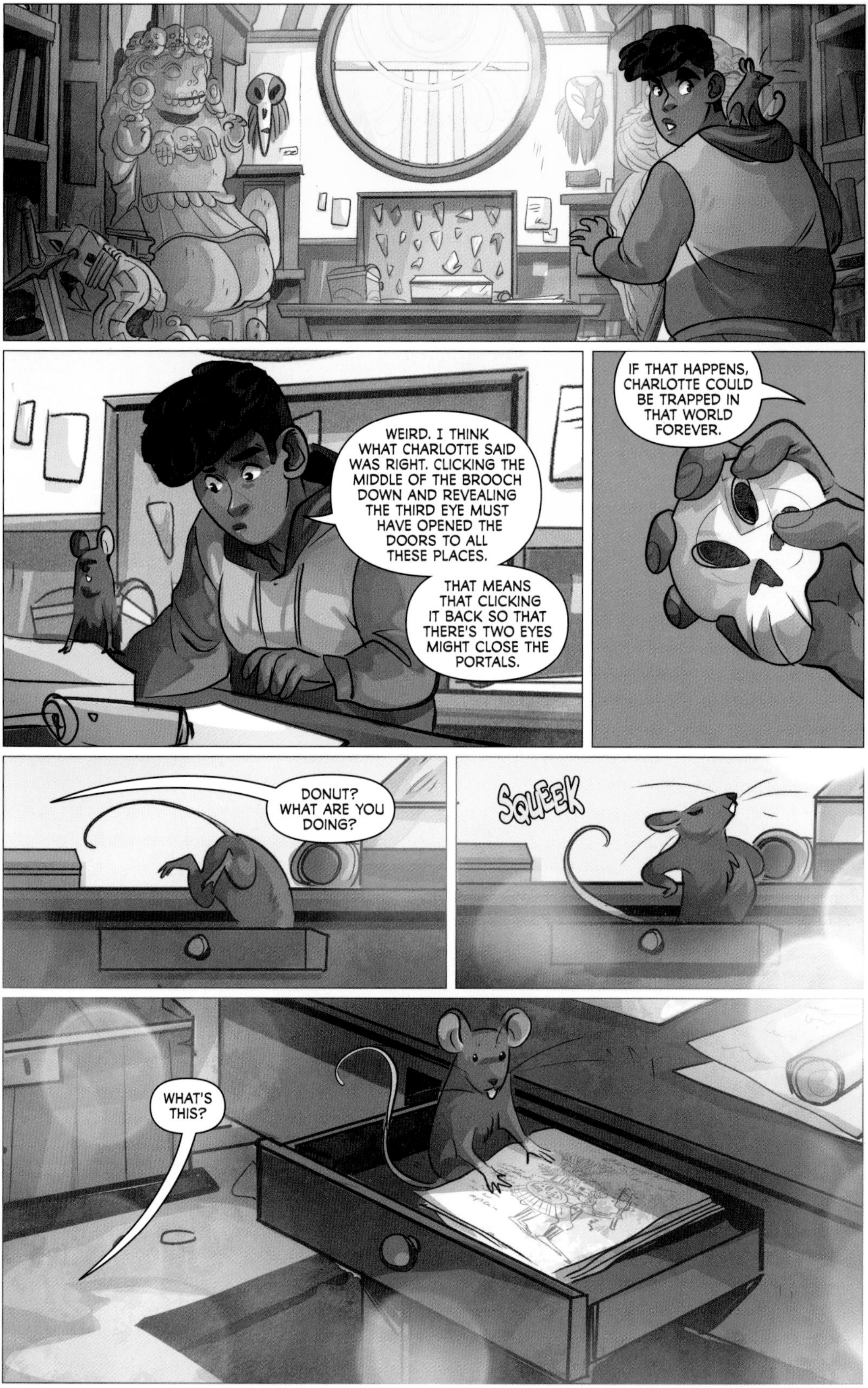
WEIRD. I THINK WHAT CHARLOTTE SAID WAS RIGHT. CLICKING THE MIDDLE OF THE BROOCH DOWN AND REVEALING THE THIRD EYE MUST HAVE OPENED THE DOORS TO ALL THESE PLACES.
THAT MEANS THAT CLICKING IT BACK SO THAT THERE'S TWO EYES MIGHT CLOSE THE PORTALS.
IF THAT HAPPENS, CHARLOTTE COULD BE TRAPPED IN THAT WORLD FOREVER.
DONUT? WHAT ARE YOU DOING?
SQUEEK
WHAT'S THIS?

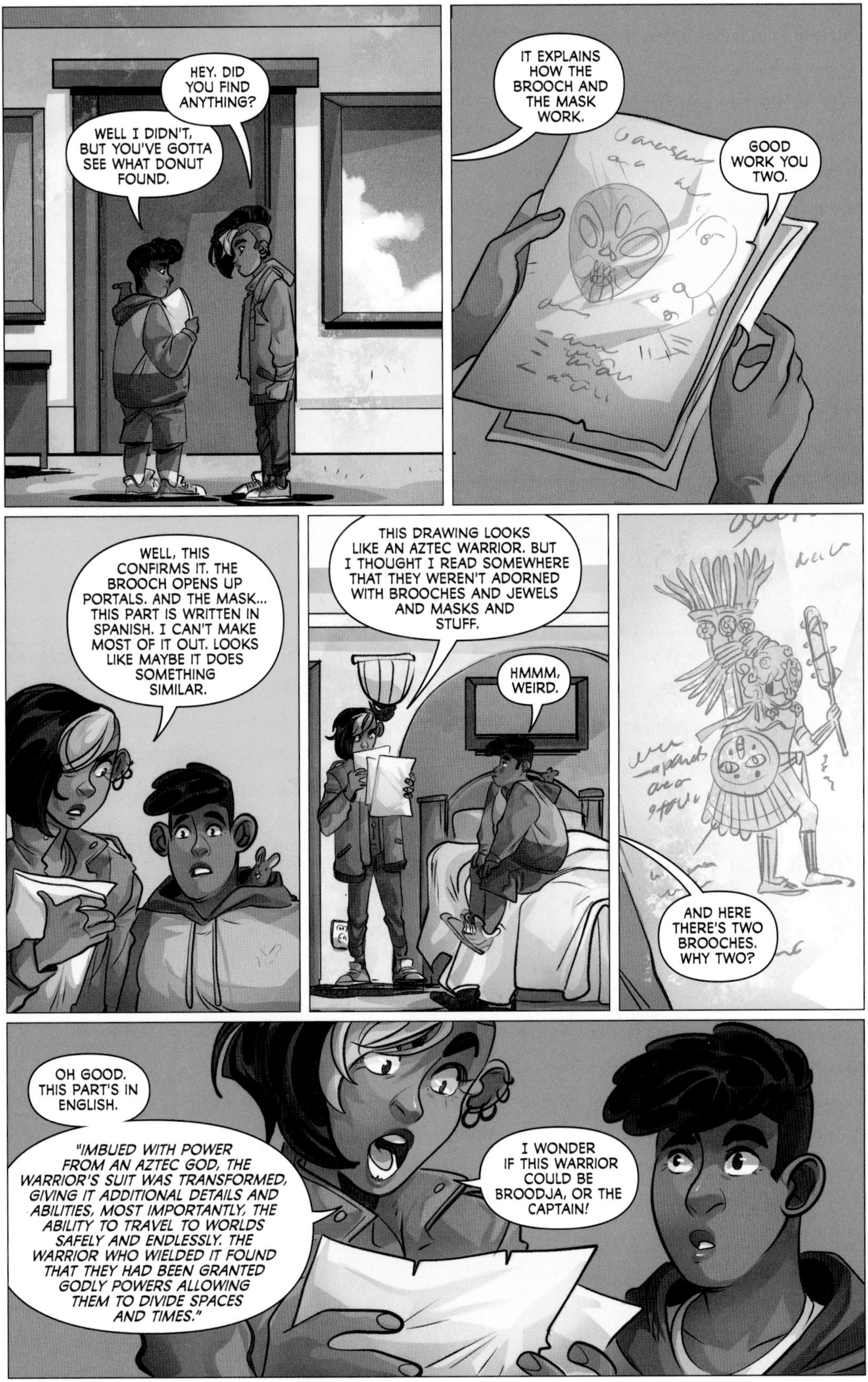
HEY. DID YOU FIND ANYTHING?
WELL I DIDN'T, BUT YOU'VE GOTTA SEE WHAT DONUT FOUND.
IT EXPLAINS HOW THE BROOCH AND THE MASK WORK.
GOOD WORK YOU TWO.
WELL, THIS CONFIRMS IT. THE BROOCH OPENS UP PORTALS. AND THE MASK... THIS PART IS WRITTEN IN SPANISH. I CAN'T MAKE MOST OF IT OUT. LOOKS LIKE MAYBE IT DOES SOMETHING SIMILAR.
THIS DRAWING LOOKS LIKE AN AZTEC WARRIOR. BUT I THOUGHT I READ SOMEWHERE THAT THEY WEREN'T ADORNED WITH BROOCHES AND JEWELS AND MASKS AND STUFF.
HMMM, WEIRD.
AND HERE THERE'S TWO BROOCHES. WHY TWO?
OH GOOD. THIS PART'S IN ENGLISH.
"IMBUED WITH POWER FROM AN AZTEC GOD, THE WARRIOR'S SUIT WAS TRANSFORMED, GIVING IT ADDITIONAL DETAILS AND ABILITIES, MOST IMPORTANTLY, THE ABILITY TO TRAVEL TO WORLDS SAFELY AND ENDLESSLY. THE WARRIOR WHO WIELDED IT FOUND THAT THEY HAD BEEN GRANTED GODLY POWERS ALLOWING THEM TO DIVIDE SPACES AND TIMES."
I WONDER IF THIS WARRIOR COULD BE BROODJA, OR THE CAPTAIN!

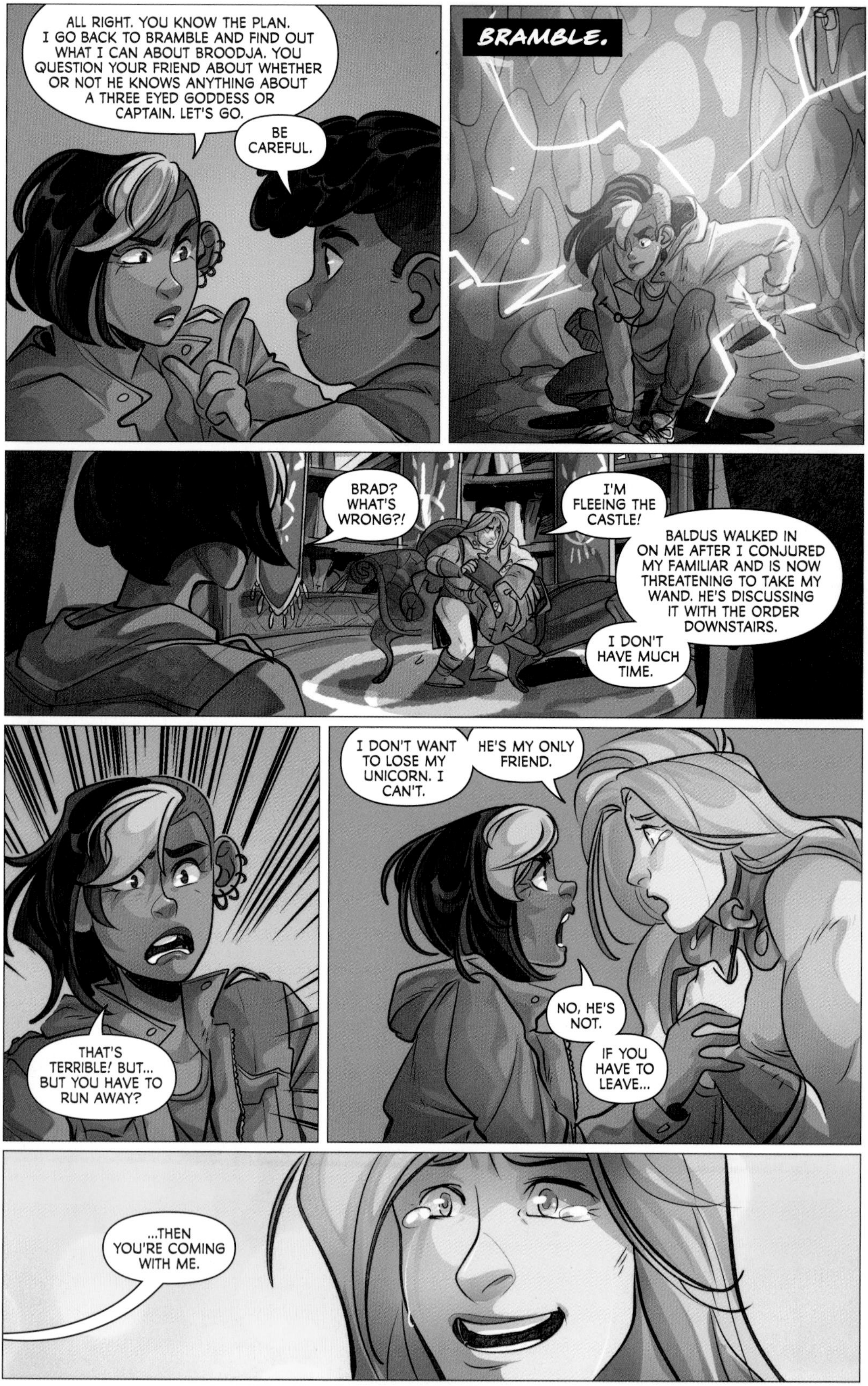
ALL RIGHT. YOU KNOW THE PLAN. I GO BACK TO BRAMBLE AND FIND OUT WHAT I CAN ABOUT BROODJA. YOU QUESTION YOUR FRIEND ABOUT WHETHER OR NOT HE KNOWS ANYTHING ABOUT A THREE EYED GODDESS OR CAPTAIN. LET'S GO.
BE CAREFUL.
BRAMBLE.
BRAD? WHAT'S WRONG?!
I'M FLEEING THE CASTLE!
BALDUS WALKED IN ON ME AFTER I CONJURED MY FAMILIAR AND IS NOW THREATENING TO TAKE MY WAND. HE'S DISCUSSING IT WITH THE ORDER DOWNSTAIRS.
I DON'T HAVE MUCH TIME.
THAT'S TERRIBLE! BUT... BUT YOU HAVE TO RUN AWAY?
I DON'T WANT TO LOSE MY UNICORN. I CAN'T.
HE'S MY ONLY FRIEND.
NO, HE'S NOT.
IF YOU HAVE TO LEAVE...
...THEN YOU'RE COMING WITH ME.

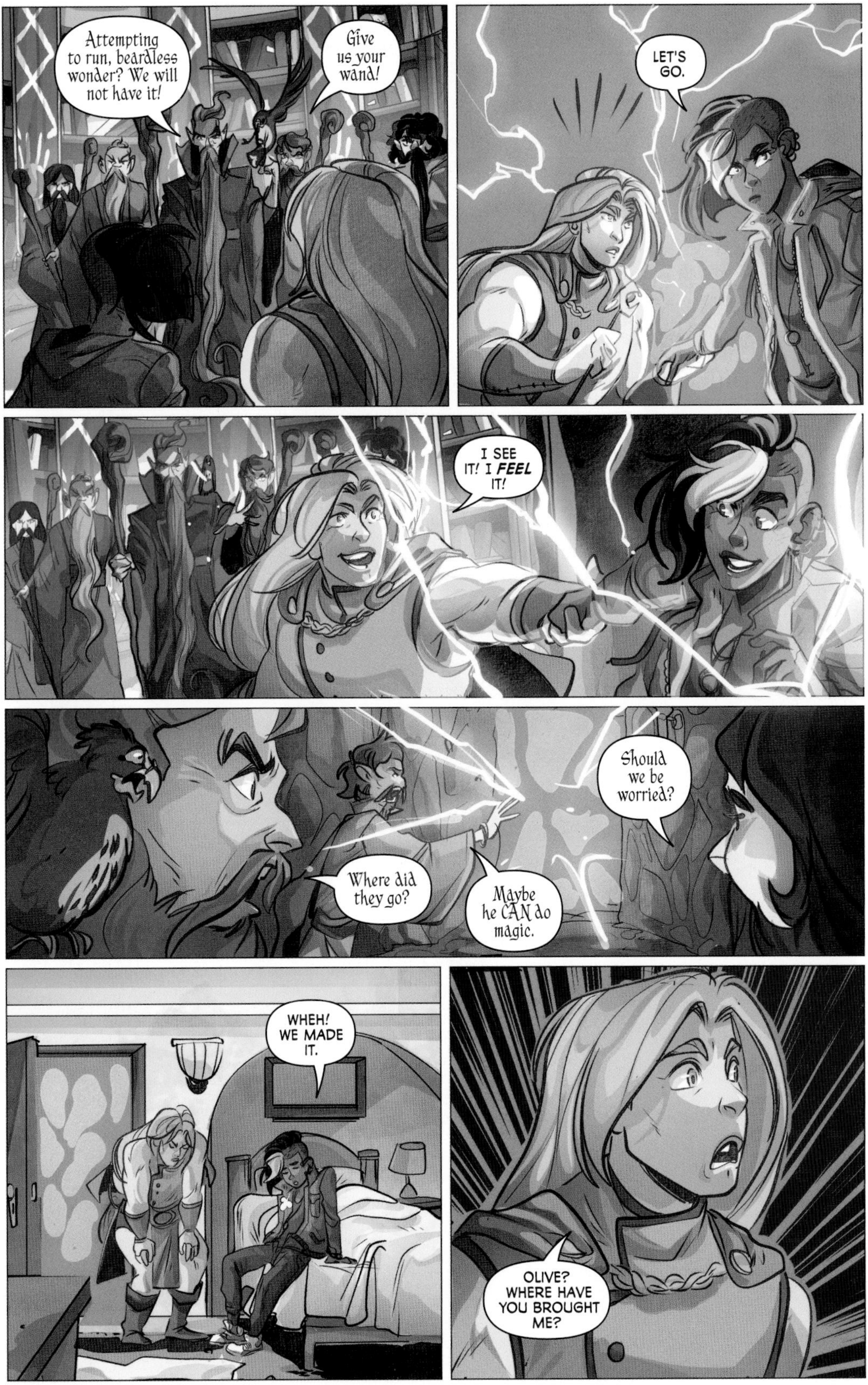
Attempting to run, beardless wonder? We will not have it!
Give us your wand!
LET'S GO.
I SEE IT! I **FEEL** IT!
Should we be worried?
Where did they go?
Maybe he CAN do magic.
WHEH! WE MADE IT.
OLIVE? WHERE HAVE YOU BROUGHT ME?

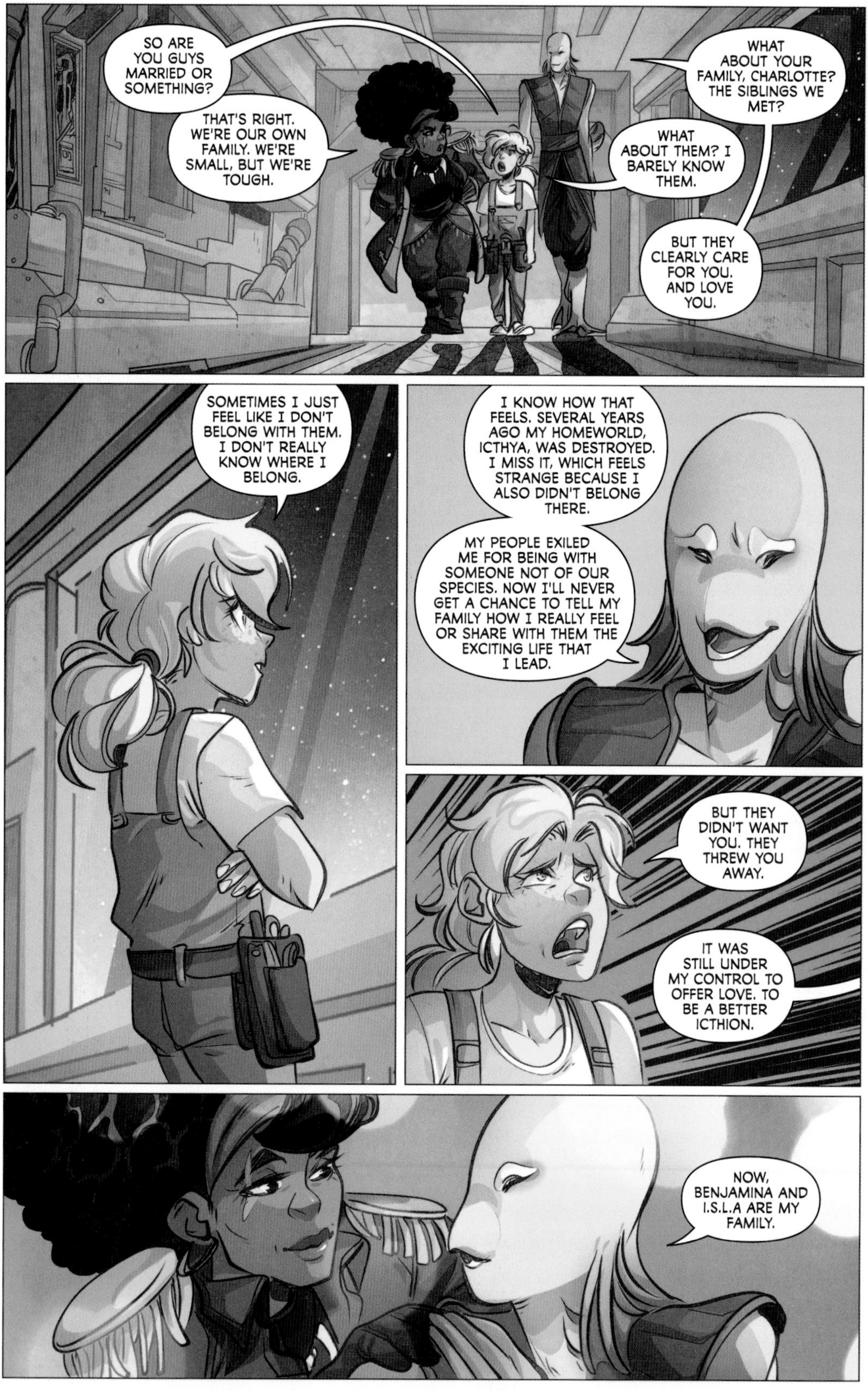
SO ARE YOU GUYS MARRIED OR SOMETHING?
THAT'S RIGHT. WE'RE OUR OWN FAMILY. WE'RE SMALL, BUT WE'RE TOUGH.
WHAT ABOUT YOUR FAMILY, CHARLOTTE? THE SIBLINGS WE MET?
WHAT ABOUT THEM? I BARELY KNOW THEM.
BUT THEY CLEARLY CARE FOR YOU. AND LOVE YOU.
SOMETIMES I JUST FEEL LIKE I DON'T BELONG WITH THEM. I DON'T REALLY KNOW WHERE I BELONG.
I KNOW HOW THAT FEELS. SEVERAL YEARS AGO MY HOMEWORLD, ICTHYA, WAS DESTROYED. I MISS IT, WHICH FEELS STRANGE BECAUSE I ALSO DIDN'T BELONG THERE.
MY PEOPLE EXILED ME FOR BEING WITH SOMEONE NOT OF OUR SPECIES. NOW I'LL NEVER GET A CHANCE TO TELL MY FAMILY HOW I REALLY FEEL OR SHARE WITH THEM THE EXCITING LIFE THAT I LEAD.
BUT THEY DIDN'T WANT YOU. THEY THREW YOU AWAY.
IT WAS STILL UNDER MY CONTROL TO OFFER LOVE. TO BE A BETTER ICTHION.
NOW, BENJAMINA AND I.S.L.A ARE MY FAMILY.

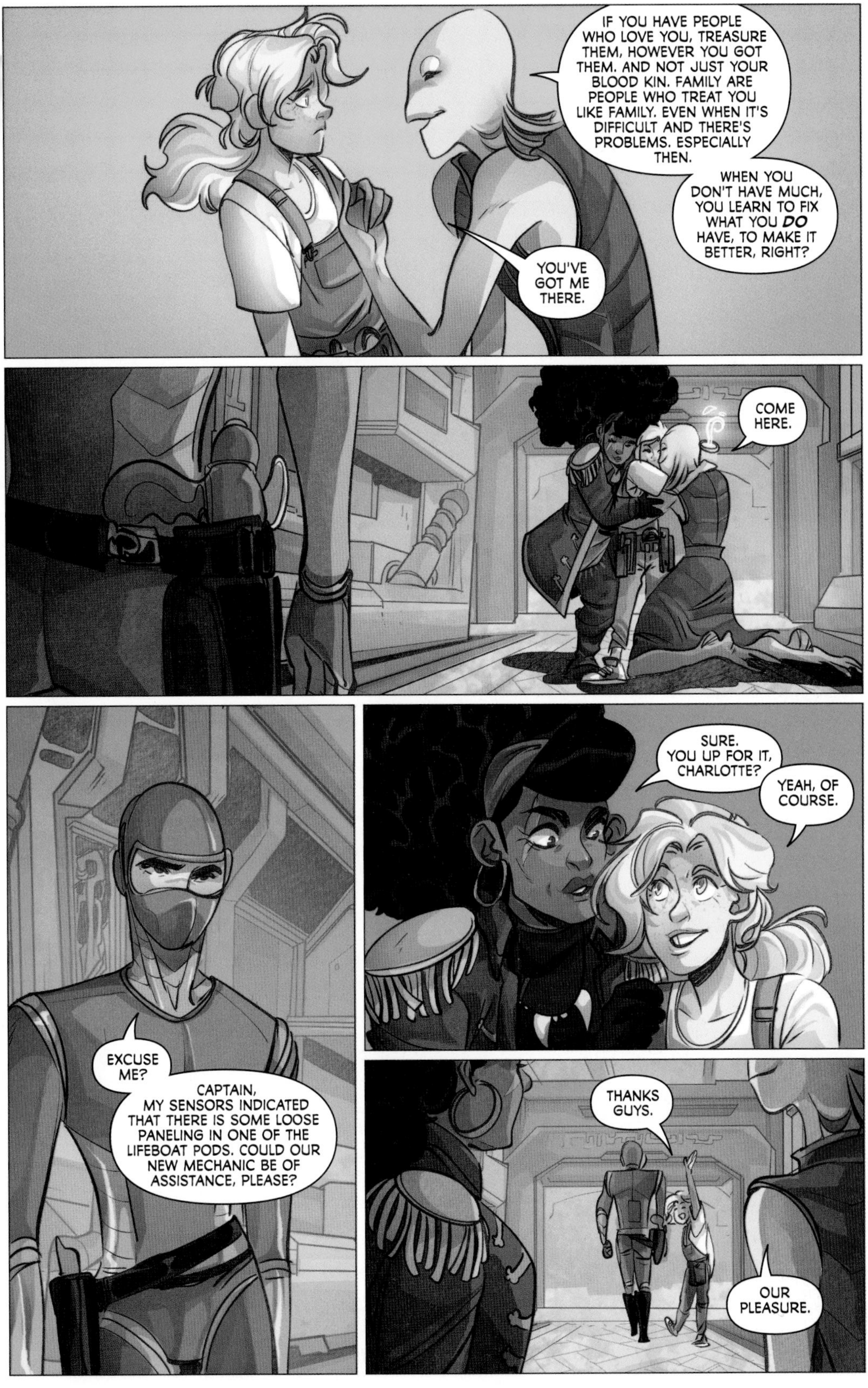
IF YOU HAVE PEOPLE WHO LOVE YOU, TREASURE THEM, HOWEVER YOU GOT THEM. AND NOT JUST YOUR BLOOD KIN. FAMILY ARE PEOPLE WHO TREAT YOU LIKE FAMILY. EVEN WHEN IT'S DIFFICULT AND THERE'S PROBLEMS. ESPECIALLY THEN.
WHEN YOU DON'T HAVE MUCH, YOU LEARN TO FIX WHAT YOU *DO* HAVE, TO MAKE IT BETTER, RIGHT?
YOU'VE GOT ME THERE.
COME HERE.
EXCUSE ME?
CAPTAIN, MY SENSORS INDICATED THAT THERE IS SOME LOOSE PANELING IN ONE OF THE LIFEBOAT PODS. COULD OUR NEW MECHANIC BE OF ASSISTANCE, PLEASE?
SURE. YOU UP FOR IT, CHARLOTTE?
YEAH, OF COURSE.
THANKS GUYS.
OUR PLEASURE.

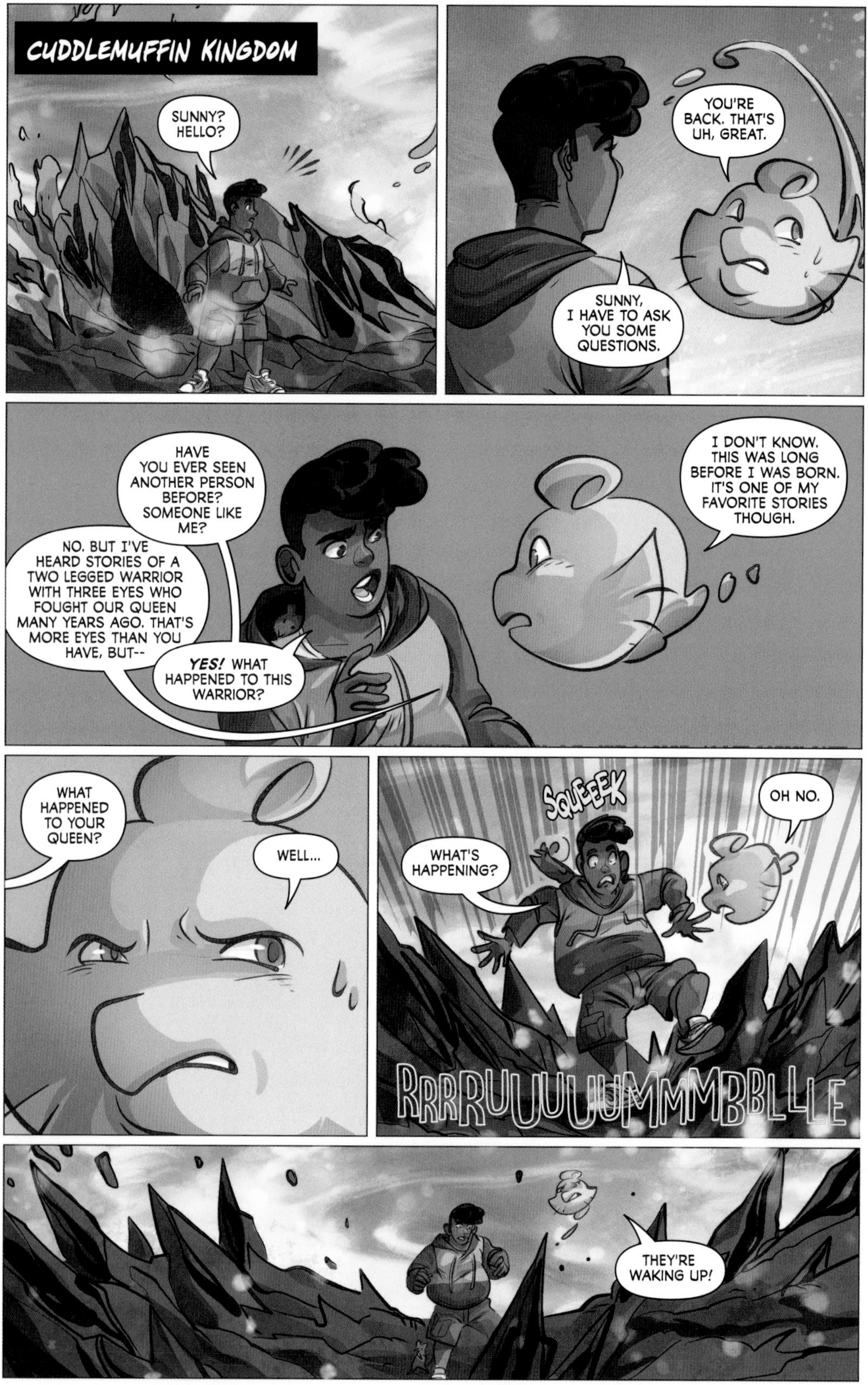
CUDDLEMUFFIN KINGDOM
SUNNY? HELLO?
YOU'RE BACK. THAT'S UH, GREAT.
SUNNY, I HAVE TO ASK YOU SOME QUESTIONS.
HAVE YOU EVER SEEN ANOTHER PERSON BEFORE? SOMEONE LIKE ME?
NO. BUT I'VE HEARD STORIES OF A TWO LEGGED WARRIOR WITH THREE EYES WHO FOUGHT OUR QUEEN MANY YEARS AGO. THAT'S MORE EYES THAN YOU HAVE, BUT--
YES! WHAT HAPPENED TO THIS WARRIOR?
I DON'T KNOW. THIS WAS LONG BEFORE I WAS BORN. IT'S ONE OF MY FAVORITE STORIES THOUGH.
WHAT HAPPENED TO YOUR QUEEN?
WELL...
SQUEEEK
WHAT'S HAPPENING?
OH NO.
RRRRUUUUUMMMBBLLLE
THEY'RE WAKING UP!

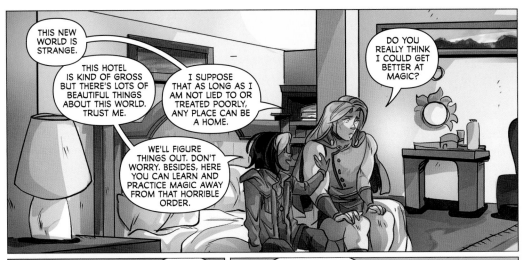

THIS NEW WORLD IS STRANGE.

THIS HOTEL IS KIND OF GROSS BUT THERE'S LOTS OF BEAUTIFUL THINGS ABOUT THIS WORLD. TRUST ME.

I SUPPOSE THAT AS LONG AS I AM NOT LIED TO OR TREATED POORLY, ANY PLACE CAN BE A HOME.

WE'LL FIGURE THINGS OUT. DON'T WORRY. BESIDES, HERE YOU CAN LEARN AND PRACTICE MAGIC AWAY FROM THAT HORRIBLE ORDER.

DO YOU REALLY THINK I COULD GET BETTER AT MAGIC?

I KNOW SO. I'VE SEEN WHAT YOU CAN DO.

I WOULD NEED INSTRUCTION. WITHOUT A MENTOR I AM NOT SURE I WOULD KNOW WHERE TO BEGIN. WHO HERE COULD POSSIBLY TEACH ME?

OLIVE, I HOPE I'M NOT WAKING YOU. I SAW YOUR LAMP LIGHT THROUGH--

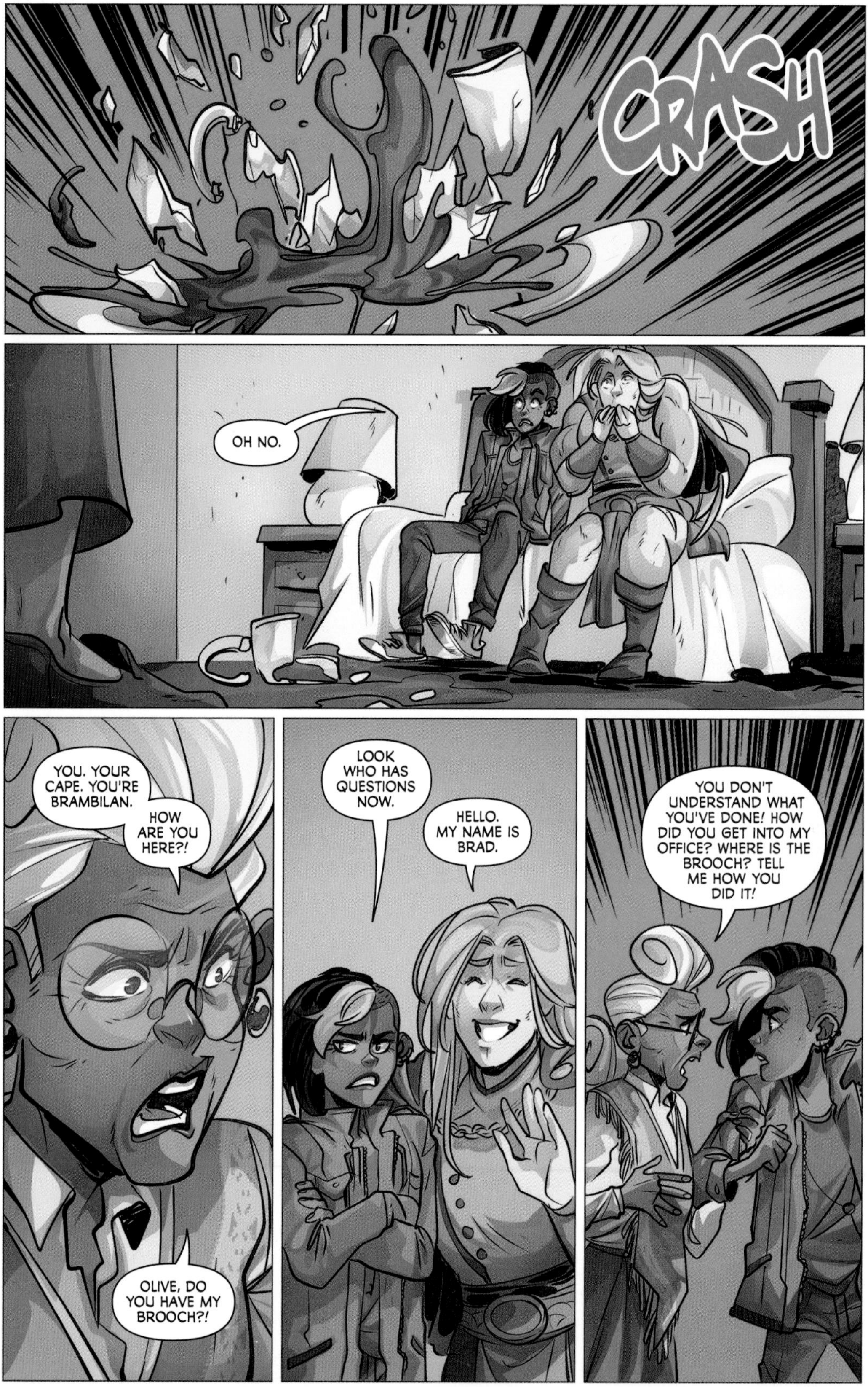
CRASH
OH NO.
YOU. YOUR CAPE. YOU'RE BRAMBILAN.
HOW ARE YOU HERE?!
OLIVE, DO YOU HAVE MY BROOCH?!
LOOK WHO HAS QUESTIONS NOW.
HELLO. MY NAME IS BRAD.
YOU DON'T UNDERSTAND WHAT YOU'VE DONE! HOW DID YOU GET INTO MY OFFICE? WHERE IS THE BROOCH? TELL ME HOW YOU DID IT!

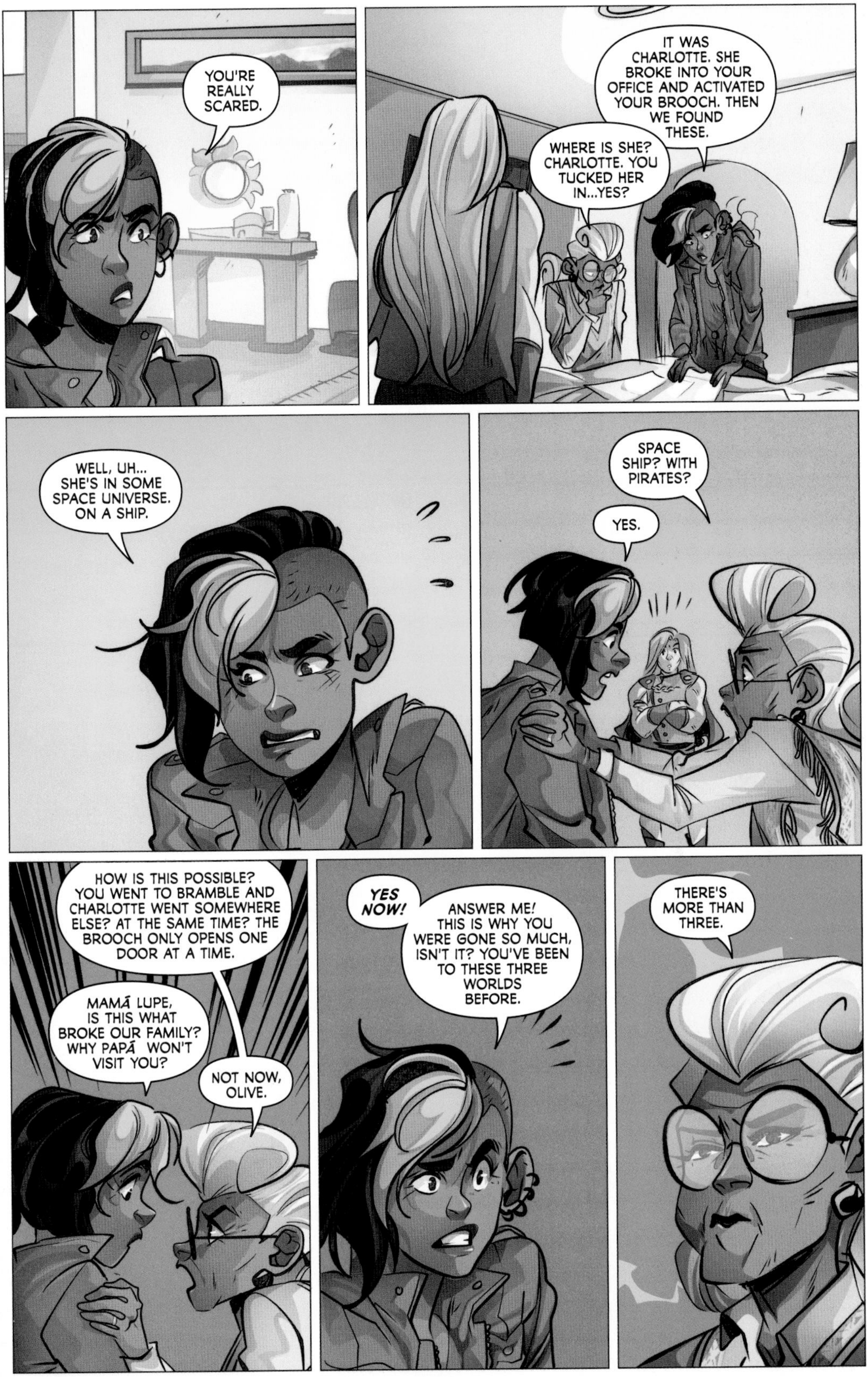
YOU'RE REALLY SCARED.
IT WAS CHARLOTTE. SHE BROKE INTO YOUR OFFICE AND ACTIVATED YOUR BROOCH. THEN WE FOUND THESE.
WHERE IS SHE? CHARLOTTE. YOU TUCKED HER IN...YES?
WELL, UH... SHE'S IN SOME SPACE UNIVERSE. ON A SHIP.
SPACE SHIP? WITH PIRATES?
YES.
HOW IS THIS POSSIBLE? YOU WENT TO BRAMBLE AND CHARLOTTE WENT SOMEWHERE ELSE? AT THE SAME TIME? THE BROOCH ONLY OPENS ONE DOOR AT A TIME.
MAMÁ LUPE, IS THIS WHAT BROKE OUR FAMILY? WHY PAPÁ WON'T VISIT YOU?
NOT NOW, OLIVE.
YES NOW!
ANSWER ME! THIS IS WHY YOU WERE GONE SO MUCH, ISN'T IT? YOU'VE BEEN TO THESE THREE WORLDS BEFORE.
THERE'S MORE THAN THREE.

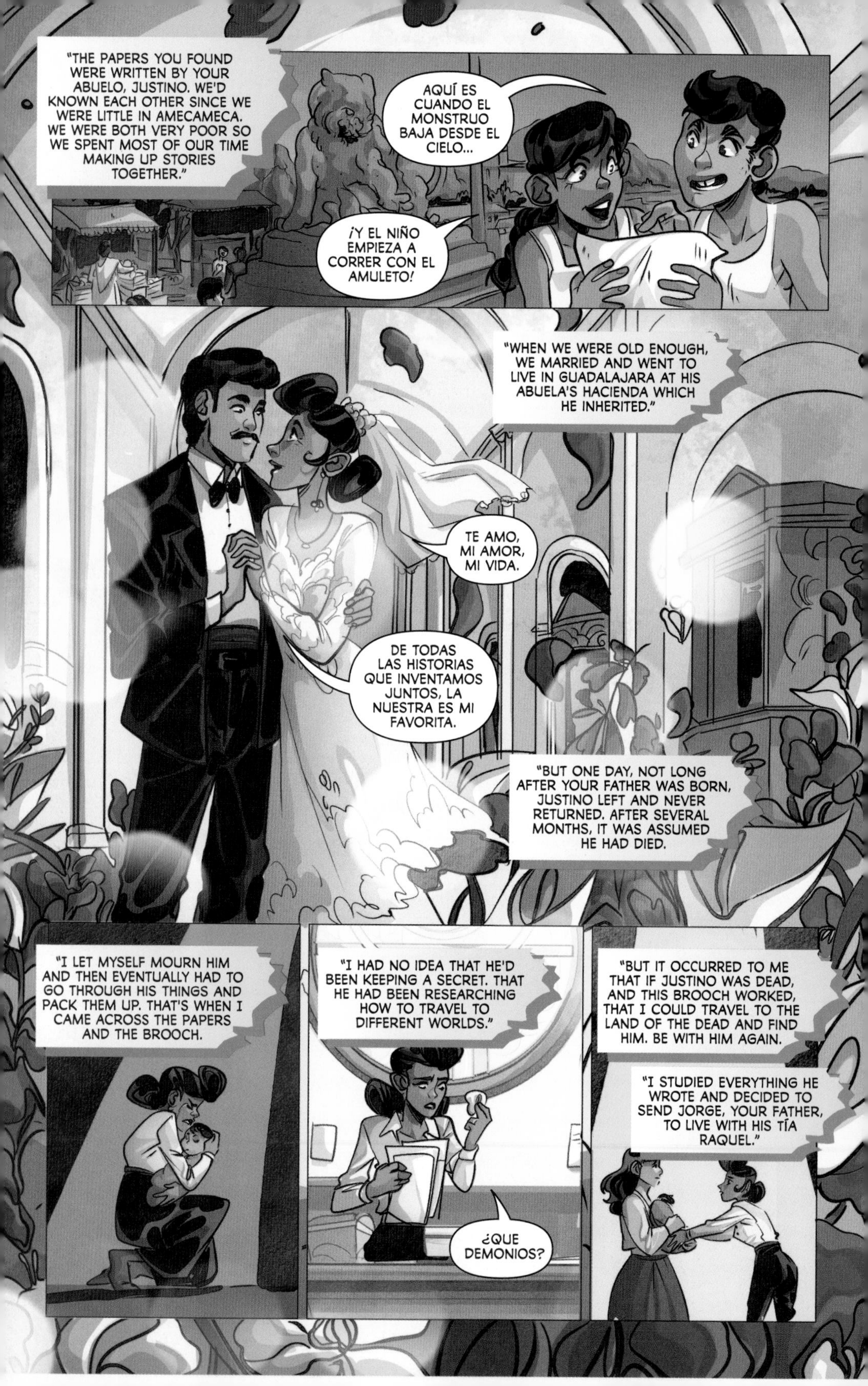
"THE PAPERS YOU FOUND WERE WRITTEN BY YOUR ABUELO, JUSTINO. WE'D KNOWN EACH OTHER SINCE WE WERE LITTLE IN AMECAMECA. WE WERE BOTH VERY POOR SO WE SPENT MOST OF OUR TIME MAKING UP STORIES TOGETHER."
AQUÍ ES CUANDO EL MONSTRUO BAJA DESDE EL CIELO...
¡Y EL NIÑO EMPIEZA A CORRER CON EL AMULETO!
"WHEN WE WERE OLD ENOUGH, WE MARRIED AND WENT TO LIVE IN GUADALAJARA AT HIS ABUELA'S HACIENDA WHICH HE INHERITED."
TE AMO, MI AMOR, MI VIDA.
DE TODAS LAS HISTORIAS QUE INVENTAMOS JUNTOS, LA NUESTRA ES MI FAVORITA.
"BUT ONE DAY, NOT LONG AFTER YOUR FATHER WAS BORN, JUSTINO LEFT AND NEVER RETURNED. AFTER SEVERAL MONTHS, IT WAS ASSUMED HE HAD DIED.
"I LET MYSELF MOURN HIM AND THEN EVENTUALLY HAD TO GO THROUGH HIS THINGS AND PACK THEM UP. THAT'S WHEN I CAME ACROSS THE PAPERS AND THE BROOCH.
"I HAD NO IDEA THAT HE'D BEEN KEEPING A SECRET. THAT HE HAD BEEN RESEARCHING HOW TO TRAVEL TO DIFFERENT WORLDS."
¿QUE DEMONIOS?
"BUT IT OCCURRED TO ME THAT IF JUSTINO WAS DEAD, AND THIS BROOCH WORKED, THAT I COULD TRAVEL TO THE LAND OF THE DEAD AND FIND HIM. BE WITH HIM AGAIN.
"I STUDIED EVERYTHING HE WROTE AND DECIDED TO SEND JORGE, YOUR FATHER, TO LIVE WITH HIS TÍA RAQUEL."

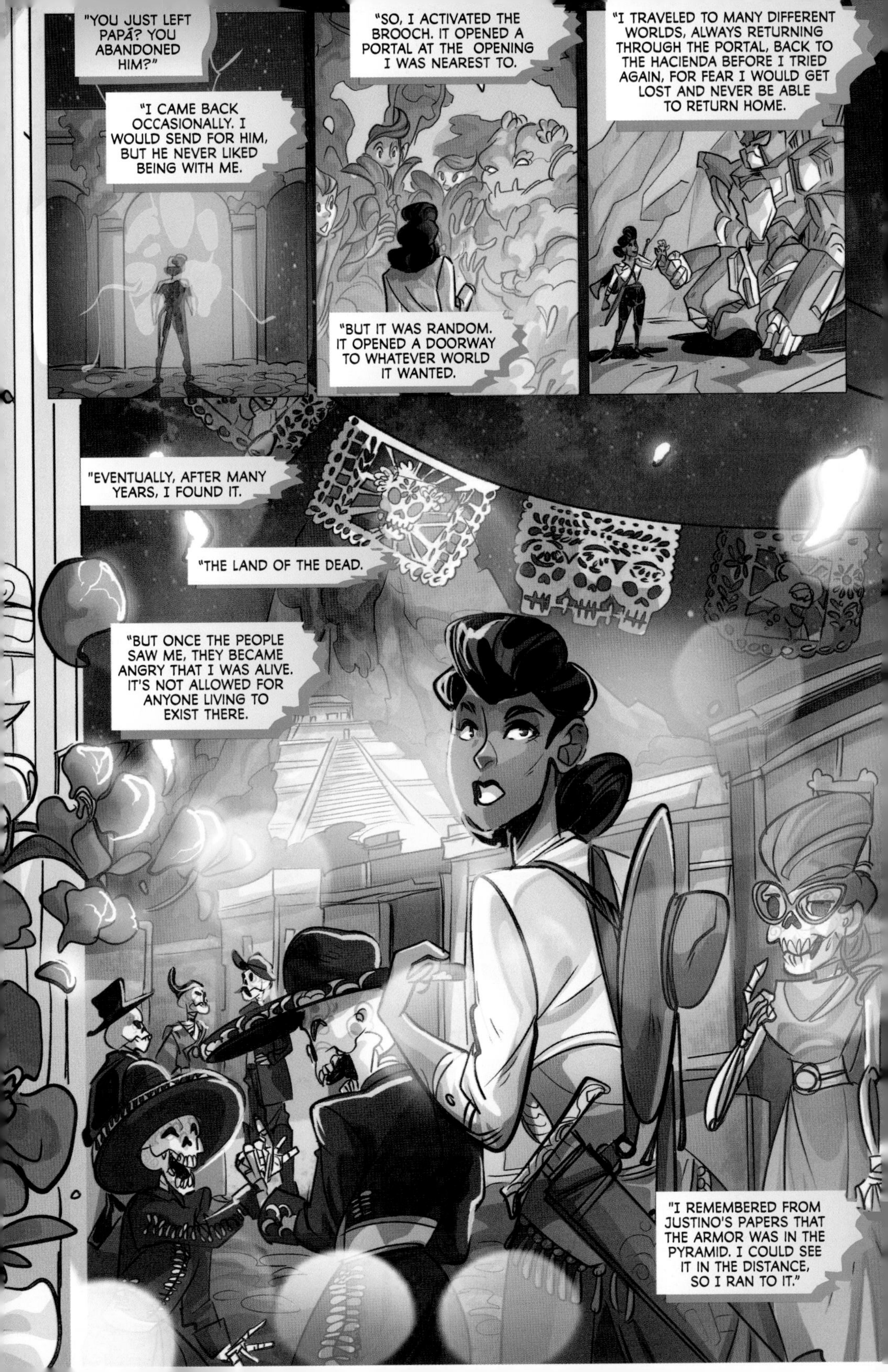
"YOU JUST LEFT PAPÁ? YOU ABANDONED HIM?"
"I CAME BACK OCCASIONALLY. I WOULD SEND FOR HIM, BUT HE NEVER LIKED BEING WITH ME.
"SO, I ACTIVATED THE BROOCH. IT OPENED A PORTAL AT THE OPENING I WAS NEAREST TO.
"BUT IT WAS RANDOM. IT OPENED A DOORWAY TO WHATEVER WORLD IT WANTED.
"I TRAVELED TO MANY DIFFERENT WORLDS, ALWAYS RETURNING THROUGH THE PORTAL, BACK TO THE HACIENDA BEFORE I TRIED AGAIN, FOR FEAR I WOULD GET LOST AND NEVER BE ABLE TO RETURN HOME.
"EVENTUALLY, AFTER MANY YEARS, I FOUND IT.
"THE LAND OF THE DEAD.
"BUT ONCE THE PEOPLE SAW ME, THEY BECAME ANGRY THAT I WAS ALIVE. IT'S NOT ALLOWED FOR ANYONE LIVING TO EXIST THERE.
"I REMEMBERED FROM JUSTINO'S PAPERS THAT THE ARMOR WAS IN THE PYRAMID. I COULD SEE IT IN THE DISTANCE, SO I RAN TO IT."

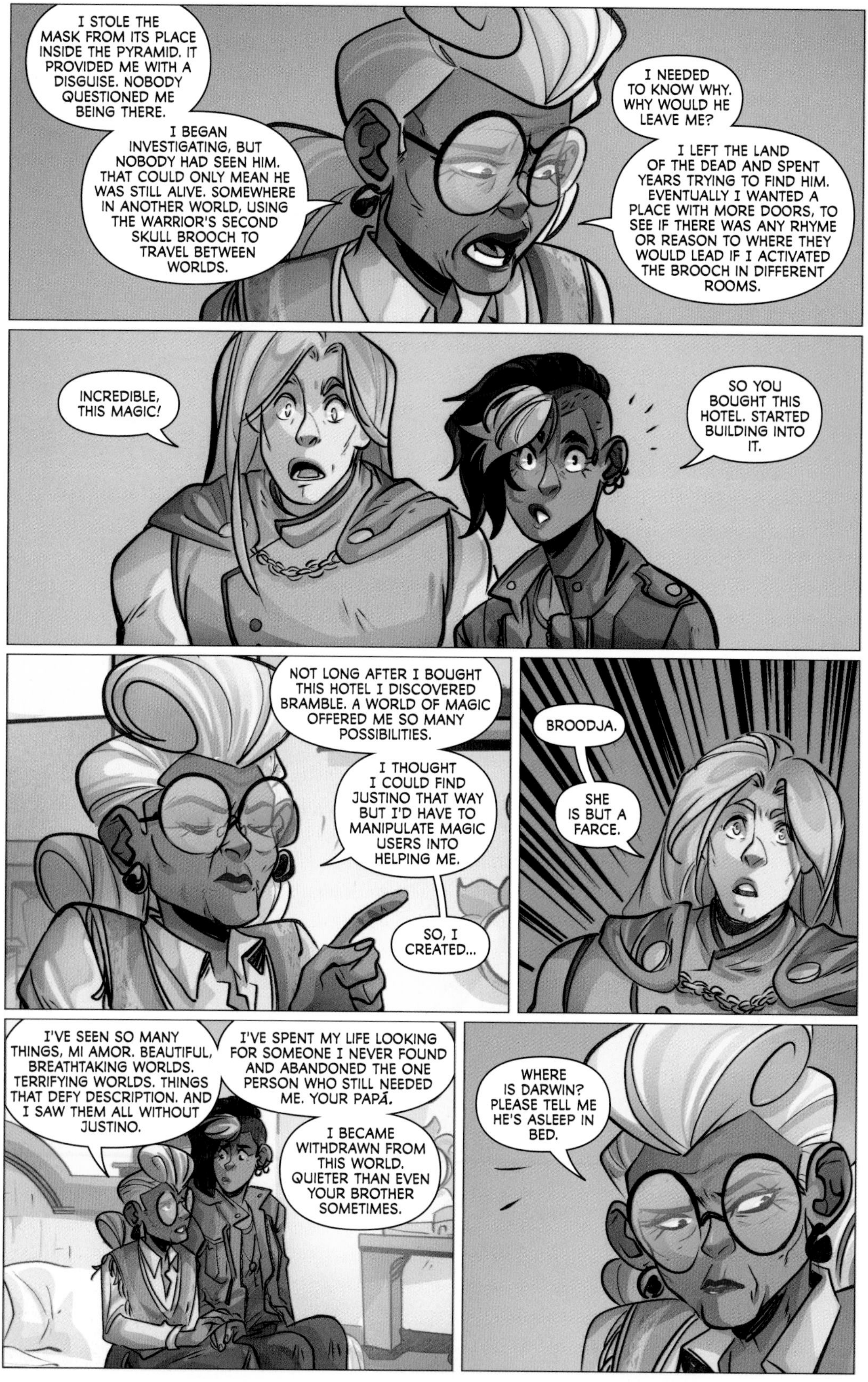
I STOLE THE MASK FROM ITS PLACE INSIDE THE PYRAMID. IT PROVIDED ME WITH A DISGUISE. NOBODY QUESTIONED ME BEING THERE.
I BEGAN INVESTIGATING, BUT NOBODY HAD SEEN HIM. THAT COULD ONLY MEAN HE WAS STILL ALIVE. SOMEWHERE IN ANOTHER WORLD, USING THE WARRIOR'S SECOND SKULL BROOCH TO TRAVEL BETWEEN WORLDS.
I NEEDED TO KNOW WHY. WHY WOULD HE LEAVE ME?
I LEFT THE LAND OF THE DEAD AND SPENT YEARS TRYING TO FIND HIM. EVENTUALLY I WANTED A PLACE WITH MORE DOORS, TO SEE IF THERE WAS ANY RHYME OR REASON TO WHERE THEY WOULD LEAD IF I ACTIVATED THE BROOCH IN DIFFERENT ROOMS.
INCREDIBLE, THIS MAGIC!
SO YOU BOUGHT THIS HOTEL. STARTED BUILDING INTO IT.
NOT LONG AFTER I BOUGHT THIS HOTEL I DISCOVERED BRAMBLE. A WORLD OF MAGIC OFFERED ME SO MANY POSSIBILITIES.
I THOUGHT I COULD FIND JUSTINO THAT WAY BUT I'D HAVE TO MANIPULATE MAGIC USERS INTO HELPING ME.
SO, I CREATED...
BROODJA.
SHE IS BUT A FARCE.
I'VE SEEN SO MANY THINGS, MI AMOR. BEAUTIFUL, BREATHTAKING WORLDS. TERRIFYING WORLDS. THINGS THAT DEFY DESCRIPTION. AND I SAW THEM ALL WITHOUT JUSTINO.
I'VE SPENT MY LIFE LOOKING FOR SOMEONE I NEVER FOUND AND ABANDONED THE ONE PERSON WHO STILL NEEDED ME. YOUR PAPÁ.
I BECAME WITHDRAWN FROM THIS WORLD. QUIETER THAN EVEN YOUR BROTHER SOMETIMES.
WHERE IS DARWIN? PLEASE TELL ME HE'S ASLEEP IN BED.

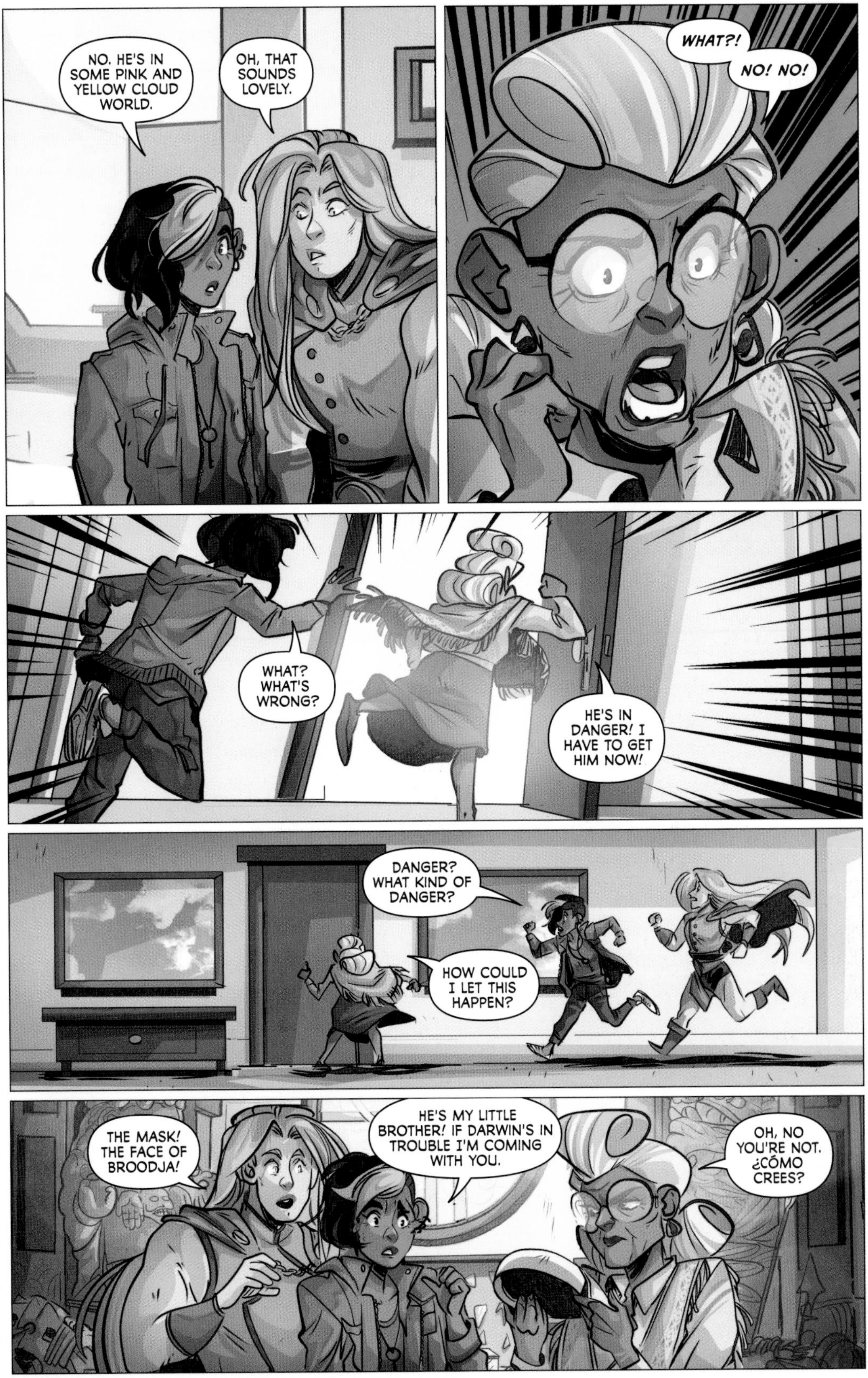
NO. HE'S IN SOME PINK AND YELLOW CLOUD WORLD.
OH, THAT SOUNDS LOVELY.
WHAT?!
NO! NO!
WHAT? WHAT'S WRONG?
HE'S IN DANGER! I HAVE TO GET HIM NOW!
DANGER? WHAT KIND OF DANGER?
HOW COULD I LET THIS HAPPEN?
THE MASK! THE FACE OF BROODJA!
HE'S MY LITTLE BROTHER! IF DARWIN'S IN TROUBLE I'M COMING WITH YOU.
OH, NO YOU'RE NOT. ¿CÓMO CREES?

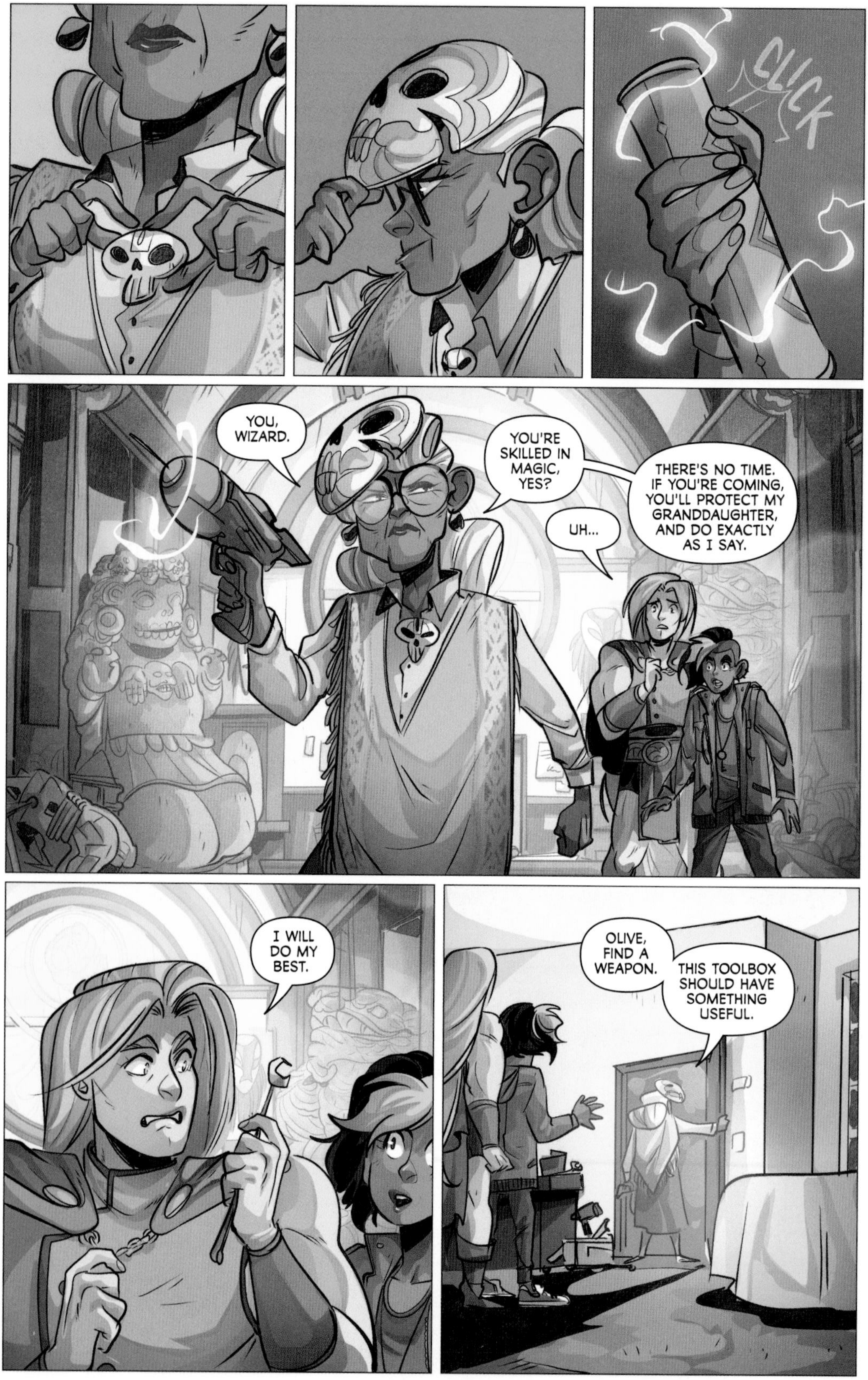
CLICK
YOU, WIZARD.
YOU'RE SKILLED IN MAGIC, YES?
UH...
THERE'S NO TIME. IF YOU'RE COMING, YOU'LL PROTECT MY GRANDDAUGHTER, AND DO EXACTLY AS I SAY.
I WILL DO MY BEST.
OLIVE, FIND A WEAPON.
THIS TOOLBOX SHOULD HAVE SOMETHING USEFUL.

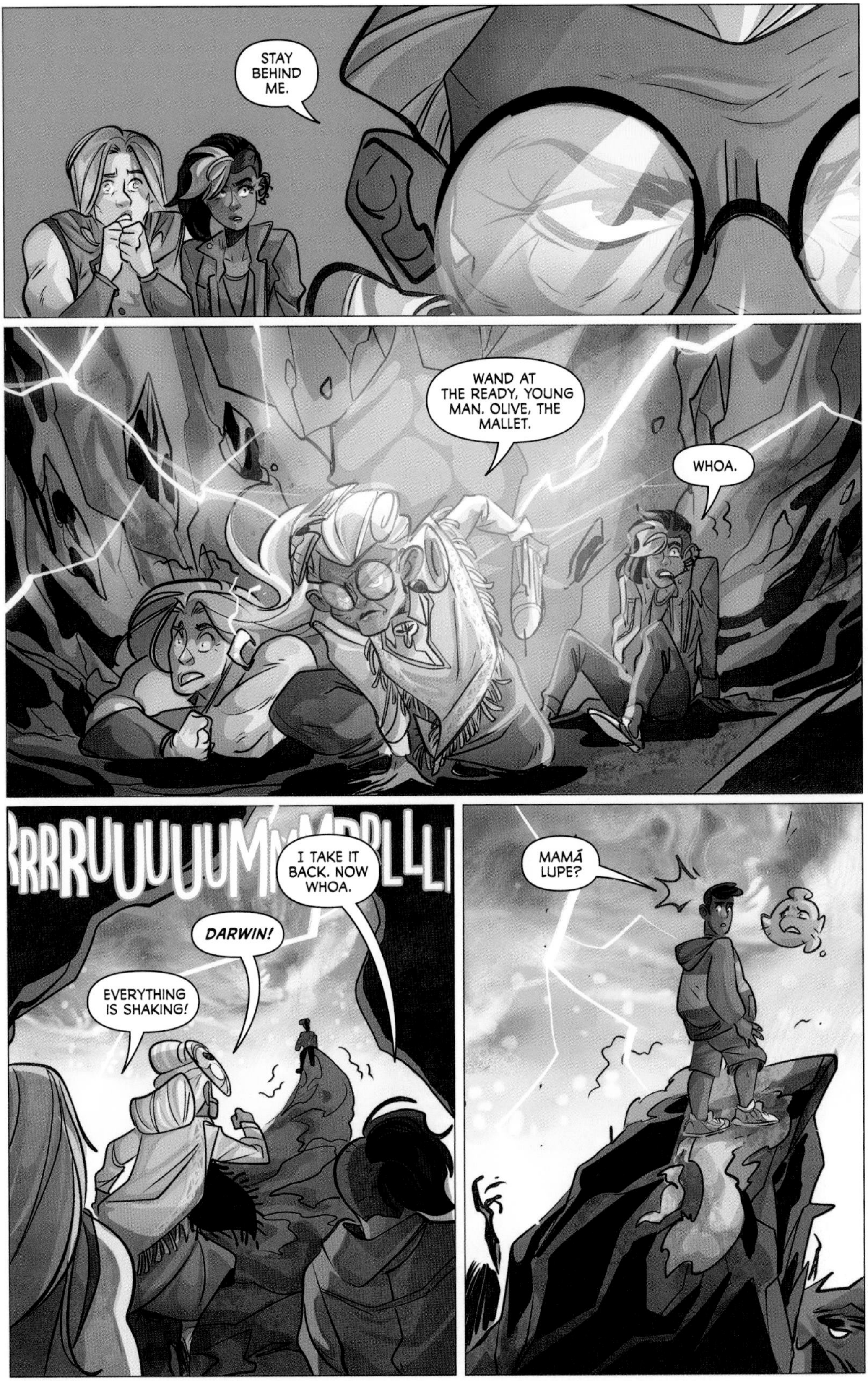
STAY BEHIND ME.
WAND AT THE READY, YOUNG MAN. OLIVE, THE MALLET.
WHOA.
RRRRUUUUUMMBBLLLL
I TAKE IT BACK. NOW WHOA.
DARWIN!
EVERYTHING IS SHAKING!
MAMÁ LUPE?

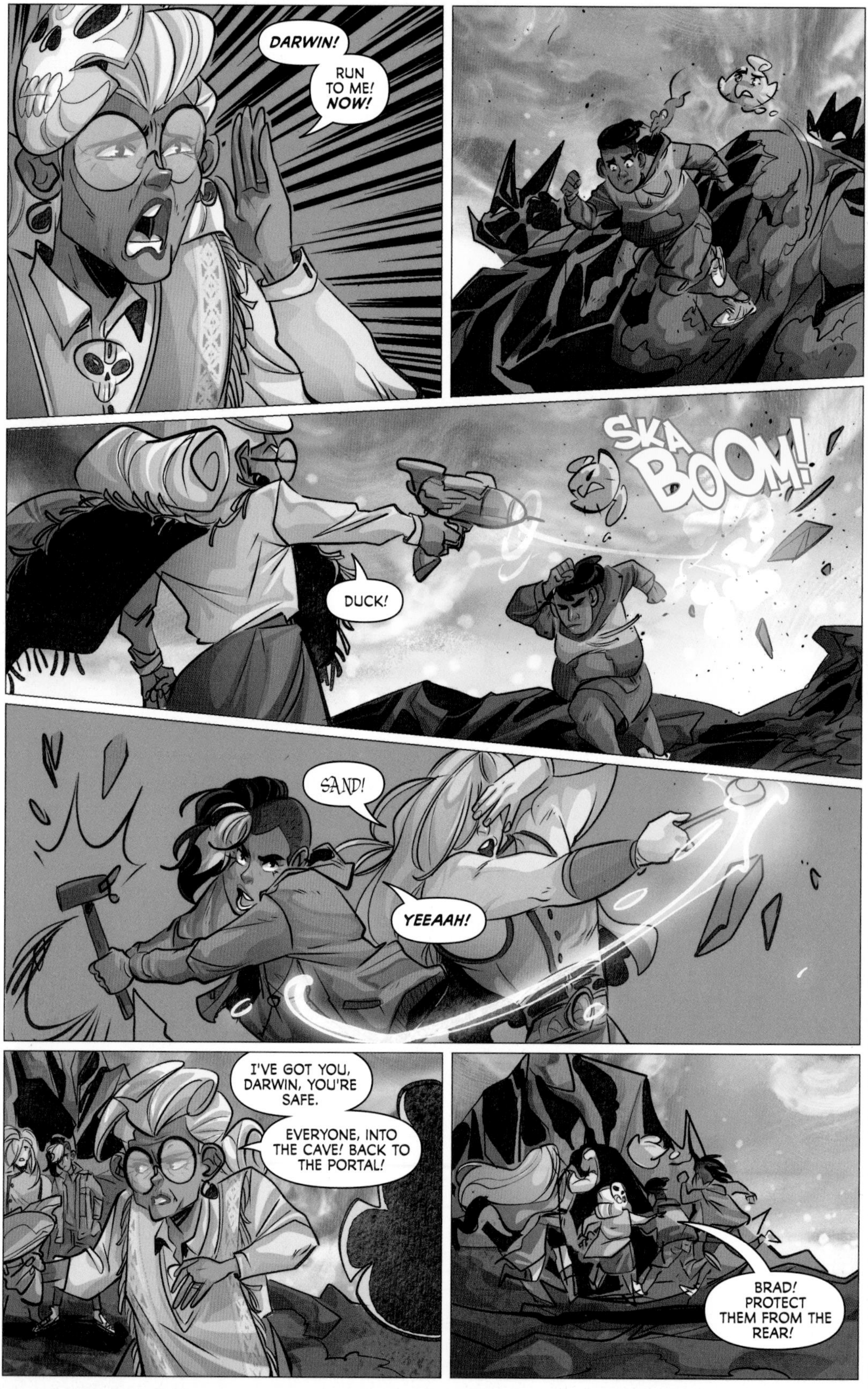
DARWIN!
RUN TO ME! NOW!
SKA BOOM!
DUCK!
SAND!
YEEAAH!
I'VE GOT YOU, DARWIN, YOU'RE SAFE.
EVERYONE, INTO THE CAVE! BACK TO THE PORTAL!
BRAD! PROTECT THEM FROM THE REAR!

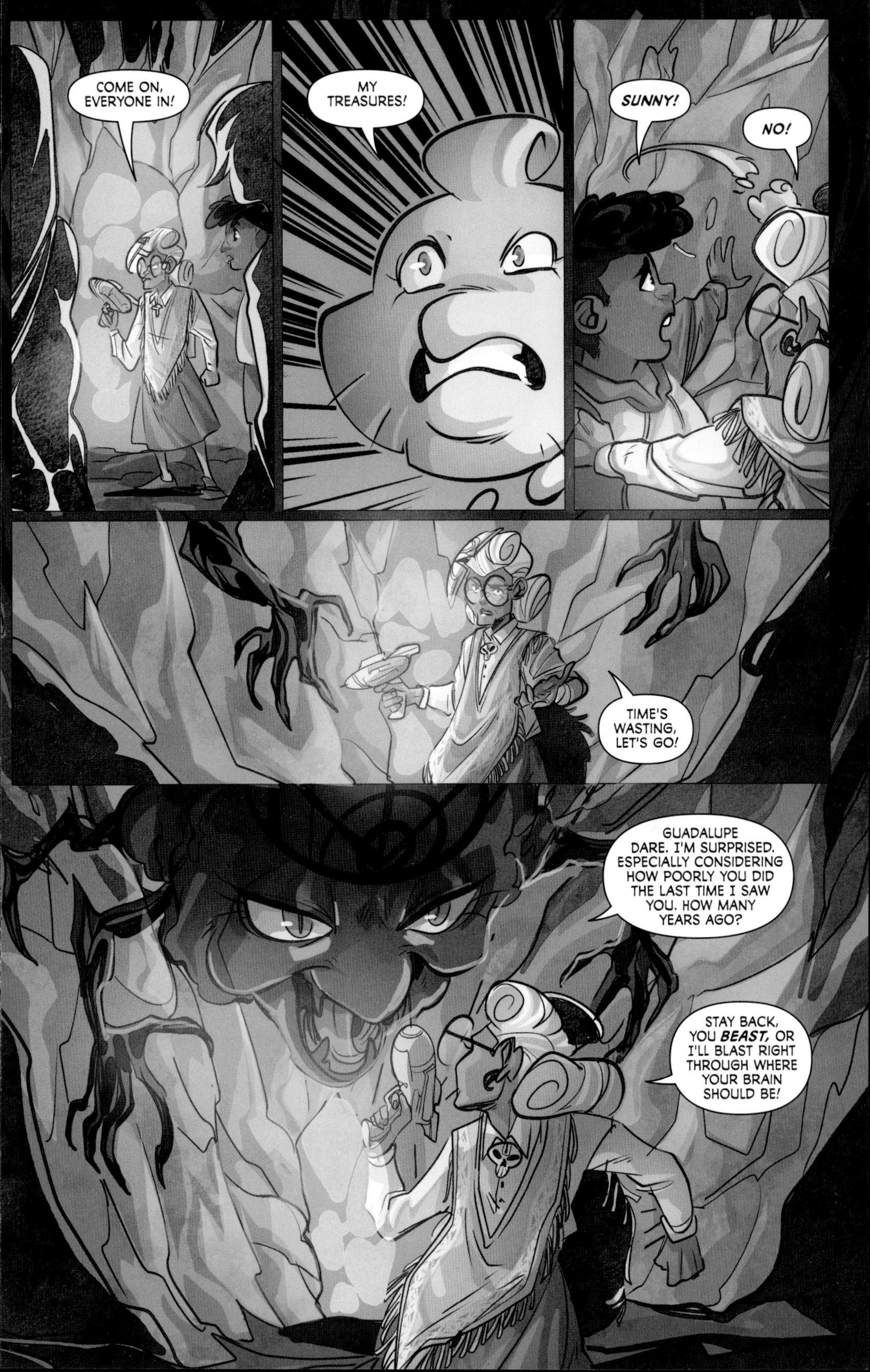
COME ON, EVERYONE IN!
MY TREASURES!
SUNNY!
NO!
TIME'S WASTING, LET'S GO!
GUADALUPE DARE. I'M SURPRISED. ESPECIALLY CONSIDERING HOW POORLY YOU DID THE LAST TIME I SAW YOU. HOW MANY YEARS AGO?
STAY BACK, YOU BEAST, OR I'LL BLAST RIGHT THROUGH WHERE YOUR BRAIN SHOULD BE!

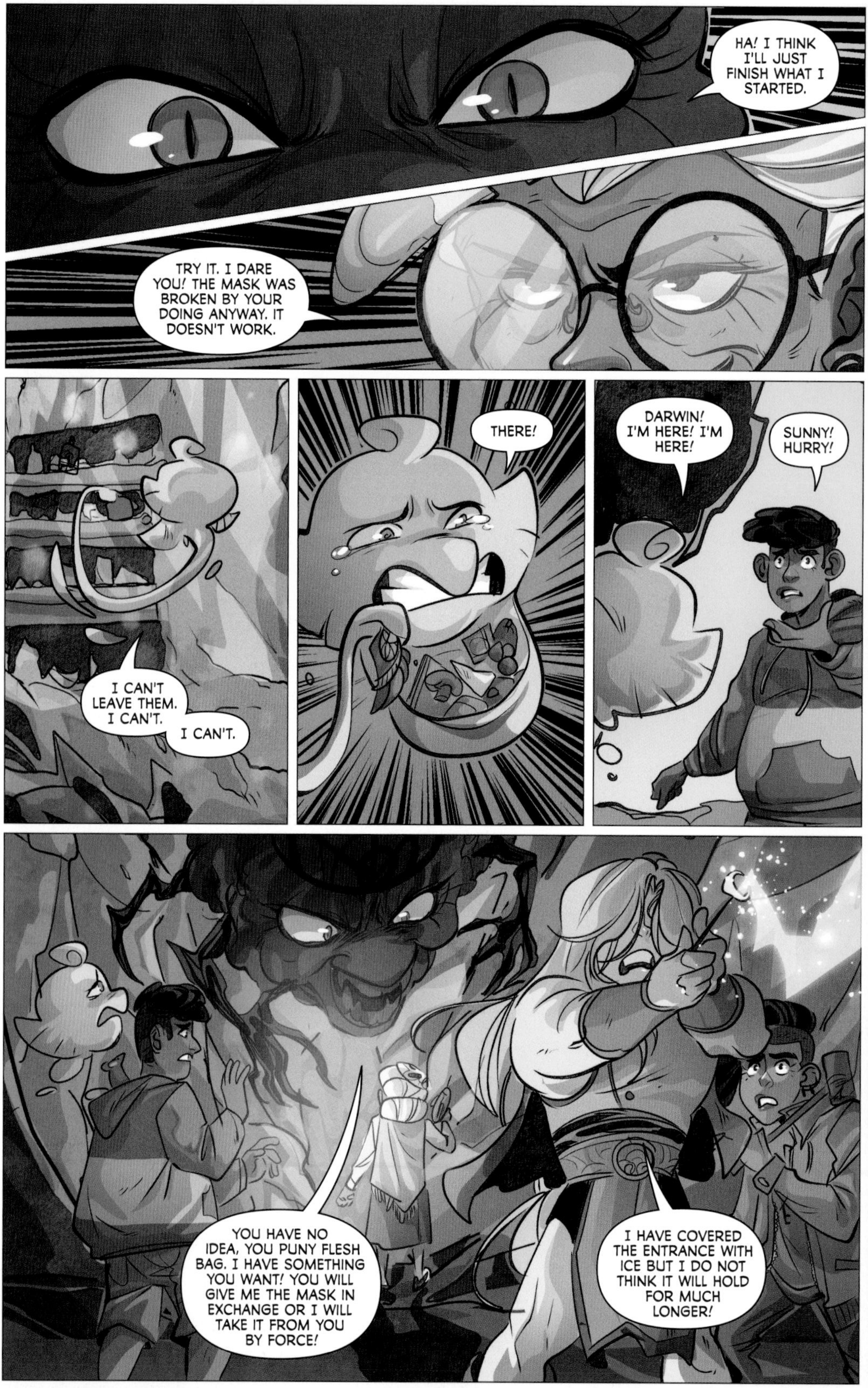
HA! I THINK I'LL JUST FINISH WHAT I STARTED.
TRY IT. I DARE YOU! THE MASK WAS BROKEN BY YOUR DOING ANYWAY. IT DOESN'T WORK.
I CAN'T LEAVE THEM. I CAN'T.
I CAN'T.
THERE!
DARWIN! I'M HERE! I'M HERE!
SUNNY! HURRY!
YOU HAVE NO IDEA, YOU PUNY FLESH BAG. I HAVE SOMETHING YOU WANT! YOU WILL GIVE ME THE MASK IN EXCHANGE OR I WILL TAKE IT FROM YOU BY FORCE!
I HAVE COVERED THE ENTRANCE WITH ICE BUT I DO NOT THINK IT WILL HOLD FOR MUCH LONGER!

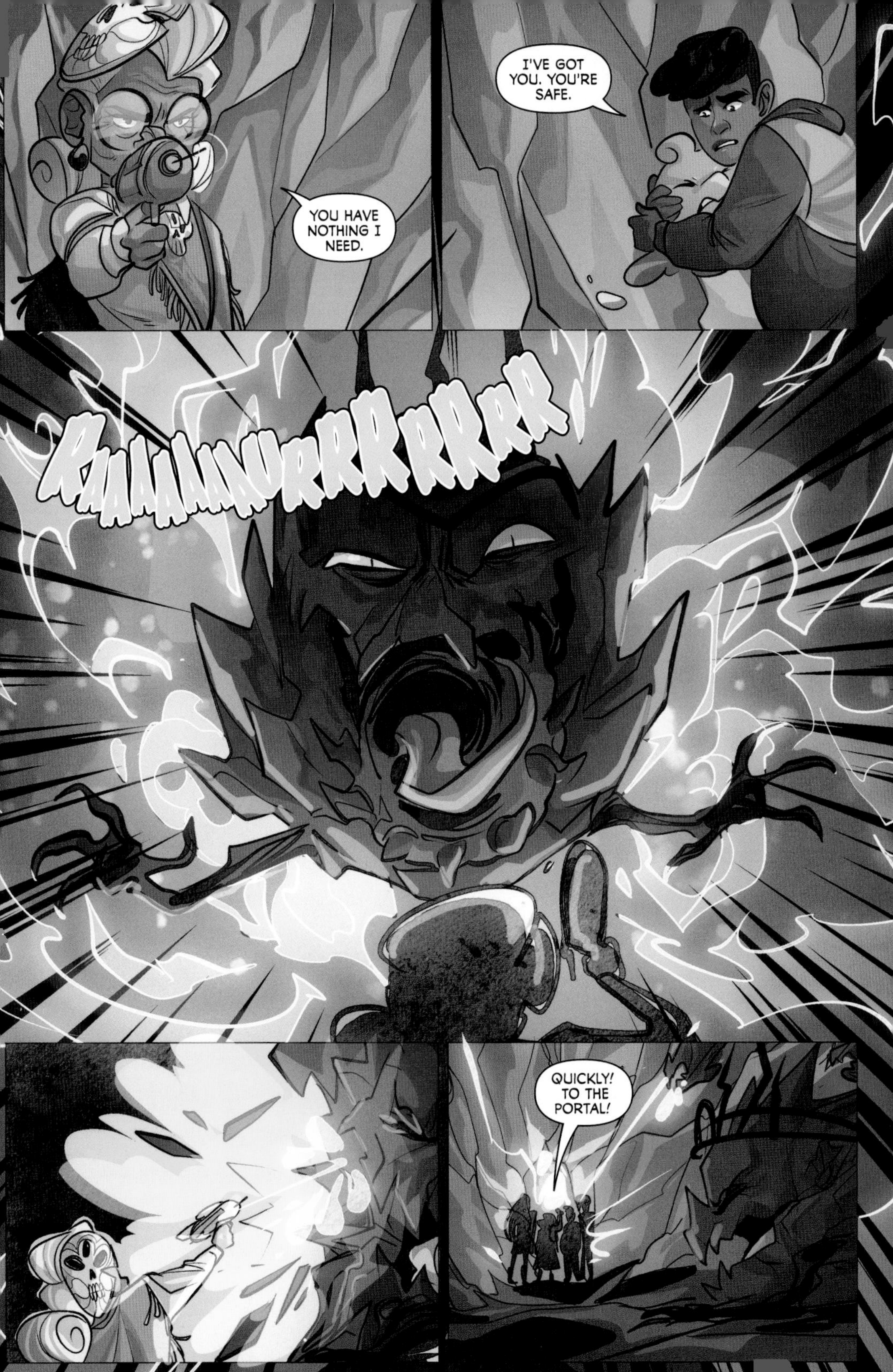
YOU HAVE NOTHING I NEED.
I'VE GOT YOU. YOU'RE SAFE.
RAAAAAAAAURRRRRRRR
QUICKLY! TO THE PORTAL!

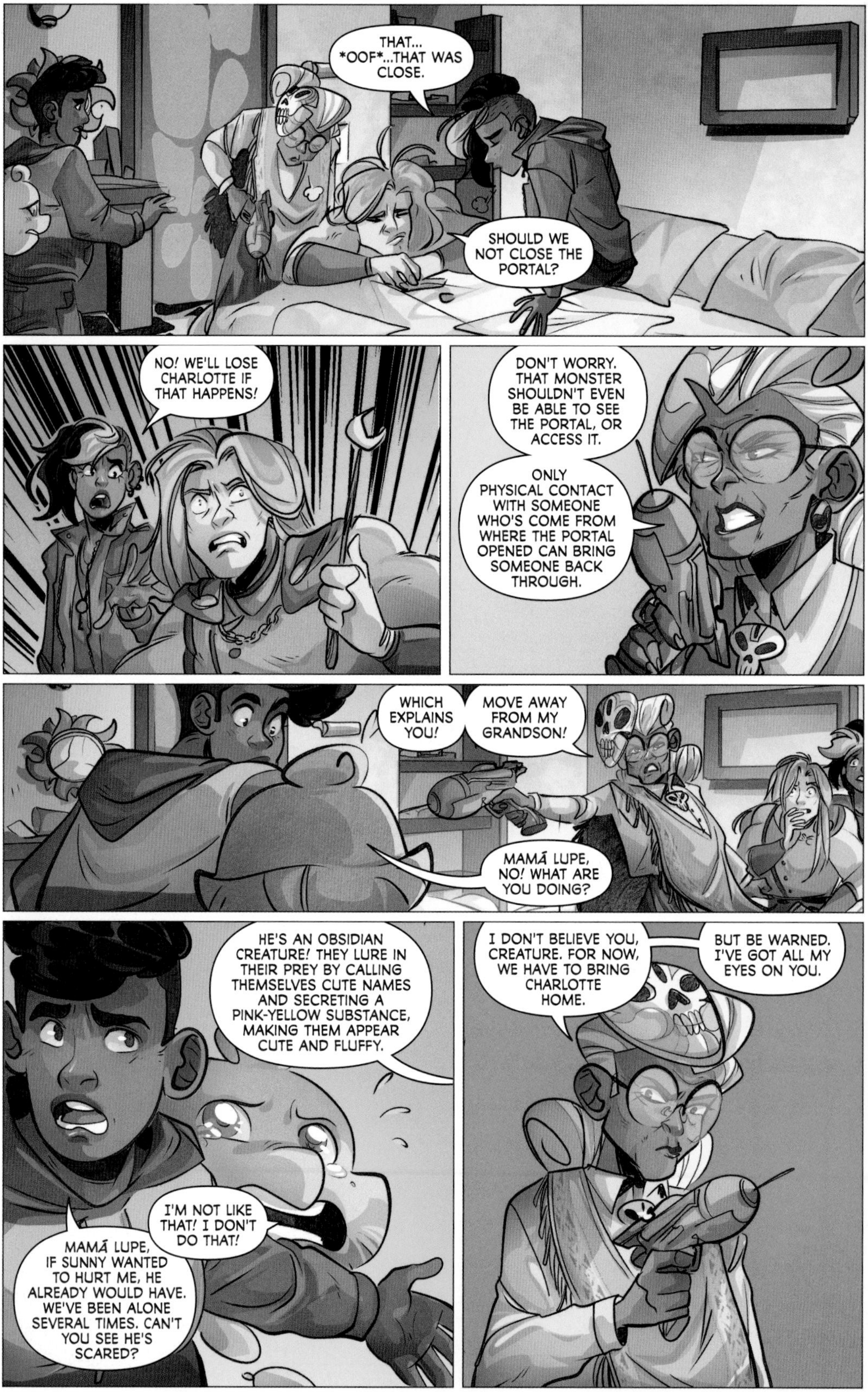
THAT... *OOF*...THAT WAS CLOSE.
SHOULD WE NOT CLOSE THE PORTAL?
NO! WE'LL LOSE CHARLOTTE IF THAT HAPPENS!
DON'T WORRY. THAT MONSTER SHOULDN'T EVEN BE ABLE TO SEE THE PORTAL, OR ACCESS IT.
ONLY PHYSICAL CONTACT WITH SOMEONE WHO'S COME FROM WHERE THE PORTAL OPENED CAN BRING SOMEONE BACK THROUGH.
WHICH EXPLAINS YOU!
MOVE AWAY FROM MY GRANDSON!
MAMÁ LUPE, NO! WHAT ARE YOU DOING?
HE'S AN OBSIDIAN CREATURE! THEY LURE IN THEIR PREY BY CALLING THEMSELVES CUTE NAMES AND SECRETING A PINK-YELLOW SUBSTANCE, MAKING THEM APPEAR CUTE AND FLUFFY.
I'M NOT LIKE THAT! I DON'T DO THAT!
MAMÁ LUPE, IF SUNNY WANTED TO HURT ME, HE ALREADY WOULD HAVE. WE'VE BEEN ALONE SEVERAL TIMES. CAN'T YOU SEE HE'S SCARED?
I DON'T BELIEVE YOU, CREATURE. FOR NOW, WE HAVE TO BRING CHARLOTTE HOME.
BUT BE WARNED. I'VE GOT ALL MY EYES ON YOU.

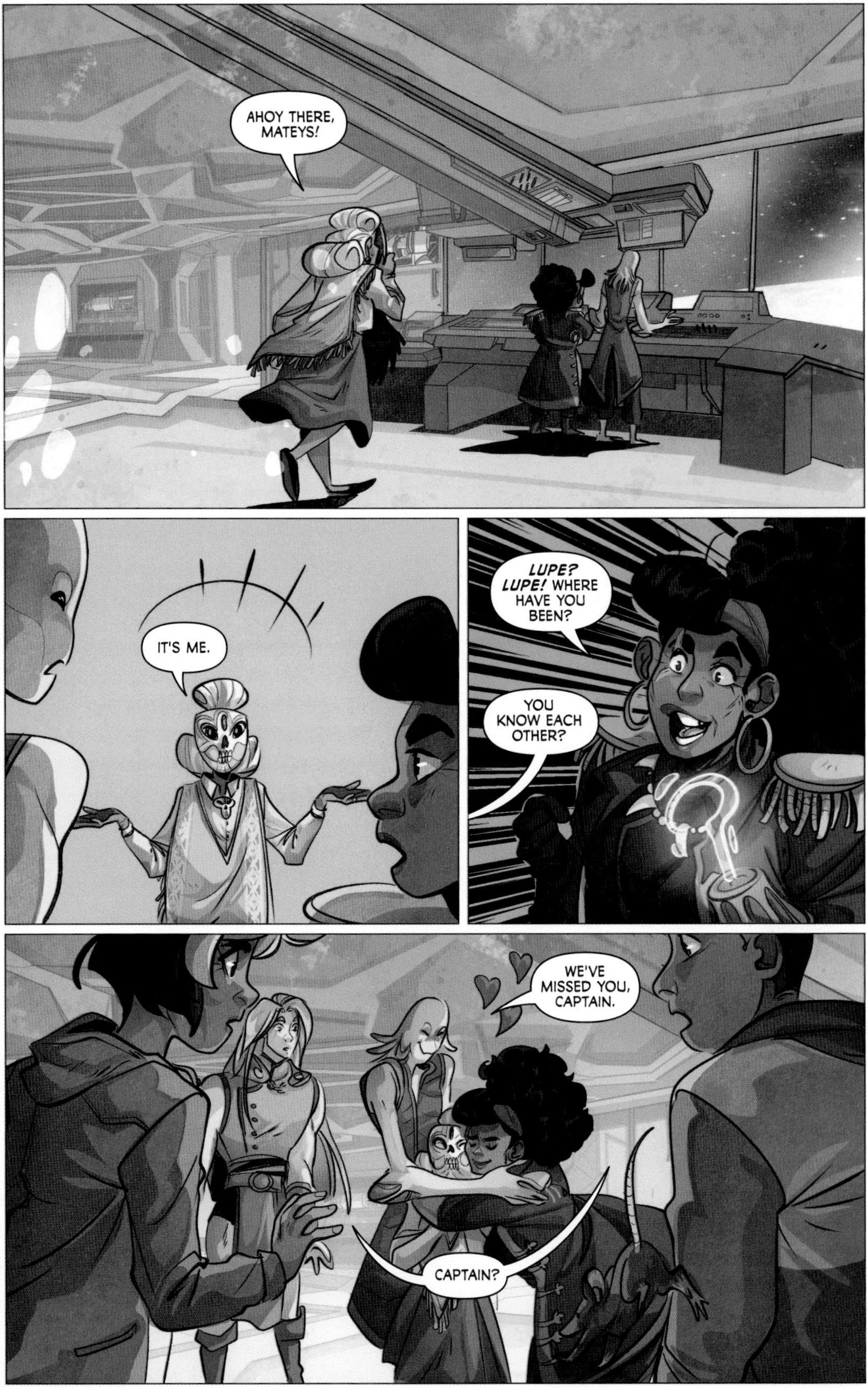
AHOY THERE, MATEYS!
IT'S ME.
LUPE? LUPE! WHERE HAVE YOU BEEN?
YOU KNOW EACH OTHER?
WE'VE MISSED YOU, CAPTAIN.
CAPTAIN?

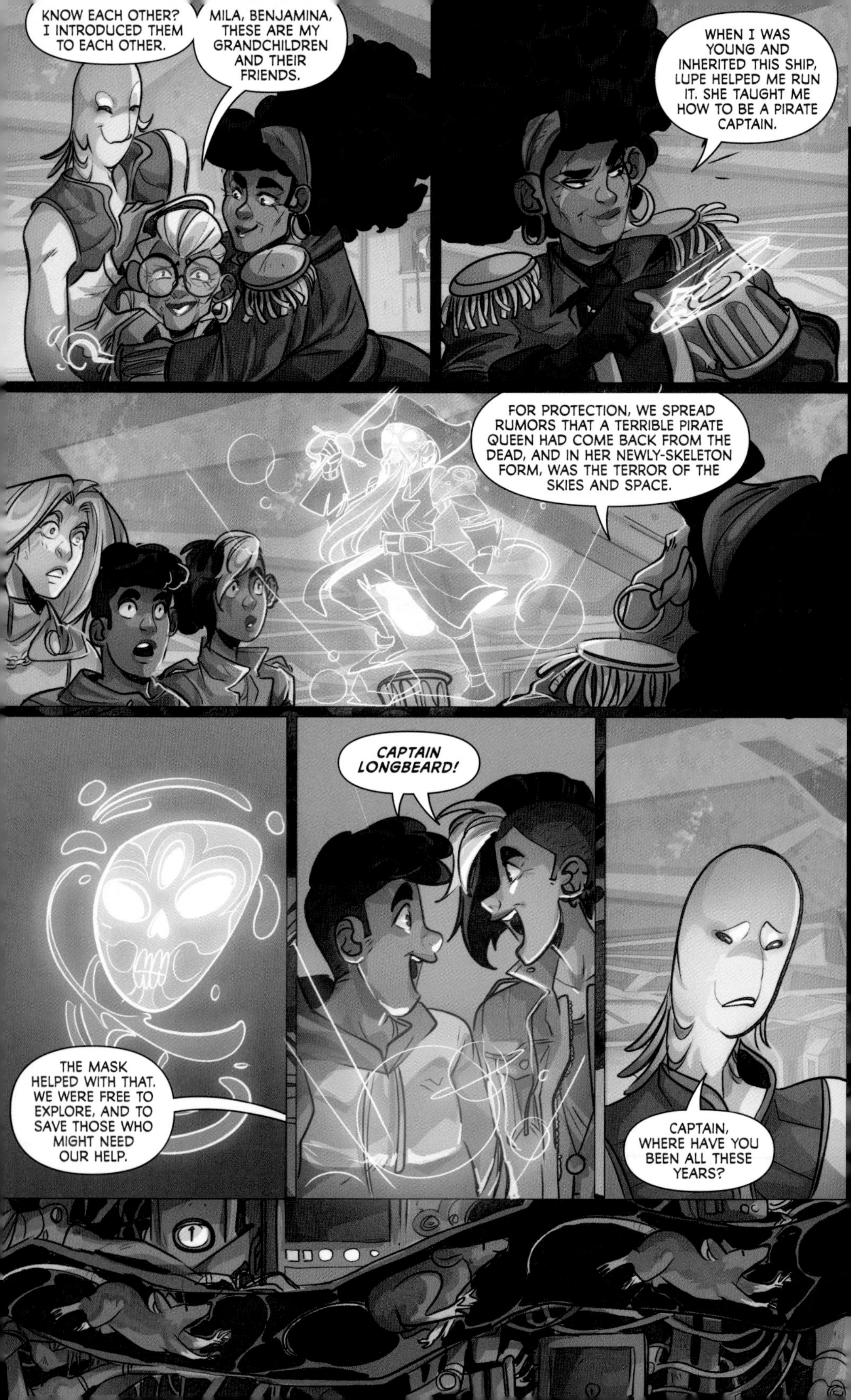
KNOW EACH OTHER? I INTRODUCED THEM TO EACH OTHER.
MILA, BENJAMINA, THESE ARE MY GRANDCHILDREN AND THEIR FRIENDS.
WHEN I WAS YOUNG AND INHERITED THIS SHIP, LUPE HELPED ME RUN IT. SHE TAUGHT ME HOW TO BE A PIRATE CAPTAIN.
FOR PROTECTION, WE SPREAD RUMORS THAT A TERRIBLE PIRATE QUEEN HAD COME BACK FROM THE DEAD, AND IN HER NEWLY-SKELETON FORM, WAS THE TERROR OF THE SKIES AND SPACE.
THE MASK HELPED WITH THAT. WE WERE FREE TO EXPLORE, AND TO SAVE THOSE WHO MIGHT NEED OUR HELP.
CAPTAIN LONGBEARD!
CAPTAIN, WHERE HAVE YOU BEEN ALL THESE YEARS?

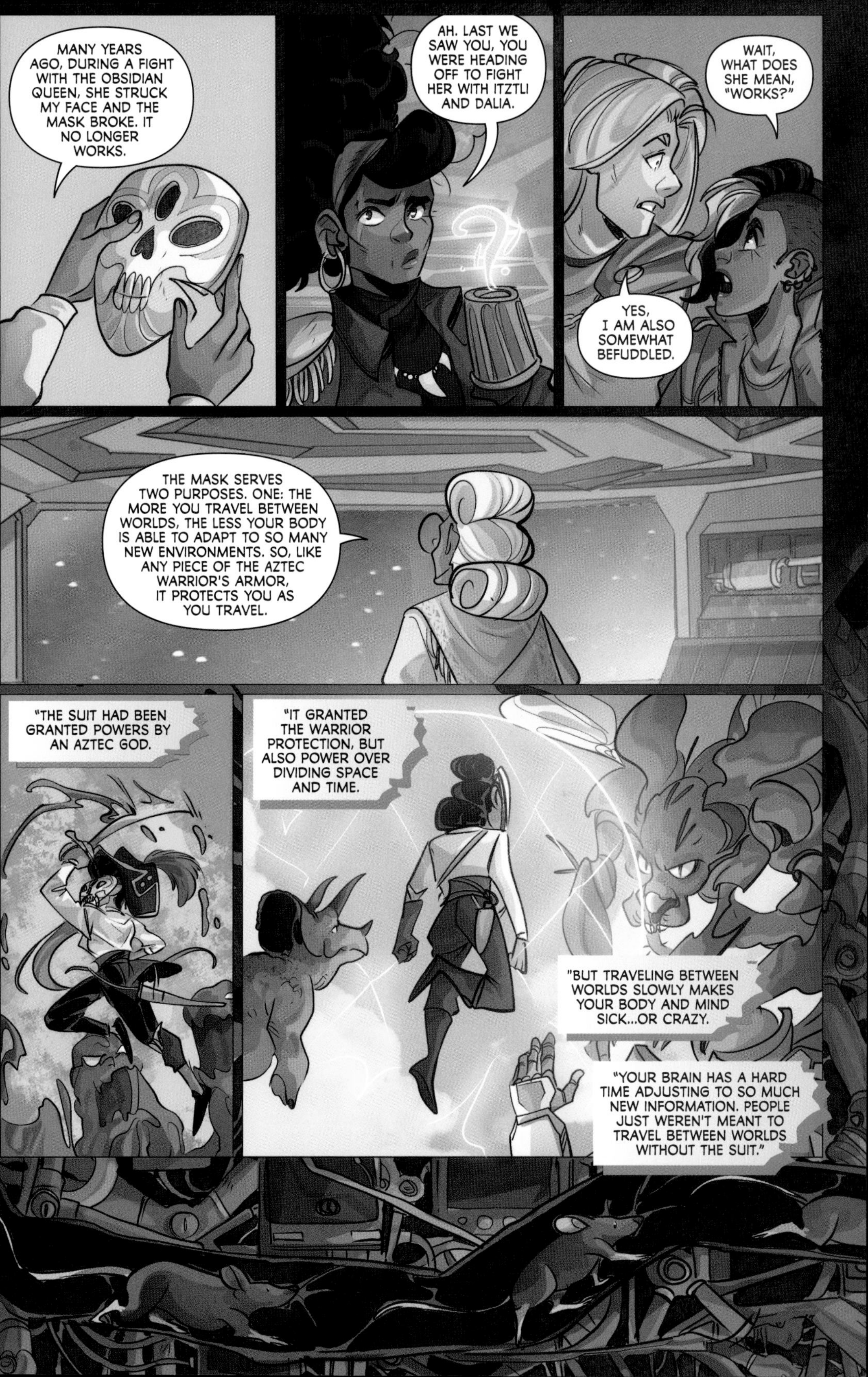
MANY YEARS AGO, DURING A FIGHT WITH THE OBSIDIAN QUEEN, SHE STRUCK MY FACE AND THE MASK BROKE. IT NO LONGER WORKS.
AH. LAST WE SAW YOU, YOU WERE HEADING OFF TO FIGHT HER WITH ITZTLI AND DALIA.
WAIT, WHAT DOES SHE MEAN, "WORKS?"
YES, I AM ALSO SOMEWHAT BEFUDDLED.
THE MASK SERVES TWO PURPOSES. ONE: THE MORE YOU TRAVEL BETWEEN WORLDS, THE LESS YOUR BODY IS ABLE TO ADAPT TO SO MANY NEW ENVIRONMENTS. SO, LIKE ANY PIECE OF THE AZTEC WARRIOR'S ARMOR, IT PROTECTS YOU AS YOU TRAVEL.
"THE SUIT HAD BEEN GRANTED POWERS BY AN AZTEC GOD.
"IT GRANTED THE WARRIOR PROTECTION, BUT ALSO POWER OVER DIVIDING SPACE AND TIME.
"BUT TRAVELING BETWEEN WORLDS SLOWLY MAKES YOUR BODY AND MIND SICK...OR CRAZY.
"YOUR BRAIN HAS A HARD TIME ADJUSTING TO SO MUCH NEW INFORMATION. PEOPLE JUST WEREN'T MEANT TO TRAVEL BETWEEN WORLDS WITHOUT THE SUIT."

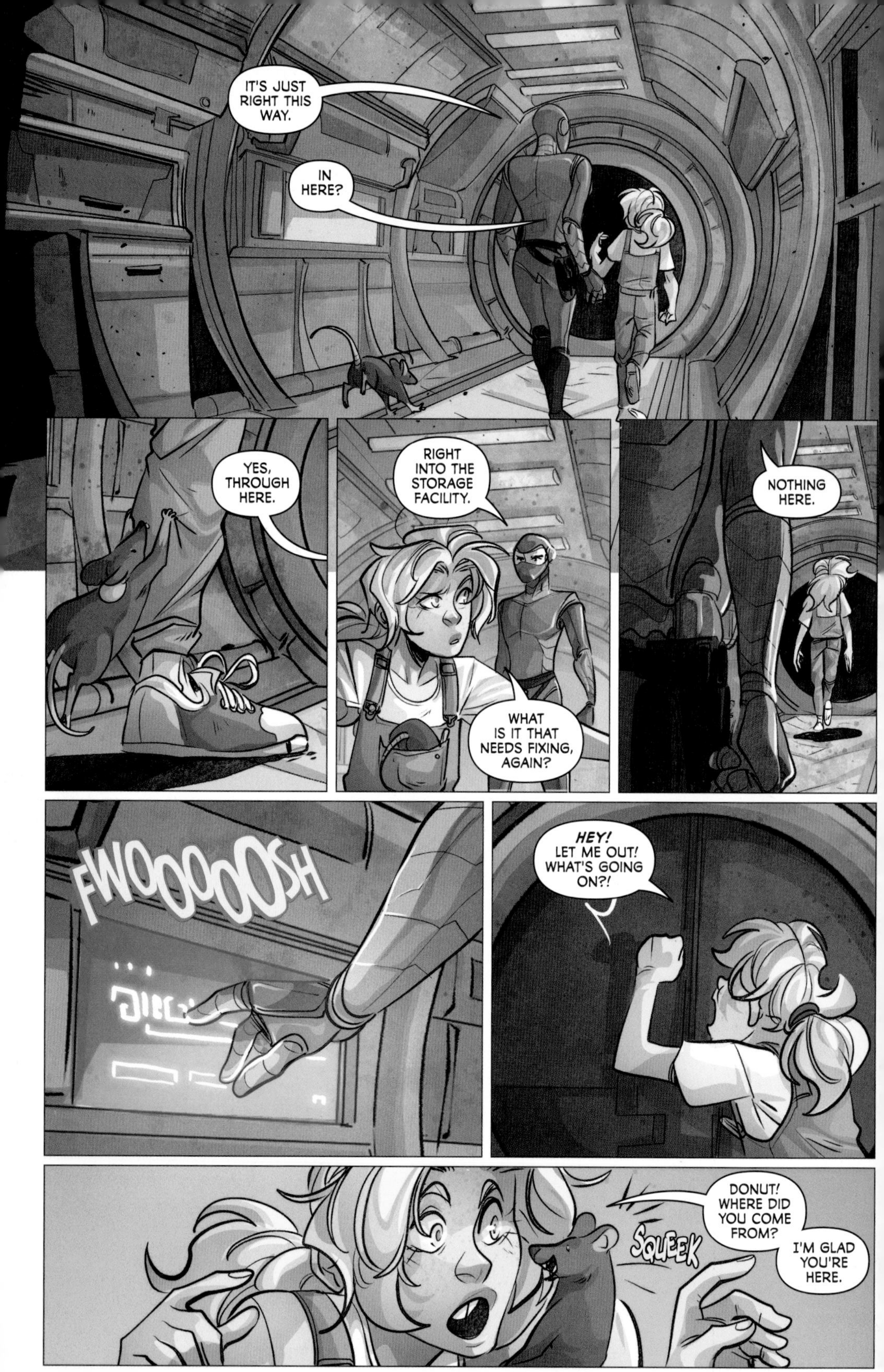
IT'S JUST RIGHT THIS WAY.
IN HERE?
YES, THROUGH HERE.
RIGHT INTO THE STORAGE FACILITY.
WHAT IS IT THAT NEEDS FIXING, AGAIN?
NOTHING HERE.
FWOOOOOSH
HEY! LET ME OUT! WHAT'S GOING ON?!
DONUT! WHERE DID YOU COME FROM?
SQUEEK
I'M GLAD YOU'RE HERE.

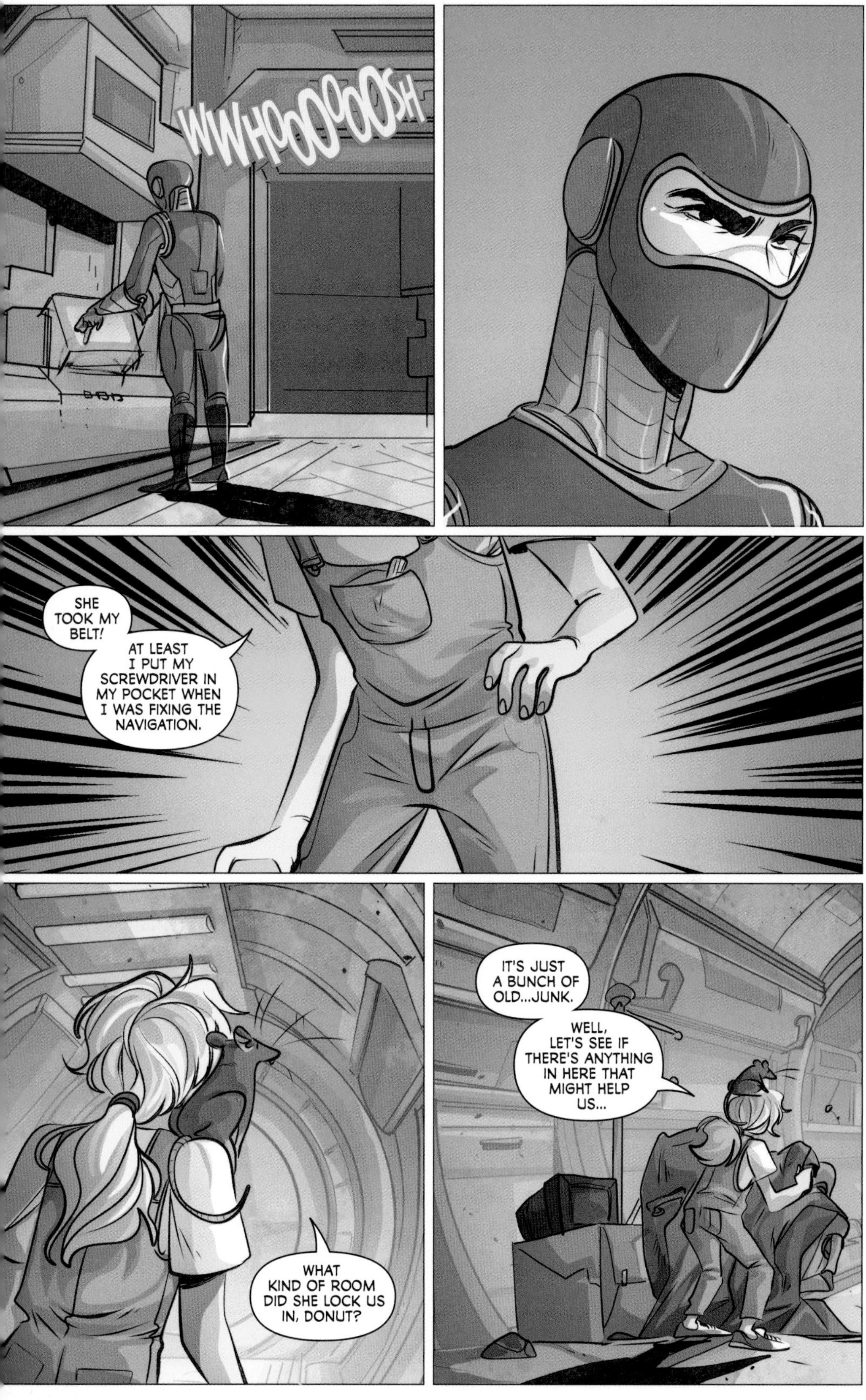
WWHOOOOOSH
SHE TOOK MY BELT!
AT LEAST I PUT MY SCREWDRIVER IN MY POCKET WHEN I WAS FIXING THE NAVIGATION.
WHAT KIND OF ROOM DID SHE LOCK US IN, DONUT?
IT'S JUST A BUNCH OF OLD...JUNK.
WELL, LET'S SEE IF THERE'S ANYTHING IN HERE THAT MIGHT HELP US...

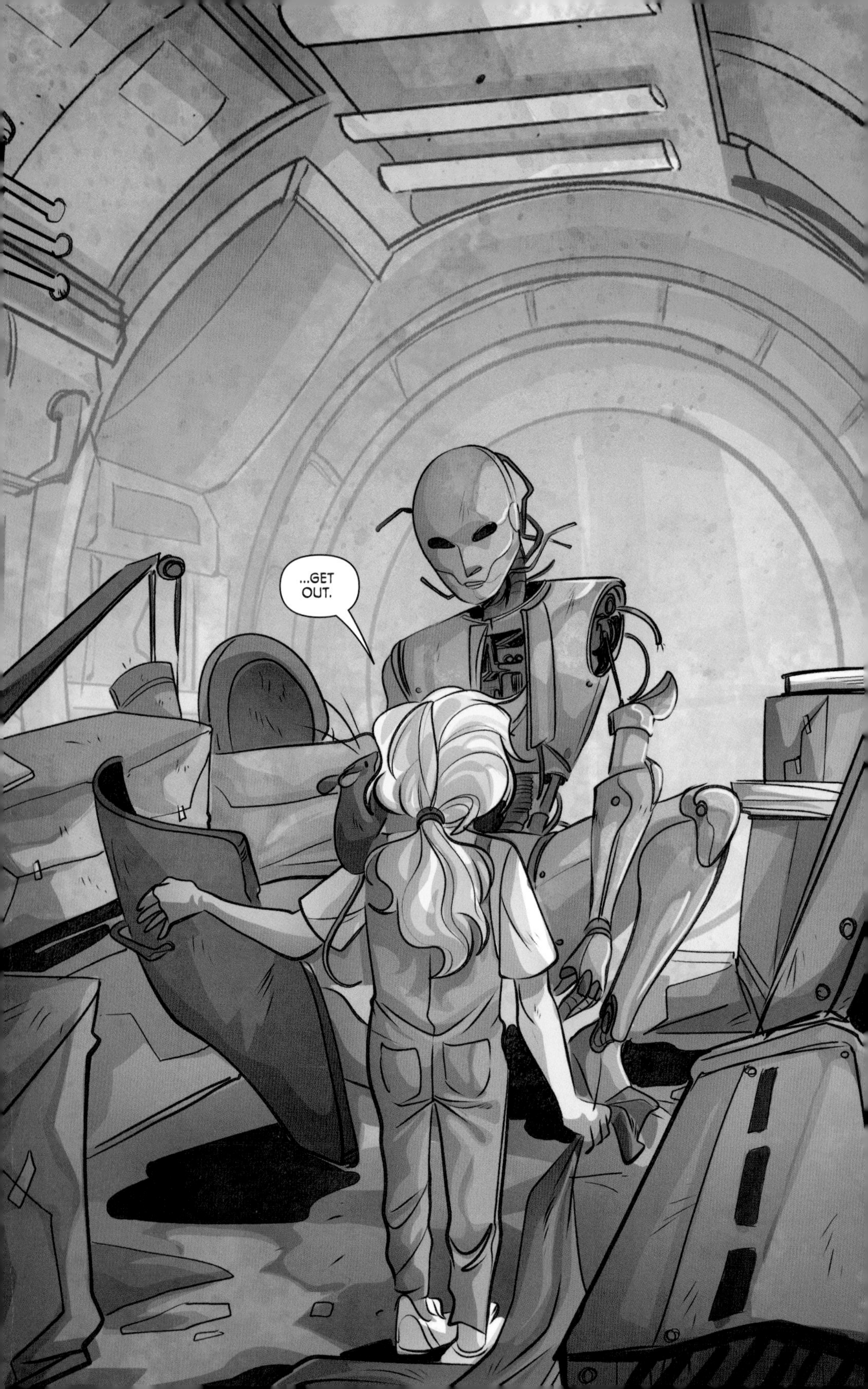
...GET OUT.

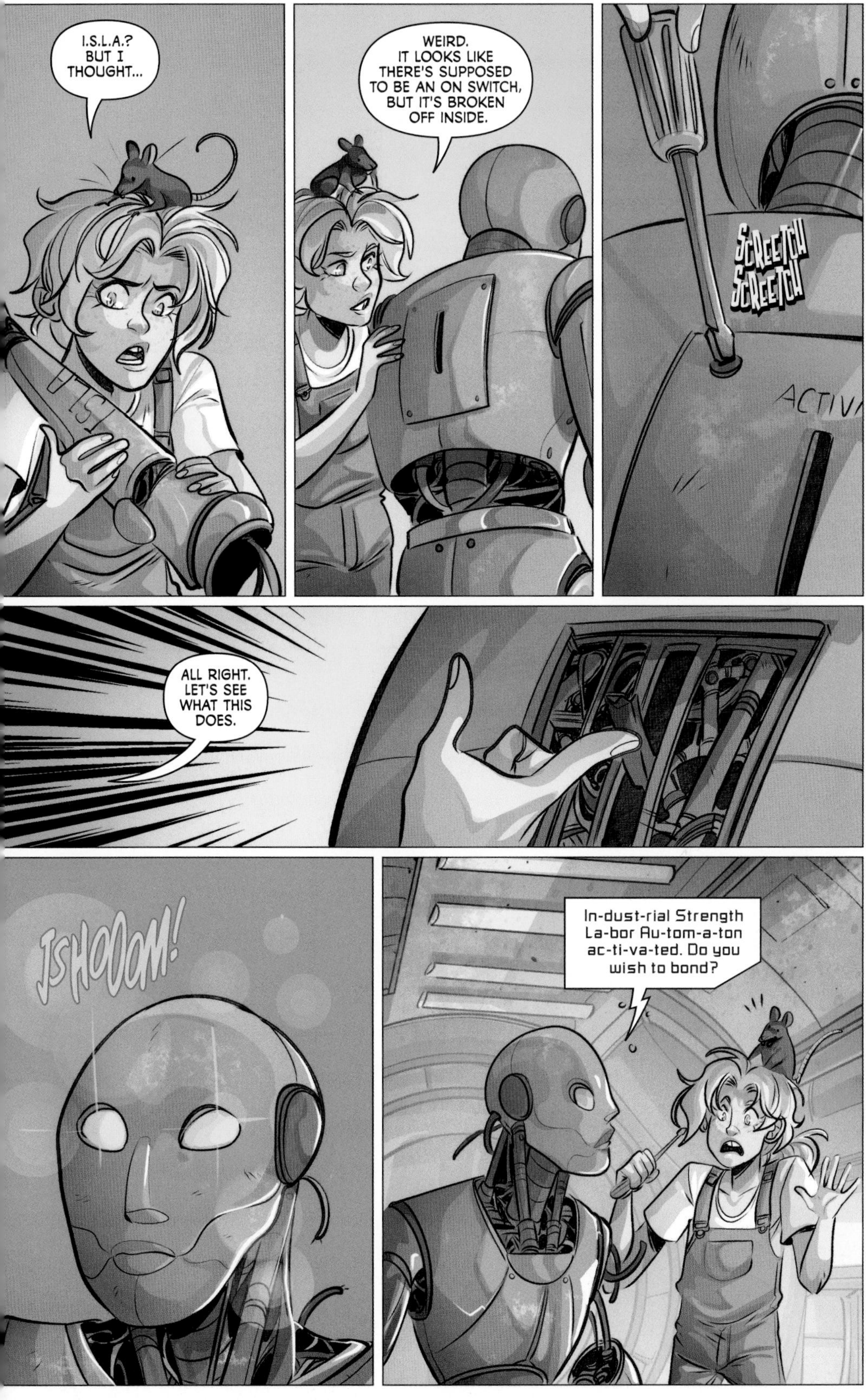
I.S.L.A.? BUT I THOUGHT...
WEIRD. IT LOOKS LIKE THERE'S SUPPOSED TO BE AN ON SWITCH, BUT IT'S BROKEN OFF INSIDE.
SCREETCH SCREETCH
ACTIV
ALL RIGHT. LET'S SEE WHAT THIS DOES.
JSHOOOM!
In-dust-rial Strength La-bor Au-tom-a-ton ac-ti-va-ted. Do you wish to bond?

"THE MASK PROTECTED MY PHYSICAL BODY, BUT ITS SECOND PURPOSE WAS THAT ON THE INSIDE, IT CONTAINED A MAP.

"THINK OF IT LIKE A WHEEL WITH DIFFERENT SEGMENTS, EACH CONTAINING A SYMBOL FOR A DIFFERENT WORLD. THE BROOCH OPENS PORTALS RANDOMLY. THE MASK LETS YOU SELECT A SPECIFIC ONE TO GO TO BEFORE ACTIVATING THE BROOCH.

"THIS SPACE UNIVERSE, BRAMBLE, AND THE OBSIDIAN KINGDOM ARE ALL "NEXT TO EACH OTHER" ON THE MAP.

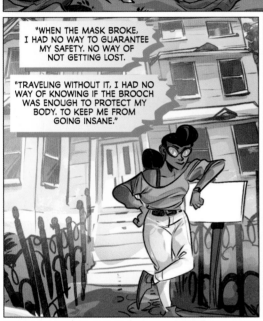

"WHEN THE MASK BROKE, I HAD NO WAY TO GUARANTEE MY SAFETY. NO WAY OF NOT GETTING LOST.

"TRAVELING WITHOUT IT, I HAD NO WAY OF KNOWING IF THE BROOCH WAS ENOUGH TO PROTECT MY BODY. TO KEEP ME FROM GOING INSANE."

HOW INTERESTING! THIS SOUNDS VERY MUCH LIKE HIGH MAGIC.

BUT WE'VE BEEN TRAVELING FOR A WHILE NOW. ARE WE GOING TO GET SICK?

NO, MI NIÑA. YOU'VE DONE IT FOR SUCH A SHORT AMOUNT OF TIME COMPARED TO ME. YOU'LL ALL BE FINE IF YOU DON'T TRAVEL MUCH LONGER. WE SHOULD GRAB CHARLOTTE AND GET HOME BEFORE ANY DAMAGE CAN BE DONE.

SPEAKING OF, WHERE IS MY GRANDDAUGHTER?

SHE'S FIXING SOMETHING WITH OUR SHIP'S ARTIFICIAL INTELLIGENCE UNIT. WE CAN GO FIND HER.

BEFORE WE DO, MILA, I WONDER IF I COULD ASK A FAVOR.

ANYTHING.

I NEED YOU TO BOND WITH THE CREATURE. SEE WHETHER OR NOT HE'S TELLING THE TRUTH.

WHAT?!

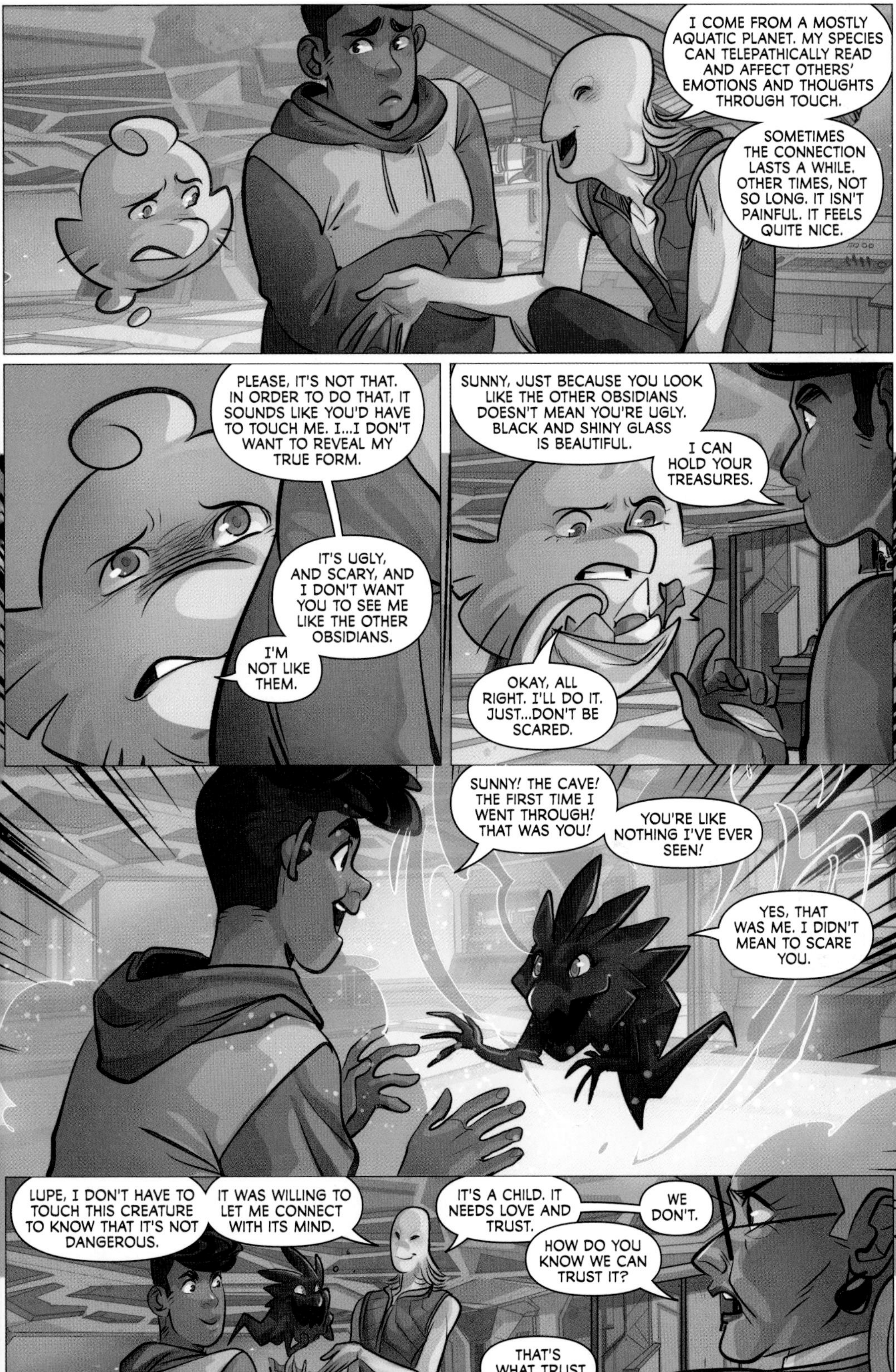
I COME FROM A MOSTLY AQUATIC PLANET. MY SPECIES CAN TELEPATHICALLY READ AND AFFECT OTHERS' EMOTIONS AND THOUGHTS THROUGH TOUCH.
SOMETIMES THE CONNECTION LASTS A WHILE. OTHER TIMES, NOT SO LONG. IT ISN'T PAINFUL. IT FEELS QUITE NICE.
PLEASE, IT'S NOT THAT. IN ORDER TO DO THAT, IT SOUNDS LIKE YOU'D HAVE TO TOUCH ME. I...I DON'T WANT TO REVEAL MY TRUE FORM.
IT'S UGLY, AND SCARY, AND I DON'T WANT YOU TO SEE ME LIKE THE OTHER OBSIDIANS.
I'M NOT LIKE THEM.
SUNNY, JUST BECAUSE YOU LOOK LIKE THE OTHER OBSIDIANS DOESN'T MEAN YOU'RE UGLY. BLACK AND SHINY GLASS IS BEAUTIFUL.
I CAN HOLD YOUR TREASURES.
OKAY, ALL RIGHT. I'LL DO IT. JUST...DON'T BE SCARED.
SUNNY! THE CAVE! THE FIRST TIME I WENT THROUGH! THAT WAS YOU!
YOU'RE LIKE NOTHING I'VE EVER SEEN!
YES, THAT WAS ME. I DIDN'T MEAN TO SCARE YOU.
LUPE, I DON'T HAVE TO TOUCH THIS CREATURE TO KNOW THAT IT'S NOT DANGEROUS.
IT WAS WILLING TO LET ME CONNECT WITH ITS MIND.
IT'S A CHILD. IT NEEDS LOVE AND TRUST.
WE DON'T.
HOW DO YOU KNOW WE CAN TRUST IT?
THAT'S WHAT TRUST IS.

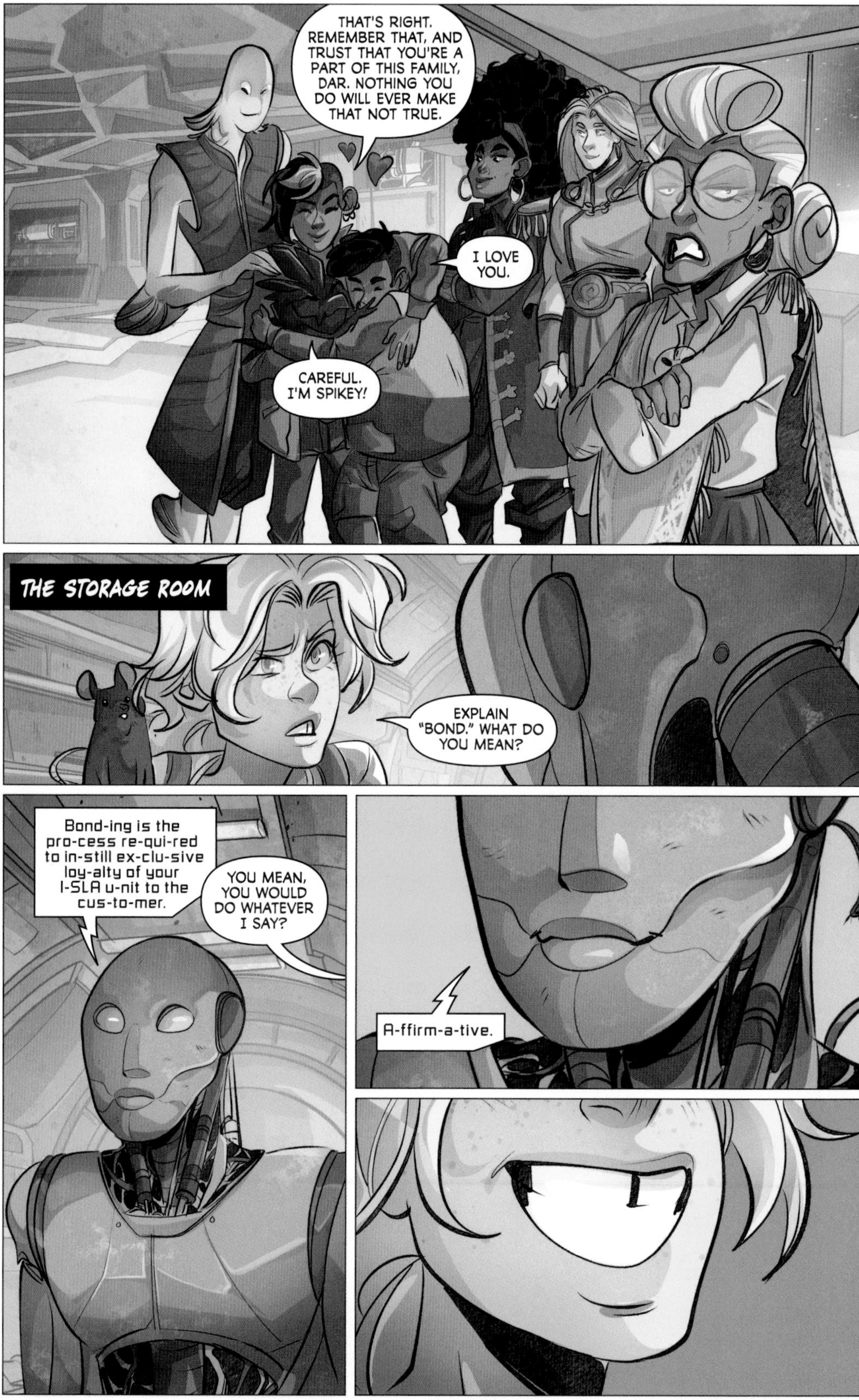

THAT'S RIGHT. REMEMBER THAT, AND TRUST THAT YOU'RE A PART OF THIS FAMILY, DAR. NOTHING YOU DO WILL EVER MAKE THAT NOT TRUE.
I LOVE YOU.
CAREFUL. I'M SPIKEY!
THE STORAGE ROOM
EXPLAIN "BOND." WHAT DO YOU MEAN?
Bond-ing is the pro-cess re-qui-red to in-still ex-clu-sive loy-alty of your I-SLA u-nit to the cus-to-mer.
YOU MEAN, YOU WOULD DO WHATEVER I SAY?
A-ffirm-a-tive.

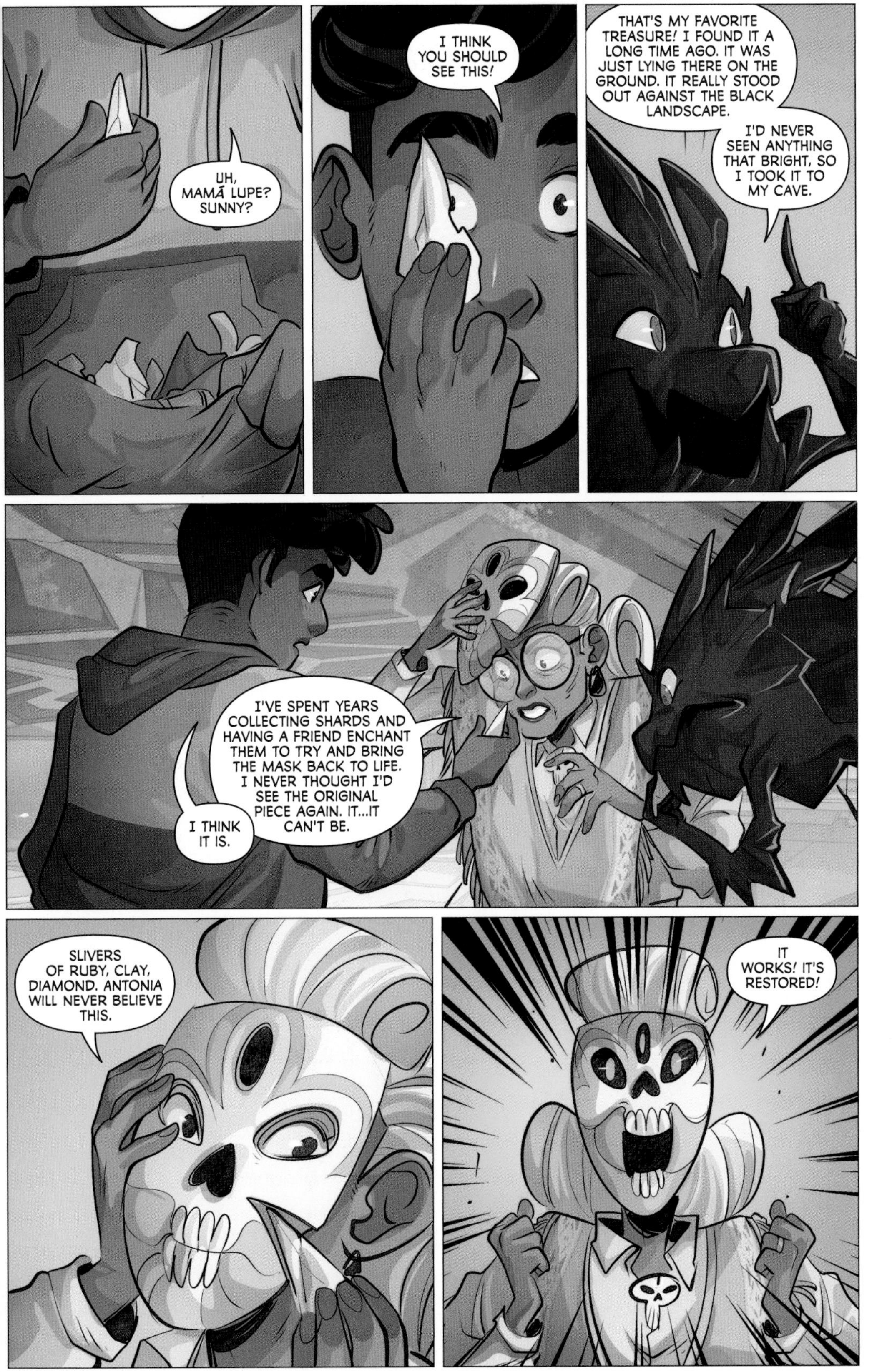
UH, MAMÁ LUPE? SUNNY?
I THINK YOU SHOULD SEE THIS!
THAT'S MY FAVORITE TREASURE! I FOUND IT A LONG TIME AGO. IT WAS JUST LYING THERE ON THE GROUND. IT REALLY STOOD OUT AGAINST THE BLACK LANDSCAPE.
I'D NEVER SEEN ANYTHING THAT BRIGHT, SO I TOOK IT TO MY CAVE.
I'VE SPENT YEARS COLLECTING SHARDS AND HAVING A FRIEND ENCHANT THEM TO TRY AND BRING THE MASK BACK TO LIFE. I NEVER THOUGHT I'D SEE THE ORIGINAL PIECE AGAIN. IT...IT CAN'T BE.
I THINK IT IS.
SLIVERS OF RUBY, CLAY, DIAMOND. ANTONIA WILL NEVER BELIEVE THIS.
IT WORKS! IT'S RESTORED!

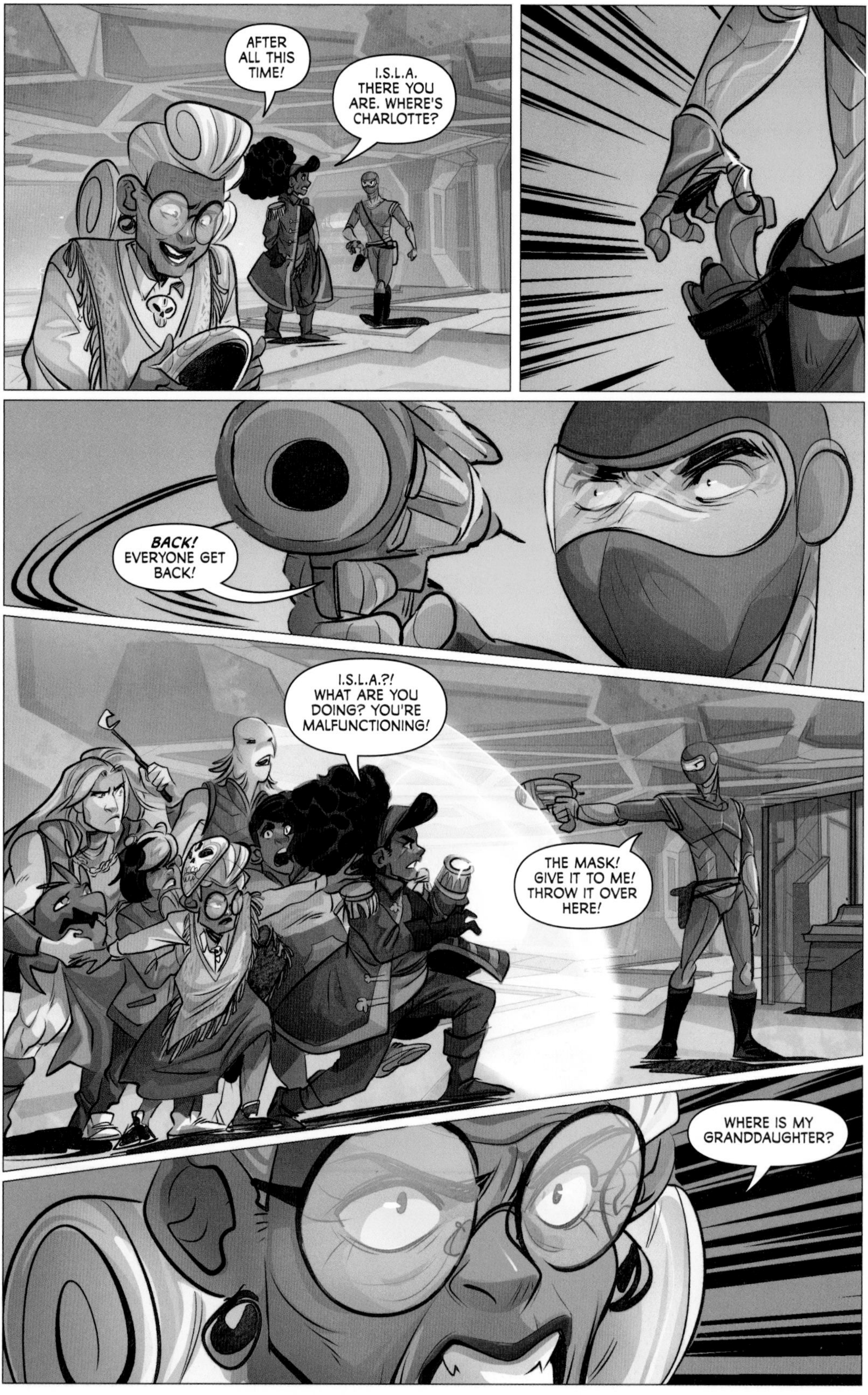
AFTER ALL THIS TIME!
I.S.L.A. THERE YOU ARE. WHERE'S CHARLOTTE?
BACK! EVERYONE GET BACK!
I.S.L.A.?! WHAT ARE YOU DOING? YOU'RE MALFUNCTIONING!
THE MASK! GIVE IT TO ME! THROW IT OVER HERE!
WHERE IS MY GRANDDAUGHTER?

YOU'LL GET HER BACK WHEN YOU COOPERATE AND DO WHAT I SAY! *THE MASK!*

DON'T HURT MY SISTER!

I.S.L.A. ENOUGH OF THIS! YOU'RE NOT OPERATING CORRECTLY. I'LL SHUT YOU OFF IF YOU DON'T--

I'M NOT A ROBOT!

I SAID GIVE ME THE MASK! I WON'T ASK AGAIN! THIS IS YOUR LAST CHANCE!

OKAY, OKAY. PLEASE. DON'T HURT ANYONE.

IF YOU AREN'T OUR ROBOT, WHO ARE YOU?

A TRAVELER. I'VE BEEN SEARCHING FOR LUPE FOR YEARS. SPENT THE MOST TIME IN THE THREE WORLDS I KNEW SHE HAD BEEN IN THE LONGEST, TO GATHER INFORMATION.

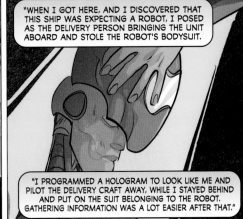

"WHEN I GOT HERE, AND I DISCOVERED THAT THIS SHIP WAS EXPECTING A ROBOT, I POSED AS THE DELIVERY PERSON BRINGING THE UNIT ABOARD AND STOLE THE ROBOT'S BODYSUIT.

"I PROGRAMMED A HOLOGRAM TO LOOK LIKE ME AND PILOT THE DELIVERY CRAFT AWAY, WHILE I STAYED BEHIND AND PUT ON THE SUIT BELONGING TO THE ROBOT. GATHERING INFORMATION WAS A LOT EASIER AFTER THAT."

YOU WERE LOOKING FOR ME? TO GET THE MASK? WHY DO YOU WANT IT?

I DON'T WANT IT. I NEED IT.

YOU AND I HAVE SPENT SO MUCH TIME IN THAT WORLD OF IDIOT WIZARDS, THE KINGDOM OF BLACK GLASS, AND HERE IN SPACE THAT THE THREE WORLDS HAVE STARTED TO BLEND AND BLEED INTO EACH OTHER.

THE WORLDS ARE BEING PULLED TOGETHER? ONE WORLD?

THEN THE BROOCH REALLY DID OPEN ONE DOOR, KIND OF. ONE BIG DOOR TO THREE WORLDS MERGING TOGETHER.

OVER THE YEARS, I STARTED TO GET SICK. I NEEDED SOMETHING TO SHIELD MY PHYSICAL BODY FROM THESE WORLDS.

THE ROBOT'S SUIT WAS ALMOST AIRTIGHT, BUT ALLOWED ME TO BREATH AND SPEAK. IT WASN'T PERFECT, BUT IT HAD TO DO.

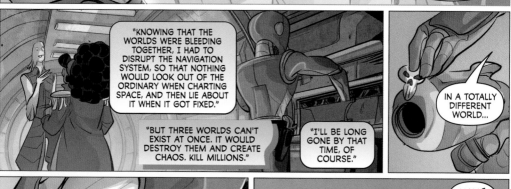

"KNOWING THAT THE WORLDS WERE BLEEDING TOGETHER, I HAD TO DISRUPT THE NAVIGATION SYSTEM, SO THAT NOTHING WOULD LOOK OUT OF THE ORDINARY WHEN CHARTING SPACE, AND THEN LIE ABOUT IT WHEN IT GOT FIXED."

"BUT THREE WORLDS CAN'T EXIST AT ONCE. IT WOULD DESTROY THEM AND CREATE CHAOS. KILL MILLIONS."

"I'LL BE LONG GONE BY THAT TIME, OF COURSE."

IN A TOTALLY DIFFERENT WORLD...

...WITH MY FATHER.

NO!

MAMÁ LUPE, WHAT?

WHO IS SHE?

SHE'S XOCHITL.

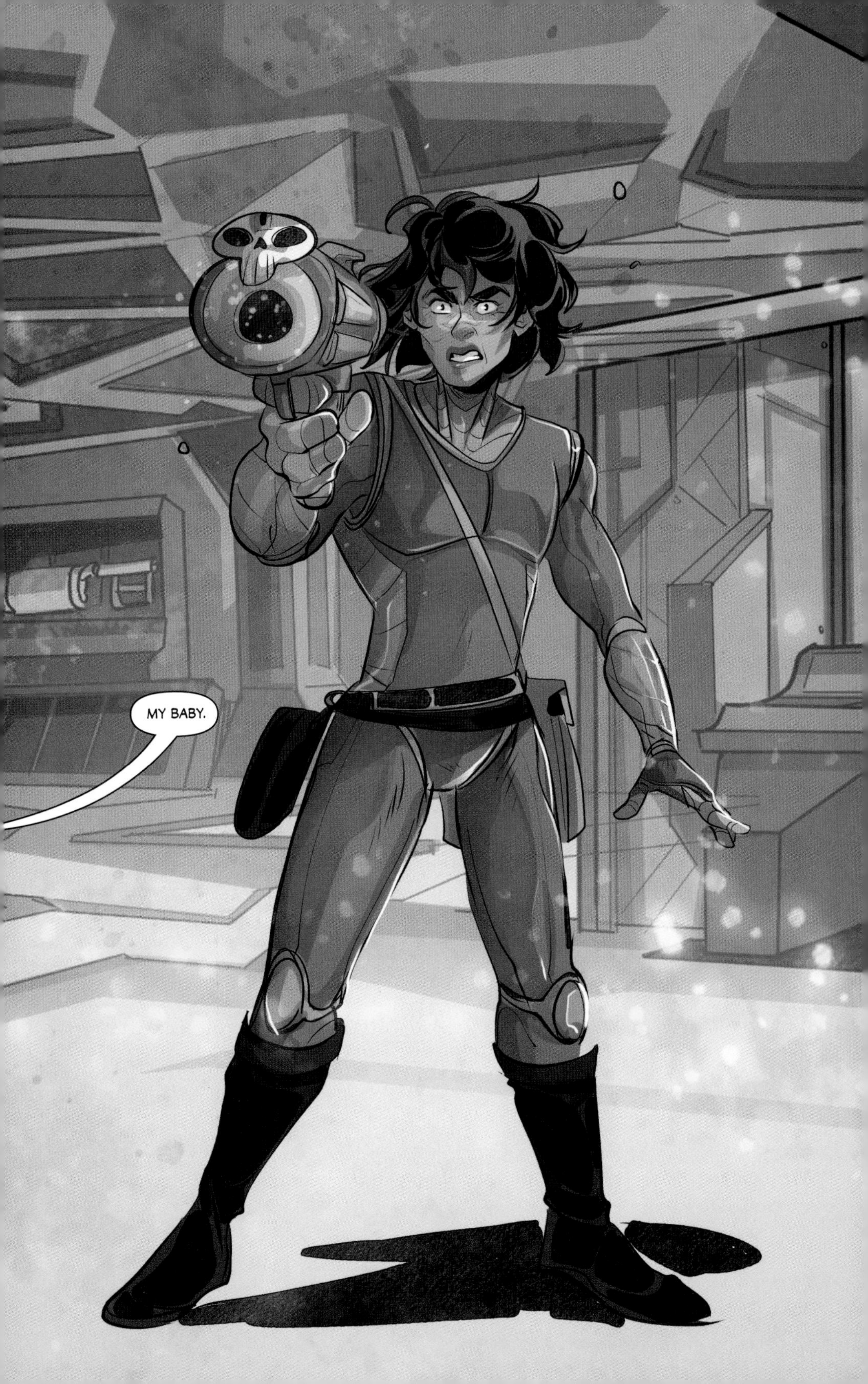
MY BABY.

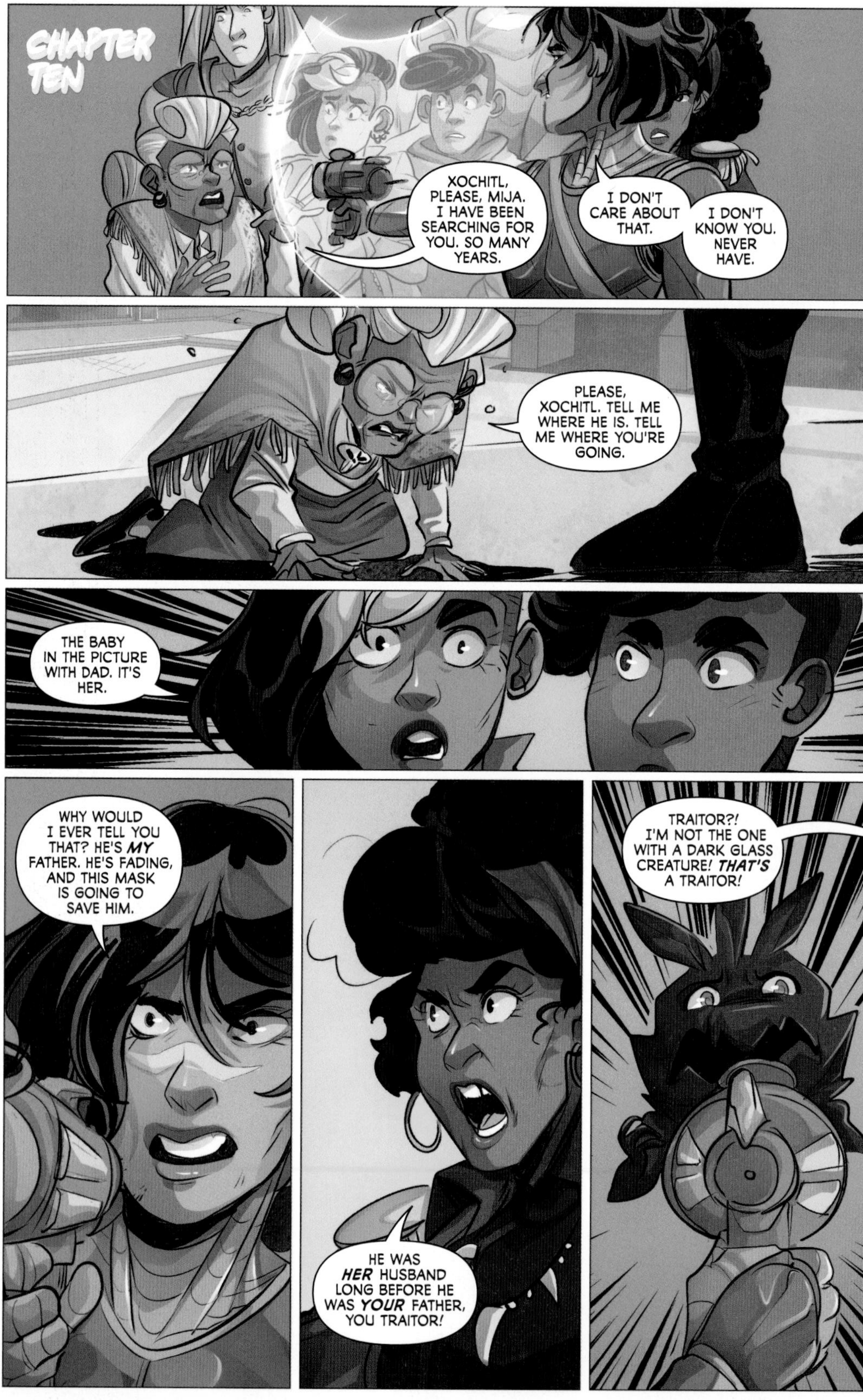
CHAPTER TEN
XOCHITL, PLEASE, MIJA. I HAVE BEEN SEARCHING FOR YOU. SO MANY YEARS.
I DON'T CARE ABOUT THAT.
I DON'T KNOW YOU. NEVER HAVE.
PLEASE, XOCHITL. TELL ME WHERE HE IS. TELL ME WHERE YOU'RE GOING.
THE BABY IN THE PICTURE WITH DAD. IT'S HER.
WHY WOULD I EVER TELL YOU THAT? HE'S *MY* FATHER. HE'S FADING, AND THIS MASK IS GOING TO SAVE HIM.
HE WAS ***HER*** HUSBAND LONG BEFORE HE WAS ***YOUR*** FATHER, YOU TRAITOR!
TRAITOR?! I'M NOT THE ONE WITH A DARK GLASS CREATURE! *THAT'S* A TRAITOR!

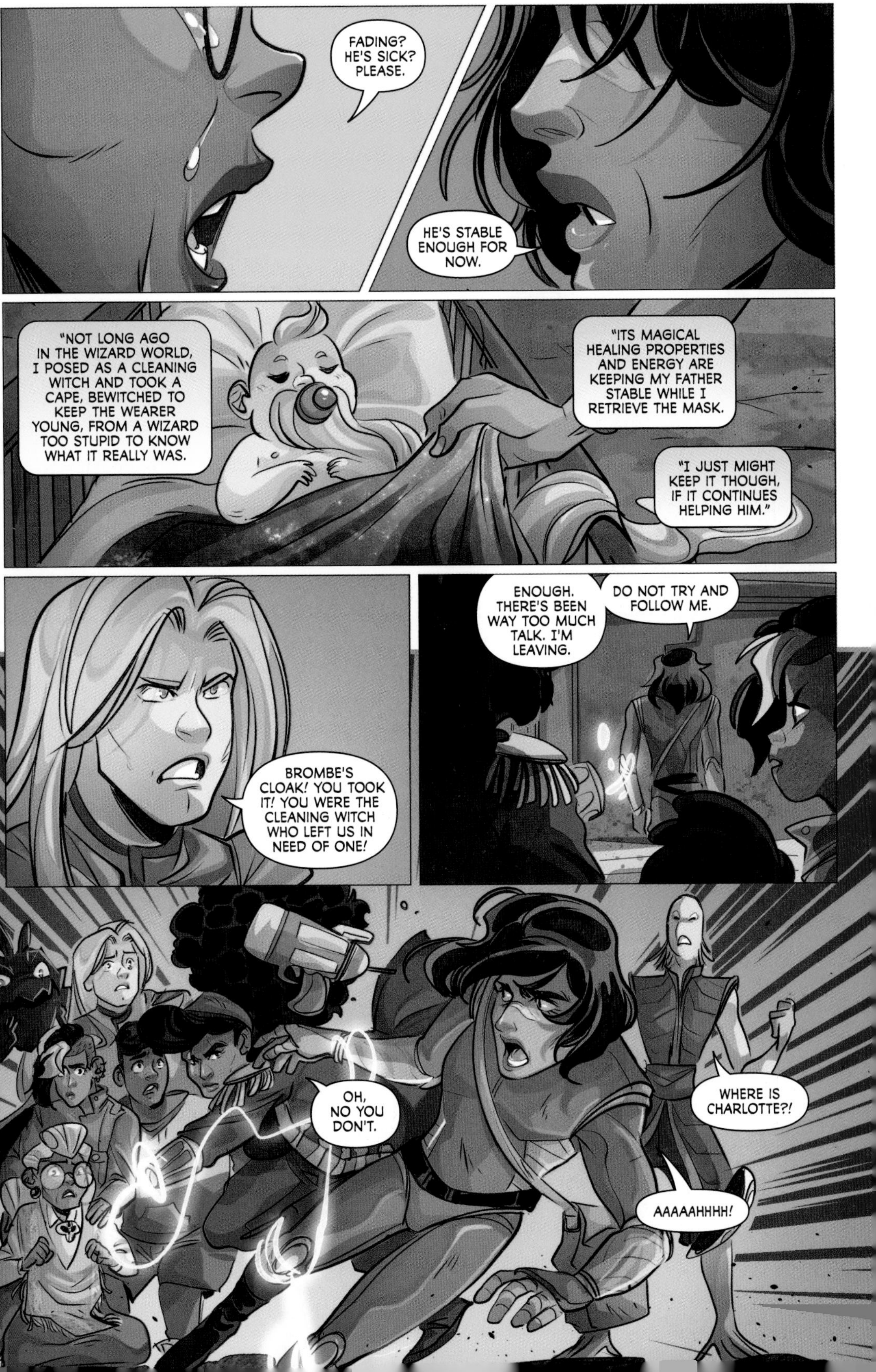
FADING? HE'S SICK? PLEASE.
HE'S STABLE ENOUGH FOR NOW.
"NOT LONG AGO IN THE WIZARD WORLD, I POSED AS A CLEANING WITCH AND TOOK A CAPE, BEWITCHED TO KEEP THE WEARER YOUNG, FROM A WIZARD TOO STUPID TO KNOW WHAT IT REALLY WAS.
"ITS MAGICAL HEALING PROPERTIES AND ENERGY ARE KEEPING MY FATHER STABLE WHILE I RETRIEVE THE MASK.
"I JUST MIGHT KEEP IT THOUGH, IF IT CONTINUES HELPING HIM."
BROMBE'S CLOAK! YOU TOOK IT! YOU WERE THE CLEANING WITCH WHO LEFT US IN NEED OF ONE!
ENOUGH. THERE'S BEEN WAY TOO MUCH TALK. I'M LEAVING.
DO NOT TRY AND FOLLOW ME.
OH, NO YOU DON'T.
WHERE IS CHARLOTTE?!
AAAAAHHHH!

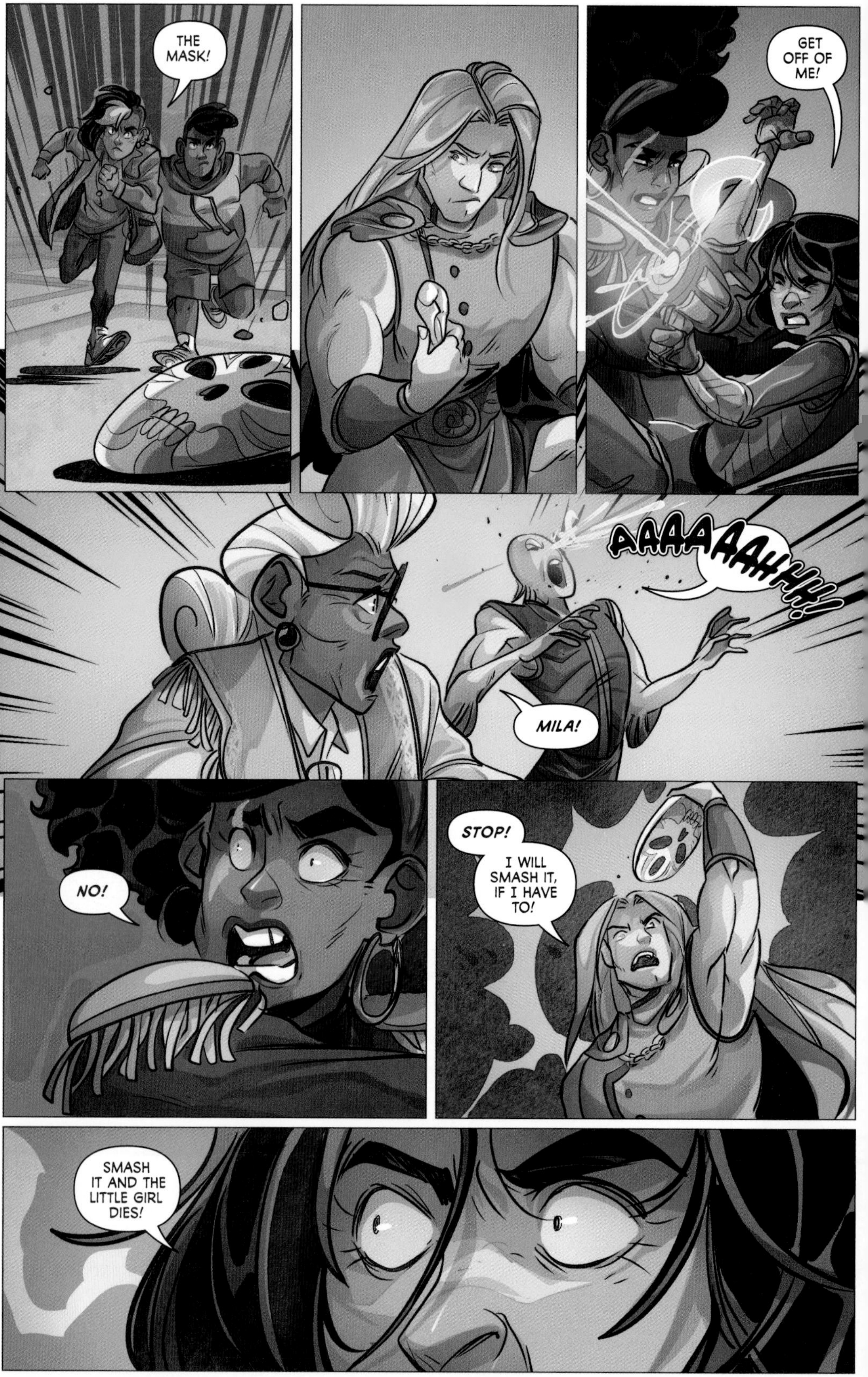
THE MASK!
GET OFF OF ME!
AAAAAAHHHH!
MILA!
NO!
STOP!
I WILL SMASH IT, IF I HAVE TO!
SMASH IT AND THE LITTLE GIRL DIES!

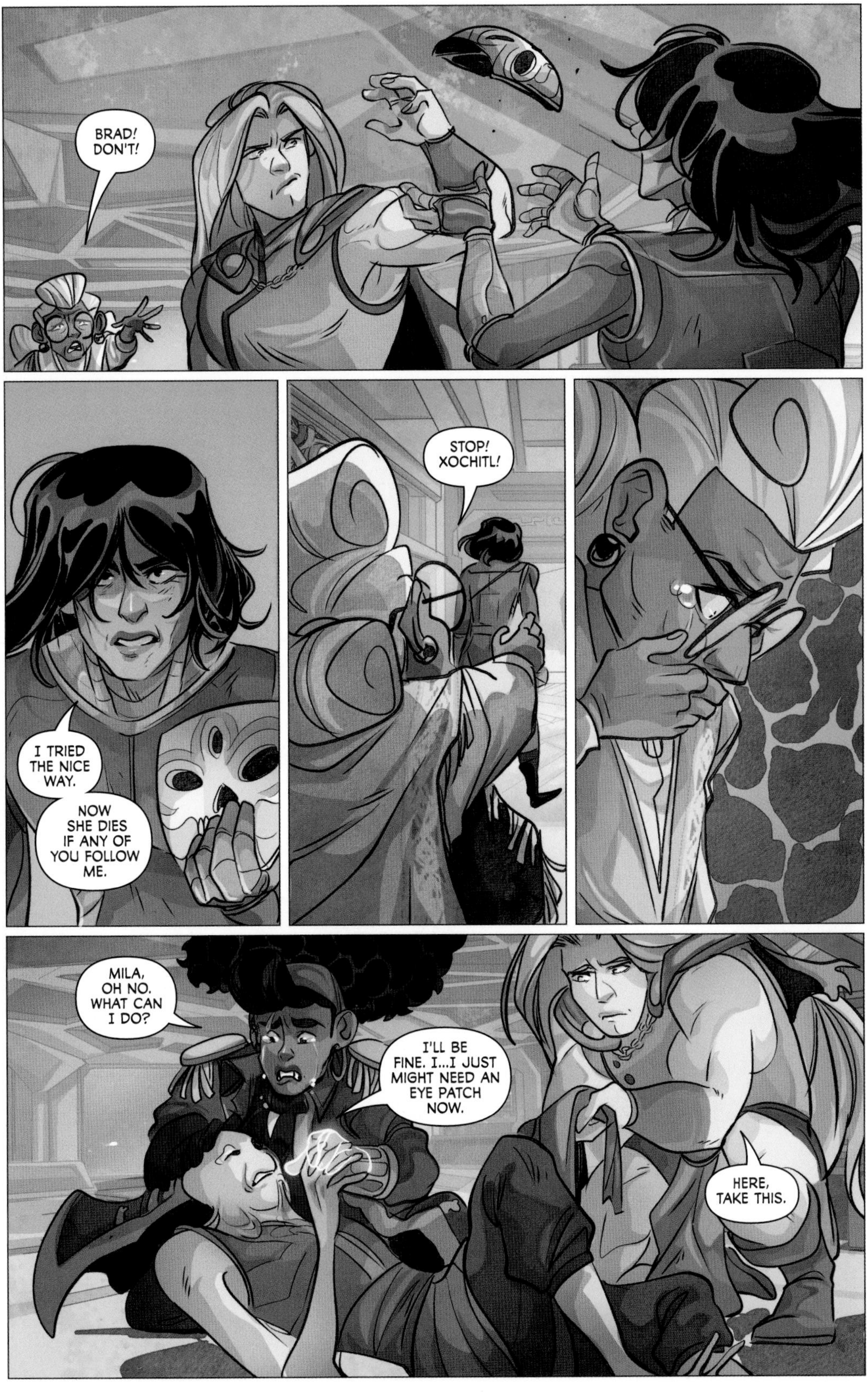
BRAD! DON'T!
I TRIED THE NICE WAY.
NOW SHE DIES IF ANY OF YOU FOLLOW ME.
STOP! XOCHITL!
MILA, OH NO. WHAT CAN I DO?
I'LL BE FINE. I...I JUST MIGHT NEED AN EYE PATCH NOW.
HERE, TAKE THIS.

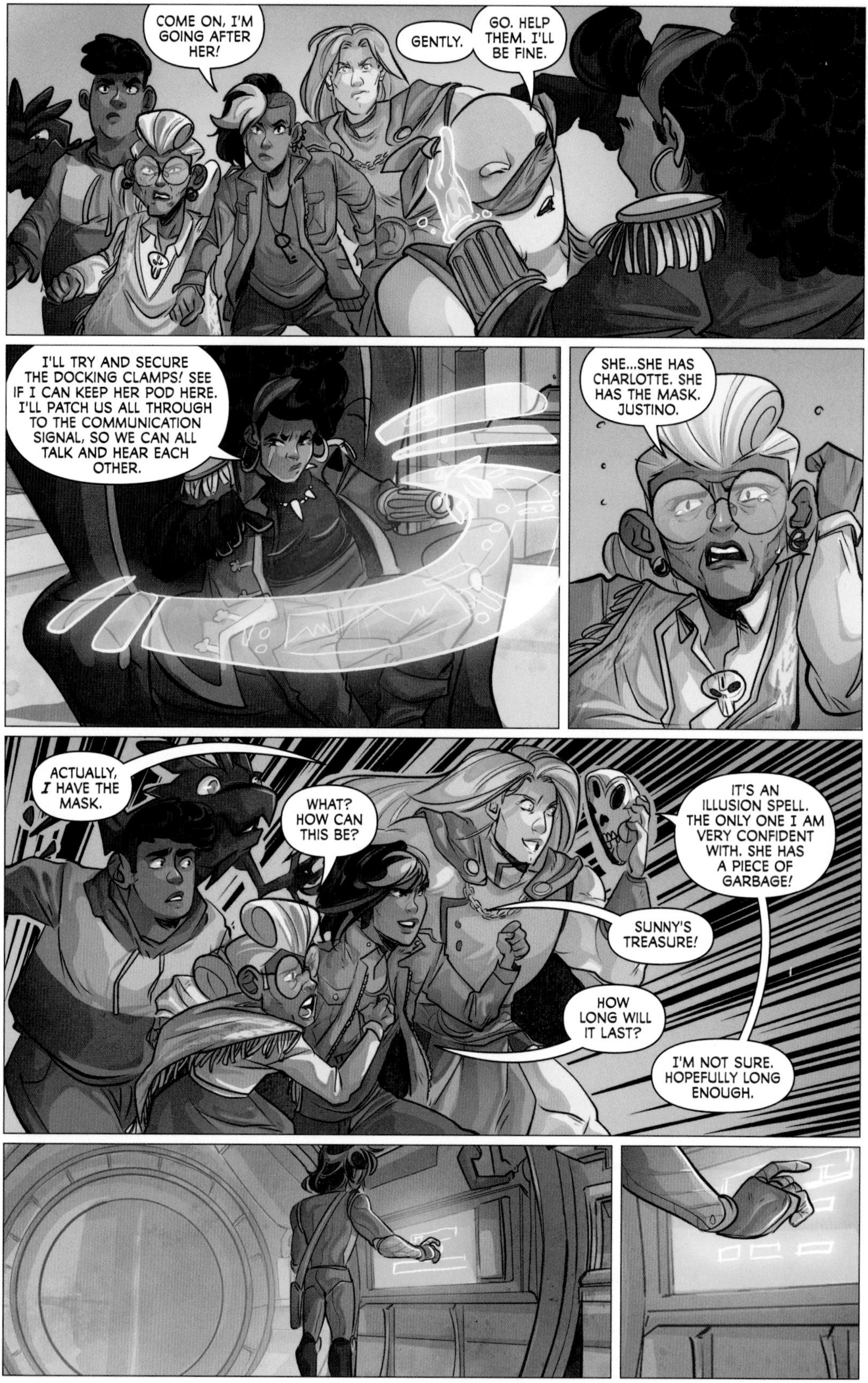
COME ON, I'M GOING AFTER HER!
GENTLY.
GO. HELP THEM. I'LL BE FINE.
I'LL TRY AND SECURE THE DOCKING CLAMPS! SEE IF I CAN KEEP HER POD HERE. I'LL PATCH US ALL THROUGH TO THE COMMUNICATION SIGNAL, SO WE CAN ALL TALK AND HEAR EACH OTHER.
SHE...SHE HAS CHARLOTTE. SHE HAS THE MASK. JUSTINO.
ACTUALLY, I HAVE THE MASK.
WHAT? HOW CAN THIS BE?
IT'S AN ILLUSION SPELL. THE ONLY ONE I AM VERY CONFIDENT WITH. SHE HAS A PIECE OF GARBAGE!
SUNNY'S TREASURE!
HOW LONG WILL IT LAST?
I'M NOT SURE. HOPEFULLY LONG ENOUGH.

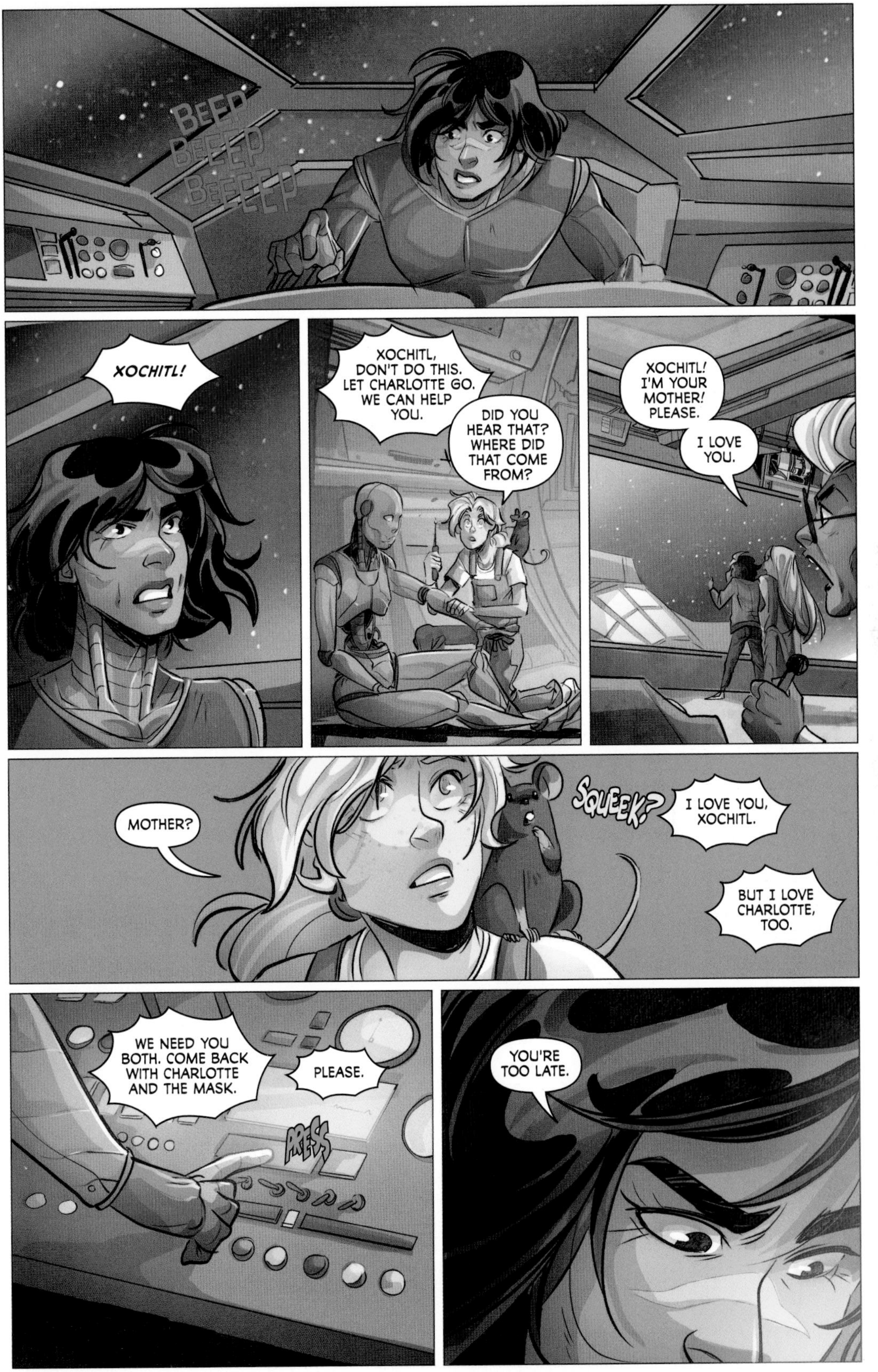
BEEP BEEEP BEEEEP
XOCHITL!
XOCHITL, DON'T DO THIS. LET CHARLOTTE GO. WE CAN HELP YOU.
DID YOU HEAR THAT? WHERE DID THAT COME FROM?
XOCHITL! I'M YOUR MOTHER! PLEASE.
I LOVE YOU.
MOTHER?
SQUEEK?
I LOVE YOU, XOCHITL.
BUT I LOVE CHARLOTTE, TOO.
WE NEED YOU BOTH. COME BACK WITH CHARLOTTE AND THE MASK.
PLEASE.
PRESS
YOU'RE TOO LATE.

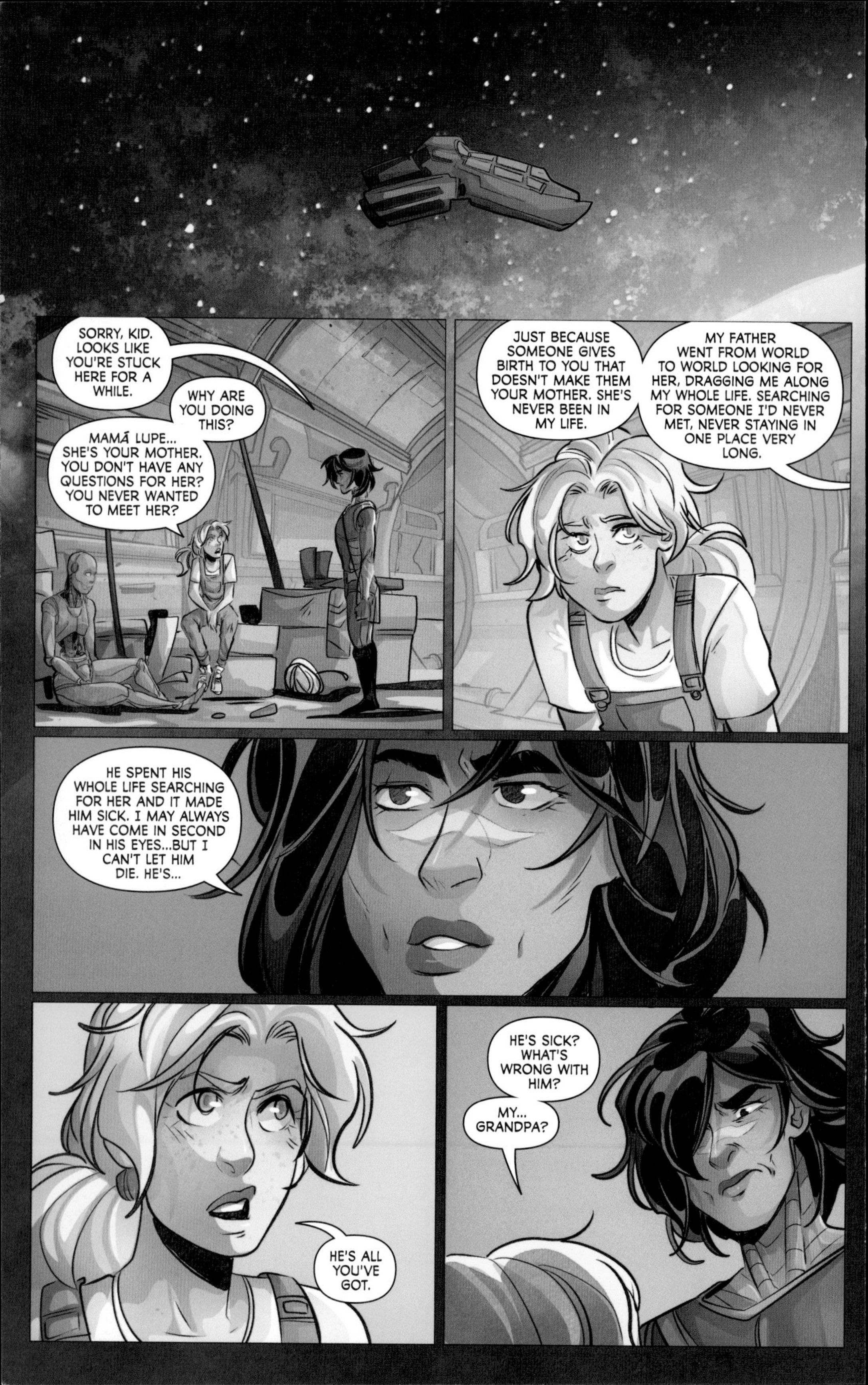
SORRY, KID. LOOKS LIKE YOU'RE STUCK HERE FOR A WHILE.
WHY ARE YOU DOING THIS?
MAMÁ LUPE... SHE'S YOUR MOTHER. YOU DON'T HAVE ANY QUESTIONS FOR HER? YOU NEVER WANTED TO MEET HER?
JUST BECAUSE SOMEONE GIVES BIRTH TO YOU THAT DOESN'T MAKE THEM YOUR MOTHER. SHE'S NEVER BEEN IN MY LIFE.
MY FATHER WENT FROM WORLD TO WORLD LOOKING FOR HER, DRAGGING ME ALONG MY WHOLE LIFE. SEARCHING FOR SOMEONE I'D NEVER MET, NEVER STAYING IN ONE PLACE VERY LONG.
HE SPENT HIS WHOLE LIFE SEARCHING FOR HER AND IT MADE HIM SICK. I MAY ALWAYS HAVE COME IN SECOND IN HIS EYES...BUT I CAN'T LET HIM DIE. HE'S...
HE'S ALL YOU'VE GOT.
HE'S SICK? WHAT'S WRONG WITH HIM?
MY... GRANDPA?

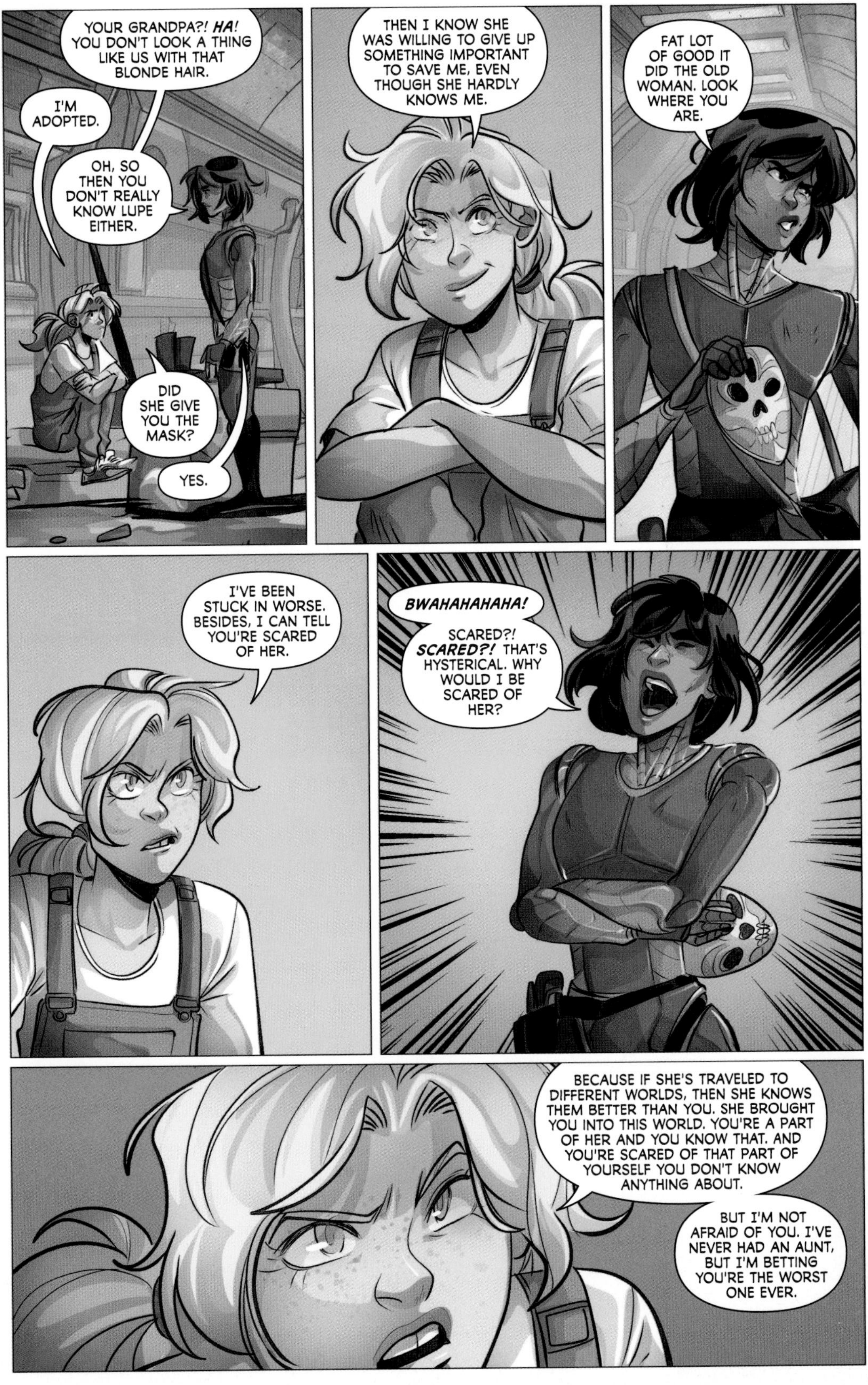
YOUR GRANDPA?! HA! YOU DON'T LOOK A THING LIKE US WITH THAT BLONDE HAIR.
I'M ADOPTED.
OH, SO THEN YOU DON'T REALLY KNOW LUPE EITHER.
DID SHE GIVE YOU THE MASK?
YES.
THEN I KNOW SHE WAS WILLING TO GIVE UP SOMETHING IMPORTANT TO SAVE ME, EVEN THOUGH SHE HARDLY KNOWS ME.
FAT LOT OF GOOD IT DID THE OLD WOMAN. LOOK WHERE YOU ARE.
I'VE BEEN STUCK IN WORSE. BESIDES, I CAN TELL YOU'RE SCARED OF HER.
BWAHAHAHAHA!
SCARED?! SCARED?! THAT'S HYSTERICAL. WHY WOULD I BE SCARED OF HER?
BECAUSE IF SHE'S TRAVELED TO DIFFERENT WORLDS, THEN SHE KNOWS THEM BETTER THAN YOU. SHE BROUGHT YOU INTO THIS WORLD. YOU'RE A PART OF HER AND YOU KNOW THAT. AND YOU'RE SCARED OF THAT PART OF YOURSELF YOU DON'T KNOW ANYTHING ABOUT.
BUT I'M NOT AFRAID OF YOU. I'VE NEVER HAD AN AUNT, BUT I'M BETTING YOU'RE THE WORST ONE EVER.

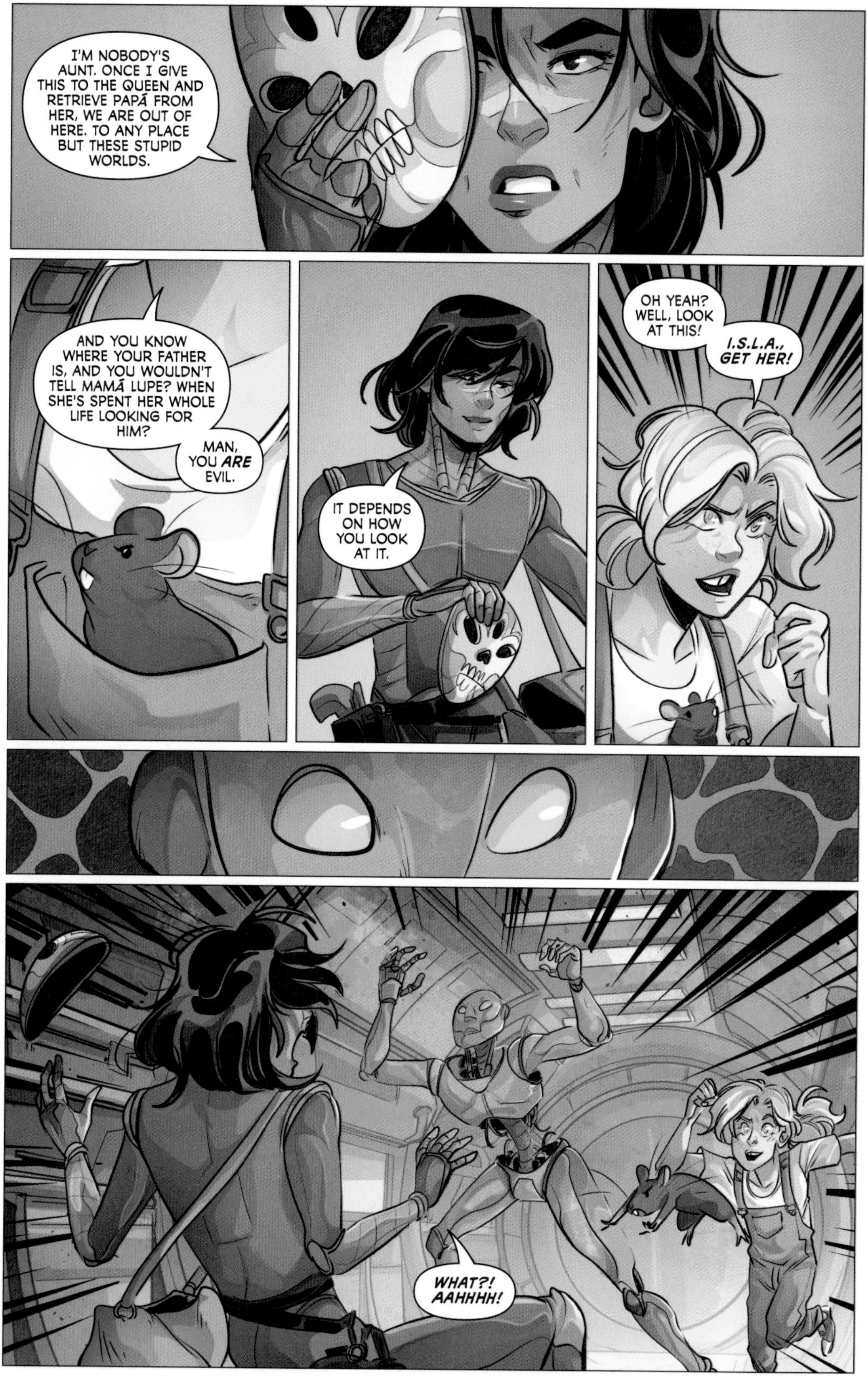
I'M NOBODY'S AUNT. ONCE I GIVE THIS TO THE QUEEN AND RETRIEVE PAPÁ FROM HER, WE ARE OUT OF HERE. TO ANY PLACE BUT THESE STUPID WORLDS.
AND YOU KNOW WHERE YOUR FATHER IS, AND YOU WOULDN'T TELL MAMÁ LUPE? WHEN SHE'S SPENT HER WHOLE LIFE LOOKING FOR HIM?
MAN, YOU *ARE* EVIL.
IT DEPENDS ON HOW YOU LOOK AT IT.
OH YEAH? WELL, LOOK AT THIS!
I.S.L.A., GET HER!
WHAT?! AAHHHH!

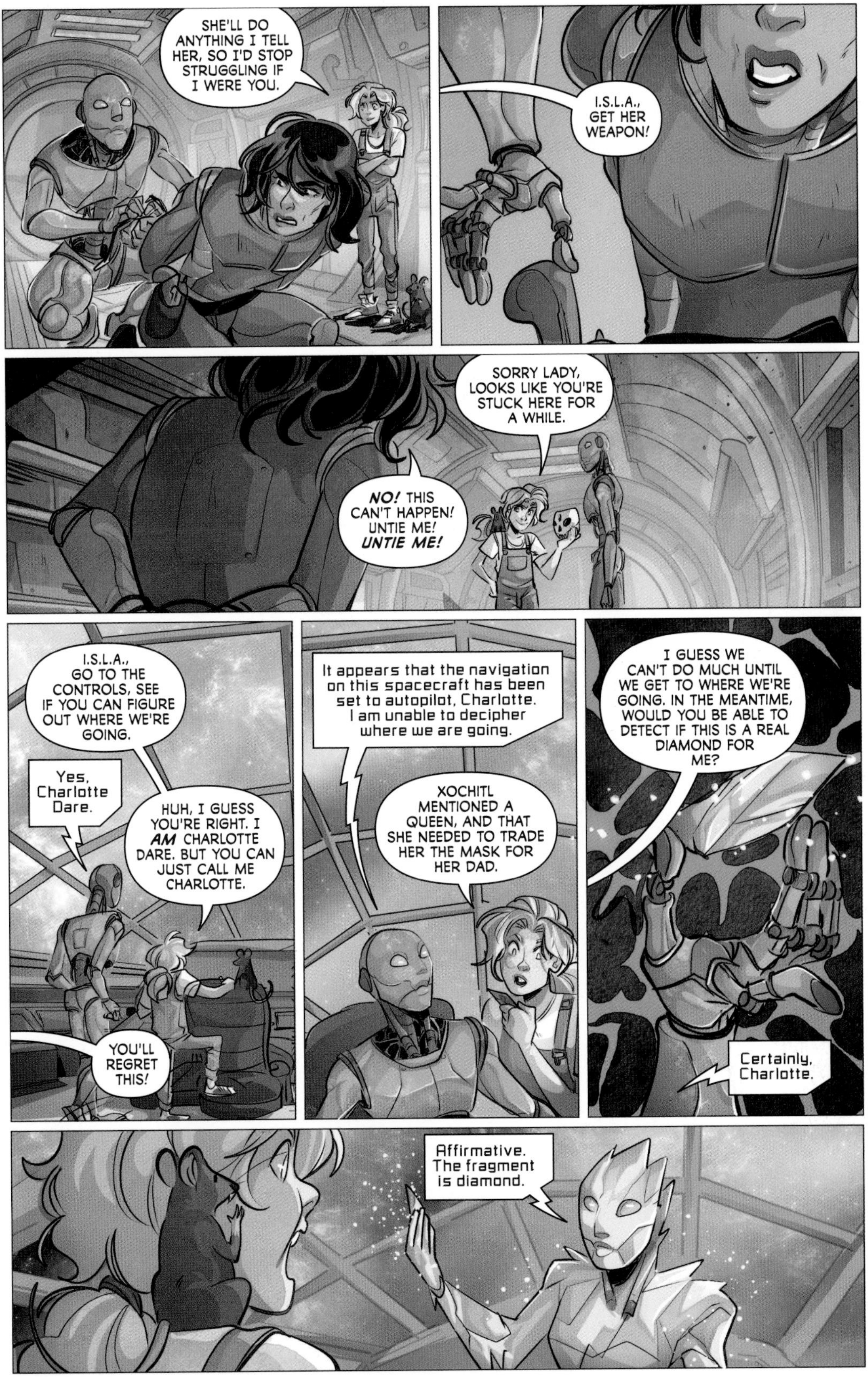
SHE'LL DO ANYTHING I TELL HER, SO I'D STOP STRUGGLING IF I WERE YOU.
I.S.L.A., GET HER WEAPON!
SORRY LADY, LOOKS LIKE YOU'RE STUCK HERE FOR A WHILE.
NO! THIS CAN'T HAPPEN! UNTIE ME! UNTIE ME!
I.S.L.A., GO TO THE CONTROLS, SEE IF YOU CAN FIGURE OUT WHERE WE'RE GOING.
Yes, Charlotte Dare.
HUH, I GUESS YOU'RE RIGHT. I AM CHARLOTTE DARE. BUT YOU CAN JUST CALL ME CHARLOTTE.
YOU'LL REGRET THIS!
It appears that the navigation on this spacecraft has been set to autopilot, Charlotte. I am unable to decipher where we are going.
XOCHITL MENTIONED A QUEEN, AND THAT SHE NEEDED TO TRADE HER THE MASK FOR HER DAD.
I GUESS WE CAN'T DO MUCH UNTIL WE GET TO WHERE WE'RE GOING. IN THE MEANTIME, WOULD YOU BE ABLE TO DETECT IF THIS IS A REAL DIAMOND FOR ME?
Certainly, Charlotte.
Affirmative. The fragment is diamond.

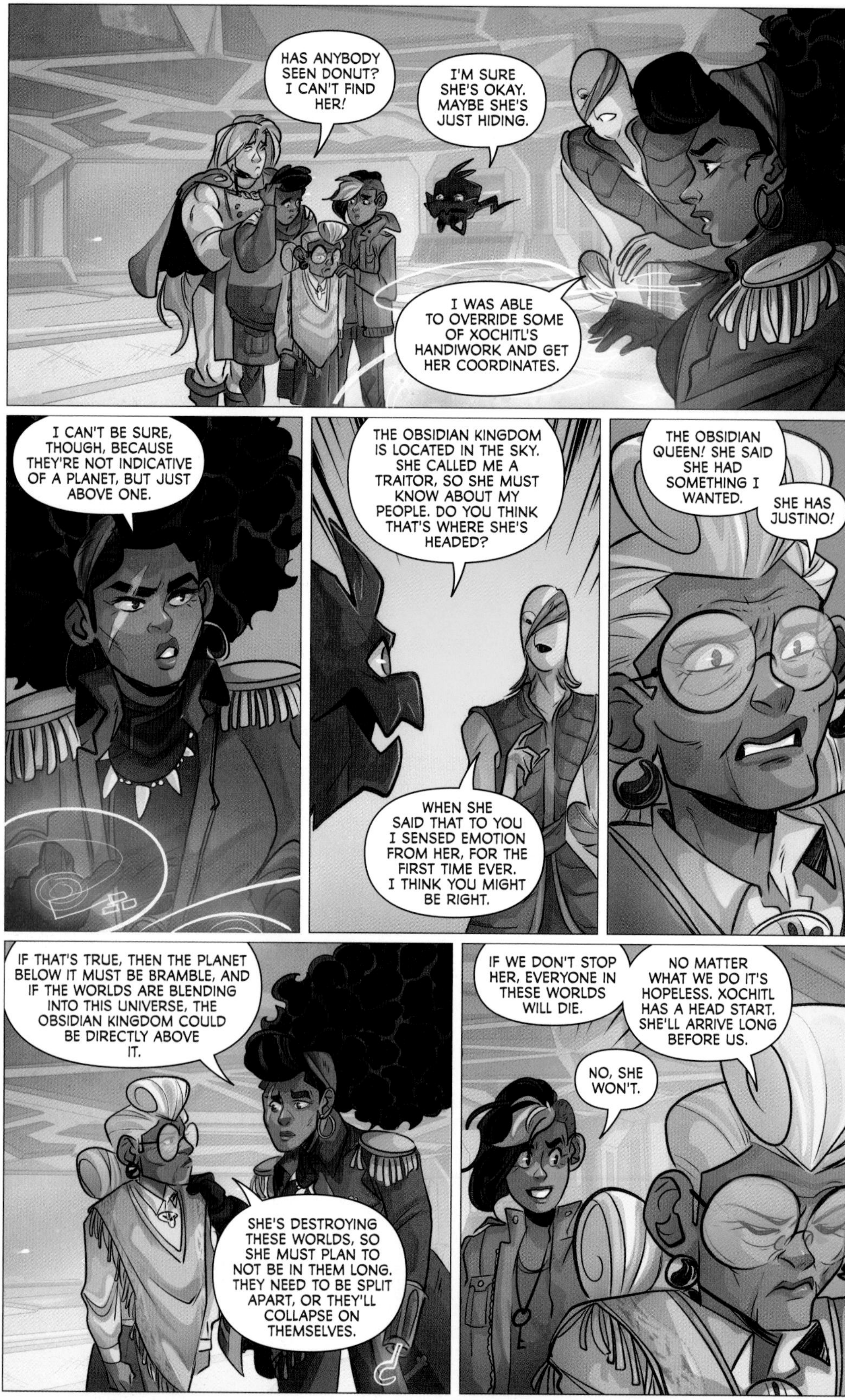
HAS ANYBODY SEEN DONUT? I CAN'T FIND HER!
I'M SURE SHE'S OKAY. MAYBE SHE'S JUST HIDING.
I WAS ABLE TO OVERRIDE SOME OF XOCHITL'S HANDIWORK AND GET HER COORDINATES.
I CAN'T BE SURE, THOUGH, BECAUSE THEY'RE NOT INDICATIVE OF A PLANET, BUT JUST ABOVE ONE.
THE OBSIDIAN KINGDOM IS LOCATED IN THE SKY. SHE CALLED ME A TRAITOR, SO SHE MUST KNOW ABOUT MY PEOPLE. DO YOU THINK THAT'S WHERE SHE'S HEADED?
WHEN SHE SAID THAT TO YOU I SENSED EMOTION FROM HER, FOR THE FIRST TIME EVER. I THINK YOU MIGHT BE RIGHT.
THE OBSIDIAN QUEEN! SHE SAID SHE HAD SOMETHING I WANTED.
SHE HAS JUSTINO!
IF THAT'S TRUE, THEN THE PLANET BELOW IT MUST BE BRAMBLE, AND IF THE WORLDS ARE BLENDING INTO THIS UNIVERSE, THE OBSIDIAN KINGDOM COULD BE DIRECTLY ABOVE IT.
SHE'S DESTROYING THESE WORLDS, SO SHE MUST PLAN TO NOT BE IN THEM LONG. THEY NEED TO BE SPLIT APART, OR THEY'LL COLLAPSE ON THEMSELVES.
IF WE DON'T STOP HER, EVERYONE IN THESE WORLDS WILL DIE.
NO MATTER WHAT WE DO IT'S HOPELESS. XOCHITL HAS A HEAD START. SHE'LL ARRIVE LONG BEFORE US.
NO, SHE WON'T.

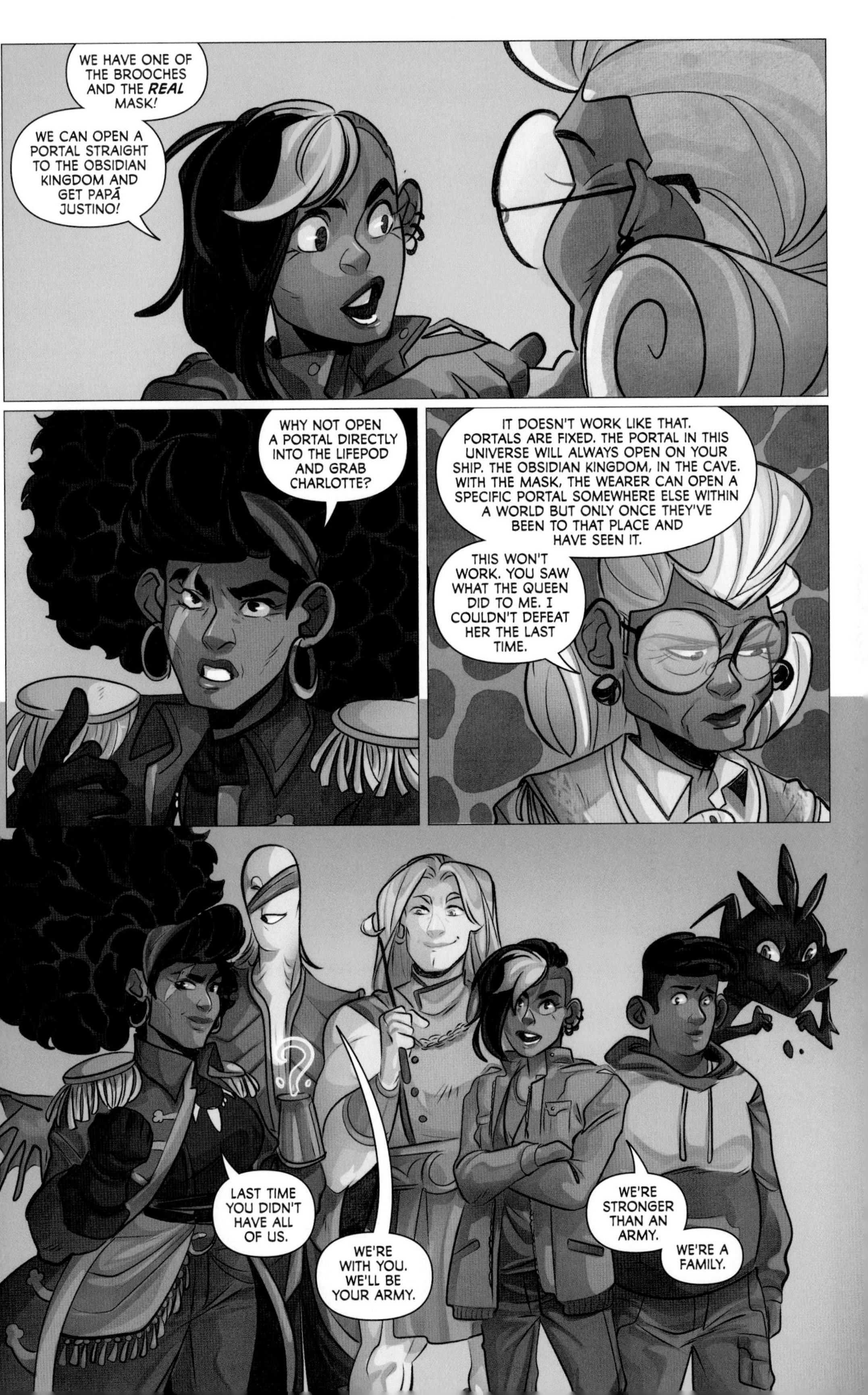
WE HAVE ONE OF THE BROOCHES AND THE *REAL* MASK!
WE CAN OPEN A PORTAL STRAIGHT TO THE OBSIDIAN KINGDOM AND GET PAPÁ JUSTINO!
WHY NOT OPEN A PORTAL DIRECTLY INTO THE LIFEPOD AND GRAB CHARLOTTE?
IT DOESN'T WORK LIKE THAT. PORTALS ARE FIXED. THE PORTAL IN THIS UNIVERSE WILL ALWAYS OPEN ON YOUR SHIP. THE OBSIDIAN KINGDOM, IN THE CAVE. WITH THE MASK, THE WEARER CAN OPEN A SPECIFIC PORTAL SOMEWHERE ELSE WITHIN A WORLD BUT ONLY ONCE THEY'VE BEEN TO THAT PLACE AND HAVE SEEN IT.
THIS WON'T WORK. YOU SAW WHAT THE QUEEN DID TO ME. I COULDN'T DEFEAT HER THE LAST TIME.
LAST TIME YOU DIDN'T HAVE ALL OF US.
WE'RE WITH YOU. WE'LL BE YOUR ARMY.
WE'RE STRONGER THAN AN ARMY.
WE'RE A FAMILY.

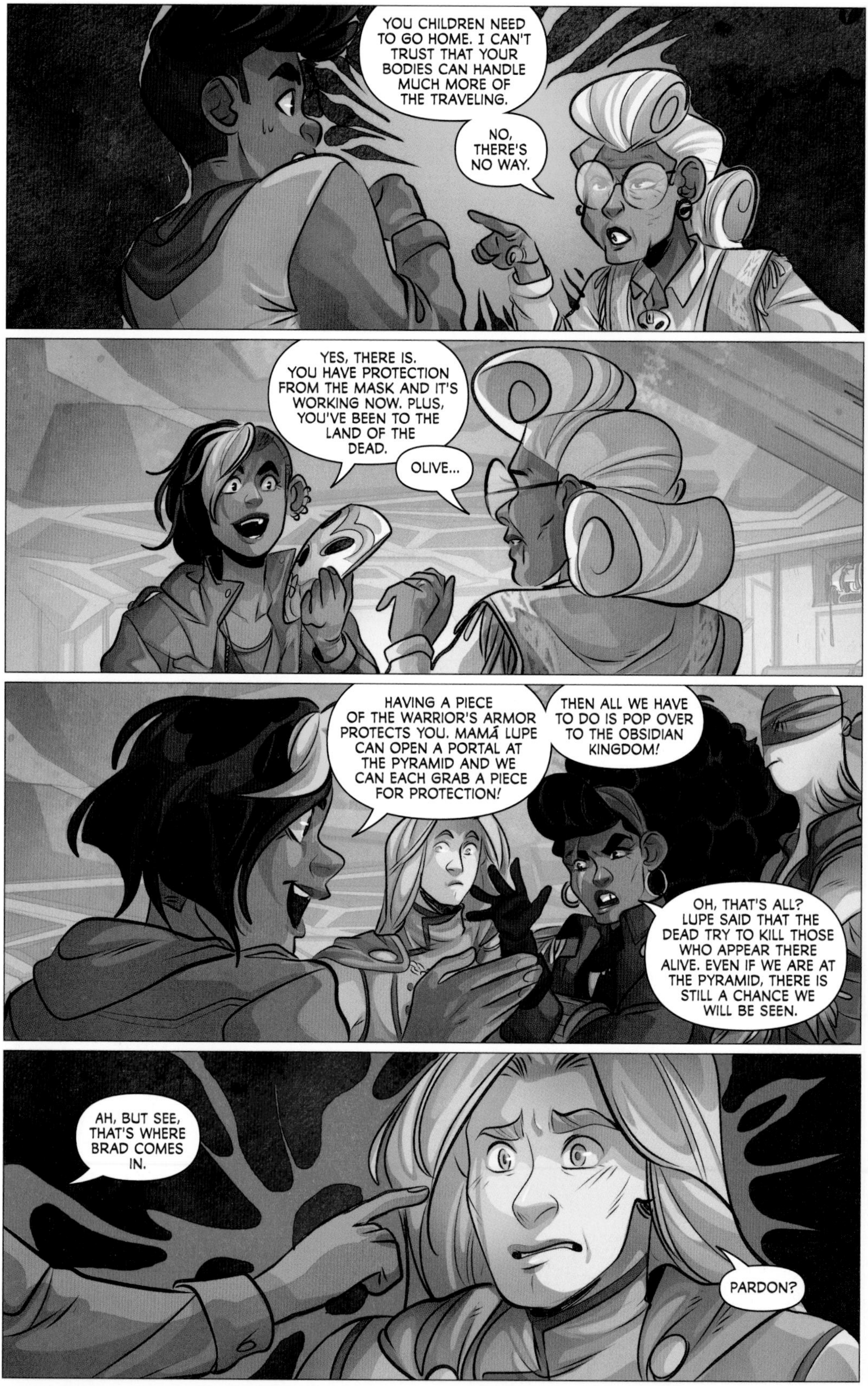
YOU CHILDREN NEED TO GO HOME. I CAN'T TRUST THAT YOUR BODIES CAN HANDLE MUCH MORE OF THE TRAVELING.
NO, THERE'S NO WAY.
YES, THERE IS. YOU HAVE PROTECTION FROM THE MASK AND IT'S WORKING NOW. PLUS, YOU'VE BEEN TO THE LAND OF THE DEAD.
OLIVE...
HAVING A PIECE OF THE WARRIOR'S ARMOR PROTECTS YOU. MAMÁ LUPE CAN OPEN A PORTAL AT THE PYRAMID AND WE CAN EACH GRAB A PIECE FOR PROTECTION!
THEN ALL WE HAVE TO DO IS POP OVER TO THE OBSIDIAN KINGDOM!
OH, THAT'S ALL? LUPE SAID THAT THE DEAD TRY TO KILL THOSE WHO APPEAR THERE ALIVE. EVEN IF WE ARE AT THE PYRAMID, THERE IS STILL A CHANCE WE WILL BE SEEN.
AH, BUT SEE, THAT'S WHERE BRAD COMES IN.
PARDON?

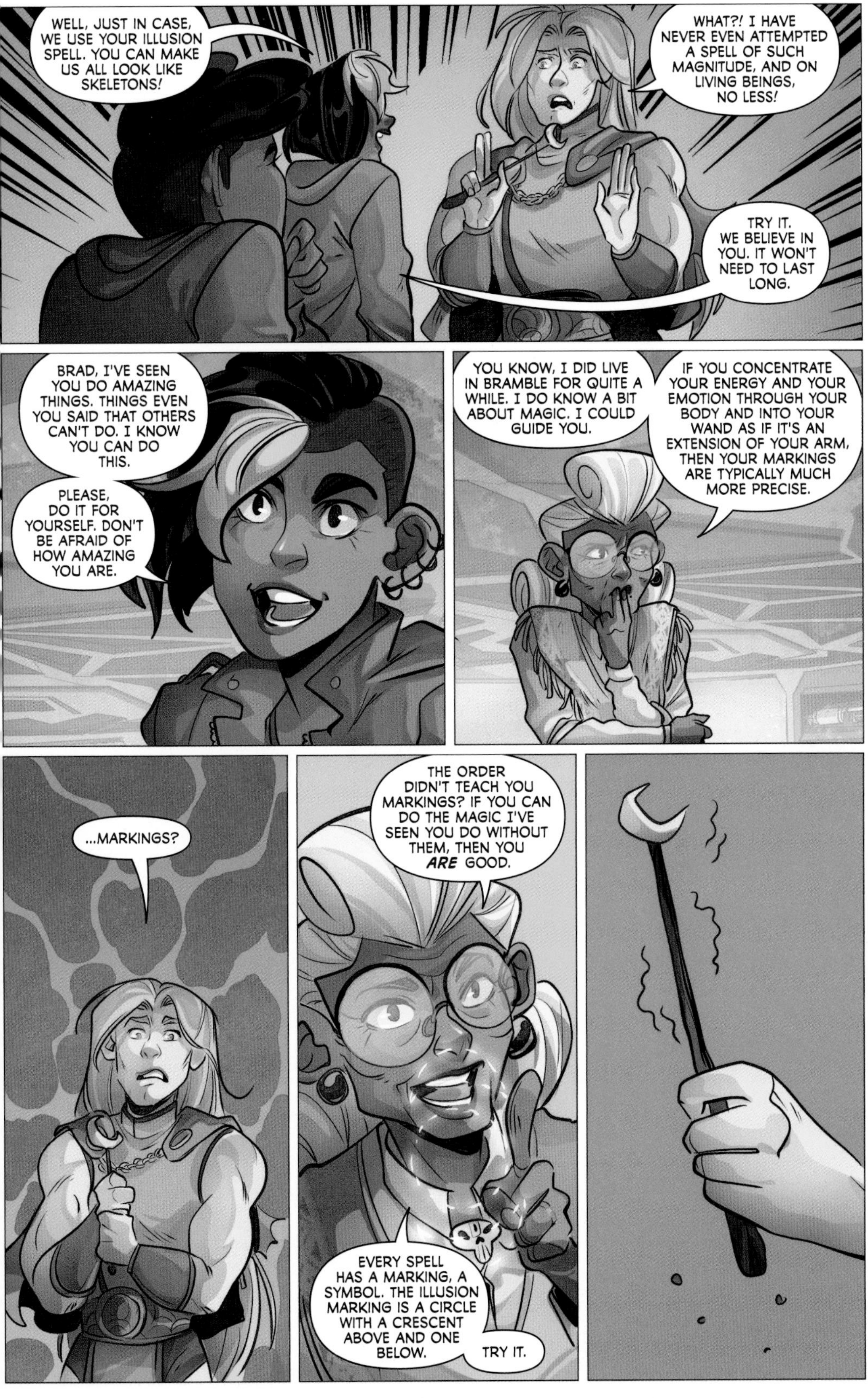
WELL, JUST IN CASE, WE USE YOUR ILLUSION SPELL. YOU CAN MAKE US ALL LOOK LIKE SKELETONS!
WHAT?! I HAVE NEVER EVEN ATTEMPTED A SPELL OF SUCH MAGNITUDE, AND ON LIVING BEINGS, NO LESS!
TRY IT. WE BELIEVE IN YOU. IT WON'T NEED TO LAST LONG.
BRAD, I'VE SEEN YOU DO AMAZING THINGS. THINGS EVEN YOU SAID THAT OTHERS CAN'T DO. I KNOW YOU CAN DO THIS.
PLEASE, DO IT FOR YOURSELF. DON'T BE AFRAID OF HOW AMAZING YOU ARE.
YOU KNOW, I DID LIVE IN BRAMBLE FOR QUITE A WHILE. I DO KNOW A BIT ABOUT MAGIC. I COULD GUIDE YOU.
IF YOU CONCENTRATE YOUR ENERGY AND YOUR EMOTION THROUGH YOUR BODY AND INTO YOUR WAND AS IF IT'S AN EXTENSION OF YOUR ARM, THEN YOUR MARKINGS ARE TYPICALLY MUCH MORE PRECISE.
...MARKINGS?
THE ORDER DIDN'T TEACH YOU MARKINGS? IF YOU CAN DO THE MAGIC I'VE SEEN YOU DO WITHOUT THEM, THEN YOU ***ARE*** GOOD.
EVERY SPELL HAS A MARKING, A SYMBOL. THE ILLUSION MARKING IS A CIRCLE WITH A CRESCENT ABOVE AND ONE BELOW.
TRY IT.

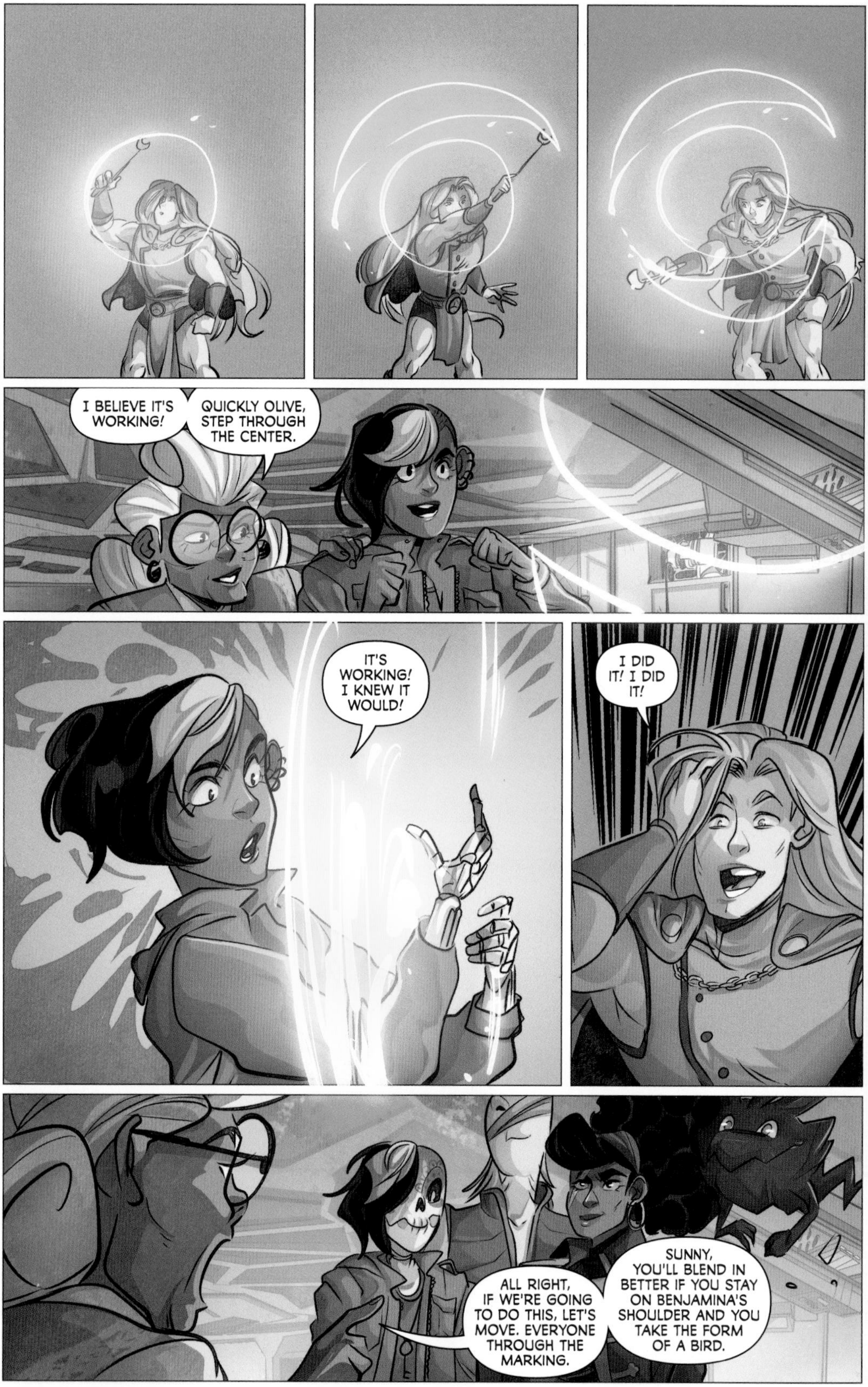
I BELIEVE IT'S WORKING!
QUICKLY OLIVE, STEP THROUGH THE CENTER.
IT'S WORKING! I KNEW IT WOULD!
I DID IT! I DID IT!
SUNNY, YOU'LL BLEND IN BETTER IF YOU STAY ON BENJAMINA'S SHOULDER AND YOU TAKE THE FORM OF A BIRD.
ALL RIGHT, IF WE'RE GOING TO DO THIS, LET'S MOVE. EVERYONE THROUGH THE MARKING.

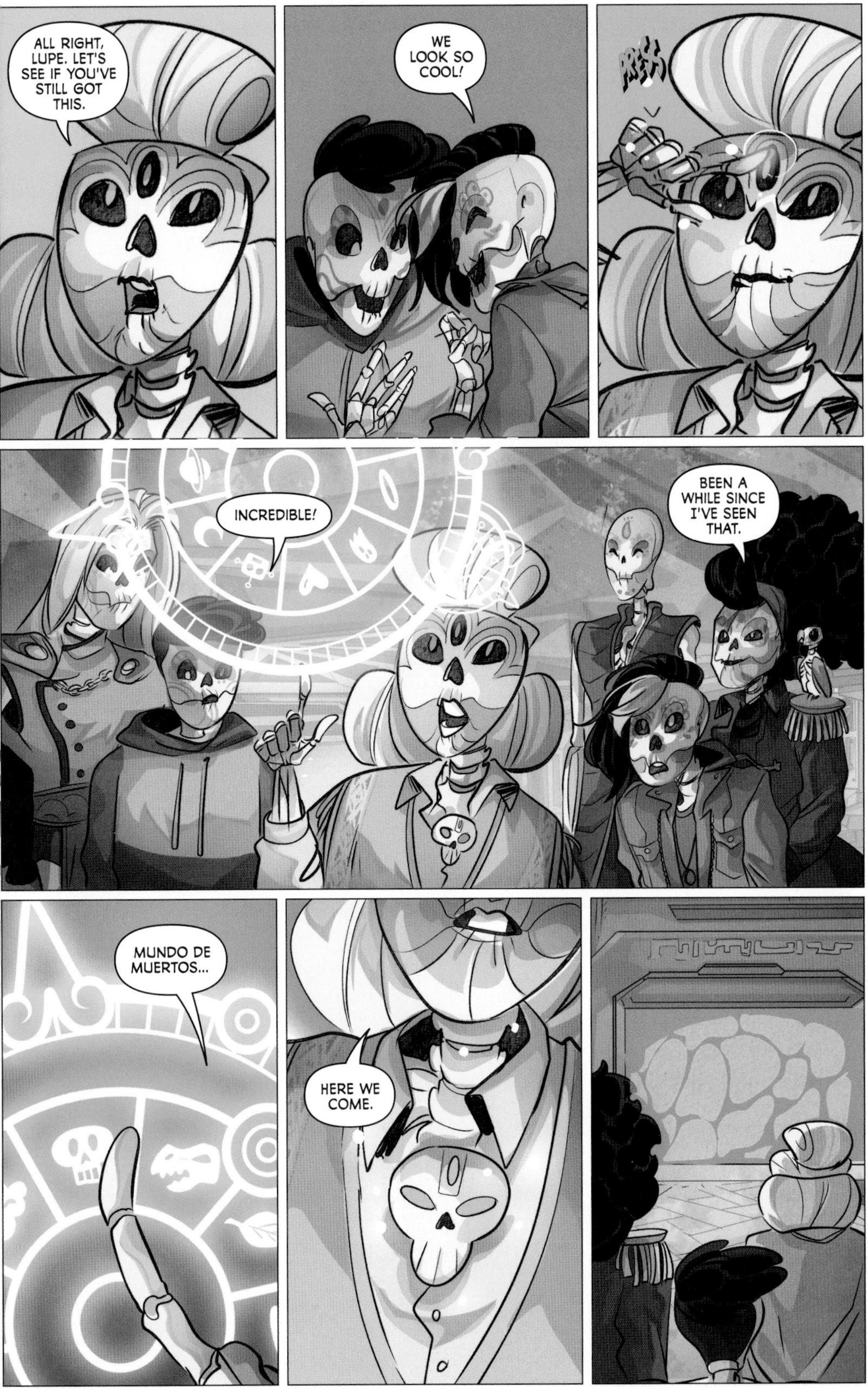
ALL RIGHT, LUPE. LET'S SEE IF YOU'VE STILL GOT THIS.
WE LOOK SO COOL!
PRESS
INCREDIBLE!
BEEN A WHILE SINCE I'VE SEEN THAT.
MUNDO DE MUERTOS...
HERE WE COME.

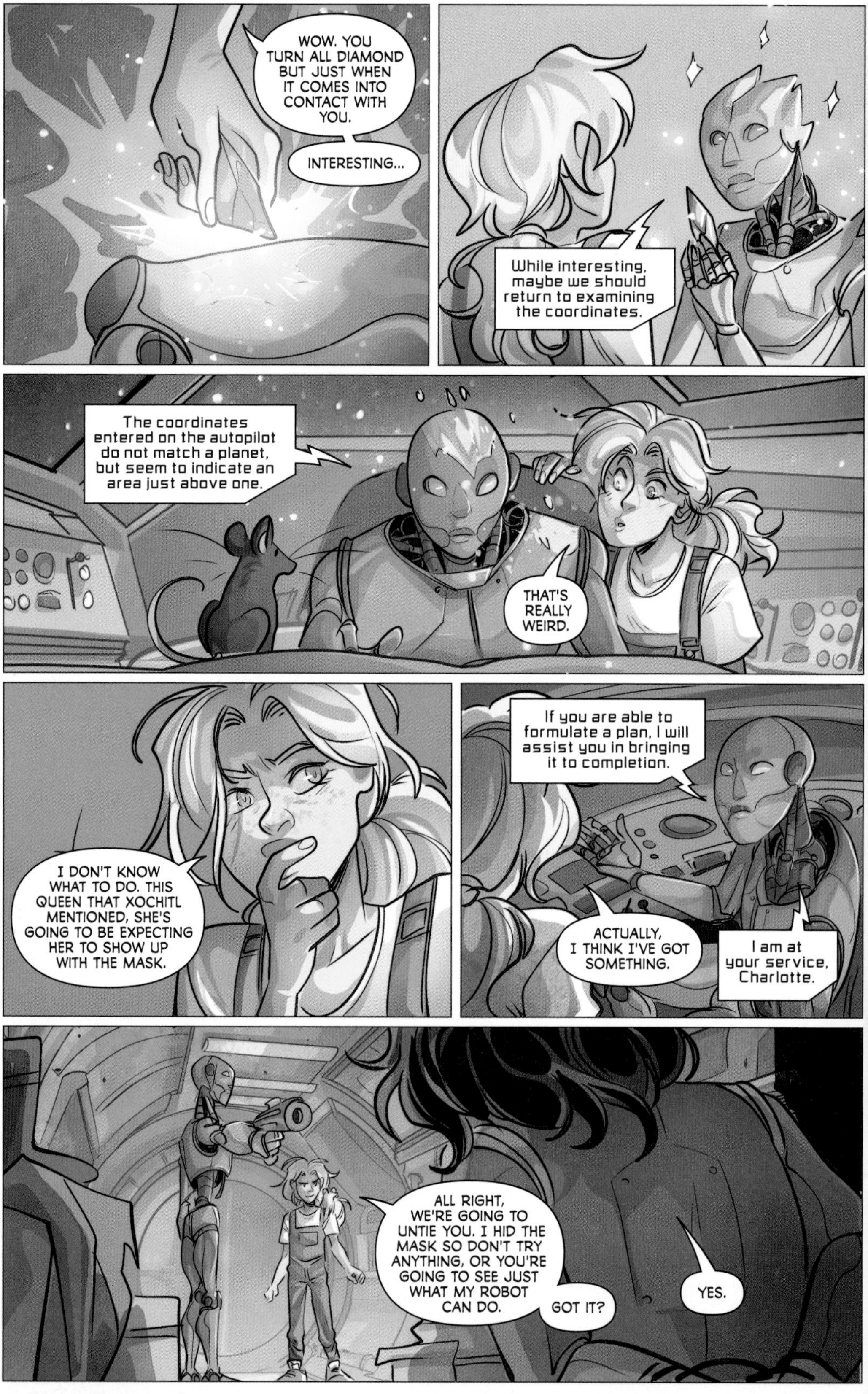

WOW. YOU TURN ALL DIAMOND BUT JUST WHEN IT COMES INTO CONTACT WITH YOU.
INTERESTING...
While interesting, maybe we should return to examining the coordinates.
The coordinates entered on the autopilot do not match a planet, but seem to indicate an area just above one.
THAT'S REALLY WEIRD.
I DON'T KNOW WHAT TO DO. THIS QUEEN THAT XOCHITL MENTIONED, SHE'S GOING TO BE EXPECTING HER TO SHOW UP WITH THE MASK.
If you are able to formulate a plan, I will assist you in bringing it to completion.
ACTUALLY, I THINK I'VE GOT SOMETHING.
I am at your service, Charlotte.
ALL RIGHT, WE'RE GOING TO UNTIE YOU. I HID THE MASK SO DON'T TRY ANYTHING, OR YOU'RE GOING TO SEE JUST WHAT MY ROBOT CAN DO.
GOT IT?
YES.

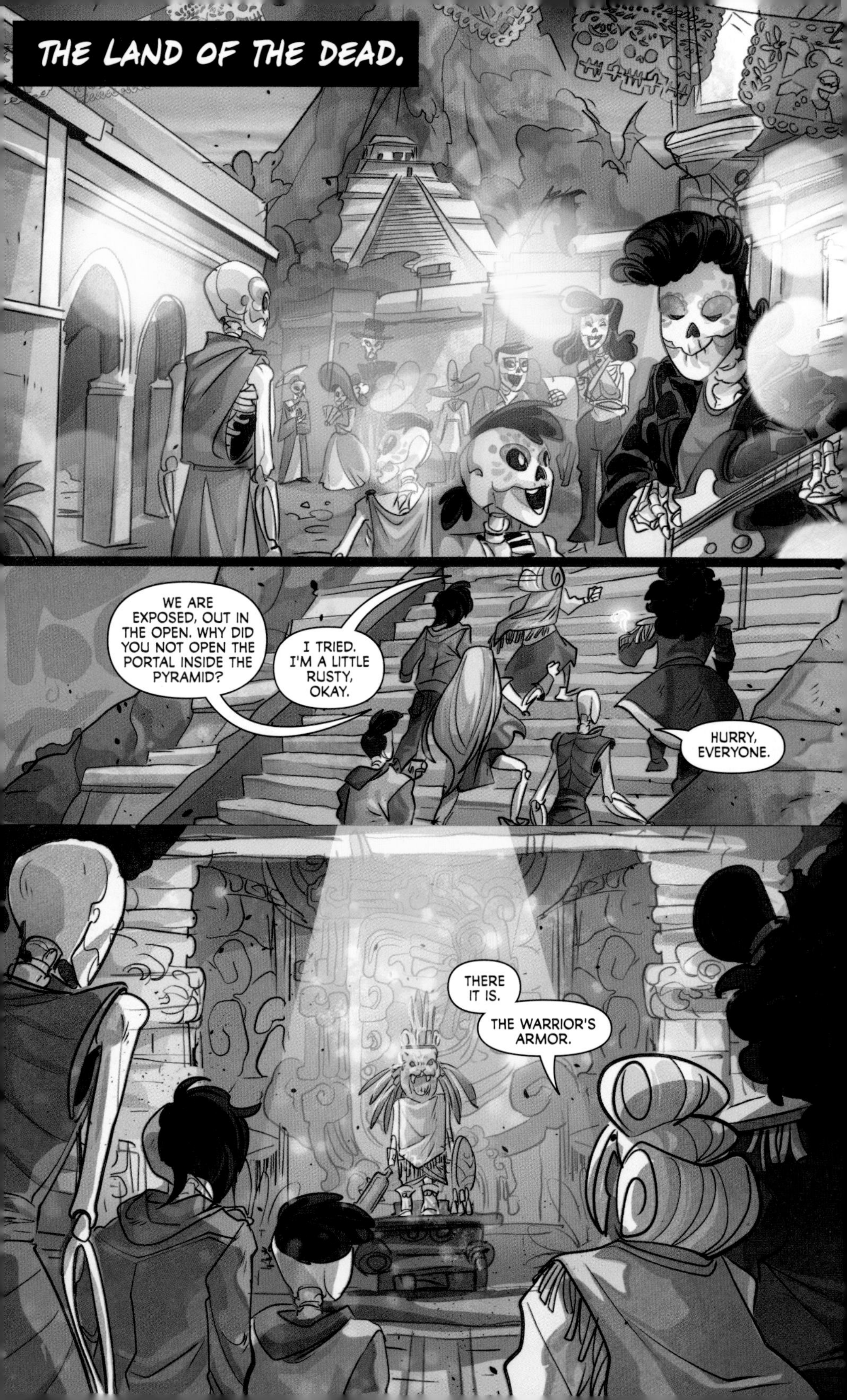
THE LAND OF THE DEAD.
WE ARE EXPOSED, OUT IN THE OPEN. WHY DID YOU NOT OPEN THE PORTAL INSIDE THE PYRAMID?
I TRIED. I'M A LITTLE RUSTY, OKAY.
HURRY, EVERYONE.
THERE IT IS.
THE WARRIOR'S ARMOR.

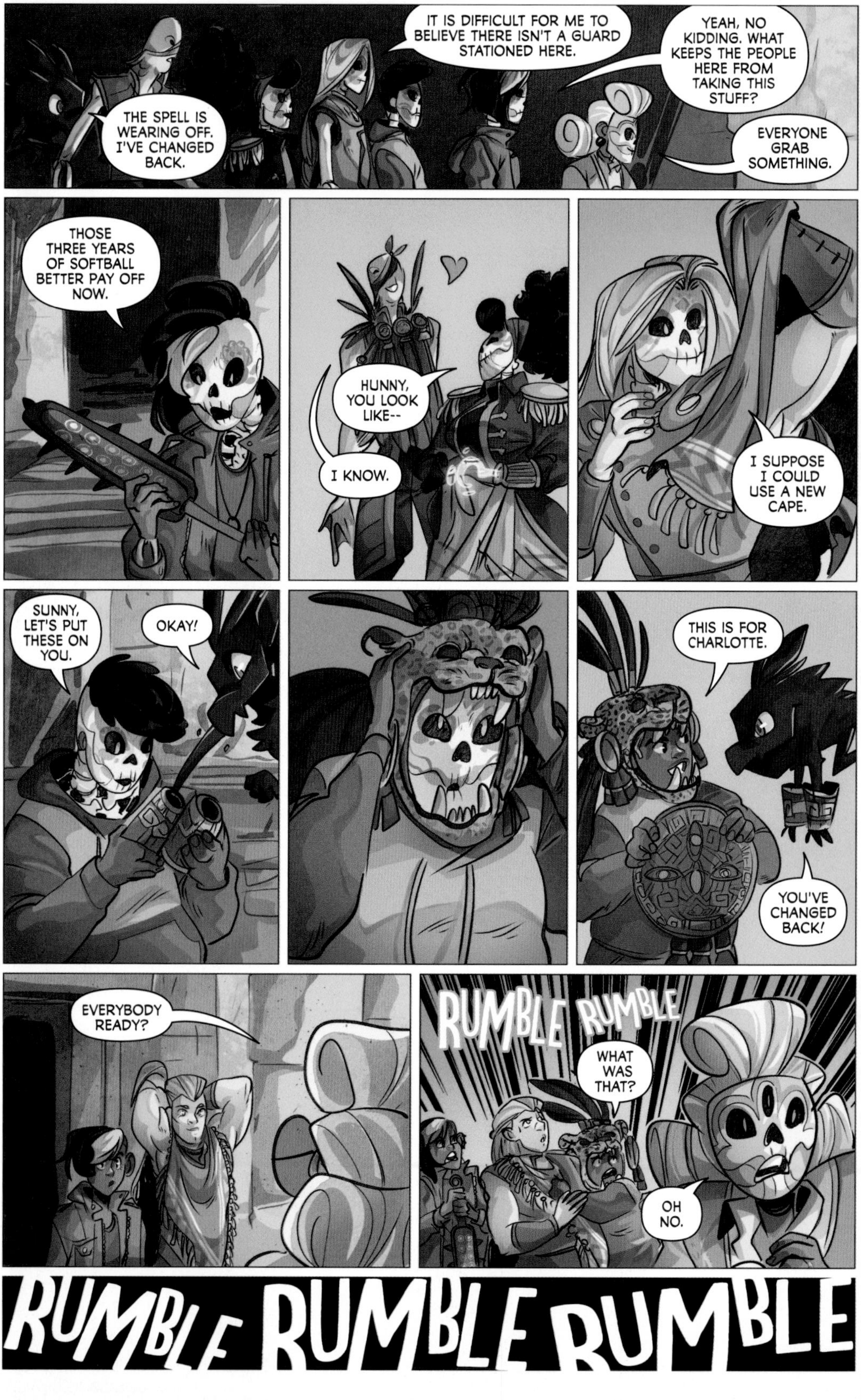
IT IS DIFFICULT FOR ME TO BELIEVE THERE ISN'T A GUARD STATIONED HERE.
THE SPELL IS WEARING OFF. I'VE CHANGED BACK.
YEAH, NO KIDDING. WHAT KEEPS THE PEOPLE HERE FROM TAKING THIS STUFF?
EVERYONE GRAB SOMETHING.
THOSE THREE YEARS OF SOFTBALL BETTER PAY OFF NOW.
HUNNY, YOU LOOK LIKE--
I KNOW.
I SUPPOSE I COULD USE A NEW CAPE.
SUNNY, LET'S PUT THESE ON YOU.
OKAY!
THIS IS FOR CHARLOTTE.
YOU'VE CHANGED BACK!
EVERYBODY READY?
RUMBLE RUMBLE
WHAT WAS THAT?
OH NO.
RUMBLE RUMBLE RUMBLE

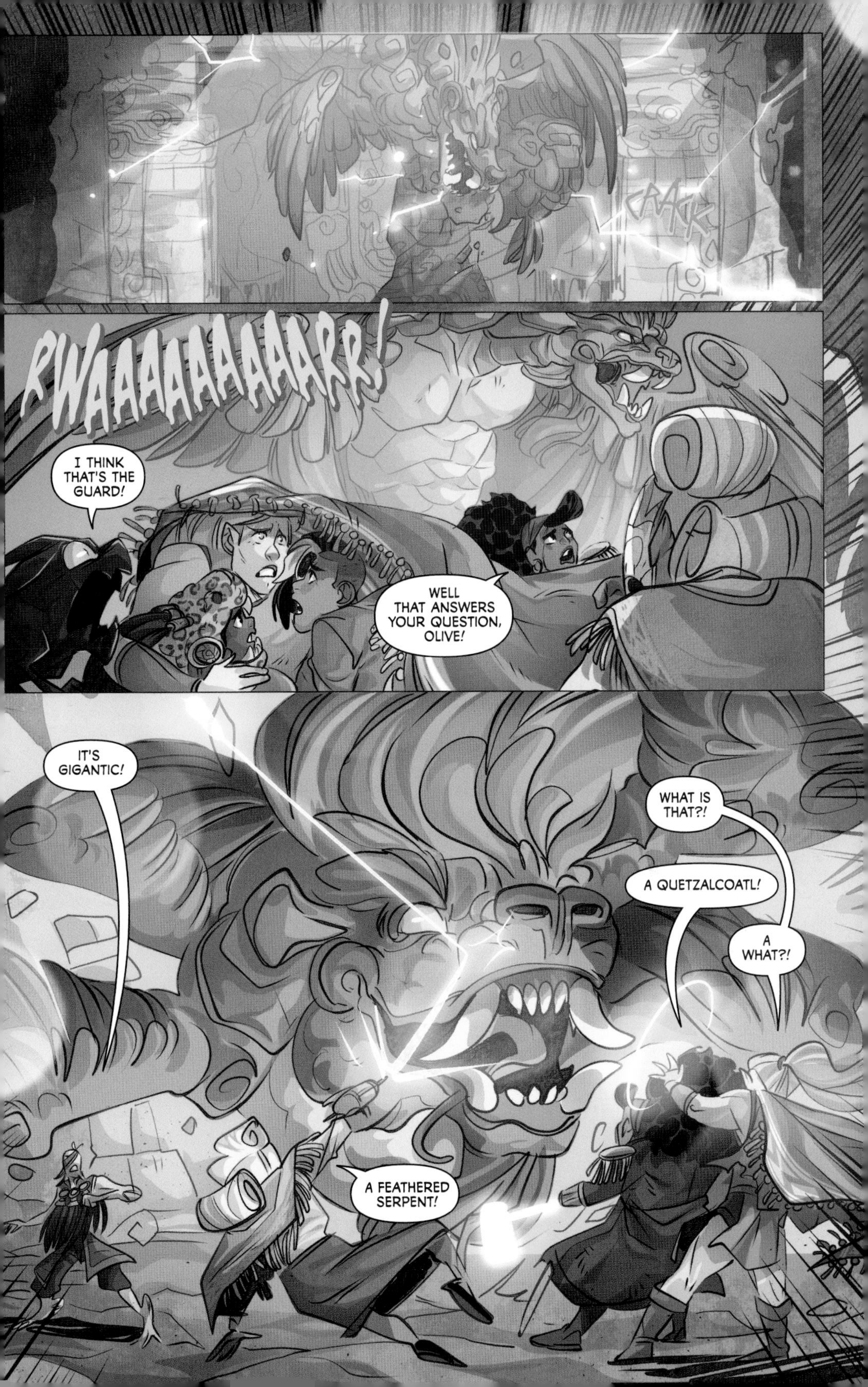
CRACK
RWAAAAAAAAARR!
I THINK THAT'S THE GUARD!
WELL THAT ANSWERS YOUR QUESTION, OLIVE!
IT'S GIGANTIC!
WHAT IS THAT?!
A QUETZALCOATL!
A WHAT?!
A FEATHERED SERPENT!

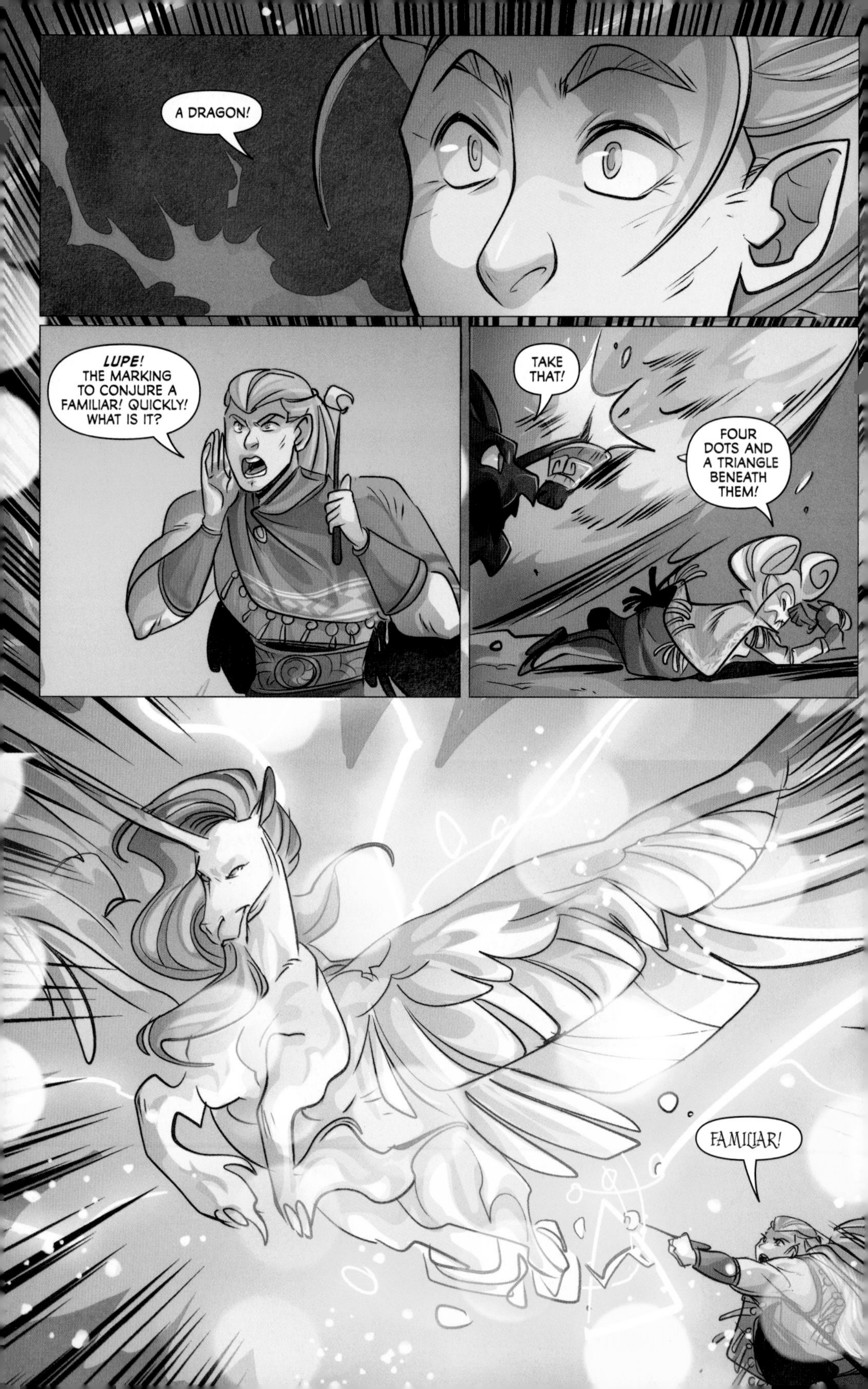
A DRAGON!
LUPE! THE MARKING TO CONJURE A FAMILIAR! QUICKLY! WHAT IS IT?
TAKE THAT!
FOUR DOTS AND A TRIANGLE BENEATH THEM!
FAMILIAR!

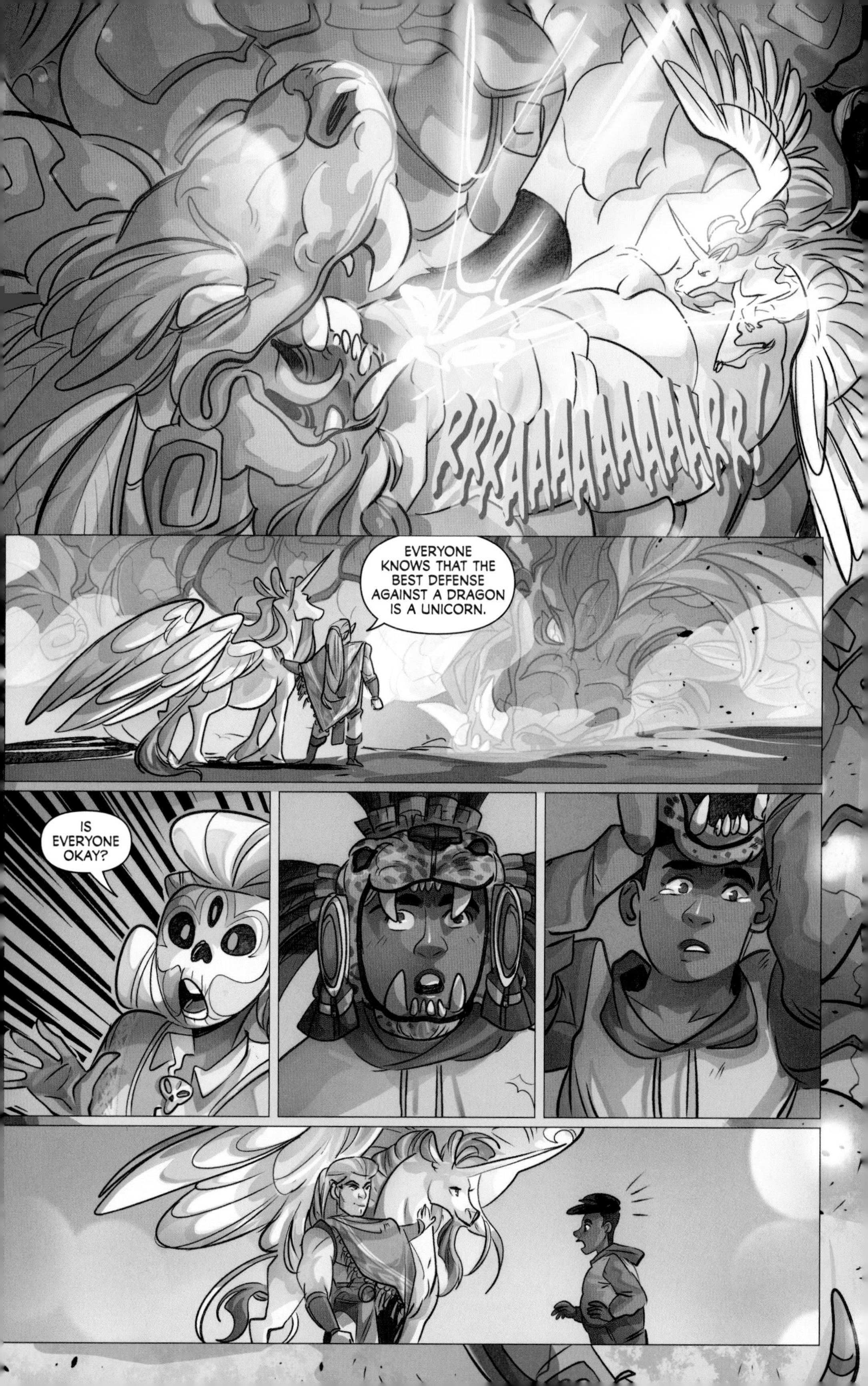
RRRAAAAAAAAAARR!
EVERYONE KNOWS THAT THE BEST DEFENSE AGAINST A DRAGON IS A UNICORN.
IS EVERYONE OKAY?

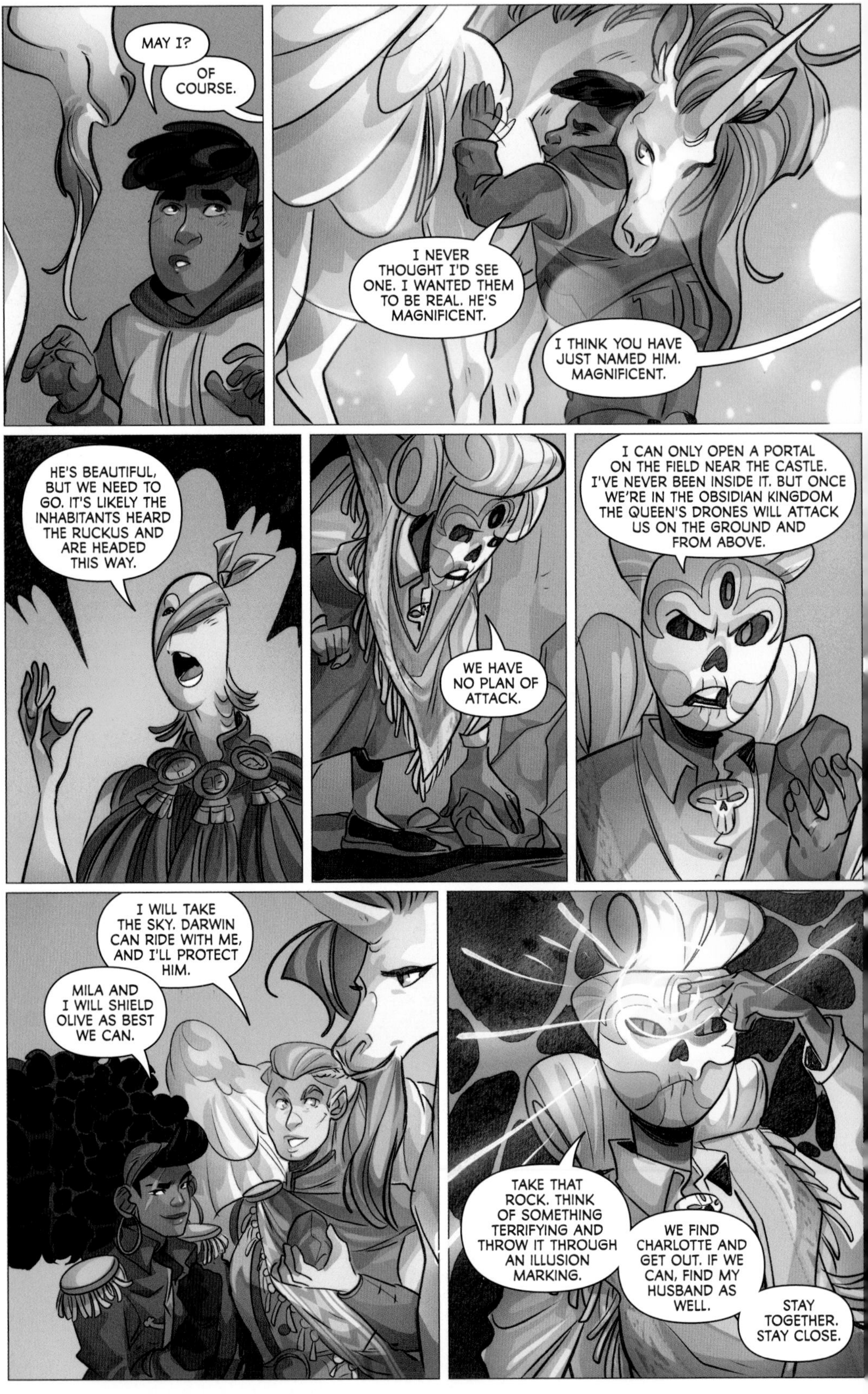
MAY I?
OF COURSE.
I NEVER THOUGHT I'D SEE ONE. I WANTED THEM TO BE REAL. HE'S MAGNIFICENT.
I THINK YOU HAVE JUST NAMED HIM. MAGNIFICENT.
HE'S BEAUTIFUL, BUT WE NEED TO GO. IT'S LIKELY THE INHABITANTS HEARD THE RUCKUS AND ARE HEADED THIS WAY.
WE HAVE NO PLAN OF ATTACK.
I CAN ONLY OPEN A PORTAL ON THE FIELD NEAR THE CASTLE. I'VE NEVER BEEN INSIDE IT. BUT ONCE WE'RE IN THE OBSIDIAN KINGDOM THE QUEEN'S DRONES WILL ATTACK US ON THE GROUND AND FROM ABOVE.
I WILL TAKE THE SKY. DARWIN CAN RIDE WITH ME, AND I'LL PROTECT HIM.
MILA AND I WILL SHIELD OLIVE AS BEST WE CAN.
TAKE THAT ROCK. THINK OF SOMETHING TERRIFYING AND THROW IT THROUGH AN ILLUSION MARKING.
WE FIND CHARLOTTE AND GET OUT. IF WE CAN, FIND MY HUSBAND AS WELL.
STAY TOGETHER. STAY CLOSE.

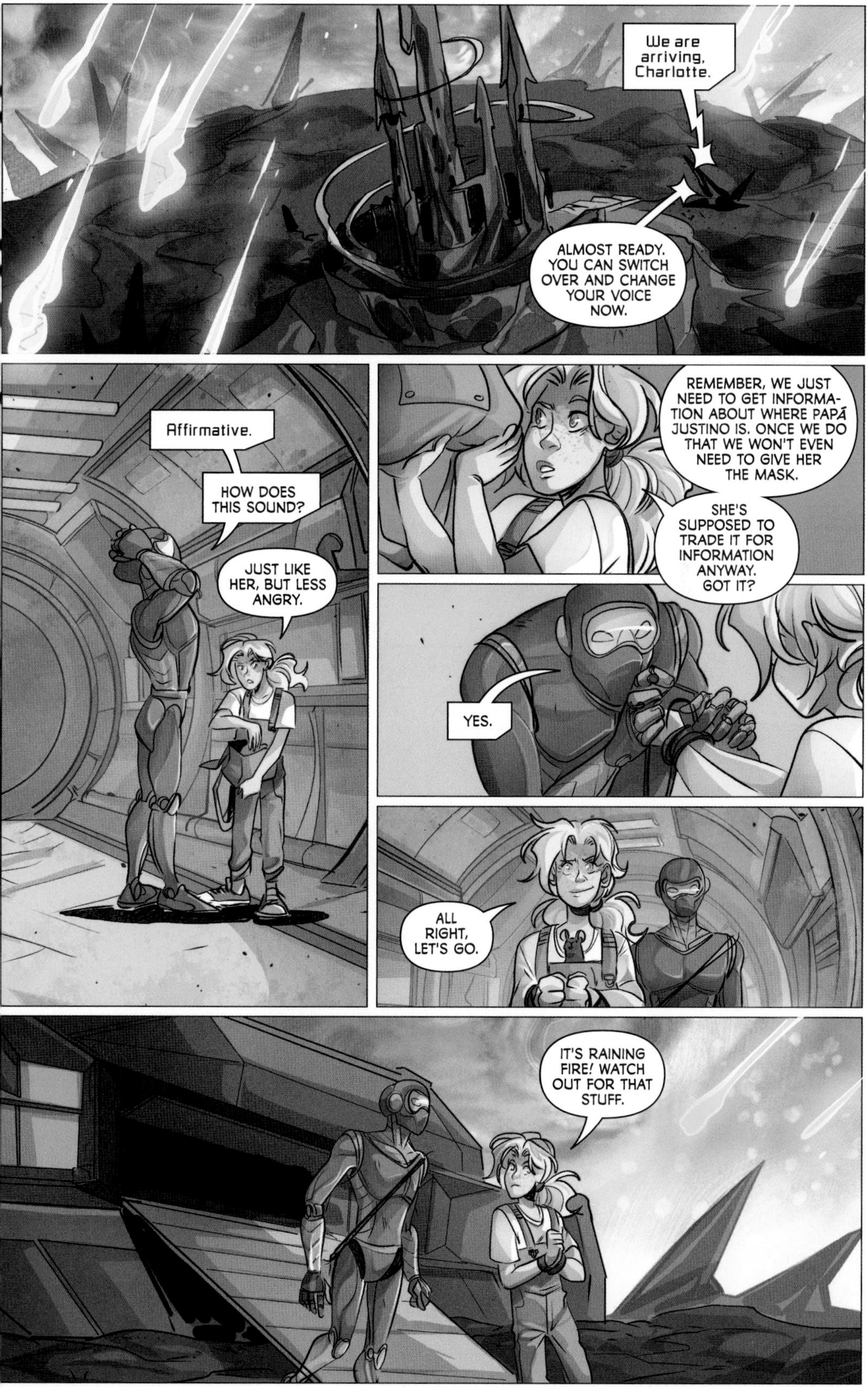

We are arriving, Charlotte.
ALMOST READY. YOU CAN SWITCH OVER AND CHANGE YOUR VOICE NOW.
Affirmative.
HOW DOES THIS SOUND?
JUST LIKE HER, BUT LESS ANGRY.
REMEMBER, WE JUST NEED TO GET INFORMATION ABOUT WHERE PAPÁ JUSTINO IS. ONCE WE DO THAT WE WON'T EVEN NEED TO GIVE HER THE MASK.
SHE'S SUPPOSED TO TRADE IT FOR INFORMATION ANYWAY. GOT IT?
YES.
ALL RIGHT, LET'S GO.
IT'S RAINING FIRE! WATCH OUT FOR THAT STUFF.

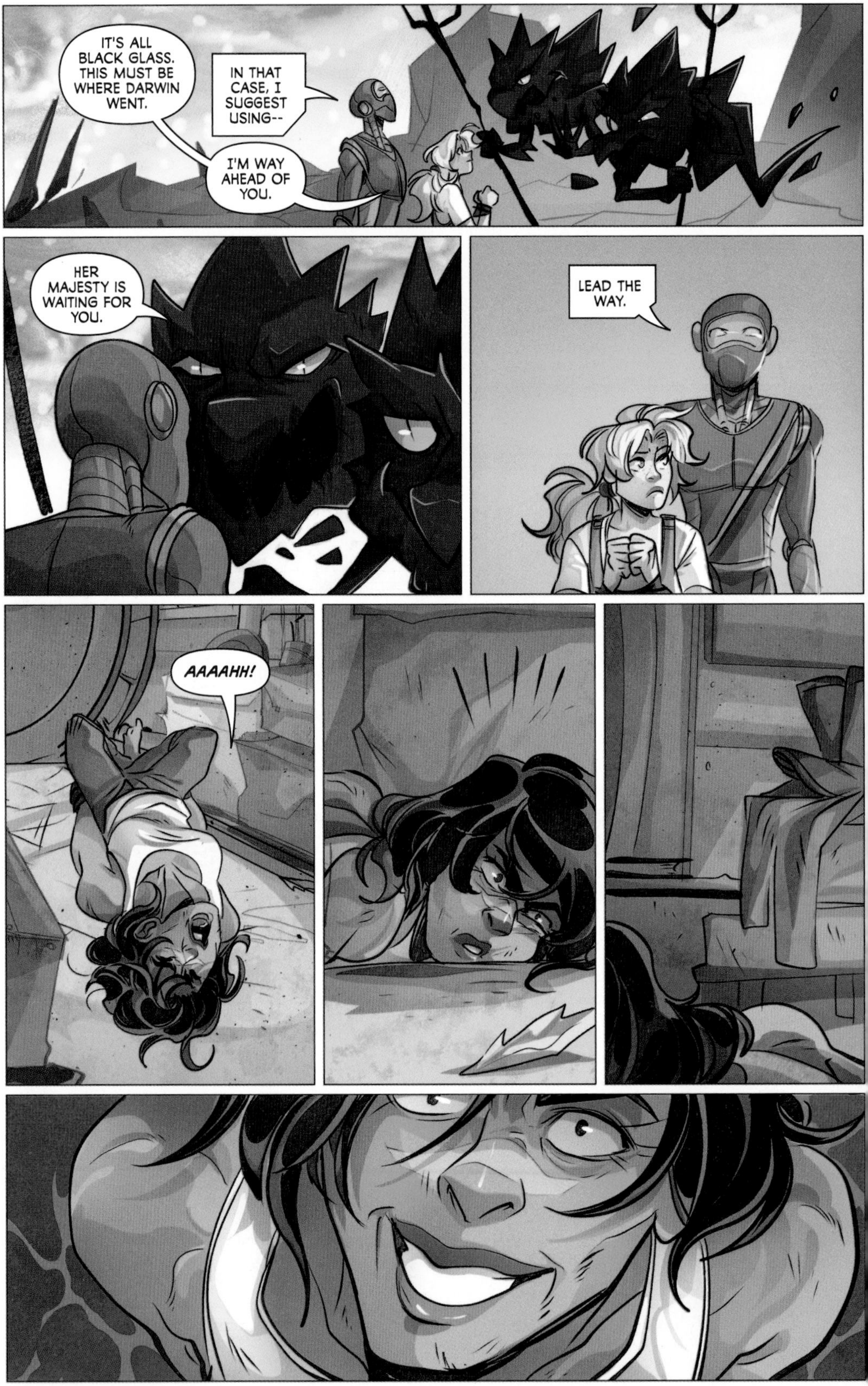
IT'S ALL BLACK GLASS. THIS MUST BE WHERE DARWIN WENT.
IN THAT CASE, I SUGGEST USING--
I'M WAY AHEAD OF YOU.
HER MAJESTY IS WAITING FOR YOU.
LEAD THE WAY.
AAAAHH!

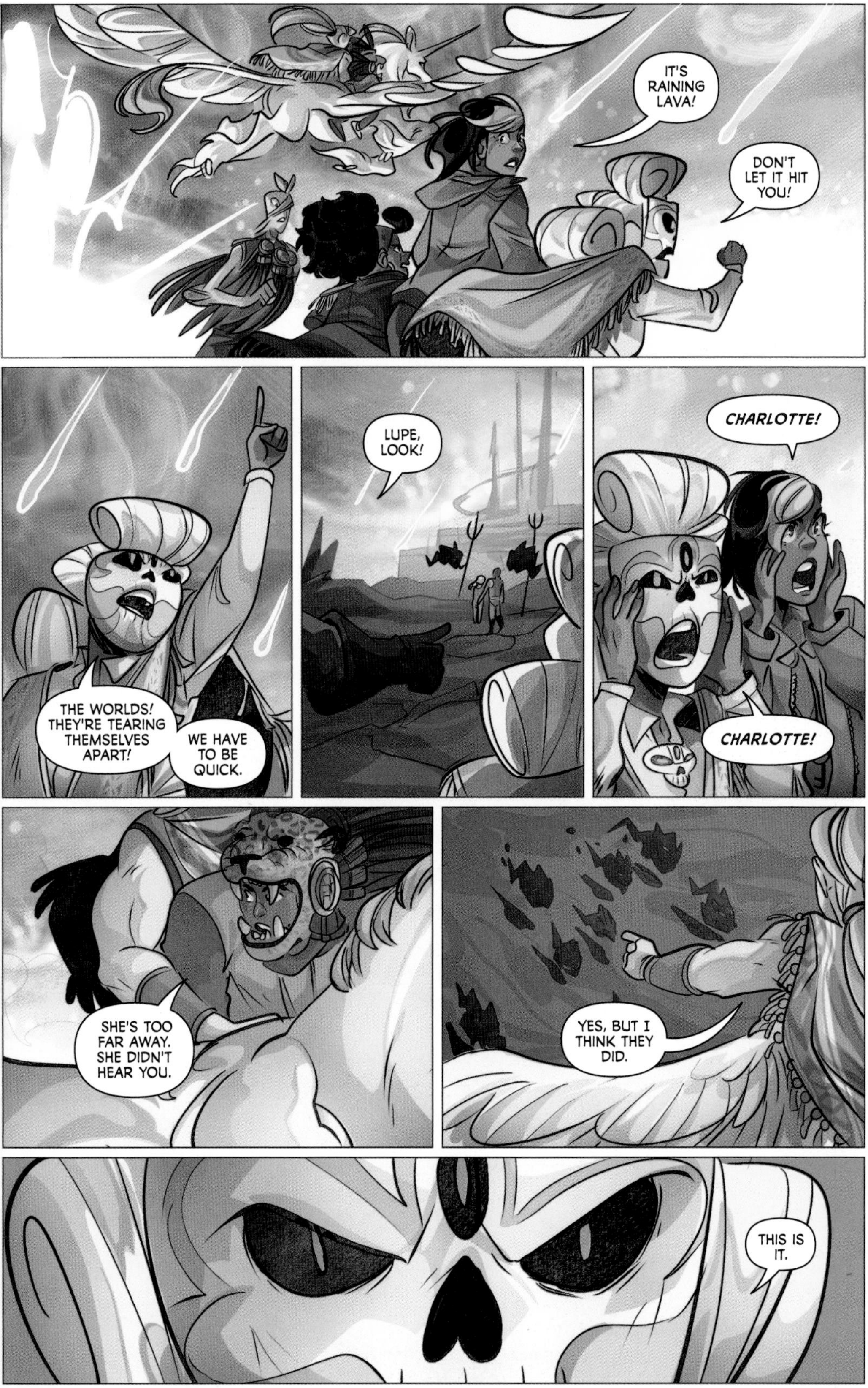
IT'S RAINING LAVA!
DON'T LET IT HIT YOU!
THE WORLDS! THEY'RE TEARING THEMSELVES APART!
WE HAVE TO BE QUICK.
LUPE, LOOK!
CHARLOTTE!
CHARLOTTE!
SHE'S TOO FAR AWAY. SHE DIDN'T HEAR YOU.
YES, BUT I THINK THEY DID.
THIS IS IT.

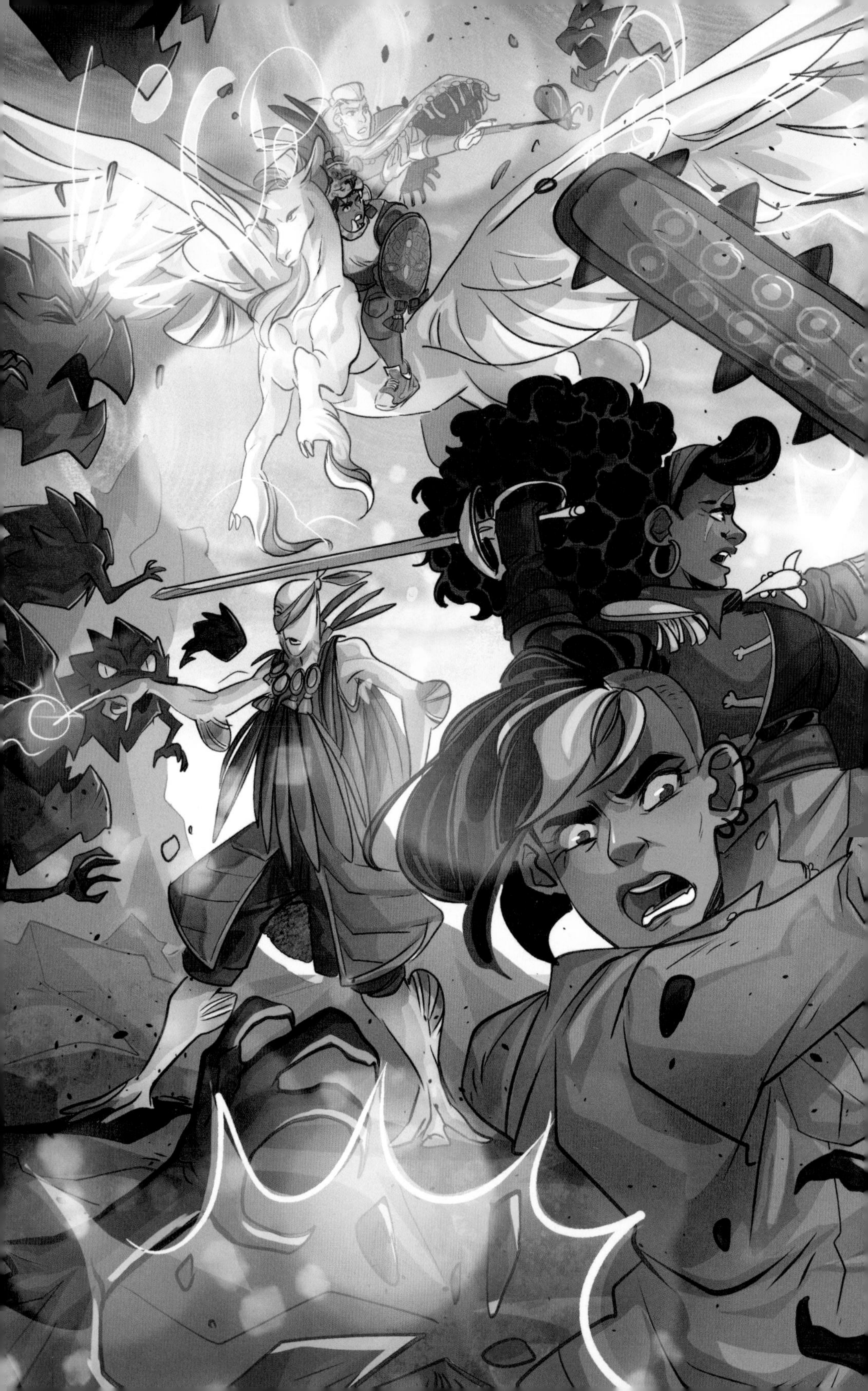

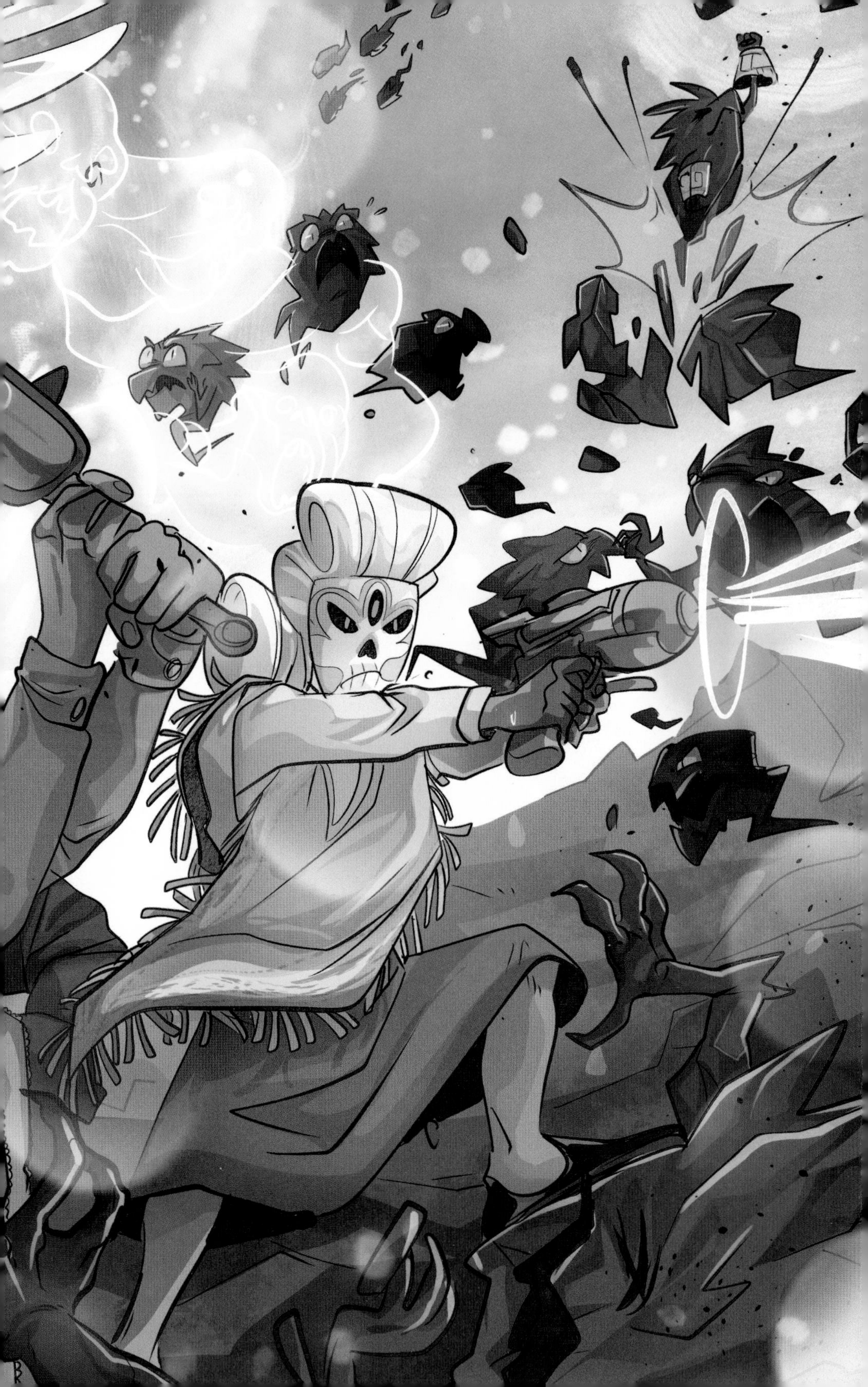

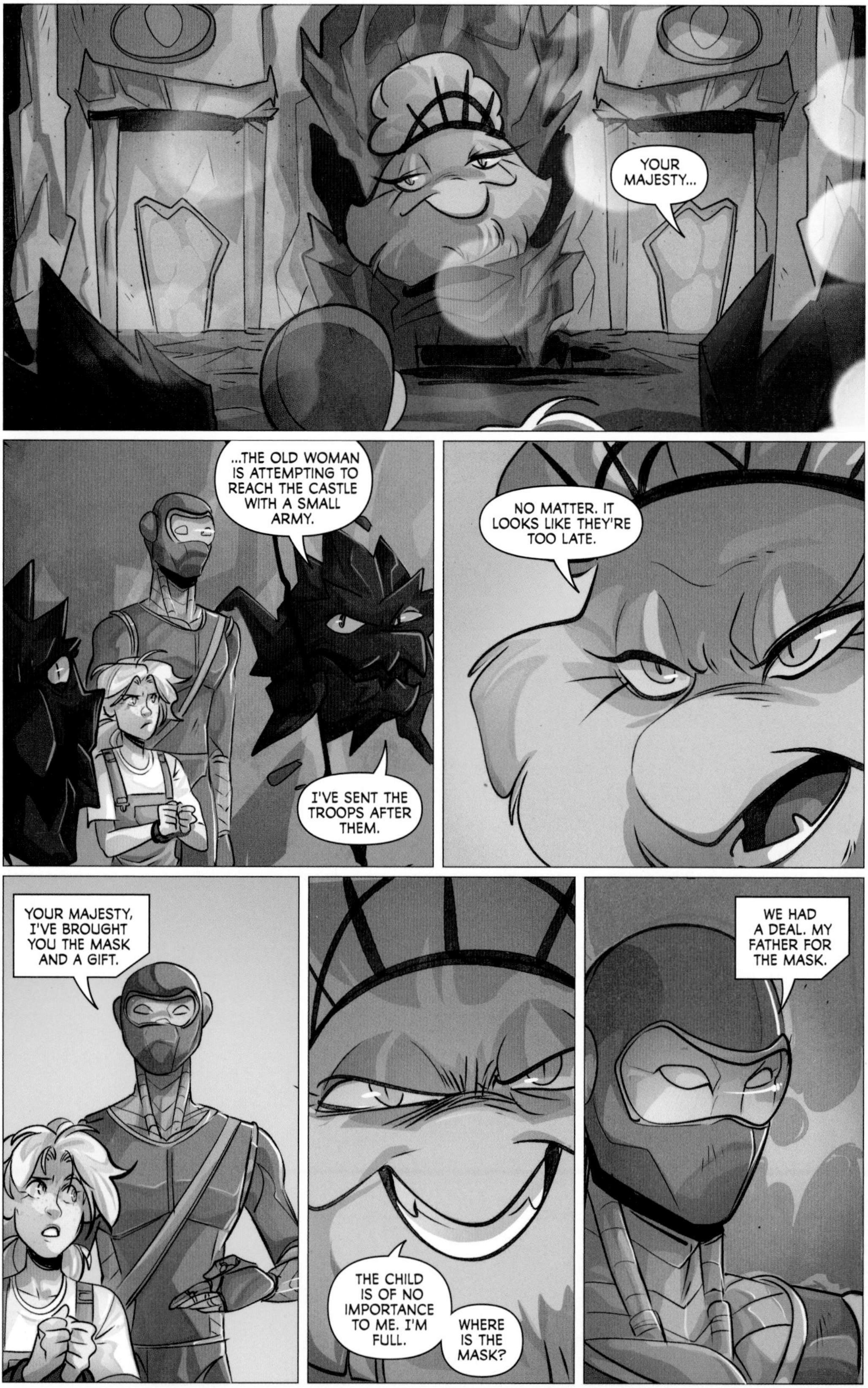
YOUR MAJESTY...
...THE OLD WOMAN IS ATTEMPTING TO REACH THE CASTLE WITH A SMALL ARMY.
I'VE SENT THE TROOPS AFTER THEM.
NO MATTER. IT LOOKS LIKE THEY'RE TOO LATE.
YOUR MAJESTY, I'VE BROUGHT YOU THE MASK AND A GIFT.
THE CHILD IS OF NO IMPORTANCE TO ME. I'M FULL.
WHERE IS THE MASK?
WE HAD A DEAL. MY FATHER FOR THE MASK.

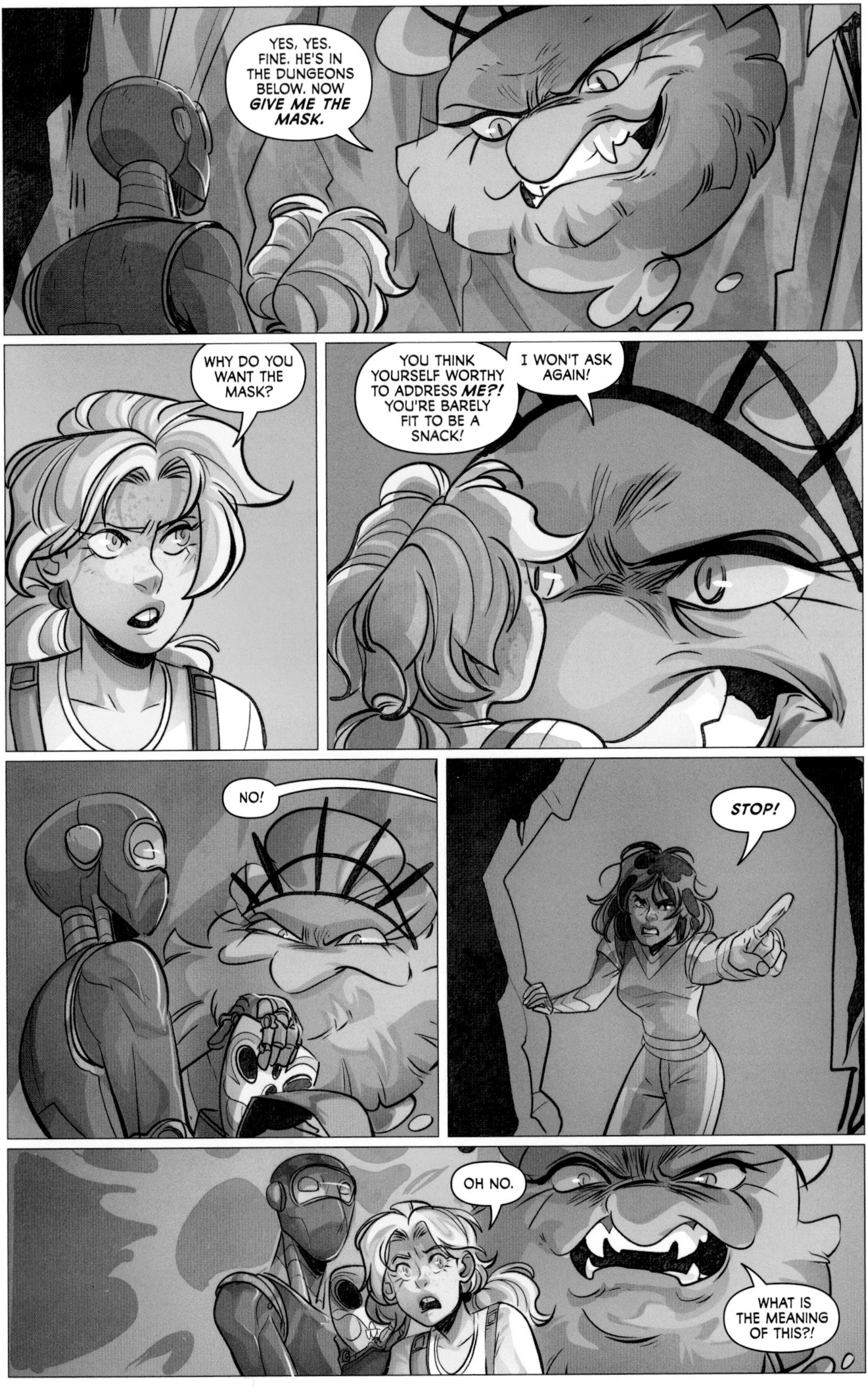
YES, YES. FINE. HE'S IN THE DUNGEONS BELOW. NOW *GIVE ME THE MASK.*
WHY DO YOU WANT THE MASK?
YOU THINK YOURSELF WORTHY TO ADDRESS *ME?!* YOU'RE BARELY FIT TO BE A SNACK!
I WON'T ASK AGAIN!
NO!
STOP!
OH NO.
WHAT IS THE MEANING OF THIS?!

THAT'S NOT WHO YOU THINK IT IS!

I'M XOCHITL! *I* MADE THE DEAL WITH YOU FOR MY FATHER!

I BROUGHT YOU THE MASK. THEY'RE IMPOSTERS!

This is a rock.

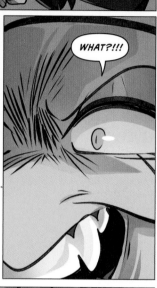

WHAT?!!!

NO! IT WAS THE MASK! WHAT HAPPENED?

TAKE THEM TO THE DUNGEONS!

HOW DARE YOU ATTEMPT TO FOOL ME!

HOW *DARE?!*

THIS IS HOW!

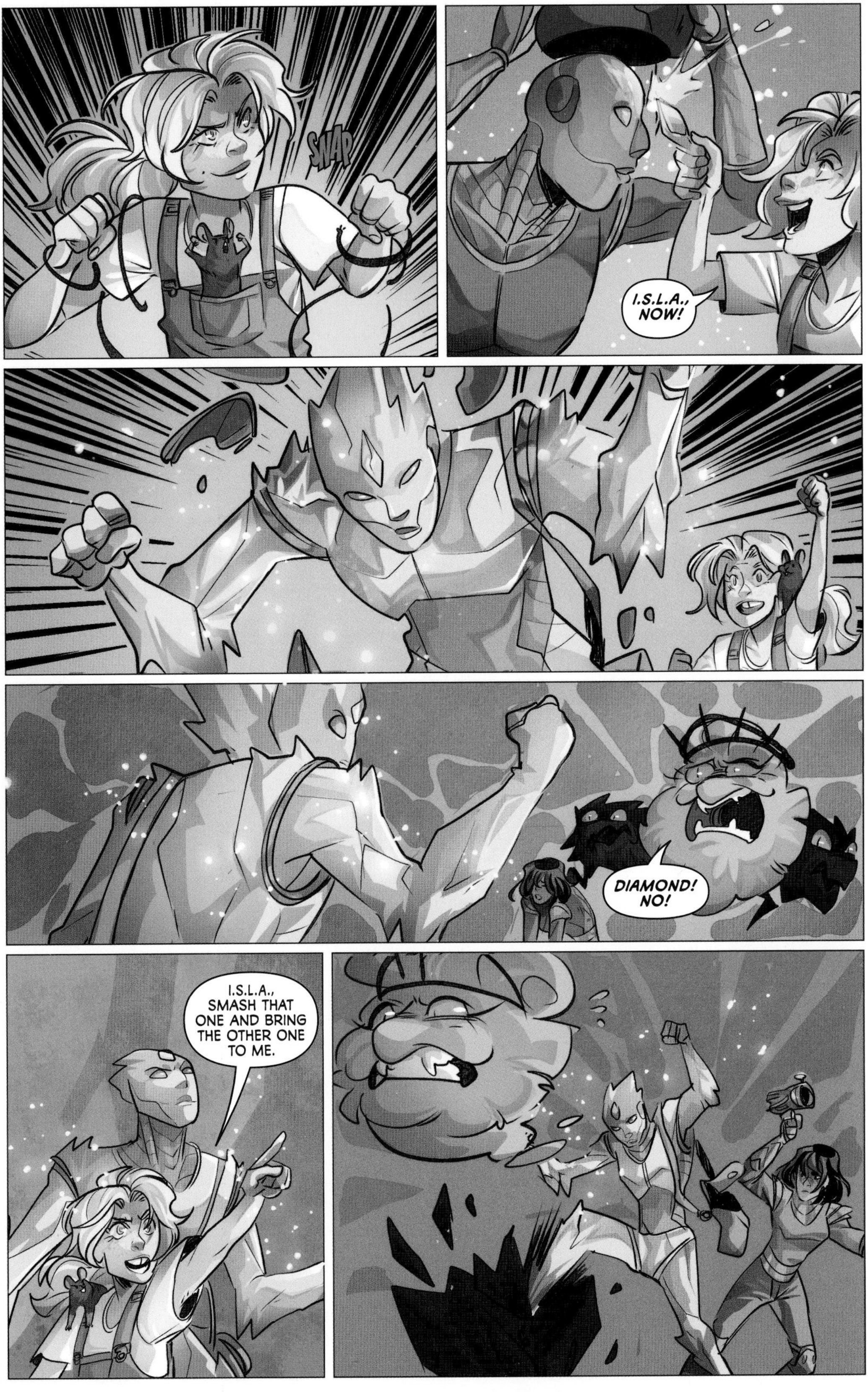
SNAP
I.S.L.A., NOW!
DIAMOND! NO!
I.S.L.A., SMASH THAT ONE AND BRING THE OTHER ONE TO ME.

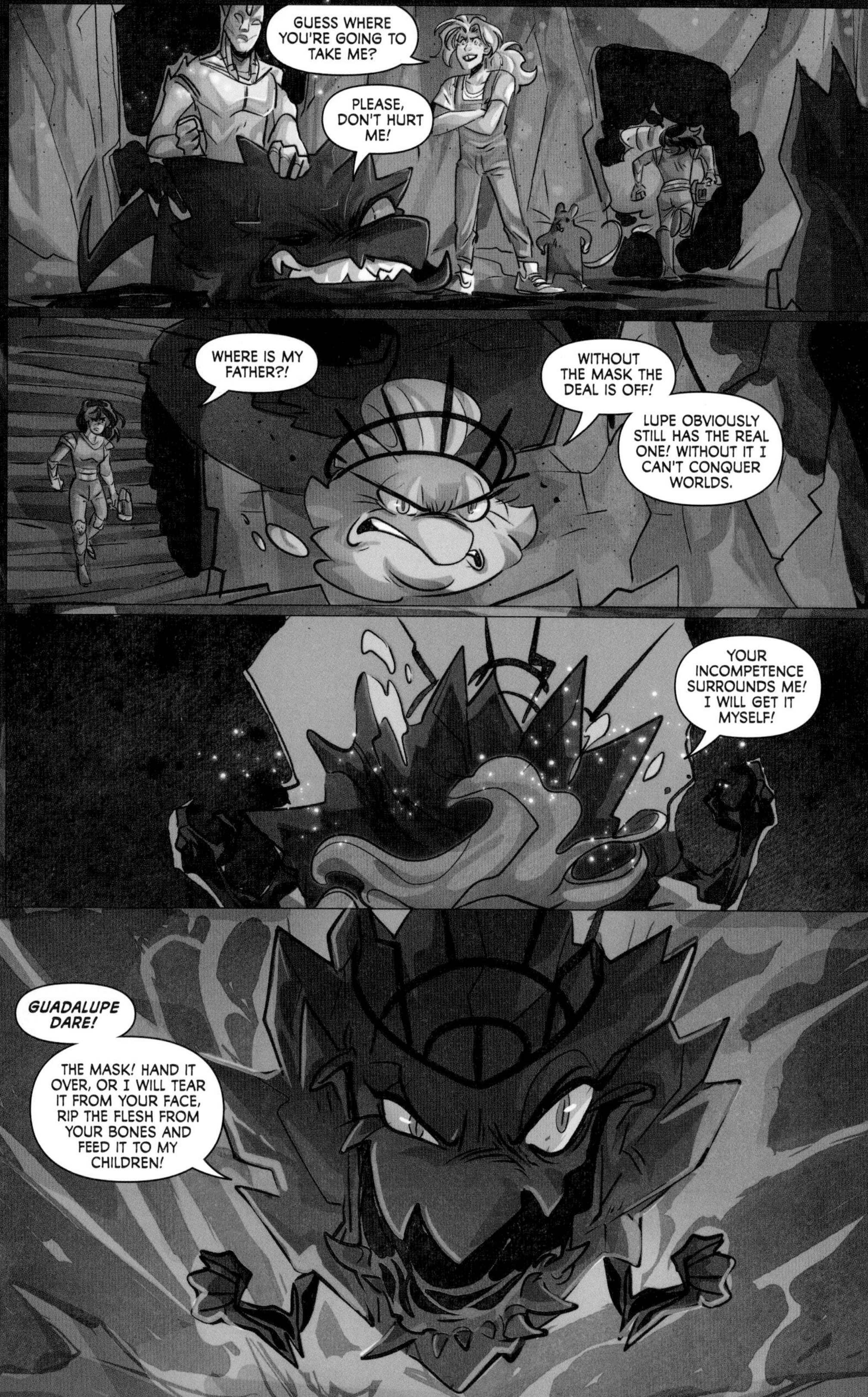
GUESS WHERE YOU'RE GOING TO TAKE ME?
PLEASE, DON'T HURT ME!
WHERE IS MY FATHER?!
WITHOUT THE MASK THE DEAL IS OFF!
LUPE OBVIOUSLY STILL HAS THE REAL ONE! WITHOUT IT I CAN'T CONQUER WORLDS.
YOUR INCOMPETENCE SURROUNDS ME! I WILL GET IT MYSELF!
GUADALUPE DARE!
THE MASK! HAND IT OVER, OR I WILL TEAR IT FROM YOUR FACE, RIP THE FLESH FROM YOUR BONES AND FEED IT TO MY CHILDREN!

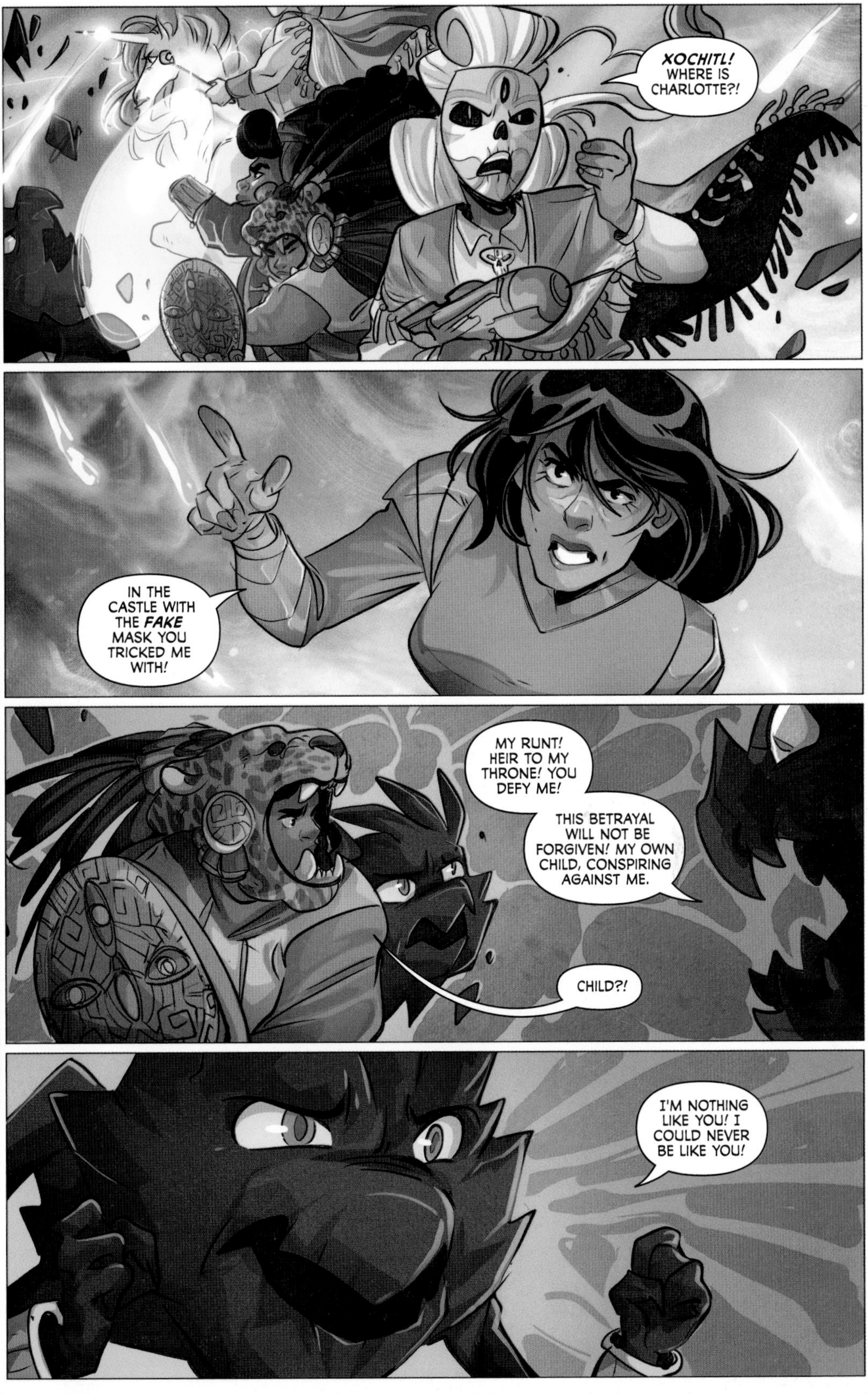
XOCHITL! WHERE IS CHARLOTTE?!
IN THE CASTLE WITH THE FAKE MASK YOU TRICKED ME WITH!
MY RUNT! HEIR TO MY THRONE! YOU DEFY ME!
THIS BETRAYAL WILL NOT BE FORGIVEN! MY OWN CHILD, CONSPIRING AGAINST ME.
CHILD?!
I'M NOTHING LIKE YOU! I COULD NEVER BE LIKE YOU!

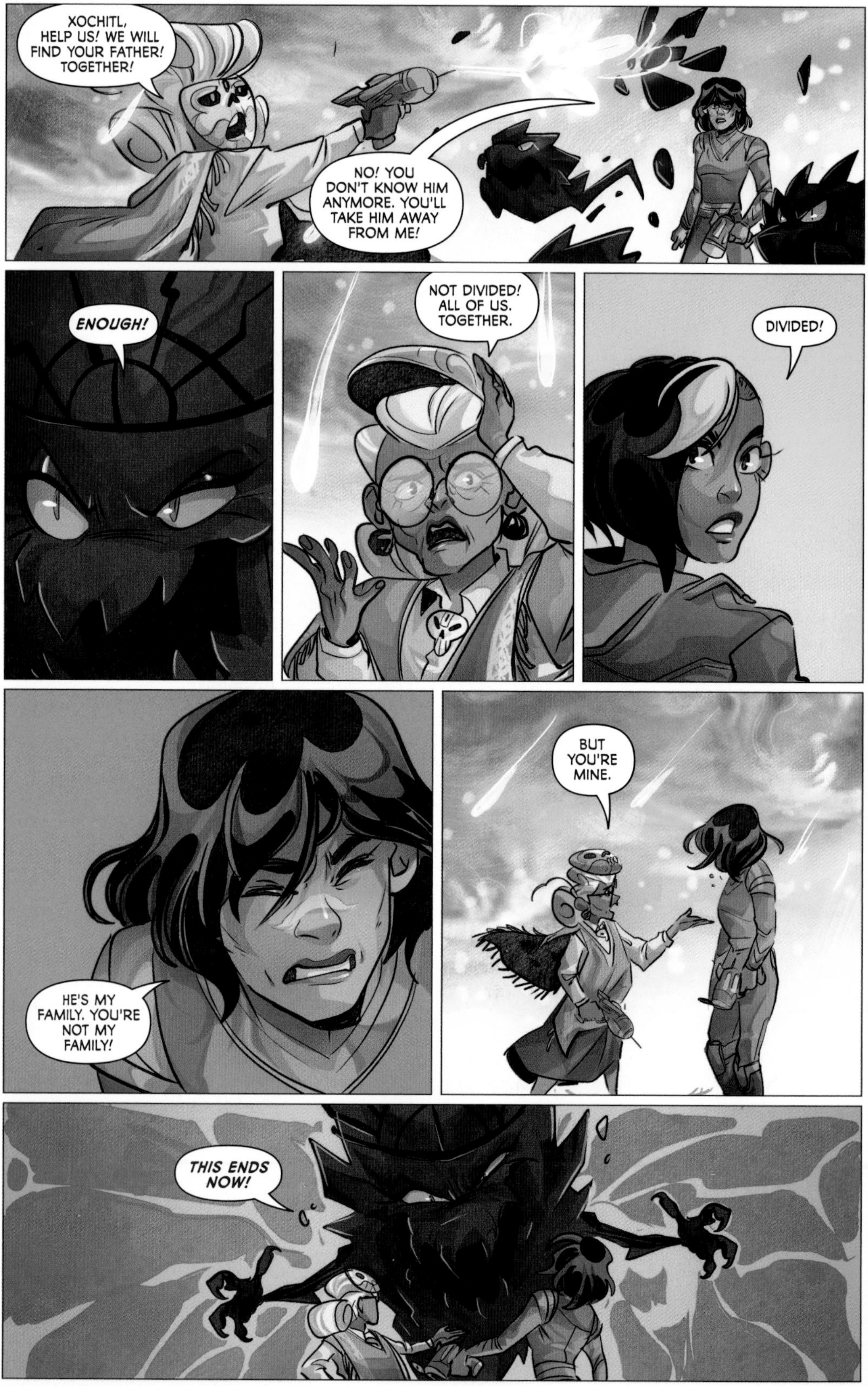
XOCHITL, HELP US! WE WILL FIND YOUR FATHER! TOGETHER!
NO! YOU DON'T KNOW HIM ANYMORE. YOU'LL TAKE HIM AWAY FROM ME!
ENOUGH!
NOT DIVIDED! ALL OF US. TOGETHER.
DIVIDED!
HE'S MY FAMILY. YOU'RE NOT MY FAMILY!
BUT YOU'RE MINE.
THIS ENDS NOW!

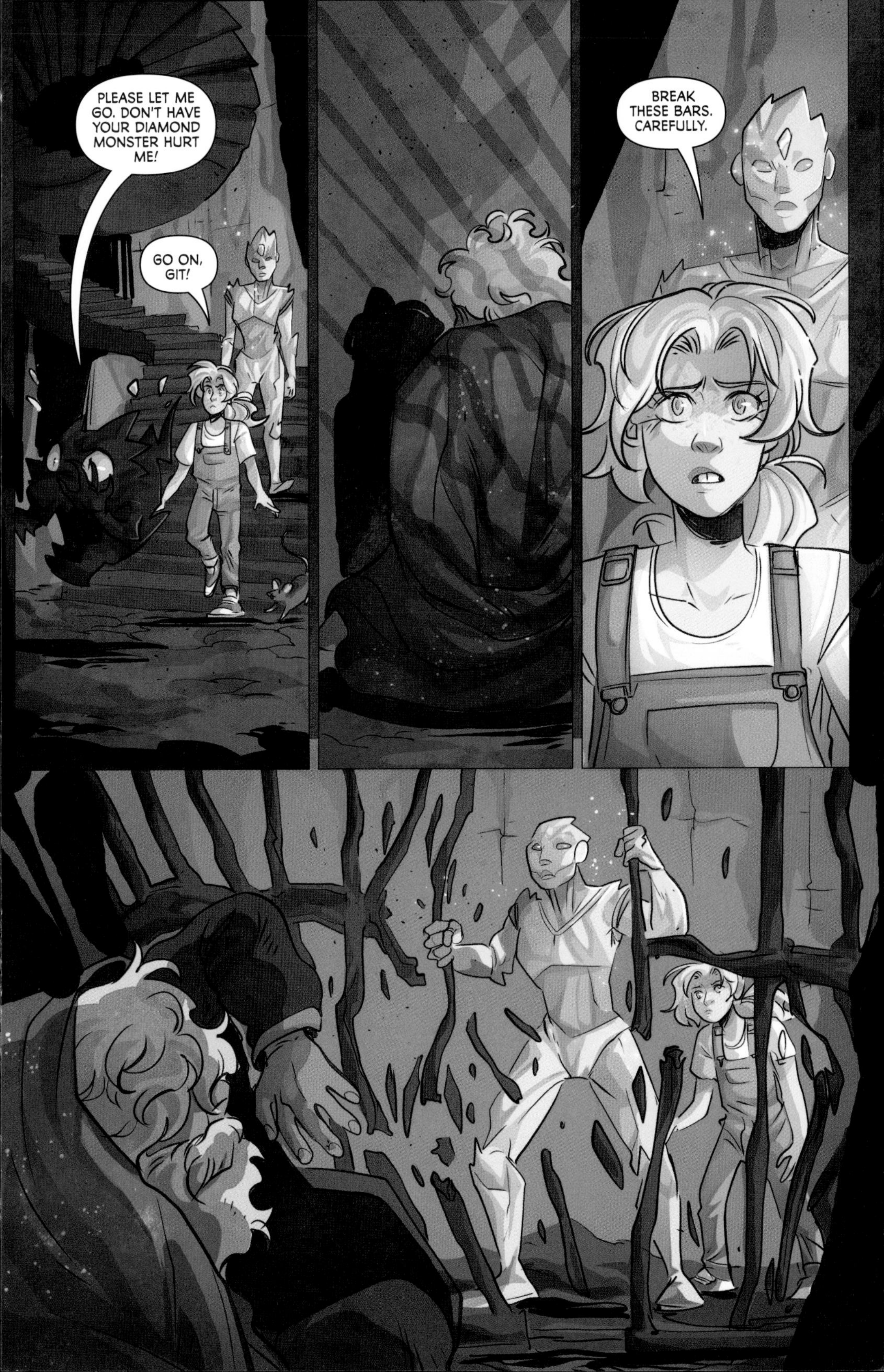
PLEASE LET ME GO. DON'T HAVE YOUR DIAMOND MONSTER HURT ME!
GO ON, GIT!
BREAK THESE BARS. CAREFULLY.

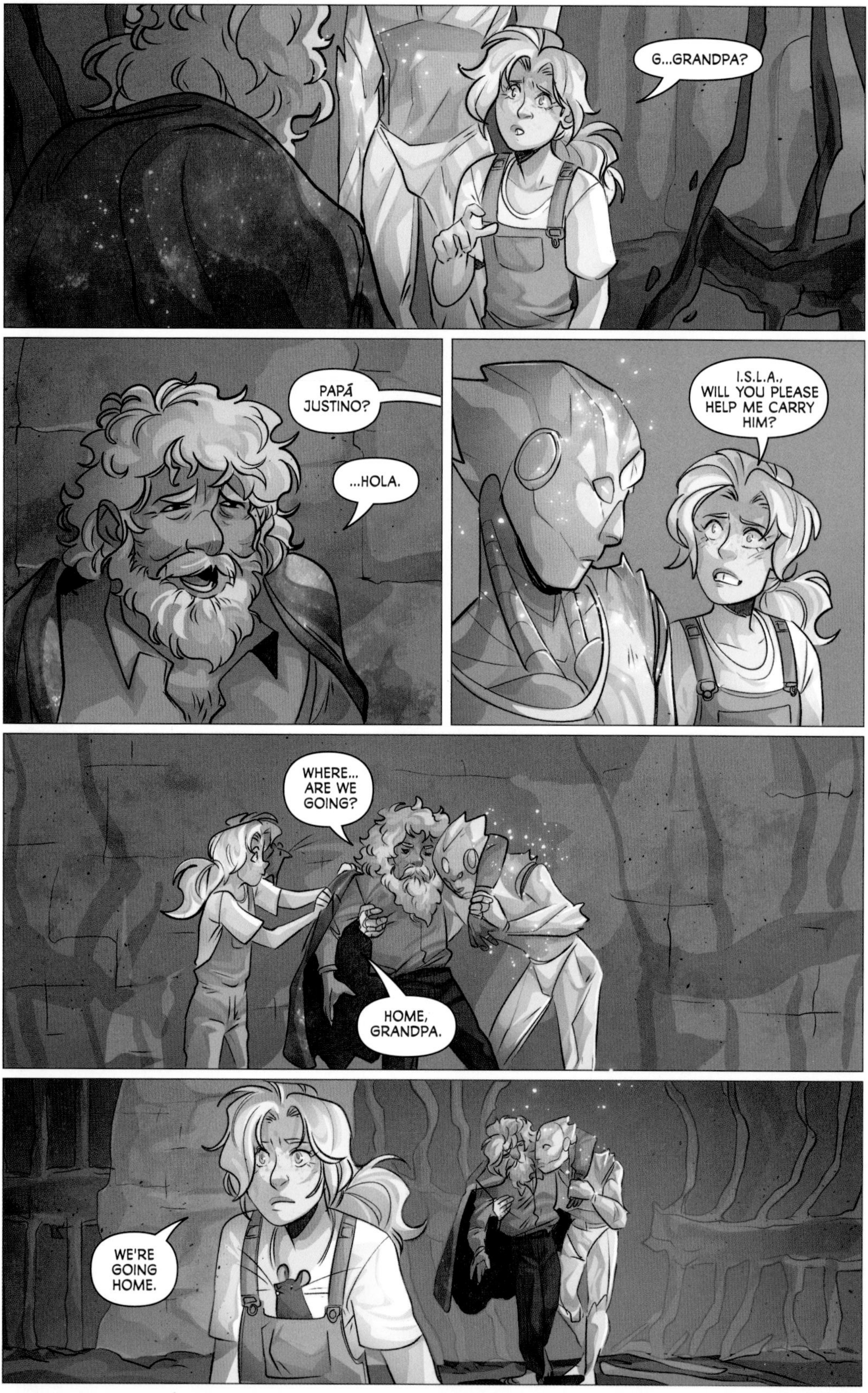
G...GRANDPA?
PAPÁ JUSTINO?
...HOLA.
I.S.L.A., WILL YOU PLEASE HELP ME CARRY HIM?
WHERE... ARE WE GOING?
HOME, GRANDPA.
WE'RE GOING HOME.

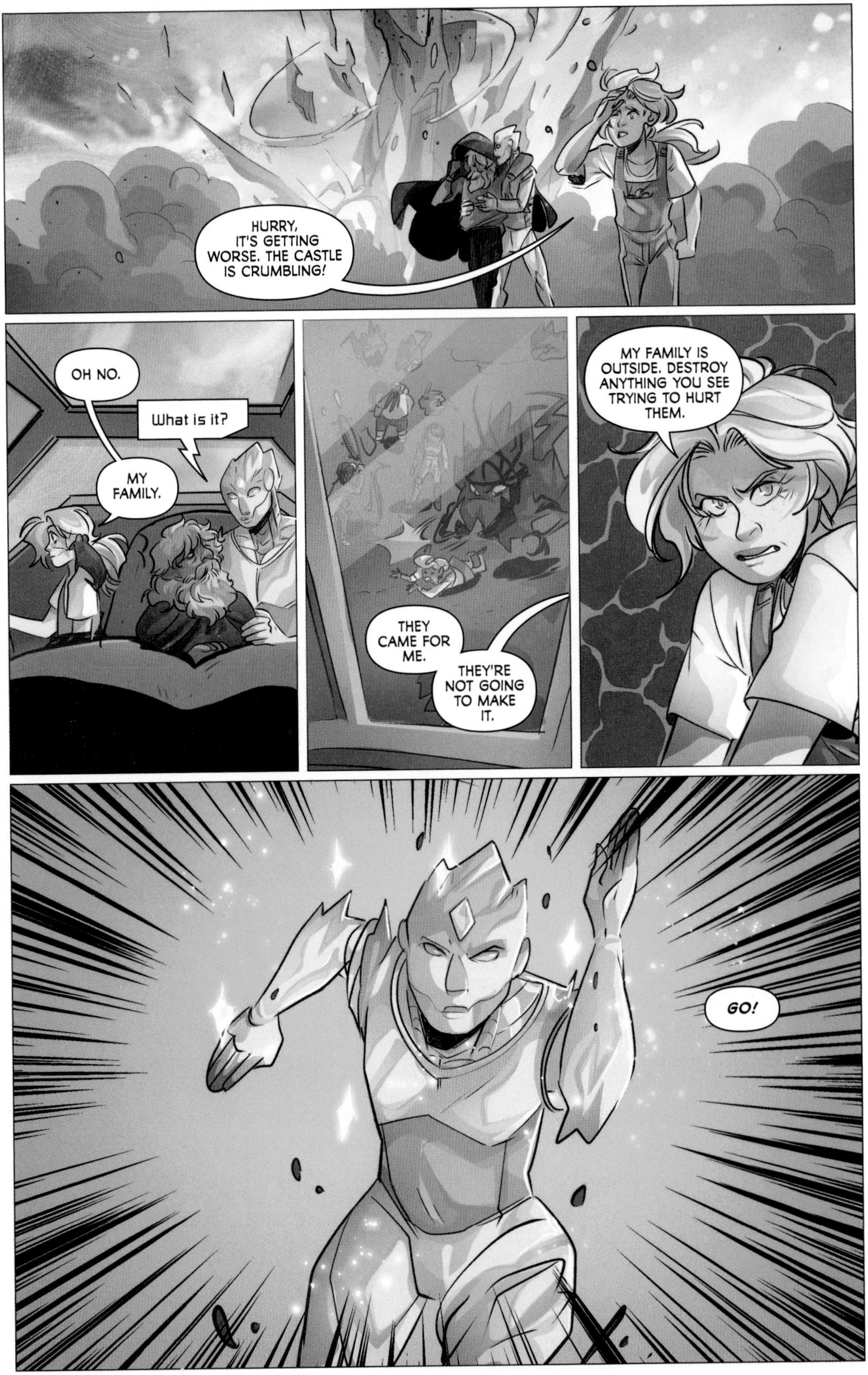
HURRY, IT'S GETTING WORSE. THE CASTLE IS CRUMBLING!
OH NO.
What is it?
MY FAMILY.
THEY CAME FOR ME.
THEY'RE NOT GOING TO MAKE IT.
MY FAMILY IS OUTSIDE. DESTROY ANYTHING YOU SEE TRYING TO HURT THEM.
GO!

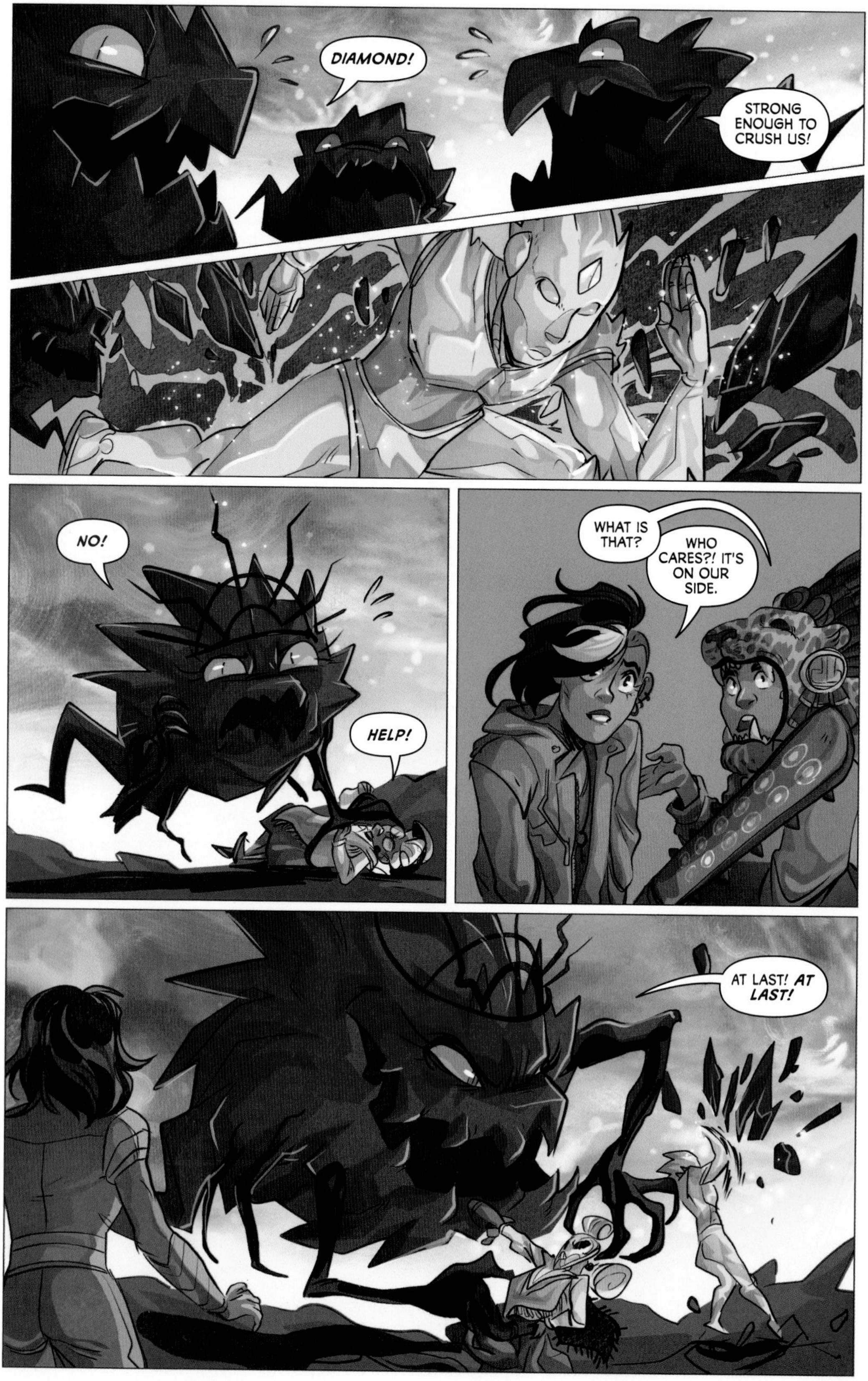
DIAMOND!
STRONG ENOUGH TO CRUSH US!
NO!
HELP!
WHAT IS THAT?
WHO CARES?! IT'S ON OUR SIDE.
AT LAST! AT LAST!

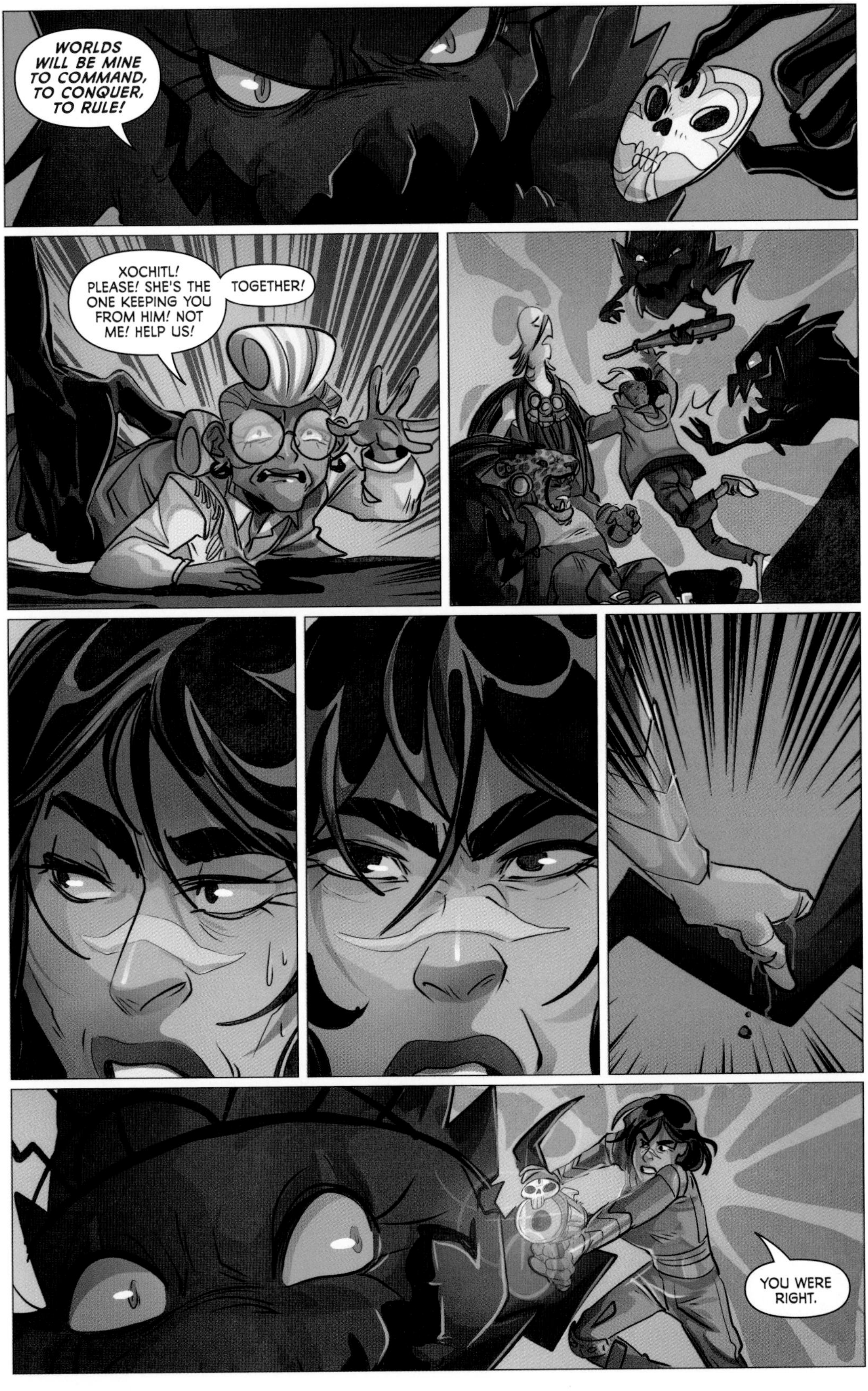
WORLDS WILL BE MINE TO COMMAND, TO CONQUER, TO RULE!
XOCHITL! PLEASE! SHE'S THE ONE KEEPING YOU FROM HIM! NOT ME! HELP US!
TOGETHER!
YOU WERE RIGHT.

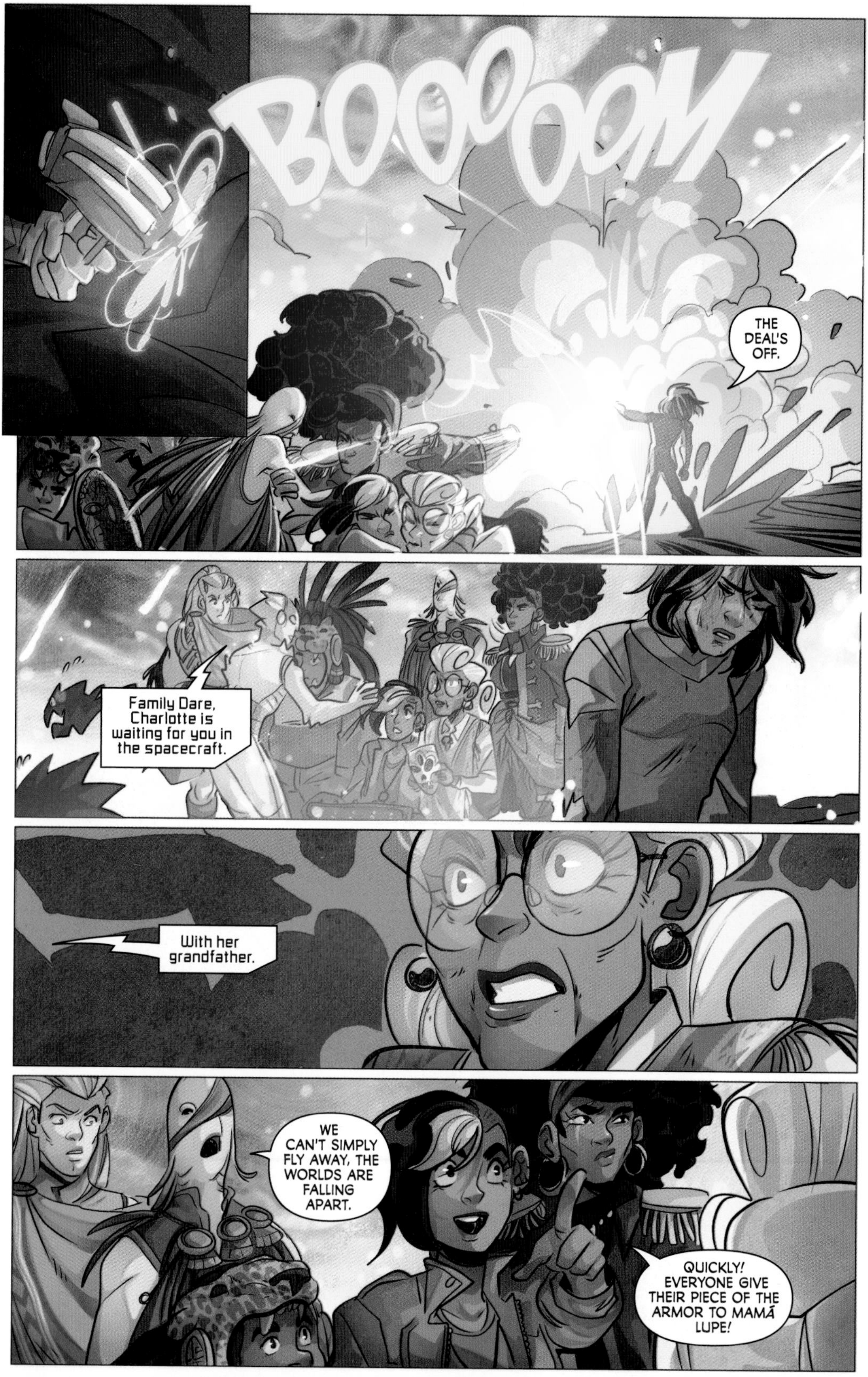
BOOOOOM
THE DEAL'S OFF.
Family Dare, Charlotte is waiting for you in the spacecraft.
With her grandfather.
WE CAN'T SIMPLY FLY AWAY, THE WORLDS ARE FALLING APART.
QUICKLY! EVERYONE GIVE THEIR PIECE OF THE ARMOR TO MAMÁ LUPE!

WHAT? ME? WHY?

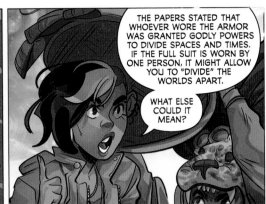

THE PAPERS STATED THAT WHOEVER WORE THE ARMOR WAS GRANTED GODLY POWERS TO DIVIDE SPACES AND TIMES. IF THE FULL SUIT IS WORN BY ONE PERSON, IT MIGHT ALLOW YOU TO "DIVIDE" THE WORLDS APART.

WHAT ELSE COULD IT MEAN?

IT IS WORTH A TRY.

DO IT FAST!

IT'S NOT WORKING. NOTHING'S HAPPENING.

YOU DON'T HAVE THE FULL SUIT.

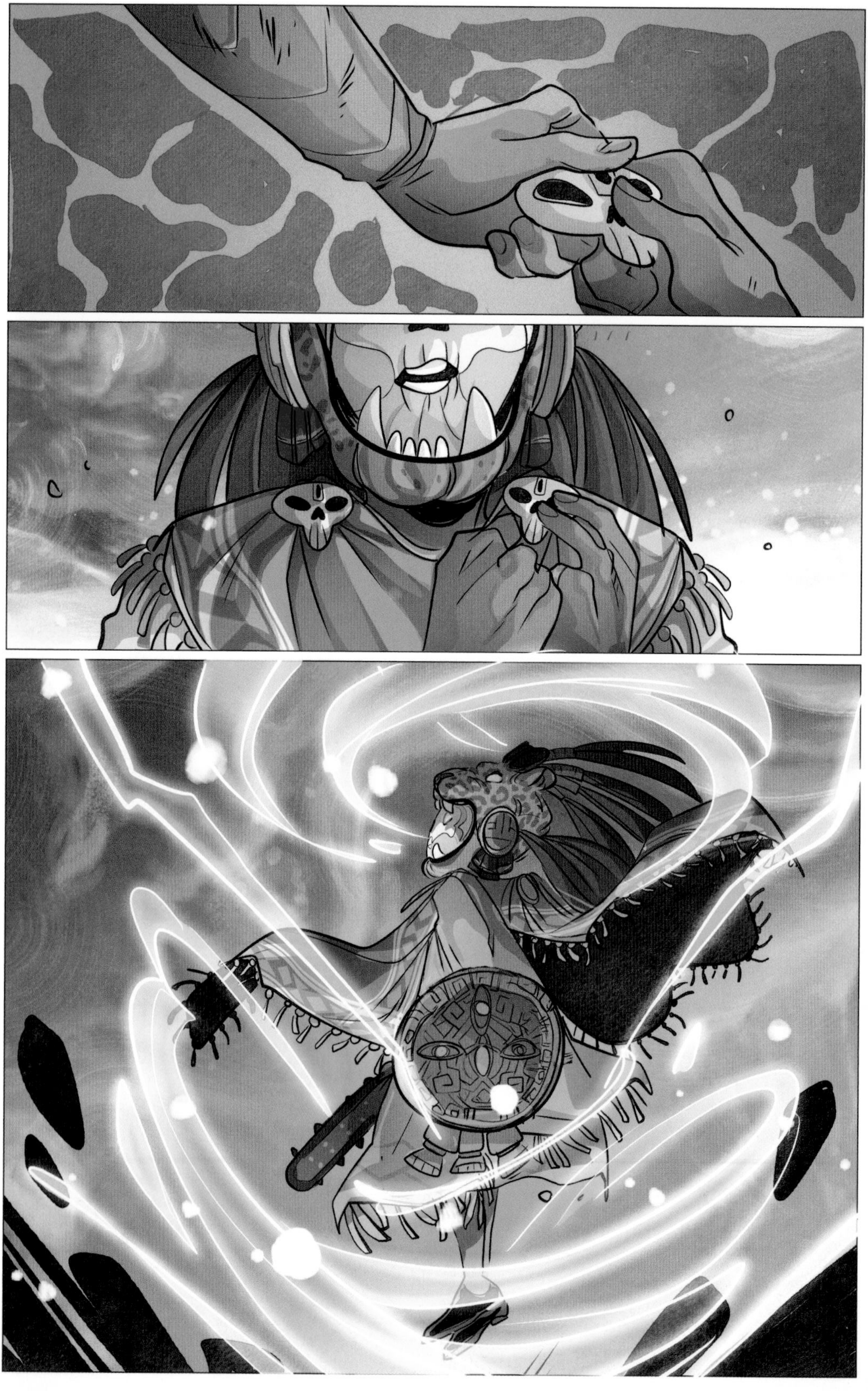

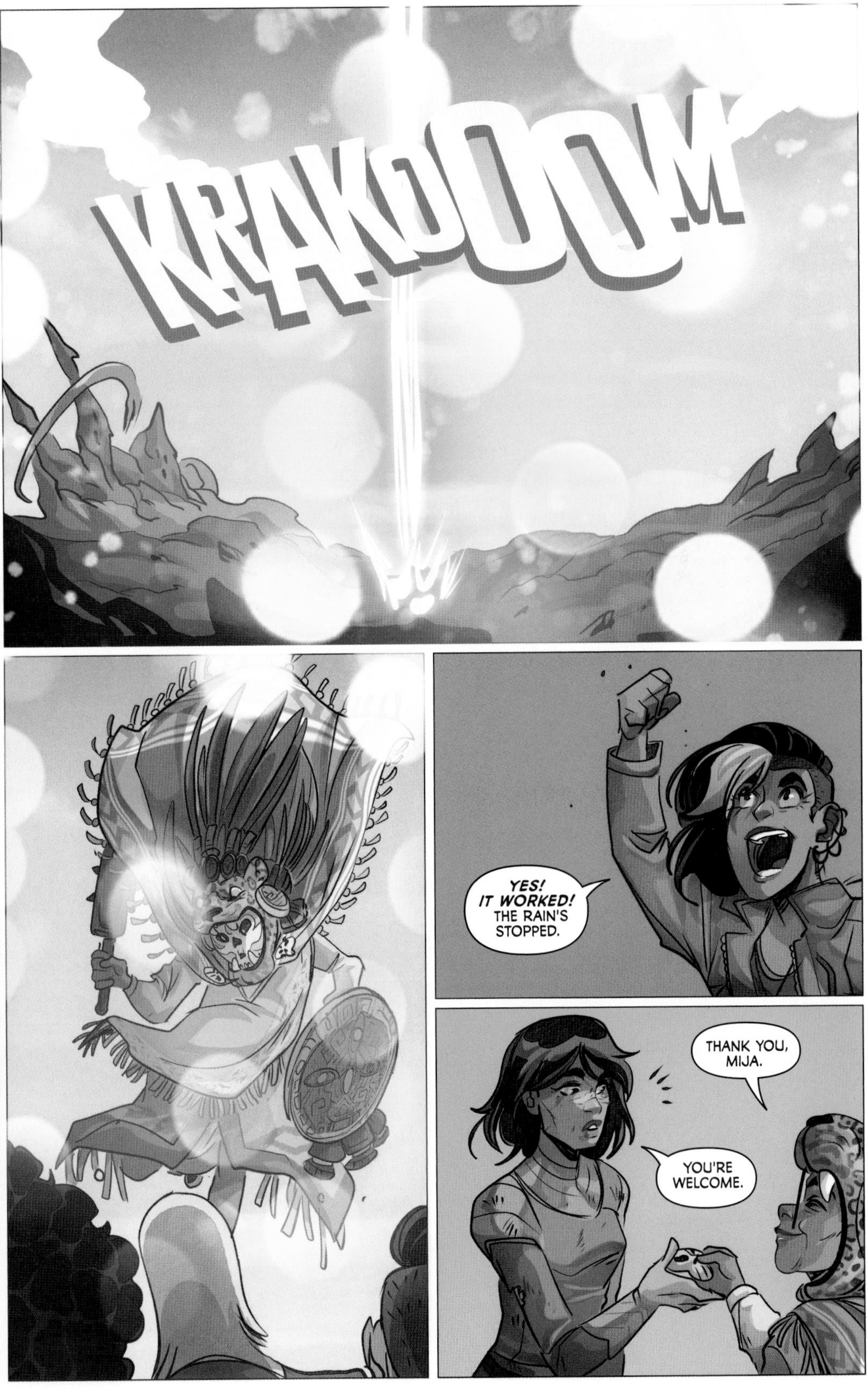
KRAKOOOM
YES! IT WORKED! THE RAIN'S STOPPED.
THANK YOU, MIJA.
YOU'RE WELCOME.

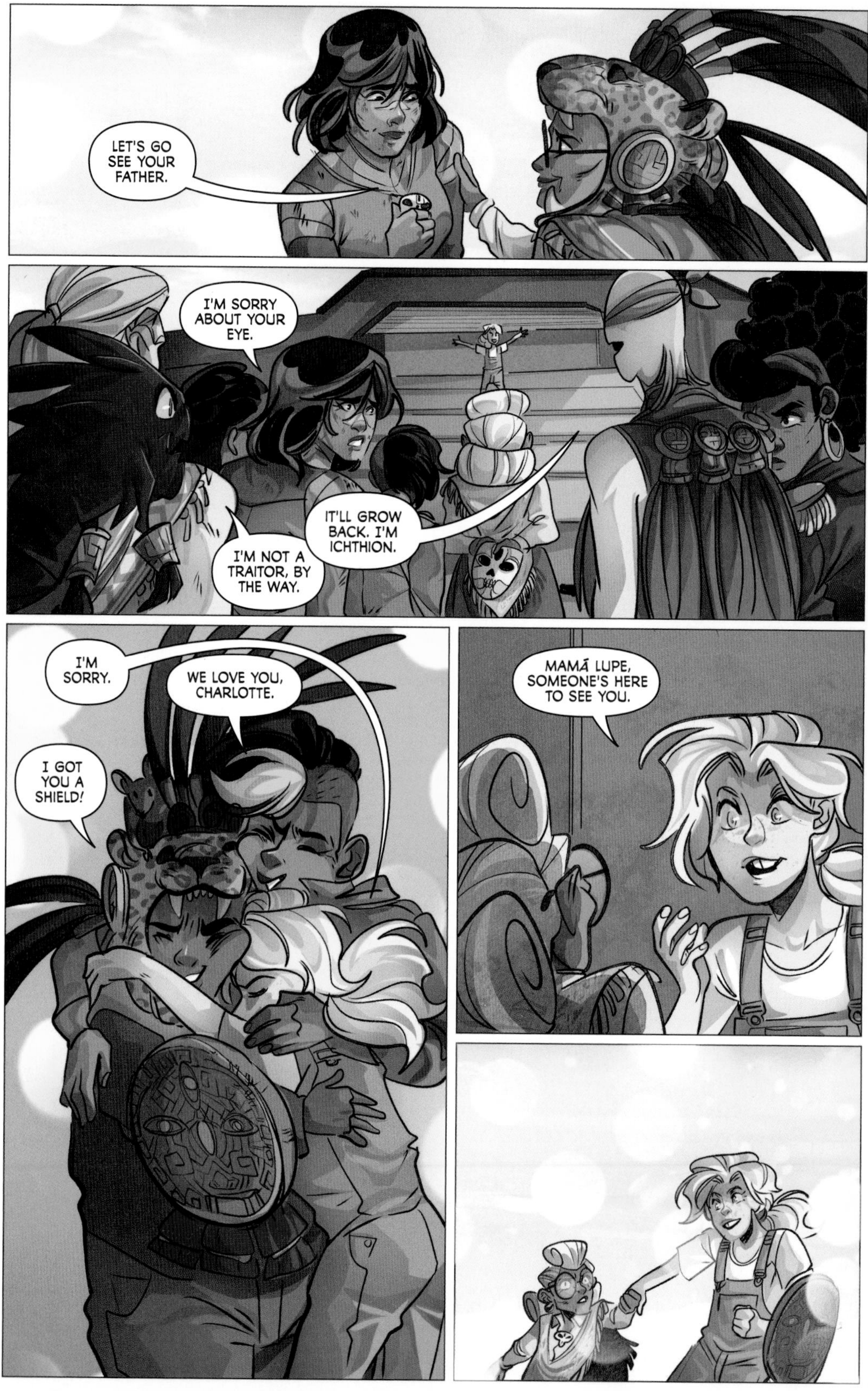
LET'S GO SEE YOUR FATHER.
I'M SORRY ABOUT YOUR EYE.
I'M NOT A TRAITOR, BY THE WAY.
IT'LL GROW BACK. I'M ICHTHION.
I'M SORRY.
WE LOVE YOU, CHARLOTTE.
I GOT YOU A SHIELD!
MAMÁ LUPE, SOMEONE'S HERE TO SEE YOU.

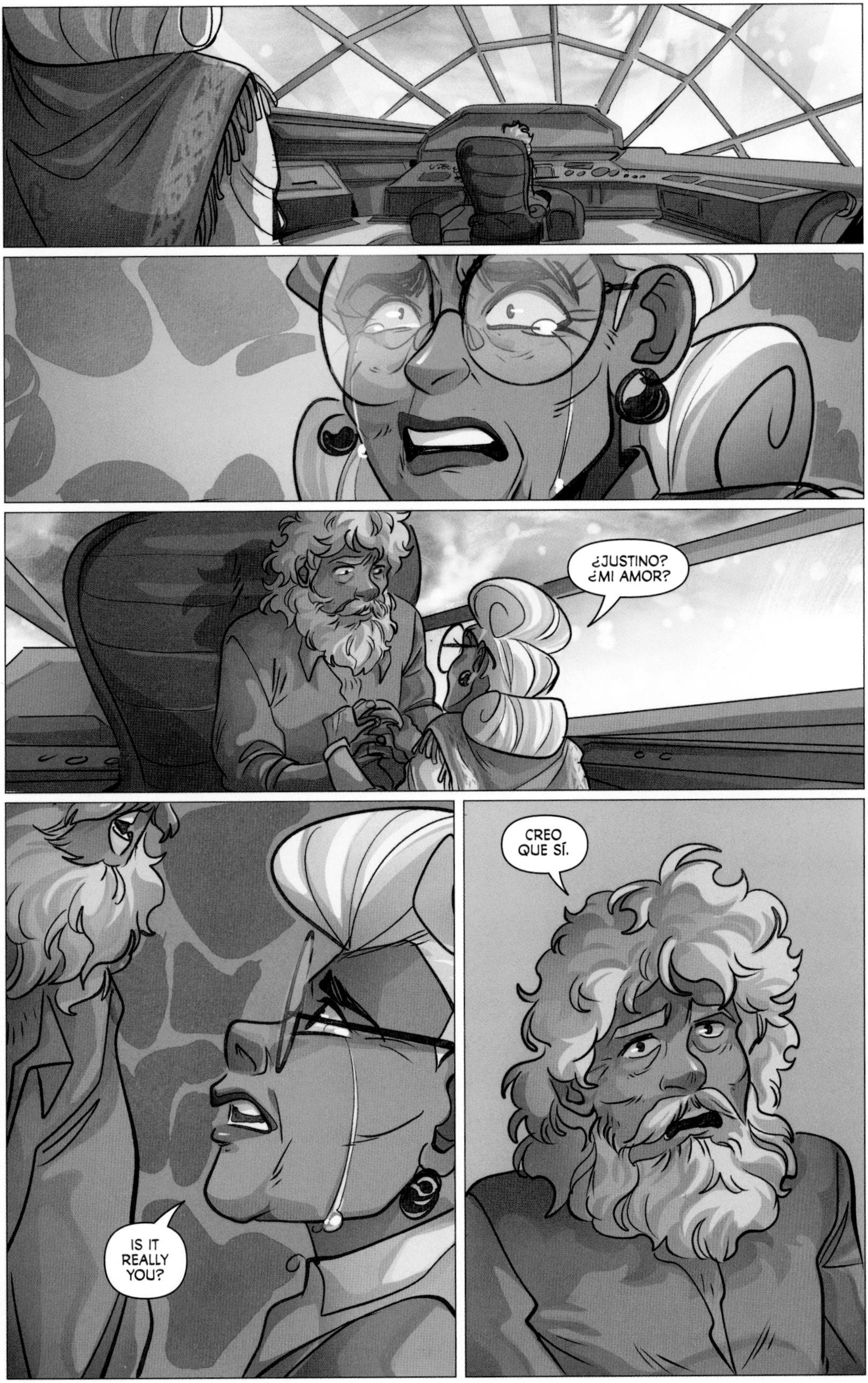
¿JUSTINO? ¿MI AMOR?
IS IT REALLY YOU?
CREO QUE SÍ.

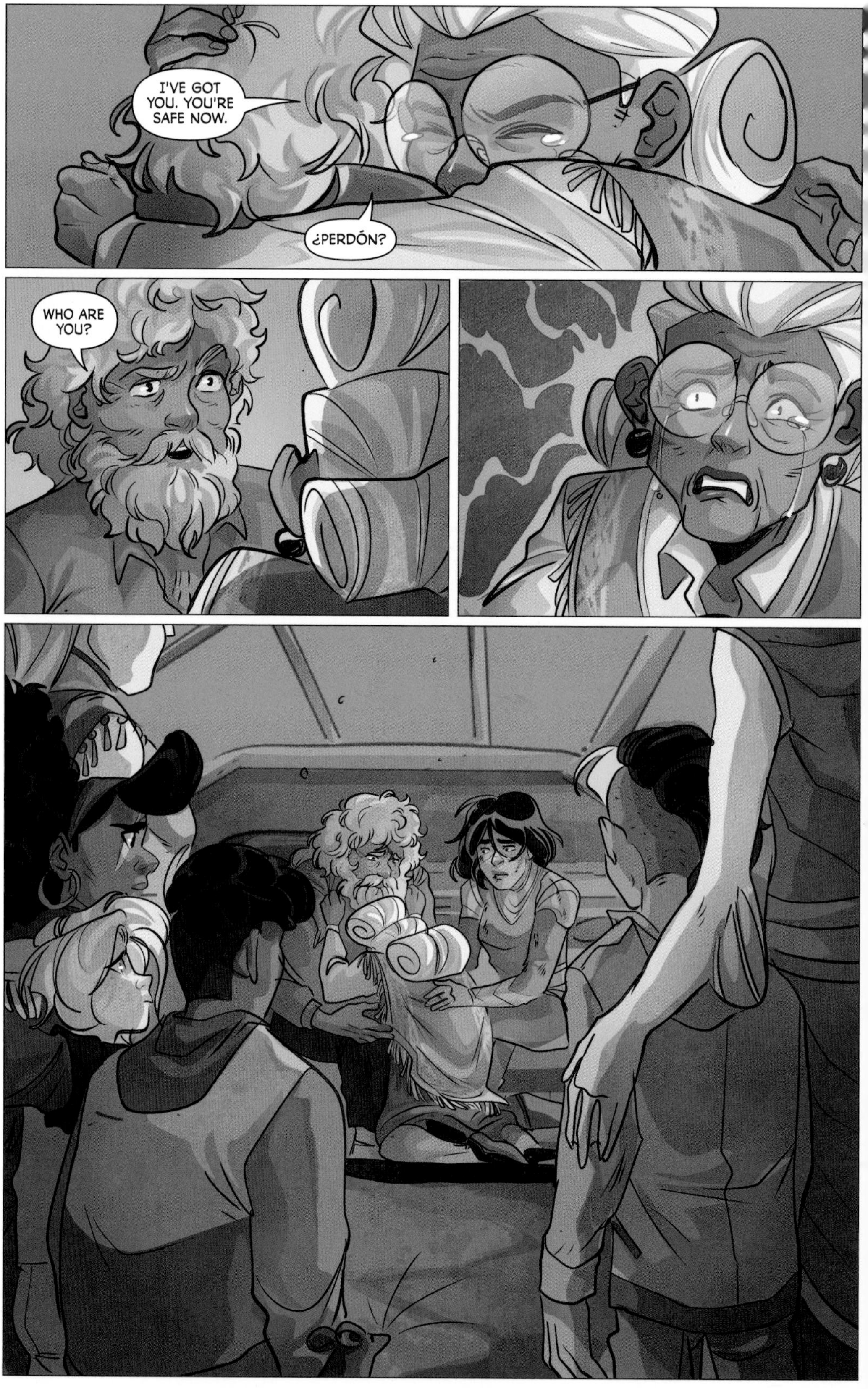
I'VE GOT YOU. YOU'RE SAFE NOW.
¿PERDÓN?
WHO ARE YOU?

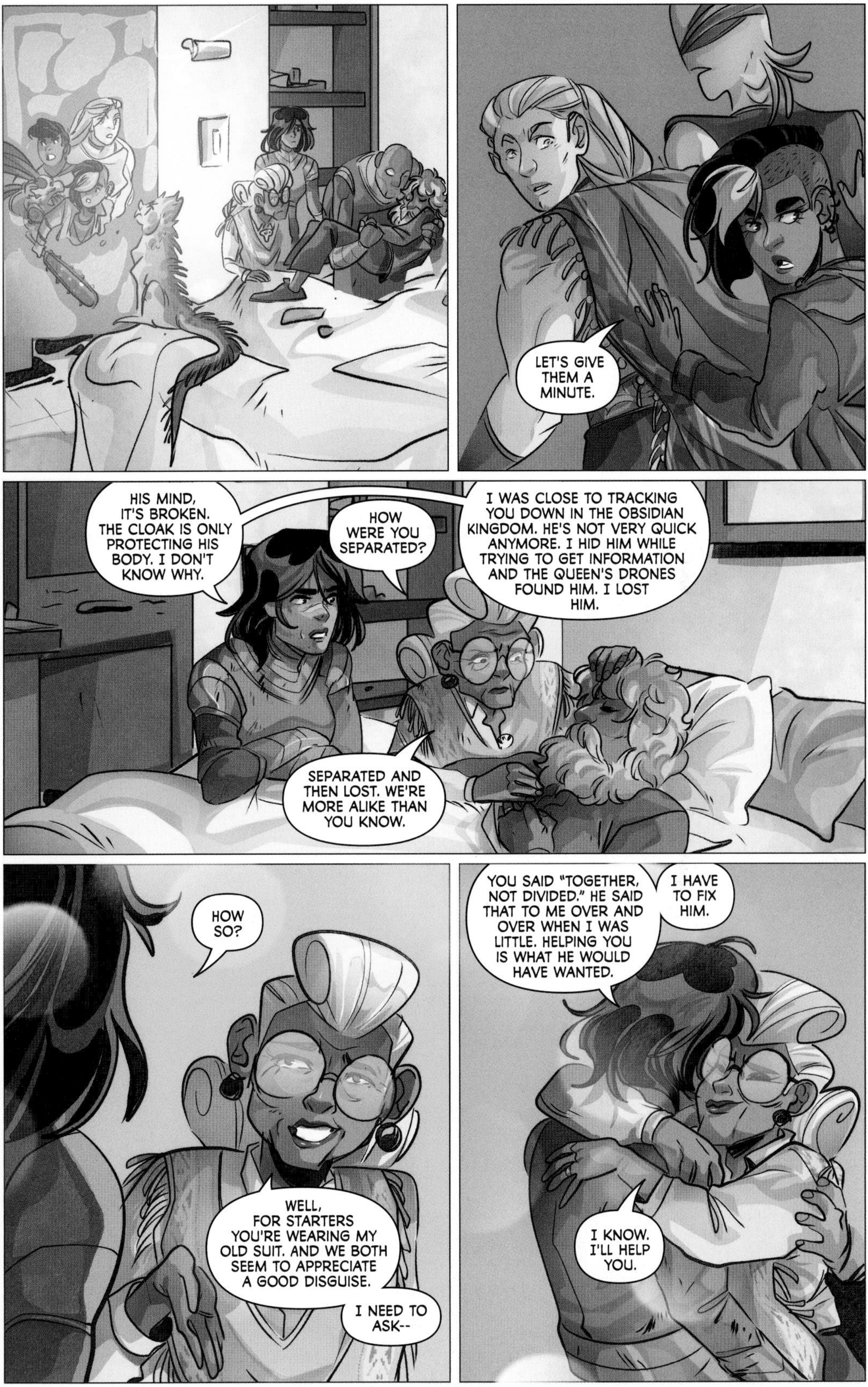
LET'S GIVE THEM A MINUTE.
HIS MIND, IT'S BROKEN. THE CLOAK IS ONLY PROTECTING HIS BODY. I DON'T KNOW WHY.
HOW WERE YOU SEPARATED?
I WAS CLOSE TO TRACKING YOU DOWN IN THE OBSIDIAN KINGDOM. HE'S NOT VERY QUICK ANYMORE. I HID HIM WHILE TRYING TO GET INFORMATION AND THE QUEEN'S DRONES FOUND HIM. I LOST HIM.
SEPARATED AND THEN LOST. WE'RE MORE ALIKE THAN YOU KNOW.
HOW SO?
WELL, FOR STARTERS YOU'RE WEARING MY OLD SUIT. AND WE BOTH SEEM TO APPRECIATE A GOOD DISGUISE.
I NEED TO ASK--
YOU SAID "TOGETHER, NOT DIVIDED." HE SAID THAT TO ME OVER AND OVER WHEN I WAS LITTLE. HELPING YOU IS WHAT HE WOULD HAVE WANTED.
I HAVE TO FIX HIM.
I KNOW. I'LL HELP YOU.

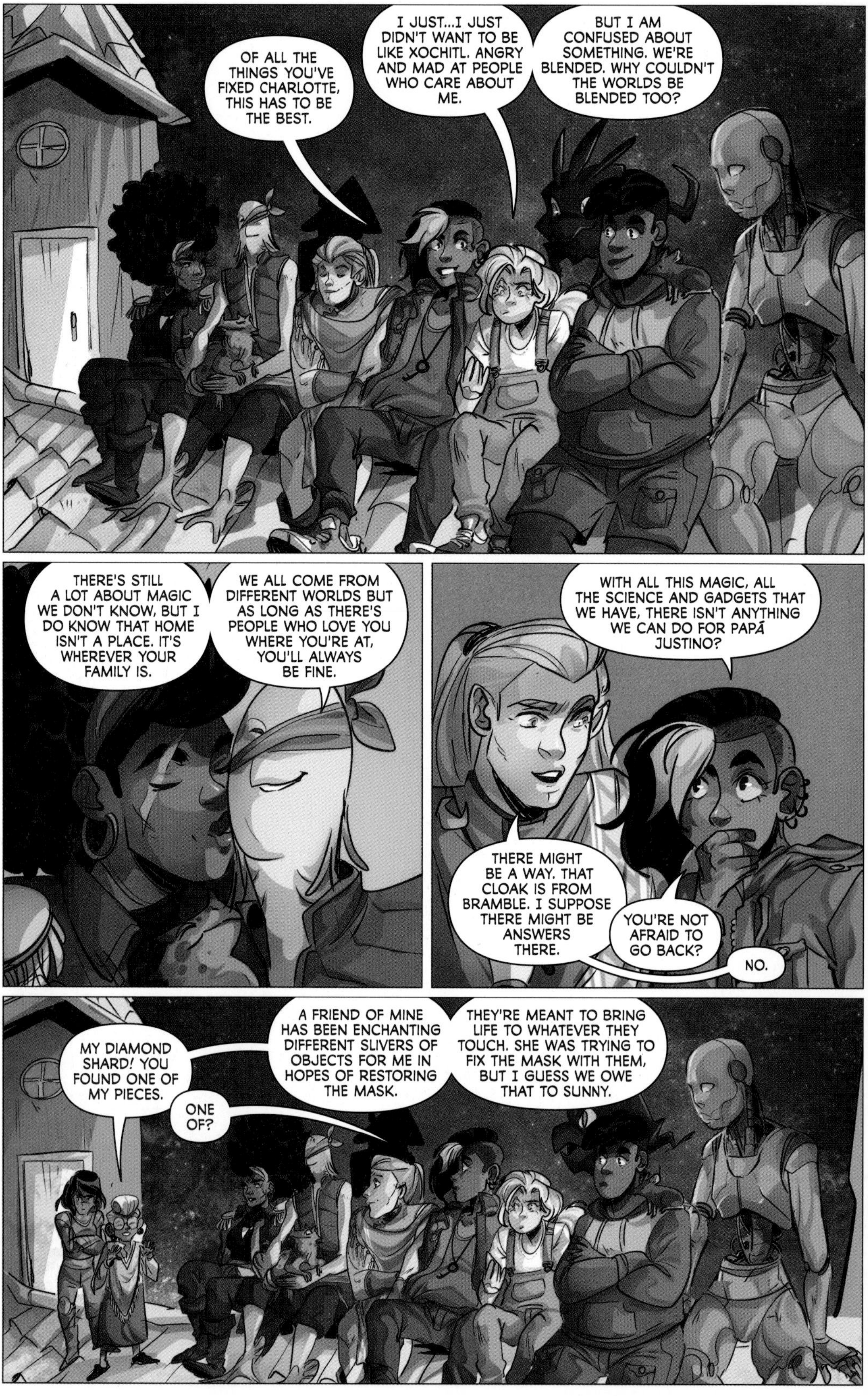
OF ALL THE THINGS YOU'VE FIXED CHARLOTTE, THIS HAS TO BE THE BEST.
I JUST...I JUST DIDN'T WANT TO BE LIKE XOCHITL. ANGRY AND MAD AT PEOPLE WHO CARE ABOUT ME.
BUT I AM CONFUSED ABOUT SOMETHING. WE'RE BLENDED. WHY COULDN'T THE WORLDS BE BLENDED TOO?
THERE'S STILL A LOT ABOUT MAGIC WE DON'T KNOW, BUT I DO KNOW THAT HOME ISN'T A PLACE. IT'S WHEREVER YOUR FAMILY IS.
WE ALL COME FROM DIFFERENT WORLDS BUT AS LONG AS THERE'S PEOPLE WHO LOVE YOU WHERE YOU'RE AT, YOU'LL ALWAYS BE FINE.
WITH ALL THIS MAGIC, ALL THE SCIENCE AND GADGETS THAT WE HAVE, THERE ISN'T ANYTHING WE CAN DO FOR PAPÁ JUSTINO?
THERE MIGHT BE A WAY. THAT CLOAK IS FROM BRAMBLE. I SUPPOSE THERE MIGHT BE ANSWERS THERE.
YOU'RE NOT AFRAID TO GO BACK?
NO.
MY DIAMOND SHARD! YOU FOUND ONE OF MY PIECES.
ONE OF?
A FRIEND OF MINE HAS BEEN ENCHANTING DIFFERENT SLIVERS OF OBJECTS FOR ME IN HOPES OF RESTORING THE MASK.
THEY'RE MEANT TO BRING LIFE TO WHATEVER THEY TOUCH. SHE WAS TRYING TO FIX THE MASK WITH THEM, BUT I GUESS WE OWE THAT TO SUNNY.

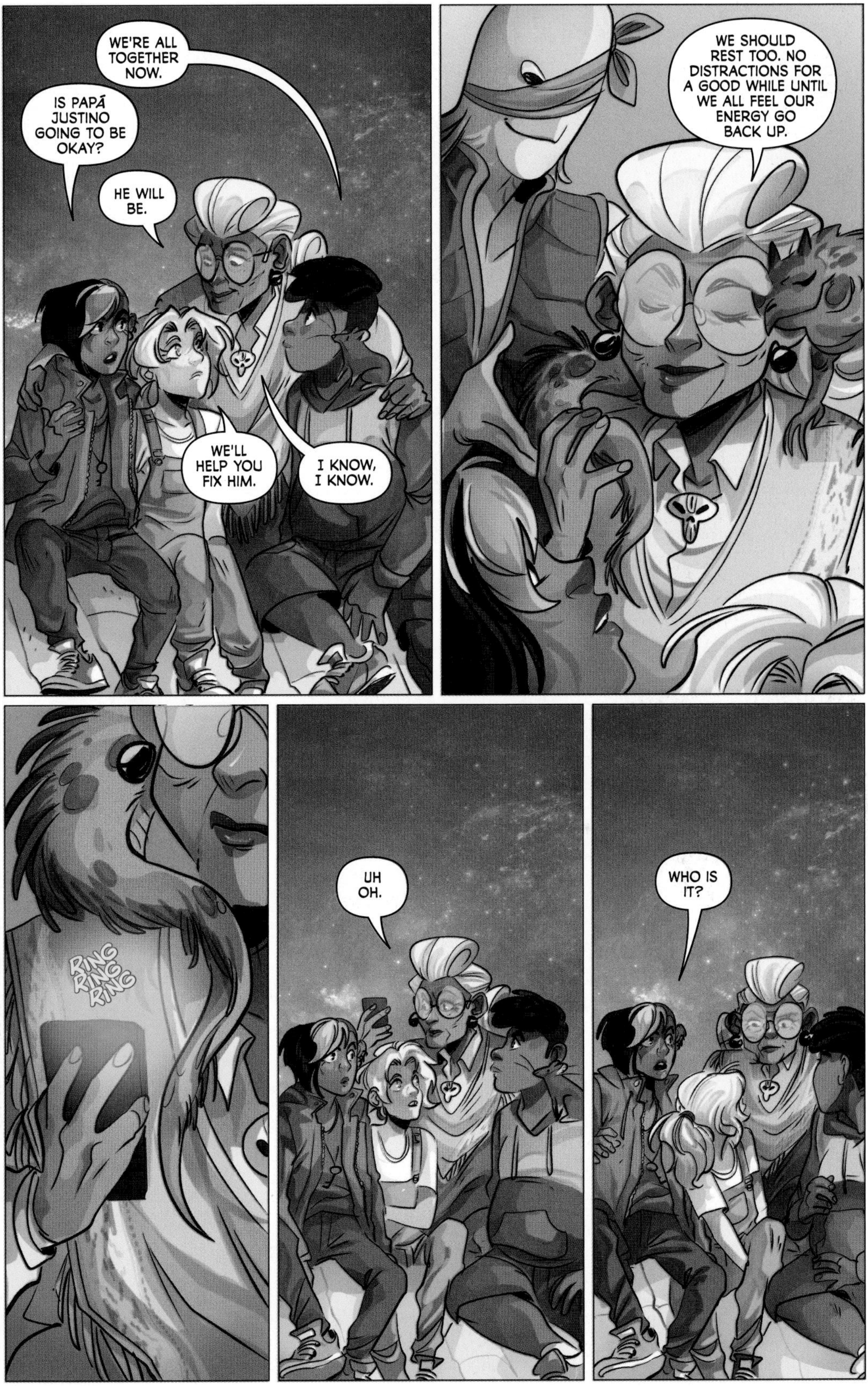
WE'RE ALL TOGETHER NOW.
IS PAPÁ JUSTINO GOING TO BE OKAY?
HE WILL BE.
WE'LL HELP YOU FIX HIM.
I KNOW, I KNOW.
WE SHOULD REST TOO. NO DISTRACTIONS FOR A GOOD WHILE UNTIL WE ALL FEEL OUR ENERGY GO BACK UP.
RING RING RING
UH OH.
WHO IS IT?

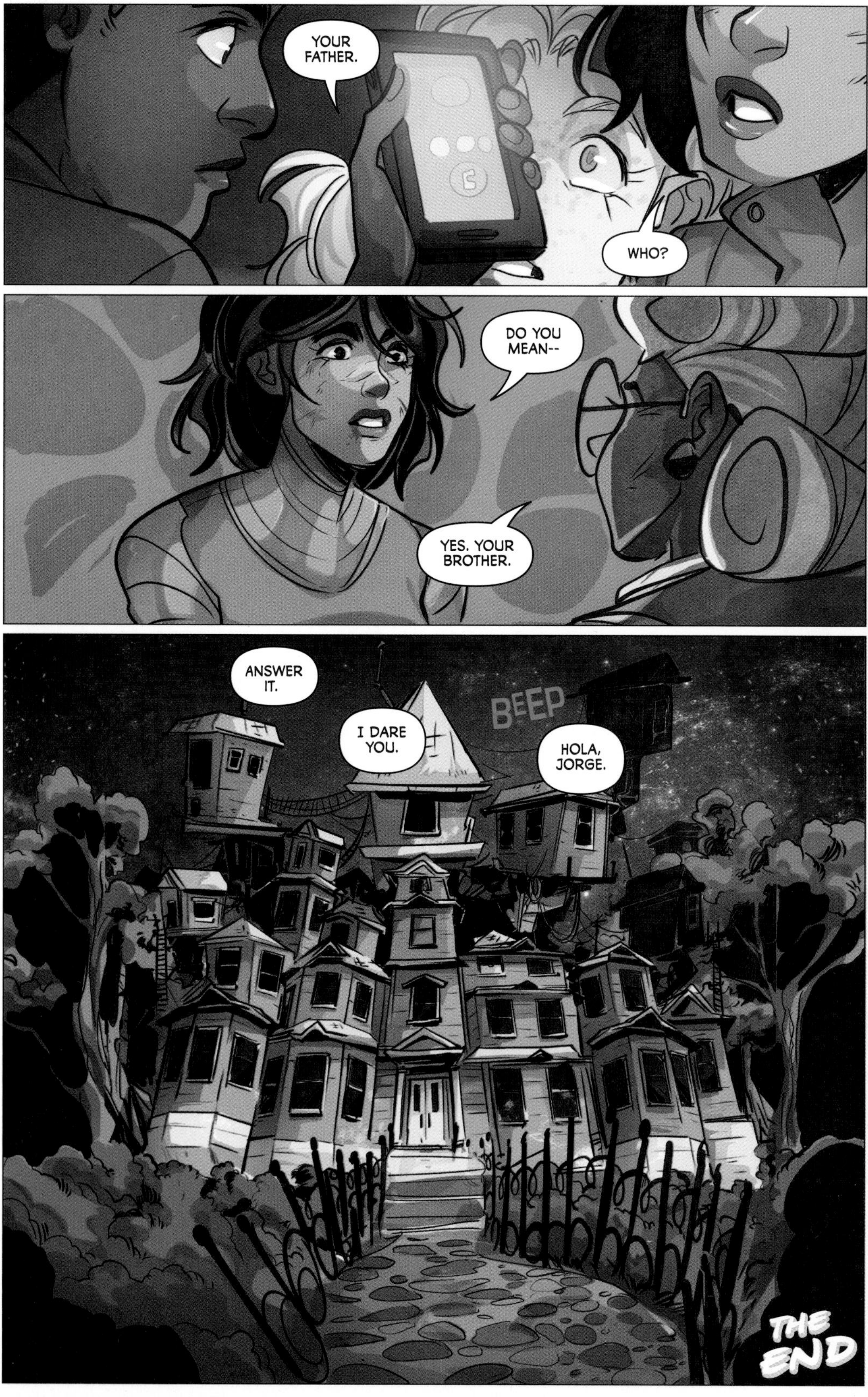
YOUR FATHER.
WHO?
DO YOU MEAN--
YES. YOUR BROTHER.
ANSWER IT.
I DARE YOU.
BEEP
HOLA, JORGE.
THE END

Terry Blas is the writer and illustrator behind the comics *Ghetto Swirl* and *You Say Latino*. His work has appeared in *The Amazing World of Gumball, Regular Show,* and *Adventure Time*. His first graphic novel, a murder mystery set at a weight loss camp, is titled: *Dead Weight: Murder at Camp Bloom. Hotel Dare* is his second book and a love letter to his childhood memories of Mexico.

Claudia Aguirre is a queer comic book artist and writer, a GLAAD Award nominee and Will Eisner Award nominee, and co-founder of Boudika Comics; where she self-publishes comics. Claudia is currently working for Black Mask, Oni Press, Legendary, Limerence Press and Boom! Studios.

DISCOVER
EXPLOSIVE NEW WORLDS

ADVENTURE TIME

Sam Sykes · Selina Espiritu · Sarah Stern
Brave Chef Brianna

KELLY THOMPSON BRIANNE DROUHARD M. VICTORIA ROBADO
MEGA PRINCESS

THE NOT-SO SECRET SOCIETY
DALEY · CRAFTS · CLARK · BRUNI

OVER THE GARDEN WALL

STEVEN UNIVERSE
VOLUME ONE

kaboom!™

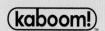

AVAILABLE AT YOUR LOCAL COMICS SHOP AND BOOKSTORE

To find a comics shop in your area, visit www.comicshoplocator.com

WWW.**BOOM-STUDIOS**.COM

Adventure Time
Pendleton Ward and Others
Volume 1
ISBN: 978-1-60886-280-1 | $14.99 US
Volume 2
ISBN: 978-1-60886-323-5 | $14.99 US
Adventure Time: Islands
ISBN: 978-1-60886-972-5 | $9.99 US

The Amazing World of Gumball
Ben Bocquelet and Others
Volume 1
ISBN: 978-1-60886-488-1 | $14.99 US
Volume 2
ISBN: 978-1-60886-793-6 | $14.99 US

Brave Chef Brianna
Sam Sykes, Selina Espiritu
ISBN: 978-1-68415-050-2 | $14.99 US

Mega Princess
Kelly Thompson, Brianne Drouhard
ISBN: 978-1-68415-007-6 | $14.99 US

The Not-So Secret Society
Matthew Daley, Arlene Daley, Wook Jin Clark
ISBN: 978-1-60886-997-8 | $9.99 US

Over the Garden Wall
Patrick McHale, Jim Campbell and Others
Volume 1
ISBN: 978-1-60886-940-4 | $14.99 US
Volume 2
ISBN: 978-1-68415-006-9 | $14.99 US

Steven Universe
Rebecca Sugar and Others
Volume 1
ISBN: 978-1-60886-706-6 | $14.99 US
Volume 2
ISBN: 978-1-60886-796-7 | $14.99 US

Steven Universe & The Crystal Gems
ISBN: 978-1-60886-921-3 | $14.99 US

Steven Universe: Too Cool for School
ISBN: 978-1-60886-771-4 | $14.99 US